THE HEN PARTY

Emily Benet

A Paperback Original 2017

First published in Great Britain in eBook format by
Little Cactus Publishing

Copyright © Emily Benet 2017
Cover image © Juan Diego Sanchez

Emily asserts the moral right
to be identified as the author of this work.

A catalogue record for this book is
available from the British Library

ISBN: 978-1-9997271-0-9

For my remarkable and talented teammate,
Juan Diego

EuroWeekly News

A British TV director was injured last night after falling five metres from an apartment block balcony in Magaluf. Joanna Kane, 37, was reportedly on a recce for the upcoming shoot of reality TV show, The Hen Party. She is currently being treated for head injuries in Son Espases Hospital. Cameraman Ricardo Molina, 39, a Spanish national, also received treatment for minor injuries sustained attempting to catch his colleague.

Despite carrying a fine of up to €1,500, the 'balconing' craze has yet to be stamped out. It involves jumping from one balcony to another, or from balcony to swimming pool, usually by holidaymakers under the influence of alcohol or drugs. So far there have been six deaths this year and countless injuries.

Sharon Wingman, Series Producer at ITV2, strongly rejects claims that Ms Kane was balconing, and will be investigating safety standards in the apartment block.

Filming of The Hen Party will be going ahead on the island with a two month delay and a replacement director. It will be the last episode in the six-part series, which treats six lucky groups of hens to a one-week luxury send off.

ONE

Kate pulled up outside the villa and turned off the engine. She let go of the breath she'd been holding and flipped down the sun visor to check her reflection in the tiny mirror.

"Stay calm," she told herself. "Stay calm, stay calm, stay calm, stay calm."

Despite the mantra, she didn't feel in the least bit calm. Her stomach was in knots. The girls would not be giving her a warm welcome this morning. If they offered her a cup of tea, she could be sure it was only because they'd laced it with poison. There wouldn't be one ally among them. Not the bride-to-be. Not her four chosen hens. Not even the crew.

Kate altered her mantra.

"Shit, shit, shit, shit..."

Opening the car door, she braced herself for the punch of manic techno beats. Instead, all she could hear was the hiss of cicadas. Even the neighbour's chocolate Labrador wasn't getting up to bark at her and pace frantically up and down the yard, tail banging against the rails. Instead it lay in the shadow of a giant cactus and dozed.

She paused as she unlocked the gates of the villa, expecting Clare to let out one of her shrill giggles, or Fiona to shriek in exaggerated panic because some dopey greenfly had landed on her arm. *Poor Fiona*, Kate thought

1

guiltily. If she hadn't been allergic to nature, they would have got on so much better.

Kate listened out for a splash of water or a clink of glasses. The cicadas stopped abruptly nearby and then started up their buzz on the other side of the street.

Should she be worried? None of them had answered their phones last night. But perhaps they'd all just run out of battery. Kate tried to silence her thoughts as she headed down the side of the villa. Maybe the heat had knocked them out. She ducked under the fragrant jasmine that was weighing down the wooden awning and took the path down to the pool.

Typical. Four days of craving a bit of silence, and now that she had it, Kate felt nothing but alarm. Even when they napped, they usually left the Eurodance blaring – songs with lyrics that sounded like they'd been composed by people in the throes of a terrible hangover.

"Hey, Gina, what rhymes with 'high'?"

"Mate, I don't even know my own name right now...what about 'fly'?"

"How about, I wanna fly so high with you tonigh'...?"

"Nailed it."

Perhaps the music had stopped while they were asleep.

"Sleeping is for the weak. I'll sleep when I'm dead!" Fiona had announced on the plane.

Perhaps she is dead, Kate thought with a shudder. These last four days, Fiona had put away enough tequila to pickle a humpback whale.

The pool was empty. Sun glittered across the surface, the bright blue tiles lending the water an inviting azure hue. A pink lilo nudged at the stone rim as if half-

2

heartedly trying to get out. At the far end, plastic bottles and beer cans bobbed up and down. Kate grimaced as she noticed the rest of the rubbish lying at the bottom. She shouldn't have done it. It was evidence that she had lost control.

If she hadn't had more pressing concerns, she would have got the net and fished it all out. She would have dived in herself and picked each piece up one at a time. But for the first time since she'd landed on the island, water pollution was not her priority. Finding the cast of *The Hen Party* television show was.

She turned her back on the pool and looked up at the sandstone facade of the villa. The first floor consisted of six rooms, three on each side of the building, each with its own decorative wrought iron balcony. On the ground floor were the kitchen, dining room and the high ceilinged living room with its luxurious leather sofas and low hanging Venetian chandeliers. Large patio doors framed by bright pink bougainvillea opened out on to a terrace with bamboo tables and chairs, and beyond that, the pool. Kate shaded her eyes as one of the upstairs doors gently swung open. No one stepped out.

She hurried to the back doors and fumbled with the keys. They had been given three sets between them. She had one, the crew of two had another, and the five hens shared the third. If the girls had gone out separately, half the party wouldn't have been able to get back in.

The stubborn door opened with a jolt and Kate stepped inside the messy kitchen. It stank of stale booze. A collection of dirty glasses had taken over the heavy wooden table. There were empty wine bottles, shot glasses stained with Jägermeister and bottles of mixers with the lids off and fizz long gone. An army of ants had followed the sticky sugar trail and were having the after party of a lifetime.

Of course Kate had expected the girls to get drunk. That was their default setting on a good day. Yesterday hadn't been a good day. They'd been disappointed and had argued, so their thirst for oblivion had evidently risen to epic proportions. She couldn't blame them, could she? They'd wanted to be treated like VIPs and she'd treated them like schoolkids on a field trip. She'd wanted to educate them, to open their eyes to the environmental catastrophe that they themselves were abetting.

She got a flashback of her forced jollity and squirmed.

However intoxicated and angry they'd been, she'd still assumed they would return to base. Wasn't there always one person in a group who could get the others home?

With an increasing sense of unease, Kate climbed the stone staircase. If they were asleep, she wouldn't wake them. In fact, as long as they were alive, then she considered her job done. She would send Ricardo in to finish off. With his camera aimed at them, he was the only one who would be able to elicit a smile after everything that had happened.

Where was Ricardo? He wasn't answering his phone either. Surely he must have calmed down by now.

The door to the first room was open. Clare's room: the smallest because she had been the least competitive on arrival. Kate stepped inside to find the room vacant but for a plump white gecko frozen still on the ceiling.

The balcony was empty. Of course it was. Despite slathering herself in factor fifty, by Day 2 Clare had a patchy red empire mapped over her entire body by the sun, driving her indoors at every opportunity. The memory of the maid of honour's puffy blistered legs brought with it another pang of guilt.

Giving in to the feeling of panic, Kate dashed into Chioma's room opposite. Her bed was unmade, her sheet trailing on the floor as if she had thrown it off in the heat of the night. There were piles of brightly coloured jangly earrings on her bedside table and an explosion of clothes swallowing up the straight-backed armchair in the corner. In Jem's room it was much the same picture, if a little neater. Her olive green summer dress hung on a hanger off the corner of her wardrobe; her makeup was organised on the dressing table. Kate stood, listening intensely, though she knew without a shadow of a doubt there was no one there. Everything was pretty much as it had been since they had installed themselves. That they hadn't left the island had to be of some consolation.

The sound of her phone ringing made her cry out. She swore under her breath and dug it out of her handbag. Were they going to be demanding rescue and compensation? Or would their hangovers have rendered them too dumb to speak?

It was an unknown number and she answered with forced confidence.

"Hello, Kate Miller speaking."

"Hi, Kate, it's Sharon Wingman here. I've just arrived in Palma Airport. Am I interrupting a take?"

Kate felt her knees weaken and she sank down at the end of Jem's bed.

"No, you're not."

"That makes a change."

"I didn't realise you were coming over."

How the hell was she going to explain to her boss that the entire cast and crew of their television show had gone missing? That she, the director, had lost the lot of them?

"I thought I'd surprise you. That's not a problem, is it?"

Kate felt the silence of the villa pressing in on her. Yes, it was a problem. It was a you-could-lose-your-job-and-never-work-again sort of problem. Palma Airport was only half an hour away. There was no way she was going to be able to locate the five hens and two missing crew members in that time.

"You've had your phone off rather a lot," Sharon added.

"Have I? It must be the...uh...bad signal in the villa."

"Joanna Kane has been trying to get in touch with you. She seems to have got it into her head that you've changed quite a bit of the original script. I don't know if maybe she's spoken to Ricardo...To be honest, I think she's still a bit concussed. Anyway, I thought I'd just pop over to make sure you felt supported and check everything is on track."

Kate fell back against the mattress so she was staring up at the ceiling. A thin crack ran across it. She wished it would open up and swallow her. Being eaten by the ceiling sounded a lot more fun than explaining herself to Sharon Wingman. She was going to have to come up with a very good story. Specifically a story that didn't make her sound like a complete and utter lunatic.

TWO

Day 1
KATE

"Attention, passengers of Monarch flight ZB226 to Palma, your flight has been delayed. Your new departure time is in approximately one hour."

The announcement over the tannoy was met with a unanimous groan of disappointment. They had arrived so early they had already been waiting two hours. Kate fought a strong urge to back away and hide in the toilets. She didn't *do* hen parties. All her friends knew that. Yet here she was, about to lead and direct a hen party abroad which would be viewed by half a million people.

She caught Fiona winking at her as she lifted her glass of champagne. "I think that calls for another bottle, am I right?"

The groans morphed into cheers.

"Another one?" Kate said, her voice coming out a little too high.

Fiona looked aghast. "Why? Is there a limit?"

"Uh no...not at all."

No limit. The girls were supposed to be pampered and treated like celebrities for seven whole days. Another cork soon popped to jubilant shrieks. Kate became aware of people turning to stare. She recognised the tense looks, the silent plea in their eyes: *please, God, don't let me be on the same flight as those women!* Everyone except the hungry-eyed blokes nursing pints at the entrance of the Wetherspoons pub. They were assessing which hen might be most up for joining the mile-high club. Kate shuddered at the thought. She had never understood the appeal of having sex in a swaying cubicle which was already sticky with the bodily fluids of past passengers.

The hens certainly stood out that morning in their pink sequined boob tubes and denim hot pants. Beneath her buoyant blonde beehive, Fiona's soft round face was a glowing tribute to fake tan. Everything about her shimmered. Her full lips were slippery with nude gloss and her thick eyelids glittered gold. She had even rubbed some sort of glitter trail down to her cleavage which made an appearance whenever her boob tube started to slip. Which it did – down over her large boobs and up over the swell of her muffin top. Kate noticed Fiona didn't adjust her top in a hurry and seemed confident with her curves.

Chioma, or Chi, as everyone called her, was also hard to miss, as nestling in her unruly afro was a headband with an erect plastic penis bobbing up and down on a coiled spring. She had further complemented her outfit with a silver bowtie and oversized sunglasses with pink lenses. With her flat stomach and tiny waist, Chioma looked much younger than her twenty-eight years. She had a striking face, with a defined angular jaw and full lips that split into a contagious toothy smile at the smallest hint of a joke. A red earphone cable trailed down her neck and she was quietly bopping to a beat no one else could hear.

Then there was Clare, who had opted for a genitalia wand rather than upset her freshly curled hair with a head piece. She waved the wand whenever she got excited, which was so often the rubbery penis was starting to come loose. To complete the Titillating Tinker Bell look, Clare was also wearing a pair of glittery wings. Unfortunately the wings had been designed for a smaller model and the elastic arm loops strained across her plump back, separating the fat into an assortment of bulges.

The sister of the groom, Jem, hadn't quite embraced the tacky fancy dress and had put her phallic accessories in her Mulberry handbag for safekeeping. She had also partially covered up with a cream bolero.

Quite possibly the guys in Wetherspoons were placing their bets that Clare would be the easiest conquest since she was reacting most quickly to the booze. Sam was out of the question as she had a copy of *Mother & Baby* magazine sticking out of her hemp handbag and was alternating her sips of champagne with gulps from a bottle of sparkling water. She'd had baby George eighteen months earlier and Kate had already heard all about the 'magical' home birth on the way through security.

"You can't get too drunk or you won't be allowed on the plane," Kate said, trying not to let the anxiety she was feeling slip into her voice. She would be held accountable if she didn't manage to get them to Mallorca. "How about a little water break?"

Fiona gasped as if she'd just been asked to drink her own urine.

"Don't give me water! It's my hen party!"

That had been Fiona's response to everything so far. At baggage drop: "Your bags are five kilos over the limit."

"So? *It's my hen party!*"

At security: "You have to put your makeup in a clear plastic bag."

"*Why? It's my hen party!*"

Kate was trying to dig deep in the hope of excavating some mutual excitement, but instead she kept coming across rocks of apprehension and regret.

"Where's the cameraman anyway?" Fiona said. "Shouldn't he be filming us? My hair isn't going to stay like this all day."

"Mine neither," Clare said, plumping up her flagging curls. "I got up at two in the morning to do these."

"Lucky you," Sam said. "I was up at two wiping a pooey bottom."

"You really spoil that husband of yours, don't you," Fiona giggled.

"It's the only way to keep them keen," Sam shot back. "Don't worry, I'll give you some marriage tips."

"I think I'm alright."

"He'll be here soon," Kate said.

The cameraman, Ricardo, was having a civilised breakfast with Mel, the sound recordist, as far away from the hens as possible. He'd warned Kate that he couldn't be around so many euphoric women until after noon. Clearly she wasn't the only person unsuitable for this job.

"*It might not be your dream job, but at least it pays the bills,*" friends had reminded her, most of them grumpily, because they couldn't see how 'working' and 'Mallorca' belonged in the same sentence.

As budgets went, a quarter of a million was low. The show had a steady audience but was constantly under threat from newer, more ridiculous realities being aired at the same time, and as a result the channel had slowly started reducing productions costs. But Kate would have been overjoyed with a fraction of that money for her documentary idea, *Plastic People*.

The seed for it had been sown during a holiday in Greece, when she'd dived under the water with her snorkel only to discover a mass of rubbish. It had had a profound effect on her. It had got her into recycling. Later, she'd been dismayed to discover there was plastic in her face creams, in her toothpaste, plastic fibres leaking off her synthetic clothing. The tiny particles were indistinguishable from plankton, which begged the question: how long before plastic made its way up the food chain and into humans' blood streams, if it hadn't already?

"Not commercial enough, I'm afraid," her agent had said about her pitch. "People are bored of bad news. But, hey, on the upside, I do have a job on a reality show. It's called *The Hen Party* – have you heard of it?"

Kate had, and except for five minutes during one Sunday hangover, she had skilfully avoided watching any of it.

"Their regular director has had an accident and their usual replacement is on her honeymoon," her agent had continued breezily. "They're pretty desperate. I'll tell them you're in, shall I?"

It was an opportunity, her agent had said. It would be great for her CV.

Opportunity. The word had swum around Kate's head later that evening. She had always felt secretly jealous of Greenpeace activists, of how they could be so courageous in the face of such powerful opposition. She was quick to

11

give donations, but what she really wanted was to take action and be like those gutsy, principled people who climbed skyscrapers dressed as snow leopards and blockaded petrol companies with passion and posters of pissed off polar bears. In that moment Kate had realised that this could be her moment to prove that she was a doer, not a dreamer.

Fiona nudged her. "I think you're missing something. Where's your glass?"

The bride-to-be was being very pally and clearly the heart and soul of the party. Kate knew she must make a concerted effort to match her enthusiasm. The woman was getting married; it was exciting. *Be excited!* she told herself.

"I'd love to, but I'd better not. I'm supposed to be working, aren't I."

"You're not working right now," Fiona pointed out. "There's no camera."

Fiona loved the camera. She switched on for it, becoming even more bubbly and high spirited than normal. Kate knew that was the real reason she had been selected for the show rather than her paragraph on why she deserved it, which had been rather sweet and also rather badly spelled. She'd bumped into her childhood sweetheart ten years after they'd separated, and after a whirlwind month together, they'd got engaged. Kate had skimmed through her entry. Fiona's dream job was: actress, singer, dancer and TV presenter. For now, she worked in the marketing department of an insurance company.

"I've got to make sure you get on this plane," Kate said.

The fourth bottle of champagne had been drained within minutes of its arrival. They were all looking flushed and happy.

"Don't worry, I'll make sure we get on," Sam said, fiercely. "I need this holiday so badly. I'm tired. Sooo tired. I found my passport in the fridge this morning. That's how tired. God, I'm tired. It's like being covered in treacle tired. Like *tired* tired."

"Is anyone else getting the impression that Sam's tired?" Clare said,

"I'm just saying…"

"No more champagne for Sam!" Chi said, holding the bottle above her head which, being as she was shorter than everyone else, wasn't all that effective.

"I didn't say that," Sam said, reaching it with ease. "I'll probably fall asleep on the plane, that's all."

"And get filmed drooling?" Fiona said, her blue eyes twinkling with mirth. "I wouldn't risk it if I were you."

Sam grimaced. "Shit. Why did I agree to this again?"

While everyone voiced their worst filming scenario, Jem disappeared to fetch a glass for Kate.

"I'm sure one glass won't hurt," she said with a reassuring smile. "I'll also make sure we don't miss the plane. My brother would kill me if Fiona didn't get her hen party."

"It's a bit early for me," Kate said, but soothed by Jem's calming presence, she took a sip.

It was too early for her. Definitely too early. She licked her lips, savouring the champagne's sweetness.

"Better?" Jem asked.

Kate narrowed her eyes. "A little," she admitted. "I didn't have you down as the bad influence."

13

Jem laughed, spots of pink appearing on her cheeks. "I'm really not. I'm just the boring older sister."

Kate wasn't sure about boring, but Jem was definitely a few years older than the rest. She guessed she and Jem were a similar age, which was nearer forty than Kate wanted to be. She caught herself glancing at Jem's hands. No wedding ring. She wondered what Jem felt about her younger brother getting hitched before her, and then scolded herself for being so old-fashioned. Not everyone wanted to get married. Anyway, perhaps she had a *partner*.

"Wait, we have to toast!" Fiona interrupted.

"Yes! Selfie!" Clare cried, tottering in front of everyone with her phone in her outstretched arm.

"No, I hate selfies. My chin is small enough as it is," Fiona protested. Instead she homed in on a white-haired man with a Swedish flag on his T-shirt who had been reading a guidebook on Paris. He obliged her request with a chuffed smile, flattered to be selected out of so many younger potential photographers. Kate couldn't help breaking into a grin as she watched the hens being silly and posing unpretentiously. She should relax a bit. Perhaps it was going to be fun after all.

She left them draining the fifth bottle of champagne and headed over to check the departure board. She stood for some time without actually looking at it, thinking about the itinerary in her bag. The channel had just assumed that she would follow it. The format was easy: get a group of girls together, play a few games, and hey presto – it's a wrap! Why would a director want to complicate things?

14

She became aware of the handsome man nearby, staring up at the screens, scanning for his flight. He had a mop of dark curly hair which fell forward over his forehead and looked like it had been styled by his pillow – the kind of disobedient hair that made her mum want to reach for a comb. Kate's hair had looked similar before she subjected it to straightening irons. Two years on, her short glossy bob and ruler straight fringe had become part of her identity, and she didn't know how she was ever going to move on to a different style.

The young man was unflustered and had the air of a frequent flyer, casual in a khaki V-neck T-shirt and dark jeans and carrying a bulging rucksack that probably held everything he needed for a week away. She guessed from his olive skin he wasn't from England. His face had an attractive symmetry, and she found she was enjoying watching him. He had high cheekbones and a strong Grecian nose. His thick lips, with their faint cupid bow, were slightly open in concentration. *Just ripe to be kissed*, she thought.

He suddenly turned, his dark eyes meeting hers. She blushed and returned her focus to the board. A gate number had appeared. It was time.

The hens giggled all the way to the gate, a sloshed Clare pretending to fly with her glitter wings and Fiona nearly performing a forward roll in her chunky pink platform heels. Chi boogied to her music and Sam made a last minute call to hear her baby's voice, her face lighting up as she asked him if he was being a *good little pirate for Daddy*. Jem stayed at Kate's side, smiling at them all from a distance.

"Fiona, Sam and Clare went to school together," she explained. "But you probably know that already."

Kate should have known, but the truth was she had been too busy making extra plans for the hen party rather than finding out who the hens were.

"Go on," she said to Jem. "So, did you know them before today?"

"Kind of. My brother and Fiona went out when they were teenagers when we all lived in the same close. I used to see Clare and Sam, mostly Clare, hanging around with Fiona. I was older than them, though, and I was also Andrew's sister, so it was a bit awkward."

"And let me get this straight: Andrew and Fiona hadn't seen each other for ten years and then they met up and got engaged within a month."

Jem glanced at her, her eyebrows raised. "I know. Crazy, right?"

"I guess when you know, you know."

The problem was when one person knew and the other person didn't, she thought.

"My brother reckons he always knew," Jem said.

They walked for a little way in silence before Kate tore herself from the memories of another lifetime.

"What about Chi?" she said. "Did you know her?"

"Oh no. She works with Fiona. All I know is that they met three years ago. Chi told me they'd bonded at a drunken Christmas party."

Kate laughed. "Easily done."

"I guess that makes me the odd one out."

"How do you mean?"

Jem smiled uncertainly. "Well, I'm the relative, not the friend."

Kate sensed her insecurity and shot her a warm smile. "Look at it this way: you're the sister of the groom. You're the second most important person here. You're going to be Fiona's sister-in-law."

Jem shook her head, her eyes widening. "To be honest, it's still sinking in."

"I'm not surprised. Have they set a date for the wedding?"

"Mid-October, apparently."

"Have you got bridesmaids' dresses?"

"Not that I know of. But I've got my eye on this grey dress in Jaeger."

Kate frowned. "Grey? Not very bright for a wedding."

"It just seems pointless getting a dress you'll only wear once," Jem said.

"Oh, I totally agree. Such a waste."

Great! Kate had already located a conscientious soul among the group. Someone who would understand where she was coming from when the time came.

"I'll cross my fingers she doesn't go for yellow and puffy," Kate said.

Jem smiled. "Thanks. Please do."

Kate moved past her towards the pile up of people at the gate.

"We shouldn't have to wait long. We have priority boarding," she explained.

They should have been in business class on British Airways. It wasn't a mistake; it was production trying to skimp after all the wasted flights two months ago. The delay had cost them.

Kate waited for the hens to quieten down before she delivered the news that they had a pre-ordered cooked breakfast to look forward to and any drinks would be paid for. They weren't the only ones making a racket. Half the passengers appeared to have had a tipple for breakfast and were planning on carrying on as soon as the drinks trolley was rolled out.

They were the first on board – Fiona, Clare and Sam in one row; Jem, Chi and the sound recordist, Mel, on the row opposite. Kate sat in a window seat a couple of rows in front. For the moment, there was no one beside her or behind her. Ricardo had sneakily upgraded to an emergency seat at check-in. Possibly he'd had second thoughts about the job after meeting the boisterous hens and was planning to throw himself out over France.

The passengers came in, noisy and excited. They called out after each other, cackling with laughter, inexplicably baffled by the seating as if reading a number and a letter required a GCSE in Maths. Kate closed her eyes to block out the hustle and bustle. The relaxing effect of half a glass of champagne had already worn off and her stomach was churning again.

I'm not supposed to be here, she thought. *I should be in Greece filming turtles.* The turtle sanctuary had lost all its funding and there was more need than ever for exposure. It made the money thrown at these hens seem so extravagant. So wrong. It was exactly why Kate had to do what she had to do. It wouldn't mean ruining the party for the girls. If she explained herself properly, they might well be understanding.

"Excuse me, you're in my seat," said a firm voice in a foreign accent.

18

She snapped open her eyes to find the attractive man she'd seen in front of the departure screens looking down at her.

"Really?" Kate said, fumbling for her phone to check her ticket number.

"Really," he said, moving into the end seat to avoid getting trampled on by a fat woman with a pod of smudged green dolphins tattooed down her arm.

She *had* got it wrong. She was all over the place this morning.

"I'm so sorry."

He didn't reply.

"I haven't had my coffee yet," she added.

That wasn't true. She hadn't stopped chugging the stuff since she'd got up at 5am. In fact, if he came any closer he would smell it on her skin. He moved back into the aisle to let her squeeze out. She felt self-conscious and like she was taking for ever. Judging by the grumbles from behind, she *was* taking for ever.

He moved past her, his aftershave lingering in the air.
"Thanks."

"No, I'm sorry. I should've...double checked," she finished weakly.

He'd already turned to look out of the window.

Kate leant back against the aisle seat. She could hear Fiona talking at the top of her voice about the time she got drunk in Brighton and lost her favourite flip-flops. Clare was trying to get a word in edgeways, because she had been on the same holiday and had a theory about the missing footwear. Sam, far from falling straight to sleep, was laughing hysterically.

Kate stole furtive glances at her handsome fellow passenger, willing him to turn around and enter into small talk with her. It was rare that she spotted someone who set off a spark in her like this. If she counted on her hands all the times she'd looked into someone's eyes and felt a rush of blood to her head, she'd still have fingers left. Perhaps that's why it had been so easy to be faithful to Matt for fifteen years. No one else had come close to tempting her. That, and because she'd been madly in love with him.

She didn't know a thing about this guy, but she fancied him. She liked the way it made her feel. It gave her a thrill to imagine leaning over and kissing him. Of course, she never would in a million years, but it was fun to daydream. If only he would turn around and ask her a question.

"Hey, Kate, how long's the flight?" Fiona shouted from two rows away.

She grimaced as her object of desire turned his head. He shot her a sympathetic smile, a *here we go* sort of look. She guessed he was in his early thirties. Younger than her. Kate decided to ignore the bride-to-be. Surely one of them knew how long the flight was.

"Every time I fly to Mallorca it's like this," he said. He pronounced Mallorca in a way that was almost unrecognisable to her ears. In others words, correctly. He had to be Spanish. "It's like they've just escaped a dictatorship or something."

She laughed. "You mean the drinking?"

She was aware of her heart racing. It was all that coffee she supposedly hadn't drunk.

"I think they start at seven in the morning," he said.

"It's because they're on holiday."

"It's still kind of crazy, no?"

"Yeah, it's a bit mad."

"You're not?" he asked.

"Sorry?"

"On holiday…"

"Oh." She let out a giggle. "I thought you were asking if I'd been drinking."

He blushed. "Maybe you have…"

"Only a couple of tequila shots in my cornflakes," she said, winking.

He grinned.

"No, I'm not on holiday. I'm going for a week's work."

"What's your work?" he said, at the same moment Fiona yelled, "KATE!"

He flinched. "Why does she have to be so loud?"

Kate squirmed in her seat. She shouldn't have let them have that last bottle of champagne. It was time she explained they were connected.

"Bloody hell, she's deaf," Fiona said.

Jem's voice piped up. "It's two hours and twenty minutes. I've just checked."

"Thank you. At least *someone* knows what's going on."

"I'd know what was going on too if you hadn't forced me to drink all that champagne," Sam said.

"Me? I wasn't the one who drank an Irish coffee this morning."

"I thought Irish meant extra foam, like a Guinness."

"Yeah, right! Nice try."

Kate let go of her breath as she heard them dissolve into giggles again.

"Well, at least we've got some space on our row," she said.

As soon as she'd said it, the lads who had been drinking at the Wetherspoons pub boarded the plane in a mist of beer and testosterone.

"WHERE ARE WE SITTING, FRANKIE?"

"I'M SITTING BY THE FIT BIRD."

"I DIDN'T KNOW YOUR MUM WAS COMING!"

Kate willed them to keep walking. To keep walking until they reached the exit door at the other end of the plane and got off again. No such luck.

A bulky bloke in a shiny football shirt came to stand at the end of her row. He looked at his ticket and then at the seat, his face an open book called: *Why The Fuck Am I In A Row On My Own?*

Chapter 1: "Why the fuck am I in a row on my own?"

His mates seemed to find it hilarious. Kate unbuckled her seatbelt. "Take the aisle, I'll move into the middle. You'll have more room."

"Are you saying I'm fat?" the lad asked, his eyes daring her to say yes.

Kate felt her cheeks burning. "No. I thought…"

He relaxed his shoulders and broke into a grin. "I'm only having a laugh. Thanks. I'll take it."

More laughter from his friends, who were settling into the rows behind.

"Hang on, mate, there's a free seat here!" one of his friends yelled.

The bloke strained his neck to have a look. "Nah. I'm going to sit by the pretty lady."

Kate let out an embarrassed laugh. The bloke gave her a funny look. "I didn't mean you, love, I meant her."

He pointed to the elderly lady on the end of the opposite row, who was in the process of removing her hearing aid. *Lucky lady,* thought Kate, miserably. She cursed production for being such cheapskates.

The Spanish guy beside her let out an audible sigh.

She buckled herself up in the middle seat and turned to him.

"I'm Kate, by the way."

"Gabriel," he replied. "Do you think we'll be able to sleep?"

"Unlikely." She lowered her voice. "There'll probably be a sing-along. Do you know any football songs?"

"No…I don't like football."

"Well let's hope you're a quick learner, then."

The blokes lowered their voices as they switched on tablets and connected earphones, and Kate thought that perhaps it would be alright after all.

There were cheers when the drinks trolley made an entrance, the lads taking the lead, then the hens joining in with high-pitched enthusiasm. The atmosphere fizzed as the male and female of the species made contact. Gabriel rubbed a hand over his face and let out a low groan.

"Almost…" he said, then broke into a yawn.

"KATE! HOW ARE WE PAYING?"

She couldn't ignore them now. She undid her seatbelt and had to prod the bulky lad a few times before he noticed she wanted to get out because he was talking to his friends in the seats behind.

The hens had gone for the mini champagne bottles. Three for Fiona and Clare, two for Sam and Chi and one for Jem. Mel was having a tonic water. Fiona also wanted money for scratch cards.

"I'm feeling lucky!" she announced. "Plus there's a three for two offer."

"OI, MUM, CAN YOU PAY FOR OURS TOO?" shouted one of the lads.

The girls shouted back at them, told them not to be so rude. It was banter. They were excited and enjoying the attention.

Certain they had enough refreshments for a return flight to Australia, Kate headed back to her seat. She was pleased to find the big guy had decided to move to the row behind after all. Gabriel tried not to look too surprised. He was obviously wondering how she was connected to the rowdy group.

"They're contestants in a reality show," she said. "I'm the director."

He covered his mouth as he broke into another yawn.

"I know," she laughed. "It's not my dream job either."

He looked alarmed. "No, I didn't mean…I'm just…I didn't sleep last night."

"What were you doing?" she asked.

The trolley stopped beside them and the lads started reeling off a list of drinks. Vodka and tonics, JDs and coke, beer. Another beer. *Make that four beers and a JD and coke.* And another beer. The stewardess's face was impassive as she served them.

"Just some research…"

"On what?"

He shot her a sheepish smile. "Rubbish."

"Rubbish?" she echoed, stupidly.

"Trash. In the oceans…recycling…that kind of thing. I was at an oceans' initiatives conference in London, it was really inspiring."

What were the chances?

"Any drinks or snacks?" the stewardess interrupted.

Gabriel ordered a black coffee, handing back the plastic cup with the milk and the sachets and the straw to mix it with to the stewardess, who looked irritated by the inconvenience of it all. Kate was about to say how she also hated all that unnecessary packaging, but one of the lads must have kicked Gabriel's seat and he jerked forward, spilling some of his coffee.

He swore in Spanish. The stewardess moved on. She didn't want to know.

Kate felt her own seat being kicked and she turned around.

"Can you stop kicking our seats, please?" she said, smiling tightly.

"SORRY, LOVE. THERE'S NO FUCKING LEG ROOM."

Kate didn't fancy the idea of an argument in a confined space with no escape. She glanced at Gabriel, hoping he felt the same. His jaw was twitching, his nostrils flared. He didn't look the type to get involved in a fight. He looked like he might write a protest blog rather than punch someone. She waited for the lads' voices to fade out and for them to get back on track.

"So, about the rubbish thing. I'm really interested, actually, because…"

But their voices were like foghorns.

"YOU KNOW THERE'S NEW RULES AND YOU CAN'T DRINK ON THE STREET IN MAGA?"

"I'LL DRINK WHERE I FUCKING LIKE."

Kate felt her cheeks burning. The hens' behaviour was also deteriorating. She could hear Fiona spouting her catchphrase, "I'll do what I like because it's my hen party!"

She shouldn't have let Fiona buy three mini bottles. She should have insisted on them buying one at a time. *This is not my job,* she thought. *I'm not a babysitter, I'm a director!*

Gabriel went to take a sip of coffee and his seat jerked again. Coffee spilled over the front of his T-shirt. There was an eruption of laughter behind him. Kate was sure it was unrelated laughter, but it compounded the situation. He sat up and turned around in his seat, his eyes blazing.

"Can you not see there are other people on this flight? This is not your private jet!"

So he wasn't afraid of confrontation. Kate felt herself tense. This wasn't going to end well. The guys didn't look like the types to respond favourably to reason.

"Sorry, mate?" one of them smirked.

"You're kicking my seat."

"I told the woman, there's no fucking leg room."

"You are KICKING it and you are shouting as if you were each in different countries."

"I wish *you* were in a different country, mate!" one of them laughed.

"And I wish you weren't going over to pollute mine."

"What did you say?" The voice sounded genuinely stunned to be told this.

"Are you racist?" another one piped up.

"Against stupid, drunk English people like you damaging my country?"

Oh God, Kate thought, her heart in her mouth.

"Yes," Gabriel finished. "I guess I am."

"WHAT YOU NEED, MATE, IS A FUCKING DRINK!" someone roared, and a second later a plastic glass of beer sailed through the air and exploded over Gabriel's head. There was an intake of breath. Gabriel looked simultaneously appalled and humiliated. The hens were up on their feet, straining to see. It felt like the whole plane was craning to get a better view of the action.

Kate jumped out of her seat, wiping at the beer that had splashed over her arms. "What the hell are you doing?"

"Sorry, I didn't mean to get you, darlin'! Just him," the thrower shouted.

An irritated air hostess was heading towards them. Her blonde hair was pulled back tightly, but even so it couldn't stop the angry lines breaking out across her forehead.

"These men just threw beer at me," Gabriel said, as if he couldn't believe it. "You should have them arrested."

The guys and hens burst out laughing. Kate heard one of the lads call, "He started it."

She felt her heart racing, the anger flooding through her arms and legs, making them tremble.

"We don't tolerate any misbehaviour on our flights and we will call the police if we need to," the stewardess said in a voice that wasn't convincing anyone.

"HOW WILL THEY REACH THE PLANE?" someone shouted.

"I'm covered in beer. What are you going to do about it?" Gabriel said, pulling at the wet patch on his T-shirt.

"I'm sorry, sir."

"That doesn't help me. You have to move me to another seat."

"And me. My seat's got beer over it, too," Kate said.

The stewardess blinked at them. "I'll bring you some paper towels."

"I don't want paper towels! I want to be in a seat where I'm not going to get attacked!"

"Please don't raise your voice to me, sir."

"I'm sorry, but I'm angry. This is unacceptable."

"WE DIDN'T ATTACK YOU. WE ACCIDENTALLY TIPPED A DROP OF BEER OVER YOU."

"It wasn't an accident!" Kate cried, losing her temper. "It was a whole glass."

Suddenly, Fiona was in the aisle, hands on her hips. "Did you throw a beer at our director? Own up! You're in trouble!"

"Please, madam, would you return to your seat."

"No, it's my hen party."

"YEAH, IT'S HER HEN PARTY, SHE CAN DO WHATEVER SHE LIKES."

"Excuse me. I'm moving to another seat. I can see one from here," Gabriel said.

Kate stepped into the aisle. She wanted to go with him.

"You can't move to another seat. You smell of beer. It's not fair on the other passengers," the stewardess said, looking around at her colleague, a short man with a puffed out chest who had just appeared. "They're throwing beer at each other like children."

"Excuse me? They threw beer at *me*!"

"If you could return to your seat, sir."

"No."

"Sorry, sir?"

"No, I'm not returning to my beer-covered seat."

"We can get you some paper towels."

Now a grey haired man in a smart navy polo shirt and chinos was approaching. Kate hoped he was aviation police and was about to handcuff the guys' wrists in a position in which they wouldn't be able to reach another drop of alcohol.

"There is a seat in my row," he said in a thick accent.

The stewards looked at him blankly. "Sorry?"

Kate wondered if they were being purposefully obtuse or if they really couldn't understand.

The man directed his next few words at Gabriel in Spanish.

"There is a free seat by him," Gabriel translated, no doubt editing out the expletives.

"Fine." The stewardess let him pass.

Kate opened her mouth to ask to move too, but closed it when she realised all the guys were staring at her. One of them winked at her and she felt intimidated.

"You don't fancy that Spanish wanker, do you?"

The stewardess patted Kate's seat. "It's pretty dry."

Kate sat down, feeling miserable. Yes, she had fancied him. But it didn't matter now.

"I'll get you some paper towels," the stewardess said with a bright smile.

THREE

Sharon Wingman was waiting for Kate in the air conditioned hotel lobby. She didn't look like she'd flown in that morning. Her mask of foundation seemed freshly applied and her tailored turquoise jacket was unwrinkled. She wore a bold silk scarf with a Picasso painting on it. It swallowed up her neck in pinks and purples, hiding the wrinkles that might give her age away. She had given up birthdays at fifty and no one knew quite how old she was.

Sharon's signature bright outfits and red-hot lipstick tended to lure people into a false sense of security, making them think her a little more fun than the other bosses. But she was as temperamental as the worst of them, and her mood could turn from sunshine to rain within seconds of hearing a decision she didn't like.

Kate felt her insides shrink. For a brief moment she'd felt like she'd scored a victory, getting Sharon to agree to meet at a hotel fifteen minutes from the villa rather than at the deserted villa itself.

"Kate!" Sharon said, her face brightening. "There you are."

Her grip was firm, her diamond rings imprinting their authority into Kate's skin. Ricardo said they were her trophies, one from each divorce.

"How was your flight?" Kate asked.

Sharon waved a dismissive hand. "Tedious. Same as all the others."

"Was everyone drunk? They were on our flight over."

"So why is there no filming going on today?"

Just like that, the small talk was over.

"It's really hot, isn't it?" Kate said. "Are you hot?"

Outside it was baking. Inside the air conditioning was set to Arctic pre-global-warming.

"I just spoke to Ricardo," Sharon said.

"Oh. How is he?"

"Where is he?" more like.

Sharon frowned, causing little fractures in her thick layer of foundation. "Shouldn't you know the answer to that?"

"Yes, of course, but it's always nice to get another opinion. He can be quite monosyllabic."

"The signal was terrible and he wasn't very articulate about why you weren't filming today. I don't think he realised I was here, actually." She reached down into her tan leather handbag and retrieved a neat wad of pages stapled together. "Now, according to the schedule, there's not a single day's break in the entire week."

"No," Kate admitted, pulling her hand away from her mouth. In the last hour she'd unconsciously nibbled half her nails off and now they were annoyingly scratchy. The kind of scratchy which made pulling up tights a perilous activity. Not that she was wearing tights. It was thirty-four degrees outside. She hoped the hens weren't stranded somewhere without shade. "The break was unplanned."

Sharon cocked her head to one side, her big green eyes firing question marks. "Well, it's not a weather-related issue. I can see for myself it's not raining."

Kate swallowed. "The hens voted with their feet."

They'd voted quite vocally, too, to be fair. From the very beginning. She'd just been determined to persuade them, so sure everything she'd planned was in their own interests.

Sharon's eyes had narrowed significantly.

"They voted with their feet? And where the hell have their feet taken them? Because it sounds like we're wasting time and money."

"Not far," Kate said, trying to sound positive. She pictured them in her head. They were slouching at the top of the steps that led to the rocky cove, groaning and moaning because all they wanted to do was flop on to some sand. "None of them are big walkers, are they?"

How would Sharon know? To her, the hens were just names on a page. Her participation had been minimal.

"You mean to say, you don't know where they are?" Sharon said, incredulous. "None of them?"

She was staring at Kate, waiting for reassurance that of course she, the director of a big television show, knew exactly where her cast was. Kate realised her teeth had another fingernail in their sights and drew her hand away.

"Not exactly," she said.

Sharon's eyes were popping out.

"But...but you've agreed on a time to...to start filming again," she stammered. "I mean, a day's break is a concern, but if you thought you'd got enough brilliant footage then maybe I could understand, eventually, but any more and…well, Kate, frankly…".

She trailed off, her mouth left open mid-sentence. Kate looked down at her feet. Perhaps it was time to admit that there had been differences of opinion with regard to the direction she had been taking the programme in.

"They can't have got very far," she said.

"You're talking like they've escaped!"

"Well…"

"Why would they want to escape an amazingly fun hen party, Kate? What happened? Why would they want to have a break from a bloody break?"

Kate could see how it must sound baffling. She hesitated, torn between telling the truth and denying everything.

"I don't really understand it myself," she said, which was partly true. "I mean, I may have pushed an environmental angle, but I don't see why being a little greener would have upset them."

Sharon's face twisted like she'd just sucked on a lemon. "What do you mean? What *environmental* angle?"

"Oh, nothing major. I just suggested we all use less plastic. The Mediterranean is in such a state."

"I don't care about the bloody Mediterranean, Kate!"

Kate grimaced. *That* was a shame. Someone environmentally conscientious would definitely see her side of the story in a more sympathetic light.

"Where are they, Kate?"

"They're nearby…they must be…"

"I don't understand," Sharon said, pressing her fingers against her temple. "Weren't they having a nice time? They had a spa day, didn't they?"

"Spa *morning*," Kate said. "That was on Day 2."

"And how did that go down, Kate?"

Kate could hear the shouting as if it were yesterday. She nodded.

"Good. It went well. To be honest, I'm as confused as you are."

FOUR

Fiona stared at Kate in disbelief. "Did you just say bull semen?"

She had woken up, willing to dismiss the bumpy first evening and get on with having the best free holiday ever. The breakfast mimosas and gold-sprinkled truffles had injected the touch of glamour which had been missing and she'd felt sure everything was back on track. But now Kate was telling the hens their luxurious spa morning involved bull semen. Had she got her shows mixed up?

"It's a very natural treatment," the director said.

She had to be kidding.

"What's so natural about wanking a bull and putting its cum all over your hair?"

"No, you don't actually have to masturbate the bull," Kate replied brightly.

"Oh, I see, that's totally fine, then."

"Great."

"I was joking!"

Chi let out a nervous laugh. "I'm thinking of braiding my hair so I don't think I need it."

"Well I'm thinking of shaving mine off now," Sam said, hands on her hips. "It's not like I ever have time to do anything with it these days anyway."

Fiona pushed away a flicker of irritation. "You have time now," she couldn't resist pointing out. Motherhood had brought out the martyr in her old friend.

35

Sam snorted. "It's your hen party, love. *You* should go first."

Kate gave her an encouraging smile. "Go on, Fiona. It's a super natural conditioner. Your hair is going to look amazing afterwards."

Fiona groaned. She wanted gorgeous, glossy hair, but this seemed too high a price.

"I don't think she needs it, personally," Jem said. "She's got amazing hair."

Aw, how sweet of her, Fiona thought.

"Thanks, honey. Neither do you."

Well, that wasn't strictly true. Jem's hair was rather wispy. If she were Jem, Fiona would get extensions. The girl had everything else going for her. Out of the five of them, she was the best looking. She had great bone structure and smooth skin which looked beautiful with nothing but a bit of moisturiser. Fiona couldn't tell Jem what her hair needed, though. They didn't have that sort of relationship. The truth was she'd really ummed and aahed over inviting her. Fiona had always got the vague impression that Jem hadn't approved of her being her brother's girlfriend the first time around. But perhaps she had been wrong, or perhaps the ten-year gap had changed things, because Jem had only been sweetness since they'd got back in touch.

"Don't you realise how many chemicals there are in normal shampoo?" Kate said, sounding a little desperate.

"I don't want *normal* shampoo. I want delicious, scented, stupidly expensive shampoo!"

Fiona was a cosmetics connoisseur. She had exhausted the testers in the Duty Free, inhaling fragrances and trying on silky moisturisers which cost fifty pounds for a pot the size of a contact lens. She had assumed that this week she would be bathed in luxury products.

"It's a really expensive treatment. She's come all the way over from New York."

New York? Fiona felt her revulsion subside a little and her curiosity grow. If it was so special, why hadn't she heard about it?

"That's quite a big carbon footprint. It'll be such a waste if you don't do it."

Carbon footprint? Fiona thought irritably. *What is she on about now?*

"I don't believe in all that."

"In what? Carbon footprints?" Kate had her eyebrows raised and was looking at Fiona as if she was an idiot. "It's not like the tooth fairy. It's science," she said with an unmistakable note of condescension in her voice.

Here we go again, Fiona thought. But she smiled patiently. It was probably best to stay on the right side of the director.

"Okay, whatever you say," she said, swallowing a hundred other responses.

Clearly that wasn't the right answer because now Kate was tutting at her. "Again, it's not what *I'm* saying, it's what science has proven."

Sam coughed. "Is it me, or is this getting boring?"

Clare burst out laughing. "Shsss, Sam! Now they'll have to cut again."

Fiona glanced over at their brooding cameraman. He was standing to one side of the camera, rubbing a hand over the dark bristles on his chin.

"Do you think we can get back to talking about the treatments?" he said.

Fiona bit her lip and shared a pointed look with the others. Clearly he thought Kate was being dull too. That was a relief since his job was the most important of them all.

"Cut," Kate said, evenly. "I was just about to say that."

The girls all turned to check their makeup in the huge wooden mirror with the hand painted ceramic tiles around the edge depicting country life in 18th century Mallorca. Fiona reapplied her lip gloss and then turned back to Kate.

"Does it smell like cum, then?" she asked.

Kate looked uncertain. "No, I don't think so. Look, I understand if you don't want to do it. There's also a hay treatment..."

"Hay?" Fiona echoed. "You mean the stuff you feed horses?"

It sounded marginally better than the bull spunk, but then Kate could hardly have suggested something worse.

"It's a very old treatment originating from Italy."

"What does that involve, then?"

"They wrap you up tightly in hot hay for twenty minutes or so."

Fiona had watched every single episode of *The Hen Party* and she couldn't remember one of them being this hippy.

"That's me out. I've got hay fever," Clare said. "Pool it is."

Fiona was aware of Kate staring at her expectantly.

"So?" she said. "Is that a yes or no?"

It was as if Kate thought Fiona was being purposefully difficult. As if she considered her a diva for delaying her answer over whether she wanted a gross hair treatment or a gross body treatment. The whole thing was weird. Yesterday had been weird too. Normally when the hens arrived at the venue there were party poppers and balloons, and they were shown a video full of heartfelt messages from the groom, family and friends. Not that anyone would have been able to persuade her dad to appear on TV, and she couldn't be sure she wanted to see her mum slurring her words after all the free drinks. But some nice messages would have been a lot better than what Kate had put on. That horrible video of a turtle getting a straw removed from its nose had been really painful to watch. Who knew turtles could bleed?

"Fine, I'll do it," she said. Perhaps the treatments were great and Kate was just an awful saleswoman. Perhaps hay was the wrong word. She should have said something like *organic stems of sun soaked pasturage*. Fiona knew a thing or two about marketing. She felt a surge of optimism and smiled. "If it's good enough for New York and Italy..."

It would be a good story at least. And how bad could it be?

Bad. Very bad. An hour later, Fiona was on a waterbed, her skin covered in soggy hay, burning with a need to be scratched. It was bringing tears to her eyes how badly she wanted to scratch. When the camera had been rolling, she'd managed to laugh at it.

"Basically, girls," she'd said, winking at her future audience, "if I can survive this, I can survive marriage. Am I right or am I right?"

As soon as the woman had wrapped the sheet tightly around Fiona, securing the hay, she'd begun to sweat and her skin tingle uncomfortably. Kate had asked her to talk about how she was preparing for the wedding. A past contestant had set up a fashion blog after appearing on the show and had gained five thousand followers in one day just by talking about styles of wedding shoes. Fiona had entertained ideas of repeating that sort of success herself, and as a precaution had practised what she was going to say. She'd had a great idea for nail art: a black and white nail silhouette with a girl blowing a kiss to a boy. She'd originally made a stencil and tried it out with Clare. It hadn't come out all that well because Clare lacked confidence and had spent the whole time muttering, *"I don't think I can do this!"* while her hand shook.

Chi, on the other hand, was a real artist and had done an incredible job in their lunch break at work. Chi had already promised to do her nails for the wedding, but Fiona hadn't mentioned that in the filming because she was worried people would wonder why Chi didn't set up the blog instead of her. Fiona had tried to sound professional and at the same time natural, but between Ricardo's solemn face and Kate's distracted one, it had been tough. She'd begun to doubt herself. Was she bad television?

She closed her eyes and felt a hundred places screaming to be rubbed. With no one around, there was nothing fun about the hay treatment at all. Without a camera rolling, there didn't seem any point in going on with it, either. She gritted her teeth as a bullet of rage shot through her. Kate had said it was an expensive treatment, but what could be expensive about it? It was hay, for God's sake. It was supposed to come from the foothills of

South Tyrol, but how likely was that, really? Kate had probably told the woman not to bother bringing it over because of the carbon bloody footprint, and to bring some average Mallorcan hay from a local barn instead. Basically, Fiona was sitting on a plastic bed covered in dry grass. For fun.

This was not a spa day, this was torture. Seriously, were there fleas in this hay? She tried to push the thought away, but it gnawed at her, much like the invisible fleas were doing to her skin. She wanted to call Andrew and burst into tears. He hated seeing her cry. He'd probably be so horrified he'd catch the first flight over. She mustn't ring him. It would be a step too far. She was getting a free holiday, but what was he getting? Nothing at all.

The top of her back was killing her. She tried to rub it against the waterbed but she just bounced. Her ankles were prickling. Her right eyelid too.

"Hello?" she called.

Where had everyone gone?

She had to get out of this. She tried, but it was like being in a straightjacket. The Italian woman who had wrapped her up had barely spoken a word of English, but surely she would recognise the sound of a woman in distress.

"HELP!"

She could hear the tinkle of laughter float up the stairs. What were they all doing down there? Had the New Yorker arrived with her jars of bull cum?

"HELLO?"

Where had the woman gone? This was totally unprofessional. Having someone on hand was the only single expense of the treatment. Perhaps she was multi-

41

tasking and she'd gone to feed the cows at her farm where the hay had come from. *She should have said*, Fiona thought. *I could have offered to roll around in her barn!* The woman wouldn't have had to drive then and Kate would have had a field day thinking about the carbon footprint saving.

"CAN SOMEONE COME HERE AND GET ME OUT OF THIS?"

She strained her ears. Her hens' absence felt like a betrayal and she tried to excuse them. Clare's hay fever had been a new one. But even if she wasn't making it up to avoid the treatment, Fiona was pretty certain it didn't mean being allergic to actual hay. And what was Sam's excuse? Was she making another phone call to George? What was the point of that when George couldn't speak? And what about Chi? She had been a bit shy with her other hens to start with, but now that she was getting on with them it almost felt like she was forgetting Fiona. And Jem? She'd excuse Jem because she'd been so nice about her hair…

She called out again, then her voice broke and she started to cry as loudly as she could. Silent tears weren't going to get anyone's attention. It was so cruel. She'd been wrapped in weeds and abandoned.

Had they already forgotten that if it wasn't for her, they wouldn't be in Mallorca?

She felt a spasm in her leg and another pressing urge to scratch. The heat was unbearable. Without moving she was sweating profusely. Self-pity turned to rage. If no one was coming to rescue her then she'd have to save herself.

Her abdominals crunched as she managed to get herself to a sitting position. Her arms were pinned to her side, her legs pressed together. She swivelled to one side and the bed bounced and tipped her over. She pushed down on her feet and hoisted herself up, hay falling on the flagstones around her. The sheet remained in place. Perhaps the woman did embalming when she wasn't smothering people in hay.

Fiona spotted the camera on the windowsill and automatically composed her face into a smile. It faltered as it dawned on her that the camera would have captured her crying for help and wailing. She felt simultaneously embarrassed and annoyed. If she'd had a free arm, she would have held up her middle finger to it. She'd tell Ricardo to edit this scene out. All that mattered now was getting out of this peasant straightjacket.

She shuffled over to the door, which was shut tight. The woman must have got used to her clients trying to escape the worst spa treatment ever invented. Fiona bent down, opened her mouth and tried to fit half a door knob in it. Her tongue made contact and she tasted metal. Was the camera getting this too? She'd want to witness Ricardo deleting this scene for herself.

Her teeth scraped against the door knob, failing to get a grip. Sweat dripped down her forehead. She felt torn between crying and banging her head against the door. In the end, destiny chose the latter. As she bent down to try to get a grip on the door knob one more time, the door opened abruptly and the handle punched into her mouth.

Pain shot through her gums. She tried to reach for her mouth, forgetting her arms were bound. She tottered, lost balance and fell with a thud on her back, her head jerking and hitting the stone. Winded by the fall, she opened her mouth but no sound came out to express the agony she was in.

"Oh my God, what are you doing on the floor, you crazy woman?" It was Sam and she couldn't have sounded less sympathetic if she'd tried. "Did I hit you? Oh my God, you're crying. Don't cry! Come on, let me get you up."

Fiona wasn't going anywhere. She was going to die on this floor. They wouldn't need to bury her, they'd just need to chuck her in a corner and throw some more hay over her.

Sam was trying to scoop her up by the shoulders.

"Oi! Someone get up here!" she yelled.

Fiona's mouth was throbbing and she could taste blood. It was metallic like the door knob.

"Get me out of this," she said, getting her breath back. "Get me out of this, now!"

"I think you've got another ten minutes, love."

"GET ME OUT OF THIS NOW!"

"Alright, don't shout at me! I get enough tantrums at home, thank you very much."

The thought flashed through Fiona's head that she shouldn't have invited Sam; that she should have left her looking after her beloved George.

"Sorry, I didn't mean to shout," Sam said quickly.

Fiona mustered a smile of forgiveness "I shouted first. I really hurt myself."

Footsteps pounded on the stairs and the closing door was thrown open again, banging into Fiona's ankle. She yelped in pain.

"Oh, sorry! Did that hurt?" Chi gasped.

"YES."

Clare called out from behind everyone else. "What's happening? I can't come in because of the hay."

"Hay fever doesn't mean you're allergic to hay, you muppet!" Sam called.

The Italian woman pushed through to the front. "No, no, no, ten more minutes!"

Before Fiona could protest, the woman's strong hands were pulling and pushing at her.

"No!" Fiona shrieked. "Get off me!"

"Come on, love, you need to get up," Sam said, trying to haul her up too.

"Get the hay off her! She's itching," Chi urged.

Fiona let them help her up on to her feet, but nudged the woman off when she tried to pull her back to the waterbed. The woman looked deeply offended by the gesture. Kate appeared at the door, wearing her regular baffled face.

"Everything alright?"

"No, it's not fucking alright," Fiona cried, feeling the tears well up again.

"Oh babe, you're bleeding!" Chi cried, covering her mouth.

Fiona licked her lips. She could taste the warm blood on them. Despite the anger, a calm voice inside her head told her to take a photo so she had proof. This deserved an apology in a form of something delicious. Like an actual spa day somewhere prestigious.

"You need lie still," the woman said, shaking her head and pointing once again at the waterbed.

"Why is she bleeding?" Kate asked.

"I hit her when I opened the door," Sam said. "But I can't have hit you in the face, can I?"

"But why was she up?"

"Because this is not a treatment, this is torture!" Fiona cried. "I'm tied up in some horrible, itchy crap and I cried for help and none of you came. I couldn't get out so I had to try to open the door with my fucking teeth. I can't move. GET ME OUT!"

Her hens moved in to find the eject button. There was none. Kate, Fiona noted, didn't move a muscle.

"Just think," she said brightly. "That's *exactly* how turtles must feel when they get caught up in those six pack plastic rings."

Fiona wasn't sure she'd heard correctly.

"What?"

"Unable to swim properly, no one to help them."

Fiona was so angry, she only just managed to splutter out the words, "Are you trying to make a point?"

"I didn't plan to, but yes, I think this is absolutely perfect," Kate said, then half turned and shouted for Ricardo.

Fiona felt the blood pumping through her like water from a fireman's cannon. Her head was aching, her mouth was tingling, her ankle was hurting and her entire skin felt like it was on fire, and this bitch was telling her it was *perfect*?

She bolted. Breaking away from the hands that were unpacking her, she ran at Kate, head first like a battering ram.

"Fiona, don't!" Sam cried.

Kate tried to move out of the way. She stepped into a little table, knocking off a glass candlestick that smashed to smithereens on the floor. At the last minute, Kate managed to dodge her, and instead of soft stomach, Fiona went flying into the wall. After that, everything went black.

FIVE

Day 5
KATE

The hotel lobby was filling up with new arrivals. They had been delivered by a bright blue double-decker coach which was currently blocking half the road outside. Groups of middle aged Scandinavian women congregated in circles, dressed in stripy T-shirts and pastel blouses, cropped trousers and soft leather sandals. Kate welcomed the disruption. Sharon let out a sigh of exasperation and suggested they move to the hotel bar.

"I could do with a drink," she added.

They sat under a smart white parasol on the veranda which looked out across the seaside. Sharon looked momentarily wistful. Kate imagined she was wishing she was in Mallorca under different circumstances; Kate had felt the same when she'd first clapped eyes on that glistening turquoise water. It was the stuff of honeymoon brochures.

Busy Cala Major beach wasn't like some of the other isolated gems, but it was still a beauty. Today it was packed with sunbathers, some opting for the shade of dried grass umbrellas, others basking in the full glory of the sunshine. Kids played on the edge of the water with buckets and spades, excavating one area to build beside it, their arms and legs coated in wet sand. A couple of teenagers were using their lilos as surf boards, running at the incoming waves and jumping before they broke.

Sharon dug out a pack of cigarettes from her bag and lit up, leaning back into her chair and turning her face to the sunshine.

"I'd offer you one, but I don't smoke."

Kate guessed that was a line she always used. Someone must have laughed at it once so now she thought it was clever.

"So let's back track."

"They were happy," Kate said.

"Don't talk about them in the past tense!" Sharon spluttered. "They had better be happy wherever they are right now, and happy to come back, and happy to spend the next forty-eight hours being filmed."

They hadn't been happy. Kate knew that much. They hadn't skipped off into the night, smiling and dancing. A witness said there had been a fight on the beach. Not just verbal, either. Two of them had fought. Which two?

"*La negra y la gorda.*" The black one and the fat one.

"A slap," a less dramatic witness said, "and lots of tears."

Fiona had been the first to disappear, Chi the last. Kate had yet to inform Sharon that the hens had made their exits separately. Imagining them all together was a lot more manageable.

"Look where they are," Kate said, waving a hand towards the beach. "How can they not be happy?"

She drowned the twinge of guilt with a gulp of cold sparkling water. She hadn't exactly let them savour the beauty of the place.

Sharon was scanning the beach as if she'd taken Kate's statement literally.

"So they're on a beach somewhere?"

"Yes."

Probably. Hopefully.

"The spa morning was on Day 2. We jumped ahead," Sharon said, running a finger over the sheet in front of her. "Let's go back to the arrival day. Day 1. That should have been pretty straightforward. Mojitos by the pool and then the soppy video with everyone sending their best wishes, etc...." She looked up expectantly. "You've got that?"

Kate swallowed. "Yes. We played a video."

"*A* video?"

"Yes."

"You said *a* video. Not *the* video."

Kate winced. She hadn't expected Sharon to catch her out so easily. Her aim had always been to get the rushes to the editor, and somehow manage to get a version of the episode so slick that the channel would let it air, in spite of the unexpected environmental angle. Clearly she'd been delusional to think there wouldn't be people tracking a quarter of a million-pound investment. She was in trouble. The question was, how much trouble?

"It was a video that had gone viral about a turtle."

"I'm not following. Did her fiancé buy her a turtle? Is it even legal to buy turtles? We don't want to be accused of supporting illegal wildlife trafficking."

"No, nothing like that."

Sharon mentally ticked off a problem in her head. "Good."

"I wanted to expand on a discussion Fiona and I had had about straws."

"Straws?"

"It's just ludicrous how they're used for less than a minute but take a lifetime to decompose."

"You weren't like this with the hens, were you?" Sharon said, looking concerned.

"Like what?"

"Preachy."

"I'm not preachy."

"Oh God. You were, weren't you."

In hindsight, Kate could have been less bossy about the whole matter of straws. She forgot that a lot of people didn't mean to be a source of great distress for the earth, but were just ignorant. Or worse, they didn't care. The top priority was always convenience, regardless of whether that convenience was killing the planet one disposable cup at a time.

"The hens were fascinated by the video," Kate soothed, "like the six million viewers who have already watched it, and the audience who will watch *The Hen Party*."

Sharon shook her head and turned her attention to the itinerary in front of her.

"Kate, you're making me feel very nervous."

"There's nothing to be nervous about."

"Then take me through step by step. Day 1: arrival at the villa. How did that go?"

SIX

Day 1
CHIOMA

An involuntary shiver of excitement ran down Chi's spine when she saw where they would be staying for the week. The villa was a vision of rustic charm with its wooden shuttered windows painted dark green, its rough sandstone walls and terracotta roof tiles. Bright bougainvillea tumbled over the back door like a cloud of pink tissue paper and two small palm trees with striped trunks and waxy green leaves stretched high above the wrought iron gate. It just needed tables laid out with white linen cloths on the patio and it would look like the perfect setting for a Mediterranean wedding. *Like Mamma Mia*, Chi thought, breaking into a smile.

"Gorgeous, isn't it," Fiona said, throwing an arm around her shoulders and leaning heavily against her. Chi could smell the booze on her breath and noted the slur. "I'm *sso* glad you could get out of your thing."

By 'thing', Fiona meant Chi's grandparents' fiftieth wedding anniversary. Chi hadn't been entirely truthful about that, but it didn't matter now.

"It's so beautiful. Thank you so much for inviting me, Fi. I know it must've been really tough to choose only four people."

"Course I was going to invite you. You're my favourite stationery cupboard person."

Chi pushed away the splinter of pain that always arose at the mention of the stationery cupboard and shot Fiona a smile.

"*Favourite?* You mean you hang out with other people in there too?"

Fiona snorted drunkenly. "Love you, Chichi."

Chi squeezed Fiona's hand, which was dangling over her breast, and felt the large engagement ring prick her skin.

"Love you too, Fifi."

Perhaps embarrassment was a better word for what she felt about that incident in the stationery room. Fiona had dragged her there to find out why she had turned up at the Christmas party with puffy eyes and smudged mascara. At the first hint of sympathy, Chi had spilled her heart out. She'd told Fiona about her cheating tattooist boyfriend whom she'd found with another women wearing nothing but their inks.

Up until that moment, Fiona had just been another colleague she'd had fleeting chats with about *Game of Thrones*. But that evening the sparkly eyed woman with the intricate braids who always dressed to the nines for work, who exuded a sense of fun, had left the party to cheer her up.

"Careful!" Chi called, grabbing Fiona's arm as she tottered forward and almost fell on her face.

Clare turned back in concern. "You alright, Fi?"

Fiona didn't answer. Her gaze was unfocused and her small mouth was hanging open.

"Oh, bloody hell, I knew I should have got her some water." Clare's square teeth raked over her chubby bottom lip which only retained a slim cover of bright pink lipstick around the edges. "I usually do. I've saved her a few times from herself before now."

Chi had noticed how proudly Clare wore the badge of loyal best friend. Clare had known Fiona longer than any of them. Since they were three-and-three-quarters, to be precise. Chi had only met her a couple of times with Fiona after work, and both times she had felt frustrated by Clare's habit of getting nostalgic and dipping into old memories she shared with Fiona, which left Chi stranded outside the conversation.

"This reminds me of her eighteenth birthday," Clare sighed.

"Like you have to go that far back!" scoffed Sam, who had stopped and was waiting for them to catch up.

"Gottossit," Fiona mumbled.

Chi felt a pang of pity for the bride-to-be. This was going to feel like a complete anti-climax once she'd sobered up and realised she'd missed the grand arrival.

"Fi, you just need to keep it together until we get in," Chi said, gently. "Got that, lovely?"

She looked towards the villa gate where the director was having a discussion with the serious looking cameraman and the friendlier sound recordist. Ricardo seemed jaded. He had barely interacted with them so far, staying away during the flight and only telling them where to position themselves in the airport. Mel, a chatty Aussie, was at least trying to get to know them. Chi could overhear them talking about the takes Kate wanted to do. She felt herself struggling under Fiona's weight. One minute she had seemed fine, the next it was like she had been hit over the head with all the champagne bottles she had drained.

They couldn't film Fiona like this. It would be so humiliating.

"Has anyone got any water?"

"I do," Sam said, rifling through her stripy beach bag.

"Come on, Fiona, drink some water," Chi urged.

Fiona was miles away now, her body growing heavier. She moved her head away from the bottle. "No, it'smahenparty," she mumbled. "Got to ssitdown."

"Okay...okay..." Chi said, looking around for somewhere she could sit. But there was only the curb. "I'm going to drop her in a minute."

"Here, let me." Sam took over, her strong arms easing Fiona against her. "Carrying George around has given my arms a workout."

"Thanks, I'm such a weakling," Chi said. She backed away, rubbing her pinched arm, and decided she liked Sam. She was practical and down to earth.

"Fiona, you need to stand up, okay?" Sam said.

Jem had turned back when she'd heard Fiona stagger and was standing beside Clare, looking alarmed. Chi had been struck by how similar Jem looked to her brother, Andrew. Both were blond and blue-eyed. Both had delicate, high cheek bones and pale skin with the softest patter of freckles over their noses.

"Oh God, is she alright? She has to sober up. She can't be filmed like that. It'll make her look so bad."

Chi imagined Jem was thinking about her brother, too – that it would be embarrassing for Andrew to see his fiancée blind drunk at eleven in the morning before the week of celebration had even begun.

"Come on, Fi, drink some water," Sam said, a little more bossily. The water missed Fiona's mouth and ran down her neck, leaving a streak in her foundation.

"What's going on?"

It was Kate. She strode towards them, her forehead knitted beneath her ruler straight fringe. "Is she alright?"

"She's drunk. That's what happens when you let Fiona drink three bottles of champagne by herself," Clare said. "You should have given us a limit."

Chi cringed at Clare's accusative tone. It wasn't as if they weren't all adults. Kate put her hands on her hips and swore. They were behind schedule already, apparently.

Fiona shrugged Sam off her and took an unsteady step forward. Sam reached for her before she could fall.

"Can't we go inside so she can lie down?" Chi said. It seemed stupid for them to be all hovering outside the gate like this.

Kate ignored her and put her hands on Fiona's shoulders.

"Fiona, are you with me?"

Fiona let out a snort which morphed into a giggle. "Yessh."

"WE NEED TO FILM YOU GOING INTO THE VILLA, DO YOU UNDERSTAND?"

Fiona nodded, a dopey smile spreading across her face. "Yesshsir."

Chi raked a hand through her hair, twisting the wiry tendrils around her finger. "Can't we wait?" She had only seen a few clips of *The Hen Party* on YouTube, but from what she had seen it wasn't a show that set out to mortify the participants. She hoped it wasn't going to start now.

"If I let her go, she'll fall over," Sam said.

Ricardo had come over now, and so had Mel.

"Maybe I could run and get her a coffee," suggested Jem.

"Good idea," Ricardo said, nodding at her. "What's your name?"

Chi noticed Jem blush as she replied.

"Jem," he echoed. "Good idea, Jem. What do you think, Kate? It's that or a cold shower."

Chi felt her eyes widen. Was he serious? A cold shower? How cruel was that?

Ricardo caught her expression and laughed. "What? The show must go on!"

Kate sighed. "Alright. There's a coffee machine in the villa. But use a normal cup, Jem. There's no need to use a takeaway cup."

"I'll come with you, Jem," Chi said. Using coffee machines was one of her superpowers. She had yet to be defeated by a model.

Jem shot her a look of gratitude.

"Alright, come on," Kate ordered. "The rest of you can wait in the back patio. Breathe in that fresh air, Fiona."

So Chi and Jem ended up having a preview of the house. They stepped into a spacious reception area, its walls hung with oil paintings of mountain landscapes. In one corner there was a vintage hat stand and a leather trunk with brass buckles. They passed along the hall of terracotta tiles and turned into a kitchen with a long wooden table and benches. It had a high white-washed ceiling with dark wooden beams running across it.

"Easy peasy," Chi said, spotting the familiar coffee machine.

"I wouldn't mind one too. Aren't you tipsy?" Jem said.

"I am."

"A bit. I had a bottle of water on the plane."

Jem looked impressed. Chi didn't feel like she deserved the approval. She knew she wasn't the measured individual Jem seemed to think she was.

"I'm usually crap," she added quickly. "But this time I really want to pace myself."

"I know. You're thinking about the filming, right?"

They shared a look and groaned. Chi was determined not to let herself down. After Fiona's engagement party, she had resolved never to get so drunk again.

"I was nervous about meeting everyone, weren't you?" Jem admitted, her cheeks quick to colour. "I met Sam and Clare such a long time ago."

"Everyone's friendly, though," Chi said.

Her game plan this week was to stay sober and to get on with everyone.

Jem smiled. "Yeah. Everyone's been lovely so far."

The button on the coffee machine stopped flashing, meaning the coffee was ready. Chi prepared a double for all of them. She and Jem were finishing theirs when Kate burst into the kitchen.

"Ricardo and I have just had a chat, and we thought we could start with everyone jumping in the pool together. That's sure to snap Fiona out of it, don't you think?"

Chi grimaced. "Not if she drowns first."

Kate laughed. "Very funny. Right. Run that coffee out to her, will you? And then it's bikini time!"

Jem shot her an apprehensive look which summed up Chi's own feelings perfectly. She had no one but herself to blame, though. She could have got out of coming. She could have insisted that she had to go to her grandparents' wedding anniversary, even if it was taking place on a different week entirely.

SEVEN

Day 5
KATE

Sharon leant forward, her eyes sparkling with the vision in her head.

"Yes, I like the sound of that. Them all jumping in the pool."

The waiter drew near and she upgraded her glass of white wine to a whole bottle. Kate was sticking to water. She hadn't finished the story yet – not that she was telling any of it all that faithfully. She had omitted the part about Fiona collapsing before they'd even got inside the villa, and the bickering over the rooms later that evening. And she knew the story wouldn't end with all the hens bursting through the hotel doors and calling out happily, "We're here!" Sooner or later, she'd have to get in the car and start searching for them.

Kate's handbag was quietly buzzing on her lap. Sharon was making notes on her schedule, so Kate slipped out her phone to have a look. *Gabriel calling.* She felt butterflies in her stomach. Nerves, too. She should have left him a note. If she didn't answer, what would he think? How would he feel? She'd never sneaked out like that before. It had been an act of unnecessary drama and she regretted it.

She cancelled the call before Sharon noticed and asked her if it was the hens touching base. Kate knew Sharon didn't really understand the situation. She didn't know that the jump into the pool she was getting so excited

60

about wasn't a very accurate representation of the unity in the house.

"What else?" Sharon said, lifting her head. "Obviously I want to see something on film as soon as Ricardo gets here, but for now I'd like an idea. What else can I look forward to? What else stands out on arrival day?"

Kate didn't have to think very hard. The events of Day 1 had stuck in her memory; they had also stuck on the floors and the walls and the ceiling. Was Sharon ready to hear about the clay fight?

EIGHT

Day 1
CLARE

At least Ricardo could only film the jump once. It was a small relief for Clare, who was acutely aware that she was double the size of the rest of the hens. She had felt her thighs wobbling against each other as she had run, and she was sure her jump had been half as high as everyone else's, but had made the mightiest splash. She dreaded to think what she looked like. Once out of the pool, she grabbed her sarong and tied it around her, even though she was sopping wet.

Everyone else had stayed in the pool. She watched Fiona and Sam laughing as they attempted handstands. Fiona flopped face first into the water then immediately came back up again, spluttering and coughing.

"Nearly!" Sam cried, before cracking up completely.

The water had done the job: Fiona was *compos mentis* again. She'd also had two double espressos, a bottle of water and an aspirin.

"I used to be really good at them," Fiona declared, splashing Sam who couldn't stop laughing.

"I bet you were. I bet you were on the Olympic team."

"Watch and learn!"

Fiona made another attempt and once again failed even to submerge her head. Clare knew for a fact Fiona had never produced a decent handstand either in water or out of it. They had grown up together, attended the same nursery, the same primary school. Fiona had been a useless swimmer, resorting to an uncoordinated doggy paddle in every game. It wasn't her fault. Her party loving mother had never been able to get up early enough to take her swimming when she was little. At the time, Clare had agreed with Fiona that the swimming teacher was picking on her, even though it wasn't true at all. The poor swimming teacher had only been trying his best to get a very disruptive little girl to stop swimming like a Chihuahua. Clare was a good swimmer because she'd had to learn quickly to escape two older brothers trying to duck her head under water when no one was looking.

Out of the pool, though, Fiona was the person everyone wanted to be friends with. She was confident and daring and more grown-up than the rest of them. She was the first to wear makeup and paint her nails; the first to send a Valentine's card, and the first to receive one. For Clare's unswerving support, Fiona had rewarded her with the title of best friend, which had proved to Clare that telling someone what you really thought was sometimes overrated. Since then, she'd always been like that with Fiona – on her side, even when she knew that Fiona was exaggerating or telling white lies.

"Clare, get back in!" Fiona called.

"In a bit. I'm knackered. Aren't you?"

"The water wakes you up."

"Yeah, come on, Clare," Sam called

Clare grinned, pleased to be missed.

"In a bit," she repeated, closing her eyes for a moment to savour the sun on her face. She knew she should put some sun cream on – she burnt so quickly and she didn't want to be red and frazzled on camera. But Ricardo had gone off to take shots of the rest of the house, so for now she could relax her tummy muscles, which she had spent most of the morning tensing.

"I love your sarong, Clare," Chi called.

Clare opened her eyes and looked down at her fuchsia sarong, forgetting which of the many she had chosen. She had brought one for every day. She had a bit of a thing for them, like Fiona had a thing for bikinis. Clare had helped Fiona pack and knew she had eight in total, including a gold sequined one which she had won for completing an online survey for *Grazia* magazine. Her friend really was a four-leaf clover.

"Thanks, I'm sure I'll be going the same colour soon." Chi laughed. "Well it's a very pretty colour."

"Get some sun cream on!" Sam called. "I've got a kids' factor 50 in my bag from our first holiday with George. We went to Greece and it rained for four days."

"Yeah, I know, I remember you whingeing about it on Facebook."

Sam stuck her tongue out at Clare. "I wasn't whingeing, I was reporting on a rare meteorological phenomenon. You should have been fascinated."

Clare had been so looking forward to spending quality time with Fiona and Sam, like old times. Old times as in before George. The last time they had met up, Sam had been unable to tear her eyes off the child, even though he had been fast asleep. Clare couldn't blame her. The boy looked like a little cherub. However, it was hard to have a conversation with someone so distracted.

Clare had been curious to see how Jem had changed, too. She remembered Andrew's older sister as being rather aloof when they were teenagers. Jem had worn a lot of black back then and had been a bit of a rock chick,

64

but her style was now the opposite. She seemed quite a conservative dresser. At the airport, she'd been the only one to cover up her boob tube with a cardigan. Clare hadn't thought her boring when they were younger, but now she suspected she was. The thought was comforting and made her feel a little surer about her own place in the group. Clare had battled with the worry that she was boring when she had been a teenager, and it still caught her off guard from time to time.

Clare watched Jem now as she kicked off from the side of the pool and swam a length under water before resurfacing gracefully. Her wet hair stuck to her slender white neck. She had flawless skin. Either that or perfect makeup. Some might think her petite symmetrical features made her a beauty. She was pretty, Clare could appreciate that much, but it was in an obvious sort of way that made her plain. Clare thought women were beautiful when their features showed character, were more unconventional.

Fiona had confided in Clare that she hadn't been sure about inviting Jem. They hadn't spoken for years; they hadn't really spoken when they were teens, either. Fiona said she just remembered Jem as the intimidating older sister of Andrew who hadn't been unfriendly, but hadn't gone out of her way to hang out with them. Of course she must invite her, Clare had said, feeling virtuous. It would make Andrew happy, plus the sister of the groom was an important ally to have in the family.

So far, Jem seemed nice enough. She didn't have her brother's easy smile or conversational skills, but she was trying. Perhaps she had other qualities that Andrew didn't have. Fiona's fiancé wasn't perfect. He certainly could have done with a bit more backbone when they were younger. But that was another time. He'd grown up. If he and Fiona loved each other now, then that was all that mattered.

Chi had been another topic for discussion. Clare had given her the thumbs up because she didn't have a big, obnoxious personality like some of Fiona's university friends. The times Clare had met her, Chi had seemed easy going, though perhaps a little quiet. That might have been because Clare and Fiona had started reminiscing about the good old days.

"Clare, sorry to disturb you…"

It was Mel, and she was holding a small black battery pack in her hand and looking guilty. Clare had immediately taken to Mel. She was friendly to everyone and had a conspiratorial smile that made you feel like she was on your side. Happy to be there, unlike Kate, who seemed to be on another planet, or Ricardo, who seemed a bit grumpy. Mel had an interesting haircut: sandy blonde, short at the back with a sweeping fringe that had been left to grow long on one side and which she curled behind her left ear.

"Do you mind if I mike you up? We're just going to do some relaxed interviews."

"If I have to take my sarong off, then yes."

"What are you talking about? If I had your body, I'd be flaunting it."

Clare blushed. "Yeah, right."

Mel shrugged. "It's true."

She sounded convincing, too. Clare took in Mel's athletic physique and supposed it was always the way – everyone thought someone else was more beautiful. Mel was wearing a sporty grey vest revealing a bony sternum and flat chest. Clare could have told her how uncomfortable it was to carry around big breasts, and how her thighs rubbed together in the heat, and she would have much rather had Mel's slim, tanned legs which ended in ankles rather than tree trunks. Instead she fell quiet as Mel clipped the microphone on to her bikini strap. She felt self-conscious to have someone so close to her breasts, though Mel was a professional and probably hadn't even noticed them. Except she had, hadn't she, otherwise she wouldn't have made that comment, even if it had just been to make Clare feel good about herself.

Mel turned her around. "Can you lift your sarong for a sec? I need to fix the battery pack on to your bikini bottoms."

Clare did as she was told, gathering up her sarong to the side. She was aware of her bum cheeks jiggling from the movement and that Mel was getting a close up of her cellulite, and God knows what other blemishes she was grateful she couldn't see.

"Mel, leave her for a moment, please! We're going to have Fiona doing the speaking," Kate called over from the other end of the pool.

It was humiliating. Clare wanted to sink through the floor. Did Kate even know her name? She was the maid of honour, didn't the director realise that?

"Well, I wasn't expecting a speaking part," Clare said, her laugh catching in her throat.

"I've got mikes for everyone," Mel called back.

Kate didn't reply. She was kneeling down beside the pool, talking to Fiona.

"Leave it on," Mel said. "I've got more."

Clare lowered herself on to the sun lounger, the battery pack digging into her side, reminding her that she didn't need to be wearing it because she wasn't Fiona. She pushed the thought aside. Of course Fiona had to be at the centre of filming. This was her party. Clare just hoped she was sober enough, because she would be furious if she came off badly on national television.

Ricardo was walking purposefully towards the pool now, his camera resting on his shoulder, his biceps swelling under the weight. He hadn't spoken to Clare once, and she'd concluded that he was one of those self-satisfied people who only spoke to someone if he thought it in his interest. On the plane the hens had marked him out of ten, Jem giving him a revealing eight points. Fiona thought he was too hairy, said she liked her men smooth-chested. Clare had yet to see Ricardo's bare chest, but judging by his thick black hair, five o'clock shadow and the dark hairs on his arms, it seemed a safe bet that he had hair on his chest, and quite possibly on his back, too. He wasn't Clare's type. Not that she knew what her type was any more. The last time she'd felt besotted by a guy, she'd been barely fifteen years old.

Clare's thoughts wandered back to the holidays of her teens. She remembered long, hot summers in suburbia, hanging around Fiona's close while her parents were out. Nothing to do, nowhere to go. The younger kids would be playing on their bikes, or kicking a ball across the tarmac, while Fiona and Clare had lain on the small patch of front lawn, painting their nails or flicking through magazines. She remembered the nerves in the pit of her stomach when the older boys had turned up on their BMXs, and how self-conscious she'd been of how she was sitting, how nonchalant she was supposed to look. Fiona had seemed unfazed by their presence, had laughed at them.

"Aren't your bikes too small for you?" she'd said.

"No, stupid, they're supposed to be small," Joe had smirked.

"For tricks," Andrew added.

It was the first time they'd heard Andrew talk. Usually he just stood behind the others, hands in his pockets, trying hard to look cool. He was one of the newest in the group, which made him the most interesting. Silky blond curtains, shy blue eyes, a light tan from a holiday abroad, and yet he didn't radiate the confidence he should have had. He didn't realise he was cute.

"Oh yeah?" Fiona said, sitting up. "And what tricks can you do?"

"Yeah, show them a trick," Joe said.

Clare always felt a little on edge around Joe because he was so bold and she felt he was going to put her on the spot. He was one of those loud-mouthed, hyperactive kids, happiest when being entertained at the expense of others. It hadn't stopped her fancying him, though.

"Nah," Andrew said, shrugging. "I can't do anything here. I need a ramp."

"Go on, mate, do a little grind," Joe egged him on.

"He doesn't want to," Clare said. She'd witnessed this situation a hundred times: Joe putting people under pressure.

"Oh, I want to see a grind," Fiona said.

Of course he had to do one after that. He had to prove himself. So he did a run up, headed for the curb, face contorted as if he was about to attempt an Olympic jump rather than mount the pavement. Miraculous, really, just how badly he fell considering how pathetically low it was. The peg jammed on the concrete, the bike stalled and he flew over the handlebars, scraping his hands against the gritty floor which peeled them like a cheese grater. Clare remembered clearly how Fiona had howled with laughter. Not even Joe had found it that funny.

Andrew had brushed himself off, his cheeks burning, and cycled out of the close, not reappearing for two weeks.

Clare snapped her eyes open at the sound of Fiona's screech and followed her gaze towards the house. Sculpted like an athlete and wearing nothing but a pair of tiny black shorts and a bow tie, a man was approaching with a silver tray laden with cocktails. She was aware of the gasps and giggles and last minute bikini and hair adjustments around her. He was so out of her league that Clare didn't even bother trying to improve her appearance as she had once done as a nervous teen for Joe and his friends.

Ricardo followed him with his camera, then panned out to include the hens. Clare instinctively held her stomach in. The gorgeous waiter stumped his foot on the tile and almost fell over.

"CUT!" Kate called.

The waiter rolled his eyes, but turned to go again.

"Hey, sexy, where do you think you're going? Bring those drinks back here!" Fiona hollered.

"Come on, girls, let's have that same response. It was really great," Kate said, clapping her hands. She was always clapping her hands. Clare knew she was going to have to be patient, because it would get irritating *very* quickly.

By the time Kate was satisfied with the take, most of the crushed ice had melted. Clare drank her cocktail greedily and then held the glass to her forehead. It had to be well over thirty degrees and she was sweating.

Instead of standing around to be ogled at, the waiter headed back to the kitchen.

"Hey, can I get a straw?" Fiona called after him.

Before he could answer, Kate shook her head. "Nope. No straws, Federico. We need to run through their lines first."

Clare became aware of the battery pack nudging into her hip and felt nervous. It was the same feeling she got when she found herself near the front at a comedy night.

"What are we doing?" Fiona wanted to know.

Clare looked at Ricardo and noticed he was frowning, as if he wanted to ask the same question.

"We're being sponsored by sustainable bamboo straws so we're going to mention them, that's all," Kate said, not looking at anyone in particular.

Clare watched Fiona's face crumple. "By *what*?"

"Relax, it won't take long. I just need you to learn a couple of lines, then Federico will bring out the bamboo straws. They're in the kitchen...do you mind, Fed?"

He shook his head. No, he didn't mind.

"And then you'll sit back in the sun and enjoy your cocktails. Sound good?" Kate finished.

Fiona looked worried. "Can't I read it? I don't think I can memorise anything right now."

"It's not much to ask in exchange for a holiday in Mallorca, is it?" Kate said with a wink that didn't quite match the tone of her voice. She may as well have said, *"Don't be so ungrateful, you selfish cow."* Clare gritted her teeth. She wished that bright and bubbly director called Joanna hadn't had her terrible accident.

"Okay…what do I have to say?" Fiona asked.

"Oh, it's simple," Kate reassured her.

It might have been simple if the person doing it was a trained actor. Fiona wasn't. She looked over the page Kate had given her and Clare could read the anxiety in her eyes.

"All this?"

"Yeah, but you can be natural. Improvise a bit."

Clare walked over to offer moral support. They'd tested each other as kids for school plays.

"Let's have a look."

"Take your time," Kate said, checking her watch. "Well, ten minutes should be enough."

According to the script, they had to recreate a conversation about how bad straws were for the environment. Someone was going to ask for one, just like Fiona had done, except now she was going to run off the facts about why they were so terrible.

"No straw, thank you! They're poisoning the planet. It's insane how they're used for less than a minute then thrown away. What is AWAY anyway? There's no such thing. Did you know that 32% of all plastic packaging ends up in the sea? Apparently one fast food chain alone uses 60 million straws A DAY."

It was strange. Clare couldn't remember previous episodes ever featuring their sponsors. Then again, she wasn't such a fan of the show as Fiona was. She preferred not to be reminded that she was nowhere near to having her own hen party.

"This is impossible," Fiona whimpered. "My head is buzzing."

"You can do it," Clare said. Her best friend always began every activity with a negative, but with Clare's encouragement she usually pulled through. "Remember how good you were in our school nativity?"

"I was a sheep! I didn't have any lines."

Clare giggled. "You were very convincing, though."

Between the sun and the early hangover, try as Fiona might, she couldn't get her head around what she had to say. She just couldn't remember more than a couple of words at a time. To cover up her inability to memorise a complete sentence, she kept making jokes or fiddling with her fishtail plait, or calling out for makeup. Kate reduced her lines, but it didn't make any difference.

"Million!" Kate cried out as Fiona said 'thousand' again. "It's 60 *million*! That's a pretty big difference."

Fiona threw back her head. "I don't fucking care how many!"

"You really can't see how catastrophic this is?"

"I don't care," Fiona repeated, and then she levelled her eyes at the director. "I still want a straw for my mojito, which is hotter than a cup of tea right now."

"I don't think you should be drinking any more, do you?"

"Yes."

"Really? Even though you had to be practically carried into the villa less than an hour ago?"

"I'm fine now, aren't I?"

The tension was palpable. Clare knew Fiona had been anticipating VIP treatment. It had been all she'd talked about prior to the trip. She'd talked about it more than the actual wedding, and Kate wasn't delivering it.

Fiona's expression slipped from anger to despair. "Can't I just do it later? I've been up since five."

"My arms are aching," announced the waiter suddenly. He'd been carrying the tray back and forward for quite some time now.

Ricardo lowered his camera and pointed at Jem. "Do *you* know the words?"

Jem was in the pool with Chi. They'd been comparing the skin of their hands which had started to crinkle like prunes. Clare had chosen to sit on the ledge at the back because she thought she looked better from a distance. It was still close enough to see Fiona's expression, which had frozen at Ricardo's question.

Kate turned to Jem and echoed the question.

"Yeah, I guess so," Jem replied, looking guilty. "Only because I do amateur dramatics and I'm used to learning by heart."

"Great!" Kate said, clapping her hands because a whole minute had passed without her doing so. "There you are, Fiona, you're off the hook."

Clare bit her lip in alarm. Of course Fiona didn't want to be off the hook. Being off the hook meant not being the star of the show. She opened her mouth to object, but Ricardo, whose temper had worn thin, announced that both his arms and those of the poor waiter were getting heavy and that not everyone was made for television. Fiona's face fell, but she didn't say a word.

Jem pulled herself out of the pool with all the grace in the world and shot Fiona an apologetic smile.

"The quicker we get this over, the quicker we can have a drink," she told her. She said 'we' to soften the blow, but it was weak and Clare could see that Fiona was upset.

With Jem upfront, the whole thing was done and dusted in ten minutes. She made it sound real rather than scripted, and the others followed her lead, showing genuine concern, with Sam saying, "I've never thought about it before, but I'll definitely be saying, 'No straw, thanks' when I go into bars from now on."

Clare declined to say her line out of solidarity to Fiona, not that Fiona thanked her for it later. She fell into a mood and only lightened up when Kate announced she had a video to show them.

NINE

Day 1
JEM

"What the hell was that?" Fiona cried, shutting the bathroom door behind them. "Is it me or was that completely inappropriate?"

Clare was shaking her head in mutual disgust. "Completely inappropriate."

Jem had a flashback of the two of them hanging out in Fiona's back garden in their pre-teens. Clare the beefy bodyguard, always ready to back her best friend up even though Fiona, with her acerbic tongue and fiery temper, was quite capable of looking after herself. Fiona was a grown-up by eleven, wearing makeup with confidence and strutting around in heels, while poor Clare had always looked slightly clownish with her over rouged face and plum lipstick. Jem could see Clare was still that fiercely loyal friend who had so often been the gooseberry in her brother and Fiona's early relationship.

"It was just for the advertisers," Chi said.

Jem liked Chi. She seemed calm and down to earth.

"But bamboo straws? I mean, come on! Why not perfume or chocolate? Or champagne?" Fiona whined.

Jem didn't think it was that bad. "At least it wasn't haemorrhoid cream," she said.

The girls laughed and Jem felt pleased with herself. Kate had said she was one of the most important people here, but she didn't feel like it. If she was honest, she felt like the odd one out. But perhaps Chi did too. It was the way Sam and Clare and Fiona got on so well. It was to be expected, though. Their relationship was another vintage. Jem had the same rapport with the friends she'd played with in junior school.

There was a light rap on the door.

"Who is it?" Clare barked.

Jem winced at the unnecessary volume. Clare took more getting used to than the others. She was like a little kid who'd had too many fizzy drinks.

"It's me, Sam."

Jem liked Sam, but she would have rather it had been Kate at the door with an order that they go downstairs. The bathroom wasn't the comfiest chill out zone in the villa. She'd opened the window but no air seemed to be coming in.

"What are you all doing hiding in here?" Sam asked, once she'd been let in.

"Rebelling!" Fiona said. "I mean, it's not just me who's annoyed, right? I know I'm the only one here who watches the show, but you know what it's supposed to be like, right?"

"Not really...I don't watch Reality TV," Jem admitted, flashing Fiona an apologetic smile. In other company she might have been a bit more forthcoming about her opinion on trashy TV, but in the circumstances, it would have been pretty hypocritical.

"Not even *X Factor*?" Clare said, frowning at her.

Jem laughed. "Don't you remember me in my Metallica T-shirt? I think I wore it for three months straight. My mum used to sneak into my bedroom at night when I was asleep to grab it and give it a wash."

"You don't look like you're into rock now," Clare said.

Just because Jem's dress sense had changed, it didn't mean her taste in music had. She'd missed out on a ticket for a Guns n' Roses concert in Berlin last week. Granted, she would have swapped her chiffon blouse for an ancient black concert T-shirt and given her coral nails a lick of red.

"George loves *X Factor*," Sam said. "He bops to all the songs."

Jem smiled. "How cute." She wasn't going to go into her thoughts on how the money-grabbing competition was ruining the music industry. She was still trying to find her place in the group and didn't want to be the one bringing down the mood. She would leave that role to Kate, who was doing a fine job of it so far.

"You should have seen Ricardo and Mel. They're totally on your side," Sam said.

Jem watched Fiona's face brighten. She looked like a little girl with her big blue eyes and round cheeks, and for a second Jem saw her through her loved-up brother's eyes.

"You heard them say that?" Fiona asked.

"I didn't need to. I could tell from their faces. They're having a serious chat with Kate now. I don't think the video was in the plan."

"I knew it! They always show one of the friends and family saying nice things."

"I wish they had. I can't get that turtle out of my head now," Chi said.

Jem had seen the video before on her Facebook feed. She'd only managed to watch half before she'd clicked through to a link and donated ten pounds to a turtle sanctuary in Costa Rica.

"They did film the other one, though," Clare said. "Us saying nice things."

Fiona raised an eyebrow. "Really?"

"Definitely," Jem said, remembering her awkward performance as if it were yesterday. "I'm so crap on camera they had to film me three hundred times."

"If you were so crap on camera they wouldn't have used you to do the bamboo straws advert," Fiona said abruptly.

Jem glanced at her in surprise. "I just have a good memory, that's all." She had sensed Fiona hadn't been happy, but she hadn't realised quite how unhappy. Should she have refused to say Fiona's lines when Ricardo had asked her to? The thought of the cameraman made her stomach flutter again.

"*Too short,*" Sam had said about him on the plane. But then Sam was nearly 6 foot. Ricardo was taller than Jem. Not by much, but enough. A good height for kissing. Jem found all his charcoal black hair rather a turn on. With his broad shoulders, strong arms and arousing scent of cedar wood and tobacco, Jem thought he was the epitome of masculinity. He had a presence about him. Not just because he was usually wielding a huge camera, but because he was clearly confident in himself and didn't seek the approval of others. Jem had caught his eye a few times and once he hadn't looked away. He'd stared back at her, and they'd had a silent staring contest without anyone knowing. His lips had finally dipped into an amused smile and he'd looked away.

"Anyway, I'm sure they'll show it eventually," she said, trying to keep things light. "The shoot was with that other director, Joanna something."

The filming had taken place a week after Andrew and Fiona's engagement party, and Jem had still been feeling guilty for not showing up. She'd had a work social, but she could have got out of it. There had been a clear moment when it would have been easy to make her excuses and leave, but instead she had accepted the offer of a glass of wine and had proceeded to listen to a colleague talk about his childhood dream of visiting Nairobi.

Fiona's face darkened. "I think we've got the wrong director. I don't like her and I can tell, for a fact, that she doesn't like me."

Jem didn't think that was true. Not exactly. The impression she got was that Kate wasn't especially interested in Fiona. She saw her as just another member of the cast rather than the star.

"Well if we're going to talk about people we don't like," Clare said, flaring her nostrils, "I don't like Ricardo."

Jem tried to mask her surprise and failed. "Why's that?"

"He's so smug."

"Really?"

"You can't see it because you fancy him," Clare said.

Jem felt the heat pour into her cheeks and wished she had a switch to turn it off. She wondered if she was as red as she felt. Everyone was looking at her with grins on their faces.

"No, I don't," she replied, weakly.

Clare gave her a pointed look. "Eight. That's all I'm saying." She was talking about the score Jem had given

Ricardo on the plane when the champagne had loosened her tongue.

Jem shrugged. "Yeah, well, maybe a bit."

"I was thinking," Fiona said. "What if we turn this whole week into a drinking game? Every time Kate says, 'Straw' we have a shot of tequila..."

"And every time she says, 'Plastic' and 'Poisoning' and 'Planet'," Sam added with a laugh.

"We'd be drunk before breakfast," Jem said, and then looked at Fiona. "Oops, you already were!"

Everyone giggled. Jem genuinely couldn't believe how Fiona could still want to drink after this morning.

"You know what this reminds me of, Clare?" Fiona said. "Your fifteenth birthday."

Here we go, Jem thought, *back to the good old days.* Clare groaned and Sam and Fiona burst out laughing. Jem sensed them all slip into a memory from their adolescence.

"I remember I wore velvet flares," Sam mused.

Fiona grinned. "Remember those mascara hair dyes?"

The memory made Jem smile. "Yes! I used to wear blue and purple."

"I had luminous green," Fiona said with a shudder. "It left my hair all covered in gunk."

"It didn't stop Andrew snogging you, though," Sam said, nudging her leg.

Jem felt sure Fiona had made the first move. It was weird to think of her nervous teenager brother kissing Fiona.

"True. And didn't Joe try it on with you?" Fiona said to Sam.

Clare's jaw dropped. "What? I didn't know this!"

"Oh my God, I remember Joe," Jem said, her head filling with memories. He had stayed over at their house loads of times when she and Andrew were young. Her mum had thought him very bad-mannered and blamed his sugar-filled diet. He had sat in her dad's chair and told her mum her chicken casserole was undercooked.

Sam was clearly reliving some memories of her own and was shaking her head, her eyes full of laugher. "I'd forgotten about Joe."

"This is not fair!" Chi cried. "I don't know anyone you're talking about."

Jem felt simultaneously sorry for Chi and relieved not to be out of the loop like her. "He was this cocky lad in our close," she explained.

"I can't believe you kissed him, Sam!" Clare said.

Sam was grinning guiltily now. "Oops...did you fancy him, Clare?"

"No! He was an arrogant little shit."

"He was," Fiona agreed. "But he was quite sexy, too, wasn't he?"

Clare looked sheepish. "Yeah, totally. Like Cristiano Ronaldo."

Jem burst out laughing. "He was not a bit like Cristiano Ronaldo! He was a skinny little thing. Your memories are warped."

"Exactly! I wouldn't have kept it a secret if he'd been hot," Sam said.

"So you hadn't *forgotten*, you big fat liar!" Clare cried. "You kept it a secret all these years."

Jem was pleased to find she was enjoying herself now. "So what exactly did you do with the young Joseph?"

"A snog."

But Sam looked too guilty for it to just have been a kiss. "You sure that's all?"

Sam covered her face, peeked through two fingers. "Fine. Second base."

Clare gasped. "Oh my God! I can't believe you never told us!"

Chi demanded to see a photo and Jem spent a few moments trying to get the Wi-Fi to work on her phone to connect to Facebook. But Kate had warned them she would turn it off and had been true to her word. She obviously didn't want them tweeting about their disappointing morning.

"So why does this remind you of Clare's fifteenth?" Jem asked.

"Don't!" Clare warned.

"Oh, come on. No one's filming." Fiona laughed and leant forward. "On Clare's fifteenth birthday, she was so nervous she got drunk before half the party had even arrived and spent the whole night in the bathroom talking to the toilet."

"It was a good party," Sam said, grinning. "Shame you missed it, Clare."

Clare stuck her tongue out. "Whatever."

A knock made them jump. Mel peered around the door with a cautious smile.

"Hey, girls...I know it's been a tricky morning, but we've got a treat for you downstairs."

Jem was pleased to see Mel. Her bum was going numb from sitting on the tiled floor and she welcomed any excuse to get up and out of the bathroom.

"Should we be worried?" Fiona asked.

"It involves clay and Federico-the-hot-waiter, so...yes, probably!"

"Well, this sounds more like it!"

Jem pushed away a sympathetic thought for her brother and how jealous he would feel if he could see Fiona's face right now. She had to remember that she wasn't here as the protective sister, she was here as one of the girls.

TEN

Day 1
SAM

Sam knew the idea was not to produce a replica of Michelangelo's *David* but she couldn't resist making an effort. She always had to forgo the pleasures of Play Doh with her nephews and nieces to concentrate on damage control. Little George would be introduced to it next and she planned to be there by his side, making appreciative noises as he wreaked havoc across the kitchen floor. She didn't regret her decision to give up the studio and become a full-time mum, but she did sometimes miss those quiet mornings pottering around, just her and her materials.

All she really needed to do was make a clay sausage and giggle along with everyone else. Yet she couldn't help herself. Federico had a beautiful muscular body, and quite honestly, his scrotum was the least impressive part of him. Not to say he wasn't well-endowed. Far from it – *David* would have been quite jealous. It was just that penises on the whole were such soggy looking things compared to a good pair of shoulders.

Sam's husband, Chris, had gorgeous shoulders. She had left a trail of kisses along them that first night they'd slept together. Even then, the thought hadn't occurred to her to draw him, or sculpt him. People thought artists were all the same: that they were 100% passion and wouldn't be able to give it up if they tried. But she had. Along had come George and she had switched off that side of her with ease. She would go back to pottery eventually, but she wasn't in any rush. While they could afford it, she would be by George's side. And if anyone said she was protective, she would point out that she had left him a whole week for a hen party.

There was a lull in the room which made her look up. Ricardo was on the other side, filming them. He had needed a couple of takes of Federico walking into the room stark naked. Their shock had been 'too quiet' the first time around, apparently, plus he'd wanted a few more angles.

Sam watched Clare fondling her lump of clay and raised an eyebrow.

"What are you doing with that poor piece of clay, Clare Williams?"

The others turned to have a look as Clare rubbed innocently away.

"I'm softening it."

"Softening it?"

The others giggled and Sam couldn't resist.

"I've always got the opposite result when I've done that."

The penny dropped and Clare pushed her clay away as if it had turned into a writhing cock. "Oh, shut up!"

Sam laughed until she remembered that all her family would be watching this one day. Then she felt the heat pour into her cheeks. She kept forgetting their banter was being recorded. With her headphones on in the corner, Mel looked like she was just listening to music rather than the audio from their individual mikes.

She coughed importantly. "I'd like to point out I'm a potter and was referring to a special technique where you agitate the clay until it stiffens."

"Not helping!" Fiona scoffed.

Clare joined in. "Yeah, put your shovel down, your hole is big enough."

Sam feigned shock. "I beg your pardon, Clare. Don't be so vulgar."

"Yeah, *I'm* the vulgar one!"

Sam knew she should shut up. She always morphed into her gobby self when she was around her childhood friends. She couldn't resist chasing the laughs. Chi appeared to consider everything she said before opening her mouth, as if she never once forgot the bloody camera was rolling. Sam set an intention to be more like her.

"What the hell is that, Fiona?" she asked, unable to keep quiet.

Fiona was making a dog's dinner of her clay. The frontal view of their sexy model had reduced her to a giggly teenager and she was just slapping bits and pieces together willy-nilly.

"It's not my fault. It's impossible. I can't get the creases."

"Creases?" Jem said, looking up at Federico. "What are you talking about? He's got flawless skin."

Oh, come on! Sam thought. *Jem was joking, right?*

"I don't think Fiona was talking about his face," she said.

Jem blushed as her eyes automatically zoomed in on his genitalia and then looked away.

"Made you look!" Sam blurted out.

Fiona snorted with laughter. Sam felt rewarded. Surely she was allowed to be silly now and then.

"Oh my God. You guys are so embarrassing," Jem said, shaking her head. "I apologise, Federico, on behalf of us all."

"There is nothing to be embarrassed about," their instructor called, sashaying back into the room. Monica was an eccentric German ex-teacher who taught life drawing and belly dancing across the island. She swished her bamboo cane around Federico's bottom. "Don't think about it so much. Just pick an area. Whatever calls out to you."

What bit doesn't call out to me? Sam thought as she reviewed his clavicles and then looked, with disappointment, down at the lumpy clay shoulders she'd been momentarily pleased with. She noticed Jem had gone for a complete figure and felt a stab of envy because it was coming along very well indeed. Perhaps she had done a class at some point. She seemed to love doing courses. Jem reminded Sam of her friend Abigail who was a Groupon addict. Abigail wasn't really after acquiring skills, though, as much as a boyfriend. Sam wondered if that was Jem's secret agenda too. Why else would you sign up to Indian Cuisine, Spanish, film club, amateur dramatics and Origami all in the space of six months?

"That's really good, Jem," she said. *Merit where it's due,* she thought. Envy was so ugly.

"Uh…thanks…I took a course once."

"Is there any course you haven't done?"

Jem laughed. "I coordinate them so I get big discounts."

"Ah, that explains it."

So many courses and still Jem hadn't met the cook, actor, origami-ist or sculptor of her dreams? It seemed unfair. What was the point of having a long-term boyfriend when you were a teenager and not having anybody when you were heading for forty? Some of Sam's worst nightmares were about being alone and afraid of getting too old to have kids. She'd wake up with a huge sense of dread, like she was carrying the world on her shoulders, and then she would hear Chris's faint snores and relief would rush over her. It was not something she shared with Clare, obviously. Instead she told her to enjoy being single while she could and that love would arrive when she was least expecting it. Privately, though, she knew that if she was in Clare's position, or Jem's, or Chi's, she would be spending a fortune on internet dating. Why were they single? They all had something special. Clare was affectionate, loyal and a great listener. Jem was clever and gorgeous. Chi was...well, Sam didn't know much about Chi, but she had let slip on the plane that she had a habit of choosing wrong'uns.

"CUT," Kate called, clapping her hands.

Sam caught Chi's look of exasperation and rolled her eyes in agreement. The filming aspect was definitely more tedious than she had expected.

"Girls, you're not saying anything interesting," Kate said.

Sam laughed. "Charming. Thank you very much."

"Remember what we discussed this morning?" their director said, looking earnest. "This is an amazing platform, an opportunity for you to make a difference."

Sam sank into her chair. What did the woman expect them to talk about while they had a naked man posing in front of them? Nudism rights?

"I've got a thought-provoking point," Clare said, looking coy.

Oh God, Sam thought. The only subject that Clare cared about was funding cuts in schools and her growing workload. Sam smothered a yawn. Education was very important to her, but she didn't get where it fitted in this scene. Cuts to the Arts? Art getting the snip? Snip, snip, snip. A model with a smaller penis? She let out a giggle; she really was regressing back to her teenage years.

"Good," Kate said, brightening. "Go on then, Clare. Let's see where it goes. And...action."

Clare straightened up and looked at Fiona. "My question is..."

"Cut! Just dive straight in, would you?" Kate said.

Sam heard Ricardo sigh behind her and suppressed another giggle. She found their moody cameraman somewhat entertaining.

Clare fluffed her hair up. "Okay."

Kate nodded. "And action."

Fiona waited for the question with her hands on her hips. Sam watched as Clare swallowed. She didn't have high hopes about the question. Clare was a wonderful friend, but she could be a bit longwinded sometimes.

"Do you think Andrew would mind you doing this?"

Trust Clare to ask something like that. Her Miss Virtuous side used to drive Fiona mad. Sam glanced at Fiona now and could tell she was irritated.

"That's not thought-provoking," Fiona said, frowning. "That's just boring."

Ouch. Sam saw Clare's face pinch. Poor Clare lived in fear of being boring.

"He'd hate it," Jem said, without lifting her eyes from her sculpture.

"That's a bit strong," Sam said.

Chi obviously thought so too. "I don't think he would," she said, speaking up for a change. "He would know Fiona hadn't chosen to do it."

"Of course he'd hate it!" Jem said with a weak laugh. "Imagine it the other way around: him making a clay model of a beautiful naked woman."

Sam conjured up in her mind a sexy brunette model with voluptuous curves and pictured Chris in front of her with a ball of clay. She waited for the jealous lump to rise up her throat. Instead, she imagined him getting up and looking for a tape measure. He would be concerned about getting the dimensions right, would probably make a scale in the corner. The thought made her smile. They were similar in that sense. They liked to do things properly. Neither was sloppy.

She knew how Chris would feel, but what about Andrew? Would he feel jealous? Insecure? Fiona had definitely worn the trousers in their relationship when they had been teenagers. One minute they were together, the next they had split up, but it had always been on her terms. She had known how to get him back.

"I really don't see the problem," Chi retorted. "It's just a body, isn't it? It's not like she's *doing* anything with him."

"Okay, forget it, forget it," Clare said, flushed and annoyed.

91

Kate clapped her hands. "CUT! You're not being natural."

Fiona ignored her. "Like Chi said, I didn't choose to do it, so he can't blame me."

"I was just making conversation. Forget it!"

"No, you're implying I'm a bad person…"

"Cut!"

"She wasn't saying that," Sam said, feeling obliged to smooth things over between the two of them. "We all know this is just a bit of fun."

"I don't think you should look like you're enjoying it so much," Jem said. "How do you think he'll feel when he watches it?"

"What part of 'Cut' don't you understand?"

"Oh, so I'm supposed to look bored?" Fiona shot back. "Yeah, because that's great television, isn't it?"

"Guys, calm down!" Sam heard herself say. "This is silly."

"I'm just saying Andrew's sensitive," Jem said.

"He's not that sensitive!" Fiona huffed.

"Yes, he is."

"The point is he trusts her," Clare said. "And that's all that matters."

"What matters is she's done nothing wrong, so he has no right to be annoyed," Chi argued.

Sam zoned out, deciding to wait for them to calm down. It was a pointless discussion. Yes, Andrew wouldn't love it, but he wouldn't split up with Fiona over it either. She remembered him as the smitten boyfriend from the days of staying over at Fiona's house when they were about thirteen. If Sam's mother had known how relaxed Mrs F was, she wouldn't have been so relaxed about those sleepovers. Penny, as Mrs F preferred to be called, hadn't just turned a blind eye to them having a boy in their bedroom. She had also pretended not to notice them raiding the drinks cabinet or nicking her cigarettes to smoke in the back garden. Andrew had told his parents he was staying at Joe's and had spent the night entwined with Fiona in her single bed while Sam had slept on the floor. Thank God they'd never done anything while she'd been there, although she couldn't be sure as she'd always been such a deep sleeper. Come to think of it, Fiona had always been pretty shameless, so quite possibly they had. Sam shuddered at the thought.

"I bet he's watched porn before," Fiona argued.

"Not on national television," Jem cried.

"So that's okay? He gets to watch porn and I'm bad if I do an art class?"

"I didn't say that!"

"Oh, shut up," Sam said, half-heartedly. "You're all making a problem out of nothing. They love each other. The end."

Sam had always been a lover of simple happy endings and had been thrilled to hear Fiona's news. It had echoed the romance novel she had been reading at the time. Chris hadn't bought it so readily.

"I'm sure you told me they were a shit couple before, so why would they be good now?" Sam swore she had said no such thing.

When she'd seen Andrew at the engagement party, all the good memories had rushed back and they'd hugged each other with genuine affection. Of course he remembered her. His mate Joe had always had the hots for her, how could he forget? Chris had been thrilled to hear this nugget of information about her teenage-hood.

"Who's Joe? Was he your little boyfriend?"

She'd blushed, a bit like she'd done earlier. A snog, she'd told Chris. Second base, she'd told the girls. The reality still made her embarrassed. If Clare's garage could talk!

Andrew had been flushed and happy at the engagement party. He'd patted Chris's arm a lot and said things like, *"You'll have to give me marriage tips, yeah? Because you're a pro, right?"* He'd got a little repetitive towards the end and Chris had mimicked him on the way home. They'd left early because the babysitter needed to leave at ten. Sam could've stayed on and let Chris sort everything out, but the truth was she'd wanted to get back with him to create a chance for some intimacy. Andrew wouldn't have been calling them pros if he'd known that they hadn't made love to each other in five months.

"You know what my brother wouldn't mind you doing, though," Jem said, one corner of her lip turning up into a mischievous smile.

"Saying the Rosary?" Fiona scoffed.

"No…"

"Cross stitch?"

"No…"

"Poetry?"

Jem yanked off one of her figure's arms and threw it at Fiona. "CLAY FIGHT!" Fiona gasped as it hit her in the chest, her eyes dilating in shock. Sam burst out laughing and ducked behind her desk as Fiona launched a counter attack against her future sister-in-law.

"MISSED!" Jem yelled.

Clare shrieked with laughter as she joined in.

"Ladies! That's enough!" the instructor cried.

For a moment, Sam was torn over whether to join in. She glanced at Kate who stood in the doorway between the living room and the kitchen with her arms folded and her jaw twitching. Her glossy hair had lost its slick look in the heat and was curling at the ends. Did she think she could get them to behave simply by looking annoyed? Only the most frightening teachers had been able to do that in school, and Kate didn't have that sort of presence. Sam felt sorry for Mel and Ricardo, and for the instructor who was being completely and utterly ignored. But then she noticed Ricardo hadn't stopped filming and was now focused on her, and if she wasn't mistaken, he was actually smiling.

Did she really want the nation to think of her as the boring one? God knows how much she must have gone on about George already. As another big piece of clay went flying through the room, Federico suddenly changed position, cupping his genitals. Sam threw back her head and laughed. As she did so a piece of clay smacked her front teeth. She snapped open her eyes to see Fiona shaking with laughter.

"You'll live to regret that!" she cried.

She took one last look at her clay shoulders then lobbed them across the room. They missed Fiona by miles, and to Sam's absolute horror, smashed into the Tiffany lamp behind her.

ELEVEN

Day 1
KATE

Kate had pretended to sleep for the rest of that flight to Palma. At one point she might even have dozed off because the voices she'd been trying to drown out were the same ones that suddenly startled her. She could tell from the gloomy feeling that she had lapsed back again to the moment in time when her world had stopped still.

"Kate, I've something I need to say," Matt had said.

She'd just arrived at the café. It was freezing outside and she was bundled up in many layers. She unwound her scarf while she scanned the menu. Insipid decor, weak coffee, and you needed a magnifying glass to locate the ingredients in the paninis. Why did her fiancé choose such unimaginative chains when there were so many independent cafés out there? Or perhaps there weren't. London was changing. It was losing its soul. She was about to mention the fact to Matt, but then the barista stopped flirting with his colleague and she ordered instead.

She couldn't believe the news, and hunger was making her even more incensed.

"It's spilling! Oil is spilling across the Arctic, just like everyone said it would. The last piece of land left that humans hadn't mucked up is ruined!"

"Yeah, I heard."

He might have heard, but Kate didn't think the news had sunk in.

"Can you believe our children are going to grow up in a world without polar bears?"

He winced. She'd thought it was because the news was hitting home and it was painful.

"I read that a toy shop is going to change the labels on their remaining stock of soft polar bear toys to 'albino grizzlies' so the kiddies won't ask any tough questions."

"That's stupid," Matt said. "They still sell dinosaurs and I'm pretty sure they're extinct."

"You should have heard Silvia this morning: '*But why do you care about the polar bears so much, Kate? It's not like they feature much in your personal life*'," Kate said, mimicking her friend. "But that's not the point, is it? That's what we've got to get into our selfish human heads. Polar bears aren't here to serve the human race and they have a right to be left in peace!"

She let out a deep breath and shot him an apologetic smile. "I'm done. Now you. What did you want to tell me?"

She reached over the table to squeeze his hand, which continued to curl tightly around the salt cellar. It was no wonder he was tense. She felt so grateful that he'd been doing all the last minute planning for the wedding so she could take some time to bash out emails and remind production companies she was still alive and accepting work. It had been a slow year and she had yet to direct a project she could really call her own.

"I can't marry you."

It sucked the breath out of her.

Matt swallowed. "The thought of getting married to you is giving me panic attacks."

She blinked at him. He couldn't be serious. They'd just spent six months of their lives planning this wedding. Kate had been growing food for it. Only the herbs and some vegetables, but that was quite an achievement for someone who hadn't grown anything since a pot of cress in nursery. Happy ingredients, Kate had insisted, and Matt had agreed wholeheartedly. Hours she'd dedicated to scrolling through websites in search of ways to make their wedding a beautiful and environmentally friendly celebration. The recycled paper invitations made locally were expensive. Her organic silk wedding dress had cost a fortune.

Cold feet? His eyes were rimmed with tears. It made the situation feel horribly real. She needed to remain calm.

"Maybe I was the person you wanted once, but I'm not any more."

So much for remaining calm. The words burst out of her. "What are you talking about? What's happened to you? Of course you're the person I want to marry!"

He looked in pain. "But Kate, I don't care the way you care about everything."

"It doesn't matter! I can care about everything for both of us!"

"I don't want that. Your 'caring'…it can be a real downer."

It was like being kicked in the stomach. The barista appeared with her order as she was sitting there, winded.

"One mozzarella panini. One cinnamon latte."

"The worst thing is…" Matt faltered, changed his mind.

She picked up her sandwich and took a defiant bite. She refused to believe this was happening.

"What?" she said. Her cheeks were burning.

"You're always going on about how bad everything is...but what do you do about it? If you care so much about the environment, then why aren't you dedicating your career to it?"

She couldn't look at him. "Like it's that easy!"

He shook his head. "I shouldn't have said that...forget I said that...I'm sorry, that's not helping..."

For a split second she thought that he was taking it all back. That the temperature of his feet had been restored and the wedding was back on.

"The point is this should be one of the happiest times of our lives," he said.

"I am happy." Tears slipped down her cheeks. "Really happy!"

"I don't think you are, and I know I'm not."

Alarm gripped her as he scraped his chair back.

"Where are you going?"

"I'm sorry," he said, wiping away a tear. She could count the times she'd seen him cry on one hand. "I don't think I can talk about this now. I think I've got to walk away."

"You can't just walk away! You can't leave without an explanation!"

He was standing up. He was backing away with his hands raised. "I'm so sorry, Kate. I can't do this now. I'm so sorry."

Before he'd even walked out the door, let alone her life, a woman had appeared and put her hand on the back of his chair.

"This is free, isn't it?"

Kate spotted Gabriel at baggage collection. He was standing a few metres away from the carousel, his rucksack at his feet. She felt a flicker of hope, willing him to look over and smile. He didn't. He smiled at his phone instead. Perhaps he had a girlfriend waiting for him outside.

"I hope we've got a pink limo waiting for us like in season two, episode three," Fiona said.

"Or a helicopter," Clare giggled. "I'm sure I saw an episode when the hens were picked up in a helicopter."

Sam laughed. "Are you sure you weren't watching James Bond?"

Kate was only vaguely aware of the conversation about transport. She was foraging through her deep handbag for a business card. She simultaneously wanted to find one and was scared of finding one. If she found one, she'd promised herself she'd go over there and give it to him.

She pulled one out and her heart began to race. All she had to do was go up and give it to him.

I was sorry we couldn't chat about the conference, I'm really interested in rubbish too…

Too earnest?

Did your shirt dry okay? I could wash it for you if you like…in my shower…we could shower together…in our shirts…to save water…I believe in saving water, don't you?

Insane?

She was a grown woman, not a nervous teen. Couldn't she just ask him out directly?

Let's go for a drink so I can prove to you not all English are hooligans. Nothing with vodka in it, though. I pick fights when I drink that stuff. Lol!

It was so frustrating because if it hadn't been for those rowdy lads, she would have got his number by now. It would have been easy after two hours of chatting. The lads were circling the hens now, wanting to know what their plans were. They could forget about meeting; Kate's schedule didn't include a drunken binge in Magaluf. She gritted her teeth as their voices grew louder. Gabriel had put his phone away now. There was a chance he'd spot her. So what if he did? He was even less likely to come over while she was standing so close to the louts.

Ricardo hoisted his camera bag on to his shoulder. "I'll go ahead and film from outside."

"Yeah. I was just thinking about that," she said, jumping to attention. It was lucky Ricardo was so familiar with the show.

"I got a call from my assistant, too. He's collected the jeep and is waiting outside."

"Great. Good."

"Make sure you all come out at the same time, yeah?"

She frowned at him. Did he feel like he needed to direct?

"This isn't my first day, Ricardo."

He shrugged, a faint smile turning the corners of his lips. "Just checking. You seem pretty distracted."

"I'm fine."

She *was* distracted. Gabriel had moved a few steps nearer the carousel. The suitcases hadn't come out yet, but the clock was ticking. His bag might well be the first one off and then he'd be gone through the security doors and she'd never see him again.

Ricardo ran a hand through his ruffled hair and replaced his faded red cap.

"See you on the other side then," he said. "Text me when you're about to go through."

Kate nodded. "Will do."

Fiona sidled up to her, wanting to know where Ricardo was going and what they were doing later. Kate heard herself explaining cheerfully enough. She was aware of Gabriel in her periphery. It excited her that he was there.

Her hand tightened around her phone, the edges of the business card she'd pressed against it digging into her palm. How often did she feel like this?

"They're coming!" Clare sang.

No! Kate felt a rush of panic. There was no time to waste. She looked over at Gabriel. He was concentrating on the carousel. But then he looked up. This was her moment. No, his eyes were back on the carousel. He hadn't seen her.

Her own bag was coming now. She decided to let it go past and follow it around, so she would bump into him. Her bag would do a double loop. She'd never let her luggage do that before, but she'd never felt so curious about a fellow passenger before, or so concerned she might not see him again.

"Isn't that your bag?" Sam said, pointing at the black Samsonite drawing near.

Damn it. Kate thought they'd all been too excited to notice her luggage.

"It's similar."

"I used to have one like that. Are you sure it's not yours?"

She couldn't pretend. "Oh yeah, you're right...Thanks."

She'd let it come to her, wait for it at the loop and then she'd turn around and he'd be right there. Their eyes would meet and they'd say hello. Of course they would. She felt her heart drumming as the bag drew near.

Hi, I'm so jealous you got moved...I think they were even noisier afterwards...

Hey, I didn't see you there. So what part of the island are you heading towards?

Hi, I think it was fate we sat on the same row...not fate that we got separated...fate's a bastard...can I have your number?

"Hey!" she gasped.

Her bag had just been whisked off the carousel. She should have put a big ribbon around it, those bags all looked the same. It didn't help that half the flight was inebriated. She waited a second for the person to realise it wasn't theirs and put it back. She couldn't see who they were because of the crowd in front of them.

"Sam's got your bag!" Clare shouted at her. Half the airport turned to look. Why did they all have to be so loud? Kate held up a thumb and smiled. She went over to get it from Sam, who had thought she was being wonderfully helpful but had unwittingly ruined everything.

Gabriel was watching her. Their eyes met and he smiled. She hovered, smiling back, thinking this was her moment to go over and say something. *Just go!* A smile was an invitation. *Go! Go!*

But then he lifted his hand and gave her a little wave. She automatically lifted her hand and gave him a little wave back.

A wave was an ending. How could she go up and say hello after that?

TWELVE

Day 5
KATE

Sharon's eyebrows had barely landed in all the time Kate had been talking.

"But it was a play fight?" she said.

"Yes."

"Was it funny?"

Kate hadn't found it funny at all. The girls had been impossible to work with. They had been incapable of having a conversation about anything remotely interesting. Of course, in hindsight she could see that Federico had been a big distraction. A very big distraction, in fact. That had been Joanna's doing. Kate had wanted to book a woman who taught rope making out of plastic collected from beaches, but unfortunately she had been unavailable for the hen party dates.

"Oh, it was hilarious," Kate said, trying out a reassuring smile.

Calm Jem had turned into a savage, inflicting bruises with the limbs of what could have been a decent sculpture. Chi had received a bump to the head from a flying buttock and Sam had smashed a Tiffany lamp. Hilarious indeed.

"You would have really laughed," Kate continued, as brightly as she could.

Ricardo had stopped following her directions early on and had filmed the whole thing. She had been heartened by his amused expression, because it meant he thought he would be able to use it. Perhaps they could if they chopped it in pieces and added different audio. She dreaded hearing herself.

"Shame about the breakages, but it's not like we haven't got insurance," Sharon said with a wry smile.

Sam had been horrified that she'd broken the lamp and had wanted to fix it herself. Kate had almost wished she'd broken it earlier because it was the only thing to shut her up. The class had ended abruptly as everyone had abandoned the room for fear of stepping on glass.

"At least it wasn't broken bones. Tell me we're not on a break because someone's in hospital with a broken leg."

Kate let out a hollow laugh. Sharon didn't need to know about Fiona's visit to the clinic after her battering ram performance on Day 2.

"No, no, just a lamp, a candlestick and a few glasses..."

As far as Kate remembered the injuries from the clay fight had been treated with humour. The girls had nursed their bruises with icy cocktails by the pool, their laughter puncturing the neighbourhood's tranquil bubble. Who could blame her for wanting to escape the villa at the earliest opportunity every day? The scream of gulls was easier on the ear than when those girls got together. Ricardo and Mel had shown great stamina, recording their alcohol-fuelled conversations deep into the evening. Sam and Fiona were very sorry they hardly saw each other any more and planned to meet up at least once a week from now on. Everyone agreed that Clare was gorgeous and needed to *put herself out there* more, and she in turn had promised she was going to embrace online dating as soon as she got back to England. Chi was going to give up alcohol because all the things she'd ever regretted in her life had happened because she'd been drunk. What things? She couldn't remember, which made everyone laugh, although she insisted it wasn't funny. As for Jem, she was sorry that she hadn't gone to Fiona and Andrew's engagement party, but was going to be there for them in the future. Kate had reviewed the recording the next day. By the end of it, everyone was saying how much they loved each other.

So when had it all gone wrong? Did she only have herself to blame?

"Your phone is ringing," Sharon said, nodding at Kate's buzzing handbag. "If it's Ricardo, tell him to drive over, will you?"

It wasn't Ricardo. It was an unknown number. She hoped it was one of the hens. She hoped it was Jem calling to tell her not to worry about any of them, that they had had their burn out and they were on their way back. At the very worst, that someone needed a morning after pill.

"Hello, Kate Miller speaking."

An agitated male voice answered.

"Is this the director of *The Hen Party*?"

"Yes...who's this?"

"Are you with my fiancée?"

It was Andrew, who was the last person she wanted to speak to, given the current situation. The only bonus was that he evidently hadn't spoken to Fiona and didn't know she had gone AWOL.

"Not at the moment," Kate answered. "But I can get her to call you when she's free."

"I don't understand. I think she's trying to break up with me. What happened out there?"

THIRTEEN

Day 2
FIONA

Fiona couldn't believe she was sitting in a hospital waiting room under the glare of fluorescents, rather than at the beach getting a suntan. It was a complete waste of her precious holiday. She had only blacked out for a few seconds. Well, pretended to. In truth she just hadn't opened her eyes because she'd wanted to hear Kate panic. And she *had* panicked and insisted on a check-up, but only because she was worried about getting sued.

Fiona's head had stopped hurting, and other than a small bruise, she felt fine and ready to get on with the party. What was a doctor going to do anyway? Hold up some fingers? Ask for her name and what day it was? She was on holiday and she wasn't supposed to know what day it was.

Clare had kindly insisted on coming along with her while Kate had done the right thing by remaining in the car with the driver.

"It's a good story," Clare said.

"Is it though?"

"Actually I probably wouldn't tell anyone if I were you." Clare stifled a giggle. "You ran into a wall!"

"I was running at Kate! You were supposed to hold her still."

"Next time, give me some warning and I'll get some duct tape."

"How about this afternoon?"

"I don't think I can take much more violence. How about tomorrow after a swim in the sea?"

Fiona didn't think she could take much more either. She was totting up battle scars. Day 1: bruises from clay fight. Day 2: concussion...*faux* concussion, but still.

"I think I should get some sort of compensation. Like a voucher I can use in a London spa."

Clare's face lit up. "Do you remember the time you won that Sanctuary voucher?"

Of course she did. Fiona remembered every win. They'd had facials. Sometimes she'd catch the whiff of tangerine and ginger and she would be back in Covent Garden on that massage bed. If she were rich she would have spa treatments every week. It was no wonder ancient celebrities looked like twenty-year-olds when they could afford such pampering.

"That was so good," Clare sighed. "I never win anything."

That's because you never enter anything, Fiona thought.

A memory surfaced of the time her dad had told a funny story back when she was little enough to sit on his lap. It was about a poor man who prays to God every week to help him win the lottery. On and on he prays. Every week, without fail. But he never wins.

"Please, God, help me!" he begs, listing all his financial difficulties. Months go by and he starts making promises to give half the money to charity if he wins. Eventually, the voice of God booms down.

"Would you just buy a bloody lottery ticket!"

As usual, the thought of her dad arrived with a dollop of guilt. She really had to get back in touch. She couldn't blame him for the divorce for ever. After this was over, she would call him.

"I think Kate does feel guilty," Clare said, thoughtfully. "She was very apologetic in the car just now."

"She should feel guilty!" Fiona cried. "She's making a mess of my hen party. If she says one more thing about turtles, I'm going to walk out."

Of course, she wouldn't. She wasn't prepared to pay one cent while she was on the island.

"Me too!" Clare gasped, and then lowered her voice as if the entire waiting room was listening in. "She's completely obsessed. She should be working on a wildlife documentary, not a hen party. I bet she gets on better with animals than people."

"I wonder if she has a boyfriend."

Clare wrinkled her nose. "I doubt that very much."

Fiona smirked. "True. If she thinks dogs have a massive carbon footprint, imagine boyfriends. Relationships are probably on her no-no list along with plastic bags and fun."

Secretly, Fiona suspected Kate might well have a boyfriend. Their director was attractive and had an amazing body. Slim but curvy. Her boobs had to be real because she didn't strike Fiona as the type who would approve cosmetic surgery. She also had a job in television, which sounded pretty sexy. Rather than being an uptight loner as they were imagining, Kate probably had a big group of friends who hung out in organic coffee shops, moaning about the state of the planet while slurping overpriced smoothies.

110

"I'm so bored," Fiona announced. "Come on, let's get some wine from the canteen."

"You think they sell wine in a hospital?"

"It's a business. They sell everything that could kill you in the same place they can cure you."

Clare looked unsure. "Maybe I should go while you wait?"

"No, I'm not making you fetch my order. Come on. They'll be ages."

Fiona perked up once they were out of the waiting room. She believed in making the most out of a bad situation, and being in hospital when you were supposed to be sunning yourself in the middle of the glistening Mediterranean Sea was definitely a bad situation. She hoped they would get around to lounging on a yacht before the week was out. The more glamorous experiences you had, the more you attracted.

There was as much wine as they could drink in the hospital canteen. Clare used her Euros to buy two small bottles, but insisted they drink them near the waiting room. By the third sip, Clare already had rosy cheeks.

"So has Chi had a boyfriend since you've known her?"

Clare had always been an insatiable gossip. Fiona had more often than not been the one being gossiped about. Chi, on the other hand, neither asked for gossip nor created any. Not since her tattooist boyfriend, at least. Since then she had been on boring dates where she had reported the guys had been polite, but there had been no chemistry.

"Nothing serious," Fiona replied. "She says she falls for the wrong ones. I think she's just too fussy."

Clare looked bored. "What about Jem?"

Fiona got a flashback of the moment before the clay fight and frowned. "God, she was a bit touchy yesterday, wasn't she? It wasn't my fault Kate stuck a naked man in front of me."

A doctor appeared in the corridor and called out a name. An elderly man with his arm in a sling hoisted himself out of his seat and followed her. Fiona sighed and glugged back her wine.

"Yeah, I don't think Jem likes you very much," Clare said.

Fiona bristled. "What? You can't just say that."

"No, not like that," Clare said, quickly backtracking. But the words had been said and a knot Fiona didn't know she had tightened in her stomach.

"I just thought she had a weird attitude. She's not a bit like Andrew," Clare clarified.

What had that got to do with anything?

"Well, you're not like your brothers. So?"

Did Jem really not like her? Fiona's ego felt bruised.

"I mean she's not quite as chatty as Andrew. She's a bit guarded, that's all I meant."

There had been some tension yesterday, but that had been cleared up the same afternoon. They'd had a drink. Jem had told Fiona how much she'd regretted not being at the engagement party. Fiona hadn't minded in the slightest. She'd been happy not to have any family there. It would have felt a bit too real otherwise. It was a big enough deal telling all your friends you were getting married.

But why hadn't Jem been at the engagement party? Was Clare right? Was it because she didn't like Fiona?

"Oh shit, you've gone quiet," Clare observed.

What had Clare expected? It was impossible to feel good after having something like that dropped on you. Oh by the way, one of the four people you invited to share your amazing win doesn't actually like you. Oops! Never mind.

"I didn't mean to say that," Clare said.

Fiona downed the rest of her wine. Clare offered to get her another. She was trying to make up for being so blunt, but this time Fiona didn't think alcohol was going to help.

"No, I'm okay," she said, tossing her bottle into the bin.

It was stupid to feel upset. She'd said plenty of mean things about Jem in the past. Perhaps that's why Clare had felt like she could say what she'd said. Perhaps she thought Fiona wanted the rivalry. She'd been a bit demented in the old days, picking fights where there needn't have been any.

"It shouldn't be much longer," Clare said, as if she had inside information. "It'll be a good story...You'll be able to tell your kids how crazy you were once."

Hi, kids, once I bumped my head on a wall and went for a check-up. The End. It was a crap story.

"If I have kids," Fiona said. "I don't want them getting beaten up by an evil auntie."

"Fiona! I didn't mean it."

Fiona let out a dry laugh.

"I don't know why I said it," Clare said, looking miserable. "I'm sorry. I'm probably just jealous."

Fiona felt herself relax. She heard the sincerity in her oldest friend's voice, could see it manifest in her blushing cheeks. Clare's words suddenly lost their substance. She felt relieved. It wasn't that Jem didn't like *her*, but Clare didn't like Jem.

"Ricardo can't take his camera off her, can he?" Clare said.

Fiona frowned. She hoped that wasn't true. She was the protagonist of the show after all.

"Anyway, it's not *if* you have kids...you've always wanted to have kids," Clare continued.

Fiona shrugged. "People can change."

Clare stared at her in alarm. "What about Andrew? Doesn't he want kids?"

Fiona had made her worry. Clare was nibbling on her corpulent bottom lip and looking at her with concern. She'd only said it out of irritation about what Clare had said earlier.

"I've got a headache," she said. "I don't feel like talking about it."

Fiona should have said she was joking, but for some reason she didn't.

"It's just quite a big deal, that's all," Clare pressed.

"It'll be fine. Trust me."

Clare's voice rose an octave. "I can't see how it'll be fine if one of you wants kids and the other doesn't. That's quite serious. People split up over that all the time."

Fiona shouldn't have opened her mouth. She could hardly criticise Clare for having no filter when she did exactly the same thing: said things to provoke.

"Clare, don't worry about it."

"Well I *am* going to worry about it. You're my friend. I want you to be happy. Getting married is a really big deal. I don't want you crying on my shoulder in a few years because Andrew wants a divorce because it turns out he wanted five kids."

Fiona spluttered out laughing. She didn't know what sounded less likely: Andrew asking for a divorce or her producing five children. He had been after her since she was thirteen. Those desperate boys from the close had spent their weekends hanging around outside her house, trying to catch glimpses of her in her bedroom. She'd felt pity for them one morning and had walked around in her bra on purpose.

"That's not going to happen," she said, reaching out to give Clare's shoulder a squeeze. "I wouldn't put you through that. Anyway, I do want kids. I don't know why I said that."

Clare smiled, her eyes brimming with tears. It made Fiona feel a bit embarrassed how emotional Clare had been since she'd announced the engagement. Fiona often thought it would make her happier to see Clare in love than being in love herself.

Fiona tried to pull her hand away, but Clare caught it and pulled it towards her. She ran a finger over Fiona's sparkling rock of a ring.

"It's beautiful," she said.

Fiona felt her insides twist. Was Clare wondering if she'd ever get one? It was so big, so over the top. Fiona probably shouldn't have brought it. It would have been a reasonable excuse to say she had left it at home for safe-keeping. Then again, how could you go on a show like *The Hen Party* without a bit of bling on your finger? She hadn't wanted viewers to feel sorry for her.

"I wish you'd..." Clare began, and then she stopped, pressed her lips together and breathed in.

"What's the matter?"

"I wish you'd let me help you choose it."

Fiona took her hand back. "I know. I'm really sorry. You don't know how you'll react until it happens. I just wanted to be on my own." She sensed there were so many things Clare wished she'd done differently. It filled her with misgivings. Fiona didn't feel this guilt when she was with Sam or Chi – Sam because she was never up to date with her life anyway, and Chi because she was so undemanding. But Clare had known her all her life. She knew where Fiona came from. With Clare, Fiona couldn't pretend to be anybody she wanted.

A different doctor in a white coat walked into the waiting area and called out a name. The other patients briefly looked up and then back down at their magazines.

"That's you," Clare said.

The woman called out again, and this time Fiona caught it. The accent had made her own name unfamiliar. She stood up. The woman said something in Spanish and then turned and walked back into her office. They assumed she wanted them to follow, so they did, stepping into a bright white room.

"Sorry? I don't speak Spanish."

The woman looked at her wearily. "Okay. What's the problem?"

"I hit my head," Fiona said. They shouldn't have come.

Beside her, Clare was trying to keep a straight face. "She ran into a wall and blacked out."

"Don't say it like that," Fiona said, flicking her arm.

"Well you did!"

"It was a form of protest!"

"It definitely had an impact."

They caught each other's eyes and started giggling.

The doctor wasn't amused. "Had you been drinking?"

"When? Now or when it happened?"

The doctor looked furious and Fiona felt a conflicting desire to laugh and a sense that she should probably behave. It was a feeling she'd had in school when she didn't know how much trouble she would be in if she answered back.

"I was having a hay treatment," she said, recovering her composure. "Have you heard of it? Don't do it, it's rubbish."

Clare leant forward in her chair. "It's her hen party. She's getting married."

The doctor blinked, waited for more.

"Aren't you going to say congratulations?" Clare asked, looking surprised.

Fiona felt a twinge of embarrassment. Clare was always reluctant to be naughty, but when she got going, she didn't know when to stop.

"Congratulations," the doctor said. "So, do you have a medical problem you want to share as well? Because you could just post this news on Facebook."

Fiona felt chastened. "I'm sorry. I think I might have concussion."

The woman nodded, relieved they were getting down to business.

FOURTEEN

Day 2
JEM

Jem sat outside on the bamboo lounger with her legs curled up beneath her. She was flicking through one of the wedding magazines that had been lying around and mentally picking her favourite dress on each page. It surprised her how drawn she was to the big meringue dresses: waterfalls of satin spilling out below fitted bodices encrusted with Swarovski crystals. Her mum would love it. She would cry the day she saw Jem in one. She would cry with joy and relief that Jem's teenage promise of wearing red and black on her wedding day had not come true after all. Jem smiled to herself and flicked over the page, landing on an advert for pink diamond engagement rings. She wondered what kind of ring she would go for.

Ricardo stepped outside with a bottle of beer and she felt self-conscious and turned the page again, pretending to flick with disinterest. He sank into a lounger opposite her. Just one day in the sun and his Mediterranean skin was doing its thing, deepening to a toasted almond. He was wearing torn jeans and a faded Guns n' Roses T-shirt. The black and white design reminded her of a Jack Daniel's label, which was probably the idea.

She swallowed back the flutter of nerves.

"So, any news from the clinic?"

Ricardo shook his head. "They haven't come out yet. Kate's still waiting in the car park."

"We must be really behind now."

"Yeah. Although it's hard to tell with Kate's schedule. She likes to keep us all guessing."

Jem knew she was the only one who felt an attraction for the cameraman. Clare had said she didn't like him, that she thought him aloof. Fiona only paid attention to him when his camera was on. Sam just thought his moodiness was funny. Chi said she didn't have a problem with him, but thought it was weird having a male cameraman to film a hen party.

Chi was currently in the pool, swimming under water. Occasionally she lifted her head to take a breath before submerging herself beneath it again. They had shared a companionable silence for most of the morning, Sam choosing to disappear to her bedroom to make some phone calls. Jem had been relieved when she'd gone. Sam didn't stop talking. It was good to have some space from the three old school friends. They were entertaining but full-on, and after a few hours Jem found herself craving escape.

Ricardo started watching something on his camera, a flicker of a smile crossing his lips. His expression was guilty, like he knew he shouldn't be enjoying it so much. He suddenly burst out laughing. The sound made her laugh too.

"Are you reviewing what you've got?" she asked.

"I shouldn't laugh," said Ricardo. But he didn't stop. He tipped the camera towards her, inviting her to watch. Jem got to her feet and moved nearer. She leant over his shoulder, resting a hand on it without thinking. She could feel his skin radiating warmth through his T-shirt. Her own body was barely covered in a loose white T-shirt that skimmed her buttocks.

Chi climbed up the pool steps and reached for her towel. She wrapped it around her slender shoulders and glanced towards them.

"What are you watching?" she asked.

Jem gasped as she recognised the scene. Fiona was wrapped up in a sheet full of hay, trying to get to her feet but having trouble with the bouncy water bed. Another bounce and she tipped over. It looked so comical, Jem couldn't help laughing.

Chi came over, grinning. "Can I see?"

It wasn't up to her. Jem expected Ricardo to hold the camera out to Chi like he'd done for her, but he didn't. He didn't seem to notice her.

Now Fiona was crying for help. One minute she was sobbing loudly, the next she was dead still, listening. Jem slapped him gently with her hand.

"This is mean," she said, trying not to smile.

"It's not my fault. It's my job," Ricardo protested. "Fiona wants me to delete it."

"Let me see!" Chi called, unable to contain herself.

Ricardo looked up, his expression suddenly wary. "Hey, you guys aren't supposed to see this."

"Oh go on, let Chi see," Jem said. She was aware that she might have a certain influence over the cameraman. Was she making the chemistry up or was it really crackling between them, sending ripples through her with each bit of physical contact?

Jem leant towards the camera again. "I hardly saw anything anyway. Show the rest." She smiled at Chi. "Look at this. It's so funny."

Ricardo held the camera further out so Chi could see too. Jem squinted in the sun. At first she was distracted by Ricardo's heady aftershave and his moody lips pursed in concentration. A moment passed, though, and she found herself focusing again on her dishevelled future sister-in-law whimpering at the camera.

Fiona was one of those people who knew how to apply makeup and position her face so that in every photo she looked like a hottie. With a video, she wasn't having so much luck. The angle was giving her a double chin, and when she leant back into her cushion, you could see the shadowy insides of her upturned nose. Her face suddenly hardened and she tipped back her head and screamed, *"Help!"* and after that she began to cry loudly. Jem bit her lip, feeling guilty for wanting to laugh. It was incredibly exaggerated.

"It's so fake," she murmured, glancing at Chi and expecting to find amusement and guilt in her fellow hen's eyes. Chi, after all, was practical and called a spade a spade. Instead, Chi looked annoyed.

"It's not fake that she bumped her head."

Jem didn't want a confrontation, but she couldn't pretend Fiona had nothing to do with the bump on her head.

"Well, she did run into a wall," she pointed out as gently as she could. Ricardo grinned.

"Did you hear what Kate said?" Chi asked, glaring at her. "She was enjoying it."

"I know. But when you get annoyed, I bet you don't sprint into walls."

"No, but I've never been wrapped up in hay either. If Fiona had had a free hand, I bet she would have slapped Kate in the face."

Jem frowned. "Like that's much better."

Ricardo burst out laughing at another dramatic performance by Fiona. His shoulders shook and he leant forward, wiping his eyes.

"Oh my God, she's so funny. I'm crying."

It was funny seeing him laugh. Jem couldn't help grinning herself. Chi had to see that Fiona had been acting.

"Are you going to delete it?" Chi said. "You have to delete it."

"No, it's going straight to YouTube," Ricardo said, deadpan.

Jem could tell he was teasing, but Chi's eyes widened in alarm.

"You can't do that! That would be totally out of order. Are you even allowed to do that? It's a hen party, you can't do this. She doesn't deserve this."

"Calm down," Ricardo said. He shot Jem a conspiratorial grin that made her heart beat a little bit quicker. "Of course I won't."

"You should delete it," Jem said, deciding it was wiser to side with her fellow hen. "Everything needs to look perfect."

She returned to her seat, arranging herself carefully, her eyes scanning for stray hairs on her legs and finding none. She was aware she looked sexy in her outfit, and that the sunshine had already given her a good base colour. Feeling Ricardo's eyes on her, she looked up to meet them. They were dark and smiling.

"Are you saying it should *look* perfect, but isn't?" he said.

The question surprised her. Quite possibly that was what she had been implying, but she hadn't expected anyone to pick up on it. But Ricardo was an observer. He was trained at reading between the lines.

"The show is never going to capture the whole story," she said with what she felt was an ambiguous shrug.

Ricardo and Chi were both staring at her now and she felt her cheeks redden. Perhaps she should leave it there, keep things nice and happy.

"You've got my attention," Ricardo said. "So what *is* the whole story?"

"I'm just saying that Andrew and Fiona..."

She hesitated. Chi had a disapproving look on her face. Jem didn't want to come across as unkind. She just thought a bit of objectivity would be good since they were chatting as friends with no camera rolling.

"...they weren't the great couple that their friends get nostalgic about."

Ricardo let out a low whistle and reached for his camera. "Can you start again? I should be recording."

"Don't you dare, Ricardo!" Jem said with a laugh. She realised it was the first time she'd said his name. It occurred to her in the same moment that she'd never dated a foreigner. She wondered if that was where she'd been going wrong.

"Okay, fine," he said. "But only because I got quite a lot of chat yesterday."

Jem groaned at the flashbacks. "About that. Can you edit out everything I said, please?"

Ricardo swayed in his chair and mimicked her voice. *"Oh my God, you're going to be my sister!"*

"Oh don't!" She covered her face. "I was very drunk."

123

"It was sweet," Chi said.

Sweet? Jem stuck her fingers down her throat and pretended to vomit. A second later, she gave up the pantomime and her shoulders sagged. She'd been trying very hard to feel chirpy about everything, but from time to time the reality hit her. Right now, she felt overwhelmed by doubts.

"What's wrong?" Ricardo asked. "What are you scared of?"

"Truth is, I find this all a bit difficult. This wedding, I mean."

Chi rushed to reassure her. "But that's normal. Your little brother is getting married. It's a big deal."

Her friends had said the same. She'd even suspected that some thought her jealous of her brother for getting hitched first. Of course she wasn't jealous of her own brother, just worried for him.

"It's not because he's my little brother," she said, trying to organise her thoughts. "I don't think Fiona is…"

Don't say it, she thought. *Don't say it. It's not nice.* This was Fiona's hen party. Once it was out, she would be a two-faced bitch, enjoying the party while secretly criticising the wedding.

"You don't think Fiona is what?" Chi asked.

"…good enough for my brother."

Jem immediately regretted her words. Chi looked shocked. Ricardo's expression barely changed, but that was probably because he wasn't emotionally invested like the rest of them.

"I mean, right for him," she said quickly.

Too late.

She had been getting along well with Chi, and now she sensed she had ruined everything. Chi was Fiona's friend first. Jem felt a rush of fear that Chi would tell Fiona what she had said as soon as Fiona arrived back at the villa, and then she would be frozen out of the group.

"I think it's because I haven't seen them together now they're older," she said, trying to justify such a strong opinion. "So I'm left with what they were like together as teenagers."

"Your brother isn't perfect either," Chi said.

So Chi thought she was biased. Perhaps she was.

"Of course he is!"

The joke fell flat. Chi was looking very serious. Jem had underestimated her loyalty to Fiona. She thought it was only Clare and Sam who defended everything she did.

"I'm afraid he's just a mere mortal like the rest of us," Chi said. "It's weird. You seem to be the only person who doesn't think it's cute they got back together after all these years."

Cute? Jem resented the description. It sparked the flame of opposition that she had been trying to put out.

"Sorry, but Fiona was a manipulative little cow when they were teenagers, so please don't tell me it's cute," she shot back, stunning herself with the force of her voice. "Sorry, but that's the truth."

"That's not what Clare says."

"Well of course that's not what Clare says! When have you ever heard Clare say anything against Fiona?"

Chi looked at her warily. Jem felt like she was being judged as the bitter sister. She didn't want that title.

"Fiona used to give my brother the silent treatment at least once a month. He used to get into such a state, wondering what he'd done wrong. She was always pointing out what other people's boyfriends were doing better."

She couldn't stop herself now.

"I remember him taking her away to the Lake District when they were sixteen. And they arrived at this cute B&B, and he'd bought a bottle of wine, and you know what she said?"

It hadn't been *"You're the best boyfriend in the whole world."*

"She said, *'It's not exactly Venice, is it?'"*

Ricardo winced. "I took a girlfriend to Paris once and she dumped me."

Chi, grateful for the interruption, looked at him with a sympathetic smile. "Seriously?"

"Yeah, but to be fair, we'd been going downhill for months."

"The point is," Jem said, wanting desperately to be understood, "my brother was an emotional wreck because of her for his entire teenage life."

Chi's face softened. "All teenagers are emotional wrecks, though, aren't they?"

"I wasn't," Ricardo said. "I was pretty together."

Jem felt a flicker of annoyance. Suddenly Ricardo seemed too smug.

"Good for you. My brother ended up in therapy."

Silence followed that revelation, bringing with it an oppressive atmosphere like a heavy wool blanket Jem wished she could shrug off. She had probably made it sound worse than it was. It hadn't been years in therapy.

He had had five sessions, and it hadn't just been about Fiona. Her brother had been a nervous boy who had lacked confidence, and their parents had thought talking to someone about his fears would help him confront and overcome them. They had always been such caring parents, and the thought that her brother could be marrying someone with a lower standard of care had niggled at Jem every day since he'd told her the news. Now her feelings were out, she felt lighter, but also a bit embarrassed.

"I shouldn't have said all that..."

"It's okay, you didn't say it to her face, at least," Chi said, looking suddenly tired. "I think we've got to trust they love each other. Everyone makes mistakes. Whatever they did to each other in the past, that's in the past."

"I know," Jem said. All her doubts weren't suddenly going to be alleviated, but Chi was right. She should trust that everything was meant to be.

She noticed Ricardo was smiling knowingly. She narrowed her eyes.

"What's that smile for?"

"Whatever happens, this episode will have a happy ending."

"Not if they split up half way through."

Ricardo nodded. "If they split up half way through, we'll shoot such a good fake reconciliation that even they'll think it's real."

"They aren't going to split up," Chi said, firmly.

"No," Jem said. "Of course they aren't."

And she knew it was time she stopped secretly wishing that they would.

FIFTEEN

Day 5
KATE

"What do you mean?" Kate said, trying hard not to let the panic spill into her voice. "Have you heard from her?"

Sharon was looking at her intently, sensing the importance of the phone call.

"She sent me a text…" Andrew's voice broke.

"What did it say?"

Sharon's eyebrows were raised in question. Kate wasn't ready to answer. On the other end of the phone, Andrew was struggling to get the words out.

"Andrew, calm down," Kate said. "It's going to be alright."

Nothing.

"Andrew, are you there?"

The words tumbled out at last. "I'm at Gatwick Airport."

"What?"

This couldn't be happening. What was it with people rushing to airports at the slightest drama? The last thing this situation needed was an emotionally unstable fiancé.

"I'm flying over."

"But why? She'll be home in two days and you can sort it out then. She was just a bit drunk, Andrew, and emotional. There's really no need for you to come over here. It might even make it worse."

"I made a mistake, but I love her and she needs to know that."

Sharon couldn't control herself now. "What is it? What's going on?"

Kate covered the mouthpiece. "Andrew, the fiancé...they had a row, apparently..."

Sharon's eyes widened. Andrew had burst into tears again. He tried and failed to articulate something else before hanging up abruptly.

"It's not serious, is it?"

"He's catching a plane over."

"Oh, for God's sake! What's it about?"

Kate shook her head. She felt wrought with guilt. She could have let them have a good time; instead, she'd pushed them over the edge.

"You're drawing a lot of blanks, Kate," Sharon said, exasperation written all over her face. "Weren't you with them the whole time?"

"Nearly the whole time."

"Nearly?" Sharon echoed irritably. "And when you weren't with them, where the hell were you?"

SIXTEEN

Day 3
KATE

It was early. Kate could tell by the gentle light filtering through the slits in the shutters. She closed her eyes again, intending to prolong her slumber for a little longer. Minutes later she was on her feet, winding up the blind. Her spare time was limited and she needed to make the most of it.

The view that rewarded her was so stunning she felt compelled to reach for her camera. The sky was streaked with golds, reds and pinks. Beneath the celestial outpouring of light and colour, the sea glistened, and right in the centre, a solitary white sailing boat shone on the horizon.

Kate spent a while in silent admiration as blue sky deepened between the burnished threads and the sun rose higher, promising a beautiful day. Ricardo would have to film it tomorrow. She should have got him to film dawn and dusk the past two days, but perhaps he could stay a couple of days longer instead. She breathed through the tension that tugged at her ribs. She needed to recharge her batteries, and the sea was calling to her.

She knotted her bikini strap around her neck and pulled her blue cotton sundress over her head. Outside the cicadas whistled and sleepy pigeons cooed. Kate felt a thrill as she headed towards the bay she had spotted on her drive back the previous night. It was early, but the temperature had already reached the mid-twenties.

The small *cala* was the second treat for the eyes that morning, with its golden sand and water a perfect blend of turquoise and deep blue. She headed down the three flights of stone stairs, her heart bubbling with excitement. There were people who did this every day. The elderly man reading a newspaper in a fold-up chair was probably a regular. There were a couple of women performing sun salutes in one corner beside a rocky outcrop. A lone towel suggested someone might already be swimming, and a young guy on a paddle board was heading off into the distance.

Kate dropped her towel and sunglasses on the sand and went straight to the water's edge. The cold water washed over her toes and she drew a breath. She took another step forward. It always seemed impossibly cold, but she knew soon she would be completely submerged and it would be wonderful. Another step.

From afar the water was such a strong turquoise, but up close it was crystal clear. She could see dozens of tiny grey fish swimming past her legs. She couldn't hold back the smile. Thank God she'd got out of bed. She already felt restored.

After the meal last night she'd felt mixed up. The rather drawn out and laboured scene with Fiona talking about Andrew's marriage proposal had brought up all her old feelings. Back at the apartment, she'd had a few drinks on her own and had ended up crying along to some of Matt's favourite songs, including Beck's melodic but sorrowful *Lost Cause*, a title which had summed up their relationship years back. By the time her tears had dried, she'd decided that she wasn't going to pursue the environmental angle any more. She was going to deliver the hen party which both the channel and Fiona had their hearts set on. Mallorca was so beautiful it didn't look like it needed her help anyway.

She adjusted her snorkel mask, took a deep breath and then plunged headfirst into the water. She swam a few metres, her legs kicking, and then floated for a moment with her eyes fixed on the sea base, taking it all in. She could see a fish nibbling at the sand and then spitting it out. For a moment, she felt profoundly happy. She thought to herself that she would do this every morning she had left on the island. It was exactly what she needed to reenergise and restore her sense of wellbeing.

Something bright blue caught her eye. She kicked her feet and propelled herself towards it. Half buried in the sand was a little plastic ice cream spoon. How rubbish. She didn't want to swim carrying it; neither did she want to have to leave the water so soon to throw it in a bin. Ignoring the twinge of guilt, she swam on. She could always pick it up on her return, if she found it again.

Towards one side of the bay, close to the outcrop of rocks, the sand was covered with a bed of sea plants which looked like giant ribbons of spinach tagliatelle. Some of her good feeling ebbed away when she saw the plastic cup nestling between the long, slippery leaves. Could she leave that too? The shore was quite far behind her now and she just wanted to swim and let her worries slip away.

As she swam under the surface, she identified more ice cream spoons and straws and bottle tops. Then she saw the transparent plastic take-away box with its lid opening and closing like a man-made clam. That brought her to her senses. Of course she was going to collect the rubbish. If she didn't, who would?

It might not be much of a contribution, but it was better than nothing. Currents would shift it otherwise and trick marine life into think it was food. Only last week she'd read about thirteen beached sperm whales on the North Sea coast of Germany. A post mortem had revealed their vast bellies full of rubbish, including a 13-metre-long fisherman's net and part of a car engine. For years, these creatures had been able to trust the oceans to nourish them. Thanks to humans, feeding themselves was now a dangerous lottery.

Kate swam towards the seabed, the water pulling and pushing at her. Her breath was dying in her throat but she was determined to pick up that horrible takeaway box. She kicked harder and reached out to grab it. Just as her fingers made contact, another hand appeared in front of hers and took hold of the other side. She pulled back in alarm and for a split second caught the look of surprise of the snorkeller staring back at her.

Kate broke the surface, gasping for breath. The other snorkeller did the same. She pulled off her mask. He pulled off his. He wiped a hand over his eyes and pushed his dripping hair out of his face. They stared at each other, recognition dawning.

"Oh my God," she spluttered.

"You're the woman from the plane."

"This is crazy!"

He held up the takeaway box, looking confused. "Was this yours?"

"No!" She laughed. "I just saw it and was going to pick it up."

He grinned. "Me too."

"Wow, this is crazy!"

"I know…so crazy…do you know how many *calas* there are in Mallorca?"

"A lot?"

"Hundreds!"

They trod water, grinning at each other. She felt a burst of happiness. What were the chances?

"There's quite a lot of rubbish," Kate said.

"Yeah…I know…I try to do a bit every time I go out."

"We need a net or something."

"Yeah…I usually bring one."

"I'm just going to get that cup."

"I'll get the spoons."

They both dived under the surface. Her eyes lingered over his lithe, muscular body as he swam past her and headed for the spoons. He was like an advert for strength and vitality; basically, a Greek yoghurt commercial.

She kicked her legs and reached out for the cup and some strips of plastic that had once been a bag and was no longer going to be a turtle's lunch. When her chest started clamouring for air, she resurfaced. He took a moment longer, appearing with his takeaway box full of packaging and spoons.

Without saying a word, they swam back towards the shore. They emerged from the water, their unappetising findings inviting a few confused looks from new arrivals to the beach. Gabriel held the lid of the rubbish bin open and they chucked it all away.

They stood side by side, the sunlight picking out the droplets of water on their skin. Kate felt good in her new red halter neck bikini. It may have cost a small fortune being by an indie brand, but at least she could be sure a small child hadn't made it in a sweat shop.

"Aren't you working?" he asked.

"Yeah, but we start quite late. The hens need to get over their hangovers."

He laughed. "A jump in the water is the best way."

"I'm sure they'll be in the pool soon."

She felt at a loss to know how to stop the morning from ending and him from leaving. At the same time, she knew it was pointless to try to keep him here. She was only here a week. What could she really expect from this encounter?

"Do you want a coffee?" he asked.

Her heart did a somersault. Why hadn't she thought of that genius question?

"I'd love one."

He nodded over at the small beach bar which was just opening up. "They do good coffee."

"Perfect. Do you come here often, then?"

"Yes, from May to June. In July and August it's swamped with tourists and there's no room to move."

They sat at one of the metallic tables on the border of the sandy terrace, with the waves rolling in just below. A waiter in khaki shorts came over and greeted Gabriel like an old friend. Kate watched Gabriel from behind her sunglasses as they chatted. The sun picked out the bleached hairs of his stubble, the salt on his lovely lips. He was attractive, even with his big, straight nose and those tiny hairs between his eyebrows that threatened to grow into a mono-brow. An easy job for a pair of tweezers.

The waiter left. Gabriel leant back, his face breaking into a contagious smile, leaving her in no doubt she fancied the pants off him.

"Kate, right?"

She was smiling too much, but she couldn't help it. "That's right. You have a good memory."

"I do. My name's Gabriel."

"Gabriel..." She echoed his pronunciation. "Gah-briel. Pronounced like that it's a girl's name in England."

He wrinkled his nose. "Yeah, I know. I've been told that before."

"I like it, though. I like the way you say it."

She could have said that she hadn't forgotten it, either, but her obvious delight in seeing him was already enough. She'd felt so annoyed with herself for being too chicken to give him her card at the airport. But now he was here, in his swimming trunks, hair wet and sun kissed and looking more handsome and far more relaxed than he had on the plane.

"I'm jealous of your life," she said, breathing in the sea air. It smelt of seaweed and sun cream and holidays.

He grinned. "It's a good life."

"What do you do all day?"

"I restore old furniture."

"Oh...I didn't expect that."

He held out his hands. She didn't know what she was looking for. Then she noticed the swollen finger.

"Hammer accident," he said, and laughed.

And the scar on his thumb.

"Electrical saw, when I was young and still experimenting." He set his hands down on the table, his fingers tapping a rhythm then stopping abruptly. He had a thin leather bracelet on his wrist which looked like it might have been there for years. It reminded Kate of her backpacking days. She'd come back with so many of them it had looked like she was wearing a badly ripped sleeve.

"My brother has a…" He frowned, looking for the word. "I guess you would call it a *lifestyle* shop. It sells lots of different things for the house, but also clothes, slippers, gifts…He sells some of my furniture there. I get lots of commissions too."

She could imagine the type of shop. White linen curtains and scented candles; rattan bull heads and distressed wooden picture frames; ceramic pots in a Mediterranean palette of terracotta, deep blue and warm yellow.

"You must be good."

"I have ten thousand followers on Instagram," he said, and laughed like he didn't take any of it seriously.

"That's amazing! You're basically a furniture-making superstar."

"I should give you my autograph."

You should give me your number, she thought, but didn't dare say it.

"I'll have to look you up," she said, which was far less efficient.

"You should."

A man who knew how to use his hands. She liked the idea of that.

"How long are you here for?"

"A week."

He looked thoughtful. "There's a bigger beach clean

tomorrow if you're free. It's happening on the coast south of Palma, near Cala Blava."

"I'd love to, but I've got five women to entertain."

"You can bring them with you. They have arms, right?"

She laughed. "They'd hate me."

"Yeah, probably. Let me guess, you're going to a beach club?"

"That's supposed to be the plan. A yacht ride first…"

He whistled. "Very nice."

"…and then cocktails at a beach club. That could change, though. I haven't been very good at following the official schedule so far."

He raised an eyebrow. "Can you do what you like?"

"No. I'm being a rebel. I was trying to make things more meaningful."

Wasn't a beach clean-up exactly the sort of thing she'd wanted? It was the universe telling her to go along with the plan.

"How? What do you mean?" he asked.

She had his full attention and he was doing an admirable job of not letting his gaze drop to her cleavage, which can't have been easy. His curious brown eyes were focused on her, little laughter lines creasing as he smiled.

"Let's just say my plan was never to direct a normal hen party."

It would be good to tell someone else. If he concluded she was mad, then she would put an end to it and start behaving like Joanna Kane, or what Ricardo claimed the show's director was normally like. Key quality: passionate about hen parties.

"I took the job because I saw it as an opportunity to

broadcast an environmental message to a big audience. It shouldn't just be serious documentaries talking about the issues; it should be in *EastEnders*..."

He frowned.

"It's a British TV show."

"Ah."

"If those characters were recycling their yoghurt pots and saying why, it might inspire the masses to get into the habit. Basically I want this hen party to highlight how short-sighted we're being every time we ask for a straw, buy food wrapped up in plastic, order a takeaway coffee..."

"Yeah, I get it. Good for you."

She was in trouble if he approved. She didn't need all that much encouragement.

"What have you done so far?"

"Little things like making the villa anti-plastic, showing them that video of the turtle with the straw up his nostril...you know the one?"

He rubbed his nose in recognition. "Oh yeah, it broke my heart."

"I was supposed to show a video of the hens' friends and families..."

"You can still show it later, no?"

"I guess so. I'll have to do something to keep them happy; so far it's been a bit up and down."

"Up and down?" He leant forward, grinning. "Tell me about it. I've never met a director before."

She filled him in on the failed sculpture class and the less than successful spa morning. She told him what the hens were like when they got drunk: how Clare's voice rose so high it sounded like she was on helium; how Sam got teary-eyed and started scrolling through all her baby photos and showing everyone and wanting to know how many babies they were all going to have. She told him how noisy they were and what a relief it was to be here, in this café, soaking up the sunshine beside the sea.

"It sounds like you're trapped on a plane to Magaluf."

She laughed. "Oh, it's not *that* bad…I'm trying to make things a little less predictable than a pub crawl."

"What are you doing today?"

"Today?" she echoed stupidly.

Oh God. While she'd been rabbiting on, she'd forgotten all about her agenda. But surely it was still really early.

"What time is it?"

He looked at his watch. "Ten past ten."

She blinked at him. "You're joking, right? How did that happen?"

It happened because she'd been having a good time.

"Oh my God, I've got to go! We're all supposed to be going out cycling."

"I can drive you wherever you need to go," he said, getting to his feet, his red shorts still wet and clinging to his brown thighs.

"I haven't even got money for the coffee," Kate realised. She'd planned for a quick dip in the sea and she'd got carried away.

"Don't worry, this is on me. You can get the next one."

She looked at him in surprise. "Oh," she said, and for a moment the panic was replaced with excitement. "Is there going to be a next one?"

He smiled, his eyes twinkling. "Well, I hope so. I want to know how the show ends."

SEVENTEEN

Day 2
FIONA

Kate nodded at Sam.

"Action."

"So were you expecting Andrew to propose?" Sam said, grinning broadly.

"Yes, since I was thirteen. I think he did once, actually!"

After the wasted morning at the clinic, Kate had finally started making an effort. The swish restaurant with its incredible view overlooking the bay of Palma was exactly what Fiona had had in mind, as were the double figure prices on the menu. She had ordered the priciest wine simply because it was the priciest wine. If she'd felt confident dissecting a lobster on camera, she would have gone for that. Instead she had gone for a steak, which she knew she could consume without any faux pas.

"Wow, you really were childhood sweethearts, then," Clare quipped for perhaps the fifth time.

"Yeah, we really were."

Fiona thought of Mandy and how furious she had been when she'd found out Andrew had cheated on her. Spin the bottle, apparently, at Joe's sixteenth birthday. They'd only been broken up a week. She hadn't spoken to Andrew for months after that.

She realised her smile was dipping and concentrated. Acting was harder than she'd expected.

"But it was a good thing that we had time apart to grow up and discover who we were," she said, remembering her lines.

Apparently, Mandy had become an air stewardess and was living in Mexico now. That was according to her mum, anyway, whom you could never trust to remember anything quite right. It sounded exotic, but it really wasn't. Who wanted to be a waitress to first class passengers? Much better to be the first class passenger being waited upon.

"Cut."

Fiona turned to look at Kate. What had she done this time? But Kate was looking down the table at Jem.

"Jem, Ricardo has just pointed out he can see you're on your phone. Can you look like you're enjoying the story, please? Even if you have heard it a million times."

Jem's face reddened and she slipped her phone into her bag. "Sorry."

Fiona remembered what Clare had said in the clinic and felt her spirits plummet. She kept forgetting how serious this was for Andrew's sister. If she and Andrew broke up, everybody here would rush to comfort her, except Jem, who would rush to her brother's side.

She pushed the thought away and turned to her wine. Ricardo announced he wanted a more eye-catching beverage in the shot, and presently a handsome waiter came over with a passion fruit cocktail and lit it ceremoniously in front of Fiona. The passion fruit sizzled as the flame flickered. It was so much sexier than a glass of Chardonnay in the local pub. She suddenly felt sad it would eventually have to end. Did it have to? Perhaps she'd win another holiday! It seemed unlikely, though, even if she had entered a ton of competitions.

"Got that, Ricardo?" Kate said. "Great. Now the proposal. Ready, Clare?"

It was very unrealistic. What sort of friends would have no idea how Andrew had proposed until they went on the hen party?

"So can you...uh..." Clare stammered. "Wait, what was I going to say?"

There were groans around the table and calls for a teleprompter.

"Stop moaning! I've got it, I've got it," Clare said, a little breathlessly. She straightened up and fluffed at her hair, which she had curled especially for the supper. Fiona smiled encouragingly at her. She knew it was a pain having to perform, especially as Clare wasn't after a career in television like she was.

"And action..."

Joanna had suggested the proposal should be lavish but personal. Kate hadn't given Fiona any instructions on what the proposal should be and seemed genuinely interested in the true story. There were calls for her to start from the very beginning. Ricardo was to the side of her, looking at her through his camera lens. He had been filming off and on since they'd arrived, but now he fell still and adopted the grumpy concentrated expression he wore when he had to capture a scene. Fiona felt her heart thumping.

"Go on! What were you wearing?" Sam called. "Did you know he was going to ask you?"

Fiona had known it would come up and had rehearsed in front of her bedroom mirror. The same as she had practised talking about her ideal wedding dress, honeymoon plans and where she saw Andrew and herself living in ten years. *The Hen Party* crew had told her not to worry about being on camera, but of course she had. If she'd left it to chance, she would have come across like a bumbling idiot. It was a bit like natural makeup – it took an unnatural amount of time to perfect.

"He called me a week before to set up a date," she began. "He said he wanted to do something special on Friday night and to be ready at seven o'clock."

"Eight o'clock," Clare corrected her. "Remember?"

As if she'd been there, Fiona thought irritably. Eight o'clock did sound about right, though. Clare had always been a hoarder of details.

"Who did he propose to? You or Clare?" Sam laughed.

"It was about seven-thirty," Fiona said, trying to keep calm. She should be grateful she had a friend who cared so much. "The doorbell rang and I went down to get it."

"So you finally fixed the bell then!" Sam said.

"Uh…"

"Cut!" Kate said with thinly veiled exasperation. "I don't want you correcting Fiona's story. I don't want to know about broken doorbells. The audience wants to hear the proposal without constant interruptions, alright? Don't break the spell, hens." Her face softened with an afterthought. "Excitement is good, but at least let her get the first bit out."

Sweat pricked Fiona's skin. She hoped it didn't show because she was pretty exposed. She'd gone for her backless silver dress. A slither of sweat was really not the accessory she wanted to be remembered for. She took a deep breath.

"We'd been back together about a couple of months at this point. We kept it quiet because we didn't want people gossiping."

She was aware of Clare squirming at her side. Perhaps she wanted to say the exact number of days.

"What did you wear?" Sam called, before covering her mouth quickly.

Kate's jaw twitched. Fiona couldn't ignore the question, could she?

"I wore my leopard print playsuit with some jangly earrings…"

"Cut!"

Fiona glanced up at Kate in confusion. "What?"

"Wear something else. That sounded tacky."

"But…"

"Say your favourite organic cotton dress."

"What? I don't have a…"

"Red," Kate cut in. "My favourite organic cotton red dress. Got it?"

There was dissent among the hens that it wasn't very romantic to change the truth.

"It sounds way classier," Kate said.

"Alright…alright…"

Perhaps Kate was right and her original outfit did sound a bit East End market.

The filming continued with the new clothes.

"I was so nervous," Fiona said. "I don't know why, I just felt like it was going to be a special night."

She swallowed before repeating the hour he'd set for the date. Eight o'clock this time as it did have a better ring to it than seven. Meeting at a Tube station sounded lame, so she decided he could pick her up at her house as if they were in an American movie.

"The doorbell rang," she said, and then she hesitated too long.

"Was he waiting outside?" Sam prompted her.

Was that lavish enough? Fiona changed her mind.

"There was someone waiting outside, but it wasn't Andrew. He'd hired a driver."

Clare covered her mouth and started giggling hysterically. "Sorry, I can't help it."

"A driver?" Sam exclaimed. "How very *Downton Abbey*."

"But it's true!" Fiona blurted out. Miraculously the hens all shut up and Kate didn't shout, "Cut!" and she was able to get on with telling her proposal story.

"Andrew was waiting by the car. It was amazing. It was a beautiful black Bentley. We got in and Andrew offered me a glass of champagne and said he wanted me to have the best evening of my life."

She felt a rush of fondness for Andrew. She wanted the audience to wish they had boyfriends like him and be as pampered and loved as she was. It was a lot of pressure keeping this up, but she knew she would have viewers hanging on to her every word.

"We drove around the centre of London. He'd made a playlist of all our favourite songs..."

She was aware of the hens all smiling at the thought. Fiona felt her own heart swell.

"It was really sweet. I already thought it was the best night ever. I didn't know it was about to get better."

"Where did you go?" Chi asked.

Fiona wasn't sure if it was Chi's line or if she really didn't know. She had told them all. All except Jem.

"After that we went to Gordon Ramsay's restaurant." Clare acted out her surprise perfectly. Her jaw dropped and she leant forward, her green eyes sparkling. "Wow, how did you get a table?"

"Oh wait...this is the amazing part," Fiona said, her hand flying to her chest. It really was a beautiful detail. "He had booked it a year in advance. He'd thought about it happening for that long."

"Even though you weren't together?" Chi asked.

Fiona felt herself bristle and kept her smile fixed. The question undermined what would have been a perfect romantic moment.

"That's the beautiful thing about it," Clare said, and Fiona felt overwhelmed with gratitude to her best friend. "He knew they'd get back together."

Fiona nodded. "Yes. He said he had always known."

There were murmurs of *aaaw*. The mood turned dreamy and wistful. The hens were no longer questioning whether it was true or exaggerated. All they were thinking was how lucky Fiona was. A feeling of relief descended over her and she beamed with joy at all her hens. Ricardo had been wrong. She *was* great television.

"He must have taken out a loan," Jem snorted, ruining the moment.

EIGHTEEN

Day 2
CLARE

Clare looked on in disbelief as Jem weaved unsteadily through the tables with her phone to her ear and left the restaurant. If she hadn't already upset Fiona that morning in the clinic, she would have spoken her mind. She thought Andrew's sister was a stuck-up, selfish cow. This was Fiona's moment and Jem was ruining it.

Her best friend was trying her hardest to look unfazed by the snub. Clare wanted to reassure her that Ricardo could edit Jem's lines out. What part of 'embellished truth' had that woman not understood? How could she have gone on like that about her brother's salary and how he couldn't possibly have supported Fiona's fantasies? Clare was quite certain her friend knew the deal. She had been doing extremely well at tweaking a truly heartfelt and generous proposal.

But did it offer much comfort if Ricardo could edit Jem's lines? He couldn't edit the reality, which was that Fiona's future sister-in-law clearly wasn't over the moon about the wedding.

"She was just drunk," Sam said firmly. "She'll sober up in a minute and feel really bad for saying that."

Clare nodded in agreement. Good old practical Sam. She was so glad she had her as an ally. Together they would make sure Fiona's hen party wasn't sabotaged by an older sister throwing a hissy fit.

"The driver was a friend of his," Fiona murmured. "He did it for free."

She looked crestfallen. Clare frowned at her. There hadn't been an actual driver, had there? She looked over at Kate. Filming had stopped and she was deep in conversation with Mel and Ricardo. Apparently they were going to record the audio of the proposal story again once they were back in London.

"Go on, Fi," Clare said, leaning across the table and squeezing her hand. "Finish the story. The real one. I bet it'll make you feel better."

"Yeah, go on," Sam urged. "I was zonked when you first told me as George hadn't let me sleep a wink all night."

Clare glanced at Chi, expecting a third voice of encouragement. Chi was furthest from them and now had an empty seat beside her where Jem had been. Clare signalled for her to move up and get involved.

"Really?" Fiona said, looking uncertain. "You want to hear it again?"

"Of course we do," Clare said.

She had been so upset when Fiona had announced her engagement in a group Facebook message. Clare had always assumed that when it happened, they would meet up somewhere fancy and buy champagne, keeping the news secret until the other person couldn't bear the suspense any longer. She would have drawn it out, making a fuss of every detail of the proposal before indulging in a good dose of speculation on the wedding, the people who would be invited, the ones who wouldn't make the cut, and of course the dress. Clare thought Facebook was far too common for a marriage announcement. She had made the mistake of telling Fiona as much, too. Even though she had said it in a jokey voice, Fiona had got upset. She had said she had been excited and had wanted to tell everyone at once. Patience had never been her virtue.

If Clare had been the one who had got engaged, she would have delighted in making the announcement really special. She had daydreamed about it plenty of times and intended to do it one day. Her plan was to buy wedding themed postcards. She would write *Guess What?* on the back in black fountain pen and send them off to her family and friends. She would then get a thrill every time her phone rang, wondering who had got the surprise and was ringing up to congratulate her, eking every bit of fun out of the event. The truth was she spent so much time thinking about things like this that sometimes she forgot one important detail: she had yet to find someone she wanted to marry.

"We had this amazing meal," Fiona resumed. "And he kept holding my hand and looking into my eyes and telling me how beautiful I was, and how happy he was…"

Fiona and Andrew. It was meant to be. They had chased each other up and down all through their youth. They had seen each other transition through different fads and styles. They had consoled each other through the death of two grandparents, a dog, Fiona's A-levels and several failed driving tests. Clare had been devastated when Fiona had told her it really was the end. They were eighteen years old. Andrew had just said he would choose a university close to home so he could be with Fiona, even though he had far better offers from Durham and Warwick. Clare had always suspected Fiona had dumped him out of love, because she knew it was what was best for him. Outwardly she had been frosty, though. Clare had been the one to wear her heart on her sleeve, crying with him, because she felt like she was losing a brother.

"Afterwards we had dessert," Fiona said. "It was delicious."

"What did you have?" Sam asked, licking her lips.

Clare switched her attention back to the present. Talking of dessert, she was ready to dive into something sweet. She had read the menu backwards and the Upside-Down Cherry Cheesecake Jar had stuck in her mind.

"It was something very chocolatey. Very fancy."

Clare shot her a withering look. "Trust you not to remember the name!" She would have photographed the menu and archived it. Later she would have looked up a recipe and recreated the pudding for a special anniversary down the line. She knew she would make such a great partner for someone one day. It was annoying that there were no men in her life whom she could begin to see herself with.

"Like chocolate what?" Sam pursued.

Clare noted Sam's flushed cheeks. Jem wasn't the only one drunker than usual tonight. She felt virtuous as she poured herself a glass of fizzy water. Fiona needed at least one of her friends to stay focused until the end of the night. She expected now the filming was over, Fiona would let her hair down too.

"I don't read books," Sam continued, with a laugh. "I read posh menus as I eat my pasta bake. It's a little fad no one knows about."

Clare raised her eyebrow at the revelation. She hadn't known Sam had any interest in good food. When she thought of Sam and food, she thought of the limp jam sandwiches of her school packed lunches.

"I do that too," Clare said. "I love reading recipes."

Fiona frowned at them both. "Sorry, I'm the opposite. I don't analyse what I eat. I can't remember what it was called. It was very tasty, whatever it was."

"We can look it up later," Clare said, giving Sam a wink. "So we can get the full feel of the proposal."

Fiona rolled her eyes. "You do that, guys, but I think you'll find Gordon Ramsay's menu changes all the time."

"So did he propose after the chocolate?" Sam asked.

Clare knew the next bit. Andrew had not proposed after the dessert. He had thought it better to do it in a more private space. Next stop: Hyde Park. There, under the stars, Andrew had got down on one knee and asked Fiona to be his wife. *Under the stars.* She was allowed a bit of poetic licence. The truth was no Londoner had seen a star in years thanks to all the light pollution in the city.

"Let's see the ring," Chi said, finally joining the conversation.

Clare waited for Fiona to explain that Andrew hadn't proposed with this ring, but with a cheaper place holder. But she didn't. She probably thought it came across better for Andrew that he should know exactly what ring she'd wanted.

Andrew had told her, *"Get the one you love"* and Fiona had done just that. She had wasted no time going to Hatton Garden. Without any advisors, without any doubts, she'd boldly chosen this one. Clare would have spent at least a week doing her research before she set foot out of the door. But that was Fiona for you. Sometimes she seemed so unsure and in need of Clare's guidance. Then there were other times when she knew exactly what she wanted. Getting engaged to Andrew was one of those times. She hadn't wavered in her decision. She had said yes even though she must have known people would think her mad for rushing into it after a decade apart.

NINETEEN

Day 2
SAM

Fuck it, Sam thought, pouring herself another glass of wine. It wasn't as if George was going to wake her up in the middle of the night and again at the crack of dawn. Plus, the crew was taking a break from filming. Ricardo was out on the terrace, getting atmosphere shots. If she wanted to, she could chug back another bottle and go out dancing until sunrise. When was the last time she'd seen sunrise at the end of a party?

She cast her mind back and a memory made her smile. Malaga. Their first holiday together as boyfriend and girlfriend. By day three, she and Chris had realised if they didn't want to eat alone, they needed to wait until ten o'clock for supper. They'd grabbed the last table on the terrace at a restaurant by the beach, full of locals talking at the tops of their voices. Sam could still taste the blistered, salty Padron peppers and the light batter on the squid that had melted in her mouth. The wine had seemed to evaporate in the heat. Two carafes later and they'd headed down to the beach, following the music to a huge concert stage.

They'd danced to everything from Spanish rock to Britney Spears covers. They'd drunk cheap beer and laughed until tears had rolled down their cheeks. Towards the end of the night, Chris had taken her hand and they'd headed off to a quieter spot to watch the light gradually spill across the horizon. She'd leant her head

154

on his shoulder and her heart had swelled with happiness because she'd known she had found the guy she wanted to spend the rest of her life with.

She'd had to wait another year for the proposal. He'd planned to surprise her with a trip to Rome, but on the very morning of their departure, she'd tripped over their suitcases so spectacularly that she had broken her arm. Instead of Rome, they had gone to St Thomas's Hospital where she had been fitted with a clumpy cast. She had been in floods of tears in the hospital car park and so he had got down on one knee there and then, pulled out the ring he had sneaked into his coin pocket for safekeeping, and told her he wanted to look after both her arms for the rest of his life.

Sam got out her phone and sent her beloved husband a drunk text about how much she loved him and how, when she got back, she planned to make more time for him. When she looked up, she saw Clare was glaring at her phone meaningfully and she tucked it away before she was accused of being as uninterested in Fiona's wedding as Jem.

Fiona was showing off her engagement ring now. It really was a gaudy thing. Gaudy? Who was Sam kidding? It was bloody fantastic. Her own stone was a fraction of the size and had still cost an arm and a leg. Fiona's ring must have cost an absolute fortune.

Clare was appraising it for the millionth time.

"It's so you," she said.

Sam suppressed a laugh. In private, Clare had said she thought the ring was a 'bit flashy', a 'bit wag'. She was probably jealous, though. Jealousy was Clare's weakness and it always made her say bitchy things that she would quickly apologise for afterwards. Sam thought it was ridiculous how hung up she was about not being invited along to choose it. It wasn't like Clare was going to wear it half the time. Sam had been thrilled that Chris had bought her ring, but if he hadn't, she wouldn't have called a bunch of friends to come along to pick one. She would have just gone with Chris.

"I know, it's so me. I love it," Fiona said, smiling.

Sam was glad she had recovered after Jem's awkward exit.

"Conflict free, I hope!" Chi said.

"Oh God, you sound like Kate," Clare replied so abruptly that Sam felt obliged to smile at Chi reassuringly and make a point of answering.

"I'm sure it is. They should all be if they're sold in proper shops."

"Yeah, true. Did you ever watch that film *Blood Diamond*? I couldn't stop crying!"

"Oh God, I'm not watching that, then. I think it'll be Disney for the next ten years."

Chi laughed and Sam felt happy. She bet Clare would have loved it if it had been just the three old school friends all week, but Sam wanted everyone to feel included. She hoped that Jem would make it up to Fiona and the rest of the week would be conflict free, like that big, juicy ring which she suddenly had a great desire to see up close. She got up out of her seat and squeezed in beside Fiona.

"Let me have another look."

"You've already seen it a million times."

"I know, but it's so amazing."

Sam had stood up too fast. Her head was swimming and she felt like she was talking a bit too loudly. She'd have some more water in a minute, but first she'd admire the ring.

"Take it off," she said. "Let me see it properly."

Fiona looked unsure. "No, you might drop it."

"I won't drop it!"

"Alright, but don't try it on. It's bad luck."

Fiona slipped it off her finger and held it out.

"You've insured it, haven't you?" Sam said. "That's the first thing I did."

Fiona started saying something, but Sam wasn't really listening. She was studying the ring. She could have sworn that there was a fine silver film underneath the diamond. Placing it in her other palm, she felt the weight of it.

"Here," she said, giving it back to Fiona. Her smile fell from her face as she headed back to her seat. She grabbed the water and topped up her glass. When she looked up, she caught Chi looking at her strangely.

"Are you alright?"

If she hadn't drunk so much, Sam would have acted more convincingly. But her expression gave her away.

"I'm fine," she said.

Chi tapped Jem's empty seat by her side. "Come over here."

Sam hesitated for a moment. Clare and Fiona were looking towards the golden horizon beyond the terrace. Sam got up and hurried around the other side of the table.

"What is it?"

Sam bit her lip. She shouldn't say anything. But perhaps Chi knew something she didn't and there was a perfectly reasonable explanation. Then again, why would Chi have asked if the ring was conflict free if she knew something? It wasn't as if she had been given the line from Kate, even though Clare was right and it had sounded very Kate-like.

"What?" Chi said, gripping her arm tightly. She looked worried now.

"The ring," Sam whispered.

"What?"

"It's..."

She didn't want to believe it, but how could she ignore the weight of it in her hand? Or rather, the lack of it. She was sure she'd felt more presence from a toy ring out of a Christmas cracker. Then there were those twinkling diamonds with the silver film. She had earrings like that which had peeled after a few months.

"I don't think it's real," she finished.

Chi's eyes widened in alarm. Her grip tightened.

"Oh my God," she gasped. "Are you sure?"

"I think so."

"What a bastard!"

Chi's reaction had the same effect as a bucket of cold water poured over her head. It sobered her up considerably. Sam had expected her to laugh and tell her that it was impossible.

"I thought there was something not quite right," Chi whispered.

"Perhaps it's a new kind." A new kind of diamond that didn't weigh anything? What was the explanation for the band?

Chi's horrified expression made Sam panic. If Fiona turned back now, she would immediately know something was wrong. Sam regretted opening her mouth.

She was no longer sure of her conclusion; she needed to see the ring again, under a microscope.

"Chi, don't say anything yet. We aren't sure. Maybe there's an explanation. Maybe it's a place holder."

And if it wasn't, it would be utterly humiliating.

"We should say something," Chi said, biting the corners of her lips.

"No, we can't. Think of Fiona. It's not something you can just blurt out in front of everyone."

"I *am* thinking of Fiona," Chi said. "I feel sick."

"We don't know for sure. We can't say anything until we're positive."

Fiona was happy. Why ruin everything?

"Alright," Chi said, nodding. "Nothing until we're sure."

"The more I think about it, the more I'm sure I'm wrong," Sam lied. "Too much wine, that's all."

But she could see Chi was lost in thought and wasn't listening.

TWENTY

Day 5
KATE

While she'd been on the phone to Andrew, someone had left a voicemail. She checked the missed call and saw it was Gabriel. What on earth had she been thinking, chasing her own private little romance? Hadn't it been enough to sabotage the show? She felt the power of her convictions weakening. She needed to believe that she had done the right thing, but the hens' vanishing act felt increasingly serious.

"I wasn't staying at the villa with them so they did have time on their own at night," Kate explained. "I had to plan each day."

Andrew had said he thought Fiona was trying to break up with him. What had happened exactly while she'd had her attention focused on a dark, handsome stranger?

"You shouldn't have had much to do. There was already a plan in place."

"I made a few changes which I thought would add depth to the show."

"Depth?" Sharon echoed, shaking her head. "It's a reality show about a hen party, not a documentary on the rise and fall of the fucking Roman Empire."

"Not just depth…for aesthetic reasons…"

"I'm going to feel nervous until I know what we've got."

Sharon was going to feel a lot worse once she knew.

"There should have been an evening meal in a fabulous restaurant in Palma."

"That's right," Kate said. "There was."

"And that went smoothly?"

They had gone to a restaurant overlooking the sea. It had been pre-booked for them – one of the few dates Kate had kept. She'd had to make up for the spa incident. Ricardo hadn't filmed a thing while they'd been at the clinic and had tried to instigate a serious conversation about her interference with the format.

"I'm all for the environment," he'd said. "But you've got to do that in your private time. We have a show to deliver."

As if the environment was something you sorted out in your private time!

And yet his words had triggered a few thoughts. Memories from her break up with Matt had bubbled up and she'd struggled to push them away. Was this about him telling her two years ago that she was all mouth and no action?

At that evening meal, she'd found herself observing Fiona, wondering how deeply she felt for the guy she was marrying. Did it compare to what Kate had once felt for Matt? For the first time since they'd landed on the island, she took an interest, started asking some questions. The proposal had been hard going, but Fiona had done a valiant job piecing it together despite all the interruptions. Apart from a few minor details, she had told the story as faithfully as she had told Joanna, who had written it up and mailed it to Kate. Everything had gone smoothly until Jem had lost her temper and revealed what she really thought about the extravagant proposal.

Kate supposed people had different ideas of what was romantic. For some people there had to be a sunset or some iconic romantic building in the background. The Eiffel Tower or the Taj Mahal. To others it was the fact that someone had spent time thinking about what would make them happy, knew what would bring a smile to their face. Their favourite flowers. A restaurant they loved. A special place. A surprise planned while they were going about their day, completely unaware.

Kate had thought that wanting to be in each other's company more than anyone else's was romantic. Although she could see how a special dinner reservation, perhaps Spanish guitar and a moonlit sky could help the mood.

She had bored her friends to death telling them how Matt had proposed.

It was pouring with rain by the time they'd reached Camber. The forecast had let them down again. August by the beach, and it looked like the first thing they'd be doing was seeing where they could pick up a pair of fleeces rather than an ice cream. But they were both determined to remain upbeat. Three days away from London. It was a treat either way.

They ate at a traditional old pub decorated with life belts and ceramic plates in the shape of fish. Kate didn't even make a note of the name because it didn't feel like it was something she would want to remember later. She regretted not ordering fish and chips. Her burger kept repeating on her as they walked along the beach

162

afterwards. Matt took her hand, gripped it tight. It was their fifteenth anniversary. Their friends were always left open-mouthed when they revealed the number even though they had been there for most of the journey. But perhaps what shocked them was how old they'd all got. They'd grown up. Kate and Matt's relationship was grown-up. Here they were, together, renting a little fishing cottage. It felt solid. It was solid.

The wind picked up as they walked across the shingle and the romanticism of it all started to lose its hold on Kate. She let go of him and dug her cold hands into the pockets of her dress. It was a little vintage smock, as warm as wearing a paper bag. She had wanted to look pretty, but now she wished she'd just thought about insulation.

"Do you ever think we'll move abroad?" she asked. It was a frivolous question. She hadn't been thinking about it. It just popped out of her mouth. "Somewhere warmer, for instance."

Matt searched her face, his expression a little perplexed. He didn't feel the cold like she did. He was one of those ruddy-cheeked outdoorsy types, happy to play rugby in the mud or get soaked up to his middle in a kayak on the Lakes. She didn't mind watching, as long as she was wearing a Canadian Goose jacket.

"Would you like to move abroad then?" he asked.

"Maybe." She thought, and then smiled. "As long as you come with me."

He stopped, his bright green eyes searching hers. Then he took her wrist, withdrew her hand from her pocket and held it in his.

"Well, that's the thing, Kate."

Her heart started thudding. She felt it. The approach of something momentous.

"I want to be with you wherever you are and wherever you go."

Then he knelt down in the shingle, which wasn't ideal because he sank a little and made her let out a nervous laugh.

"Will you marry me, Kate Miller?"

She'd resigned herself to never hearing him utter those words. She had thought she had accepted it too. They were a modern couple; they didn't need a bit of paper proving their love. That's what she told people when they teased. Clearly she'd never believed it, because now that it was finally happening there was a little girl running around her heart, screaming for joy and punching the air and crazy dancing. Tears pricked her eyes and a big smile spread across her face. And cold? What cold? She'd never felt a warmth like it.

"I thought you'd never ask," she said, and then she dropped to her knees, took his face in her hands and kissed him.

The wind blew and the seagulls screeched and the sea rolled in. *This is it*, she thought. This was going to be a moment she would remember for ever.

Grinning like idiots, they walked back to their apartment and drank the wine they'd brought with them. It made her wonder if he had planned it at all. He could have easily sneaked some champagne and a box of chocolates into the boot of their car. Not that she was high maintenance, but it was a big deal and it wasn't like she would ever have said no. It was funny because in a way she had instigated his proposal. If she'd never asked that hypothetical question, how would their walk have unravelled?

At the time it had just been a passing thought. She had got the man of her dreams, who cared what they were drinking? It was a cold August evening; red wine was more warming than champagne, anyway. But after the day he broke her heart in the café, the thought would ambush her. A little catty voice would remind her that he hadn't meant to ask her in the first place. It had been a spur of the moment thing that he had probably regretted the very next day.

She had told everyone how romantic it had been. How perfect. But it hadn't been. Not really. It was a walk along the beach in the cold.

TWENTY-ONE

Day 3
FIONA

Fiona sat at the edge of the pool, drying off in the sun. She'd felt like a zombie until she'd jumped in. It was incredible how instantaneously the water peeled away the thick coating of a hangover. It was another perfect day on the island as far as the weather was concerned. The sky was a brilliant blue. What wasn't perfect was Fiona's mood. She had a ball of anxiety in her gut which no amount of deep breathing seemed to be able to dissolve.

It was half past eleven and Kate still hadn't turned up. This should have been a positive thing considering her feelings for the director, but for some reason it was getting on Fiona's nerves. What was Kate doing? Why had they still not been on a yacht? Or a private cruise? Why had they not stepped inside a fancy beach club and been given goody bags of Chanel perfume and Pandora charms like past contestants had? *Anyone* could rent a villa with a pool. It was very pleasant, but *anyone* could do it. The show had always promised and delivered luxury. It was infuriating that Kate was making so little effort to make this show glamorous.

Ricardo was also getting on Fiona's nerves, specifically the way he was only talking to Jem. There wasn't anyone in this house who deserved less attention. She was sitting there, giggling away with him as they slurped bottled beer, even though on the plane Fiona could have sworn that Jem had said she didn't like beer. How dare she act so cheerfully after her performance last night at the restaurant? So much for not wanting to be on camera! Fiona was going to have a hard time convincing Ricardo to edit that out, along with all the other parts she wanted deleting.

Sure, Jem had said sorry. But it was too late. It was like Clare announcing Jem didn't like her and then backtracking. Some things, once they were said, couldn't be taken back. Fiona had got the message loud and clear: Jem didn't want her to be marrying her brother. Good. Fine. She'd wasted enough time worrying over whether Jem would fit in with everyone, whether she would have a good time. Well now Fiona didn't care about Jem's feelings, whatever they were or were not going to be.

Sam sat up on the sun bed and took her earphones out.

"Are you alright, Fi?" she asked. "Do you want me to get you a drink?"

Fiona realised she must have been scowling and rearranged her face into a smile.

"Yeah, I'm fine. I'm just wondering where our bloody waiter is."

"Oh God, that's my fault. He got injured when I smashed the lamp."

Fiona snorted with laugher. "Shit, I'd forgotten about that."

"It's his busiest time of year too," Sam said, looking guilty. "He refuses to get naked after September. Too cold."

"There must be more than one hot waiter on the island."

"I know."

"I don't even care if he's hot. I'd be happy to be served by the hunchback of Notre-fucking-Dame if he knew how to make a cocktail." Fiona sighed. "Don't you think there's a real lack of…"

Glitz? Sparkle? Show?

"Staff?" suggested Sam.

"Yeah, that too. I just think it's all so badly organised."

"Oh, it's not so bad. We've done quite a lot if you think about it, and it's probably better not having every minute accounted for. Look, I'll get you something. I can be the replacement waiter."

Sam was being extra nice this morning. She was the only person who had seemed to have survived the night of drinking. Both Clare and Chi had underestimated the potency of the bottle of Hierbas – a yellowish green liquor which had looked like washing up liquid and had tasted of aniseed – the waiter had left on their table. Fiona had steered clear, while encouraging everyone else to down their shots. Chi, whom she had caught sipping water at every interval on the first day, had ended up getting really wasted, her toasts becoming more bizarre as the night progressed.

"To Fiona for inviting us all to share in this amazing holiday!"

Yes.

"To living in the moment!"

Fine.

"To Compeed plasters!"

Okay.

"To second chances!"

Why?

"To seeing the wood for the trees!"

What?

"I'll have a gin and tonic if you're going," Fiona said.

"Coming right up."

Sam had never been a very demanding person, or ambitious. She could have done so much with her pottery, but she had always seemed half-hearted, like she had been doing it to waste time until she had a baby. Lying beside a pool was enough for her. She didn't expect five-star beach clubs or luxury manicures. Fiona should be pleased Sam was content. She looked like she needed this holiday. She hadn't been looking after herself. Her skin had regressed back to her dry, flaky teenage days. Fiona made a mental note to give her one of the face creams she'd won for commenting on a lifestyle blog.

Fiona took another deep breath and tried to let go of the restlessness plaguing her. It was only Day 3 and she needed to enjoy herself. But her mind kept wandering to the fact she would be going home in four days and what needed to be done. Andrew had texted her a few times about ideas he'd had. She hadn't expected him to take such an interest in things like wedding favours and table decorations. It sounded like he was spending his days scrolling through wedding blogs. Wasn't that only what girls did? She'd told him to wait until she got back. She couldn't think about it now.

Mel came outside and stood with her hands on her hips.

"She not here yet?" she asked Ricardo.

He gave her a pointed look. Fiona strained her ears.

"Have you called her?"

"No, I'm not calling..."

"It would have been nice to work out how we're going to do it."

"That's amateur directors for you," Ricardo muttered.

Mel exhaled and then retreated back inside again. Fiona pressed her palms against the hot stone, lifted herself up and slid into the cool water. She swam as far as she could holding her breath, which wasn't very far. She'd never got the hang of opening her eyes under water and hated not seeing where she was going. Turning on her back and kicking her legs, she looked up at the bright blue sky. It was a beautiful day, and yet she couldn't completely enjoy it. *Amateur* directors? Is that really what Ricardo had said? Not for the first time, Fiona wondered if it was worth all the stress.

TWENTY-TWO

Day 3
CHIOMA

His warm smile disarmed her as she walked through the bar. She hadn't felt like coming out until that moment. It had been a long week and she'd been craving a night in, curled up on the sofa. The stranger held up the champagne bottle, eyebrows raised in mischievous suggestion. He had the bluest eyes. She grinned back at him, butterflies in her stomach. Everyone always said it was when you stopped looking for someone that you found them. Perhaps this was him. He looked so clean, so wholesome – the opposite of her ex with his beard and porous skin and tattoos creeping up his neck.

"Hi, I don't think we've met," he said. "Glass of champagne?"

"Has anyone ever said no to that question?"

He laughed. "You are here for the engagement party, right?"

"I am, I am..."

The pink champagne fizzed as he poured. Her heart was pounding. She didn't want the drink any more. She just wanted him. The rest of the bar seemed to melt away as she leant forward and kissed him. But before their lips had touched, he was backing away, the smile wiped off his face.

Chi woke up with a start, her heart racing. She was aware of a wet sensation between her legs and knew it must have come. She breathed a sigh of relief. It was over. She

171

could erase him from her memory now. One night of madness that would never happen again.

Despite the realisation, she didn't immediately jump out of bed. She wanted a little more time in the safe cocoon of her sheets. Her head was aching from too many shots and she didn't feel ready to face the other girls, who would no doubt remind her of the stupid things she'd said when she was drunk. Some people seem to find their own drunkenness so funny. Not her. After a big night out she always woke up with a feeling of shame. She had told herself the solution was very simple: don't drink so much! But it was easier said than done.

She heard the muffled voice of Sam talking on the phone in her bedroom and her heart sank further. Sam had said the engagement ring wasn't real, and though Fiona may have embellished the proposal, Chi knew that she was in love with her ring. Fiona had sent pictures of it to everyone with sparkling heart emojis. Sam had told Chi not to say anything. She had backtracked and said that she was probably wrong, but Chi had sensed that Sam was lying because she was worried Chi was going to blurt it out there and then.

It wasn't something Chi could just brush away and pretend she hadn't heard. She had to make sure Sam was wrong. She would pick the most well-known high street shops and scour their accessories section. If she didn't find a match, then she would lock what Sam had said in a compartment in her head and throw away the key. After all, she was proving quite good at pretending things had never happened. Her new motto seemed to be: *as long as no one saw her act like an idiot, then she hadn't done it.*

But this was different. This wasn't something *she* had done. This was something Andrew had done while cold sober. Was he really capable of doing something like that?

Chi frowned up at the ceiling as she tried to imagine what could have been going through his head. She concluded there was a big chance that Sam was talking bollocks; she'd been pretty drunk last night. Perhaps pretending to be a connoisseur of fine diamonds was what Sam did when she had too many. Everyone had their thing.

"It's jus' so big," Sam had drawled.

She'd shown Chi her own engagement ring: a small twinkle on a white gold band. Compared to Fiona's it was really modest.

She's envious, thought Chi, suddenly. That was it. Lovely Sam was finally showing a crack in her loveliness. It wasn't that the ring wasn't real, it was that Sam didn't want it to be real, because she didn't think it was fair.

Alcohol, Chi thought grimly, *that's what it did*. It brought out the worst in everyone. It made people say and do things completely out of character. And yet the conclusion left her feeling dissatisfied. Regardless of whether Sam fancied a bigger ring or not, she didn't strike Chi as a person who would make things up.

Chi reached for the glass on her bedside table and emptied the remaining droplets of water down her throat. Another hour in bed. That's all she needed to pull herself together.

She remembered her period had come and tried to relax. It could have been so much worse. Her hand flew up to her wooden charm that hung from a leather thong around her neck. It was a square with a spiral on it that her grandmother had given her. Lucky charms could only do so much to protect her. She needed to learn from her mistakes. If she couldn't control herself when she had too much to drink, then she shouldn't be drinking at all.

The thing was, though, until she'd met him, she'd thought she did have control. She'd never been one to be persuaded into one night stands with slippery fingered strangers. But she'd trusted him. She'd assumed he'd do the right thing.

She turned over and pressed her face into her pillow. Her thoughts returned to the ring. If Sam didn't think they needed to say anything, then she wouldn't say anything. It was easier that way. She ran her fingertips along her crotch. Everything could be easier now.

Thankfully she'd brought tampons so her period wouldn't need to interfere with her enjoying the pool. She got up and headed to the bathroom. A moment later, she was looking in dismay at her clean panty liner. She swore under her breath and sat back down on the toilet. The pressure had been mounting gradually these last two weeks. She had always been regular. She had always been careful. Getting in touch with him again would be admitting it had happened, but if her period didn't come soon, she might not have a choice.

TWENTY-THREE

Day 3
KATE

Kate was panicking by the time she got to the villa. She didn't know how it had got so late. It felt like she and Gabriel had only been chatting for ten minutes instead of the best part of an hour. It was gone eleven o'clock and she was already very late to meet the cycling operator. She'd arranged the cycling trip weeks before and had forgotten to fill everyone in. If she'd stuck to the plan, or if she'd involved everyone in her new one, she wouldn't have had to remember everything.

Pep was leaning against the bonnet of his van, smoking a cigarette. For someone who cycled every day he didn't look all that fit. He was in his fifties with grey hair and a substantial paunch.

"I'm so sorry about this," Kate said, again.

He'd already told her how early he'd got up to be at the bike shed. A lot of traffic, apparently. She hadn't encountered any so far on the island and was sure he was just trying to eke out as much guilt as possible to get a good tip.

"I'll round them up then we can be off," she said.

He shrugged. "It doesn't matter to me. But noon is the worst time."

"I know. I couldn't get out of a conference call."

"If you prefer to do it tomorrow...although I will have to charge you two days."

"We can't tomorrow. We've got to be at the beach."

He frowned at her. "But it doesn't matter what day you go to the beach, no? The beach isn't going anywhere."

"There's a special event we're going to."

"What event?"

"Just a special *thing*..." She trailed off. Why did she have to tell him?

Kate rang the bell. Ricardo and Mel were already there. She could see their jeep parked out on the street. She rifled through her bag to find the villa keys. Just as her fingers curled around them, the door opened. It was Mel, dressed in denim shorts and a black T-shirt with a vintage microphone on it.

"Morning, I was about to send out a search party," she said with a tense smile.

"You knew we weren't going on the boat, though, didn't you?"

"Yes. Ricardo said you'd swapped boats for bikes."

"Exactly. That's not a problem, is it?"

"Hopefully not, but it would have been good to talk it through. I like to be prepared."

"I'm sure you'll be fine."

"No offence, but that's easy to say when you're not using equipment."

It looked like Kate was going to spend the entire day apologising. Quite possibly she would have to prostrate herself in front of the hens to get them to do what she wanted. But no regrets. This wasn't about her. Anyway, what they were about to do was a treat. Yes, they would be happy. Thrilled even.

"Morning, everyone!" she shouted up the staircase. "Can we have everyone in the kitchen, please?"

There was no response. They were probably all in the pool. Good. They would be refreshed and ready to spend a day cycling...in thirty-three degree heat...at noon, because she had completely forgotten what she was supposed to be doing. On the upside, she had a new phone number in her contacts under the letter G. She snorted at the thought. Every time she thought about Gabriel, she felt her face wanting to break into a smile.

Her good spirits evaporated when she saw everyone outside, lounging in the sun, already on the alcohol. Was there no limit to how much they could consume? Sam and Fiona were lying side by side on the sunbeds with what looked like Gin and Tonics. Ricardo and Jem were under the parasol, sharing something on their phones, two beer bottles on the table nearby.

How on earth was she going to move them?

"Don't get too comfortable, everyone!" she said, forcing a laugh.

Sam and Fiona stopped talking and looked over at her.

"It's time for our first activity of the day."

Seeing their suspicious faces, Kate felt very tempted to go outside, pay the guide what was owed and leave them all alone. But that would make for a crap episode and she had a reputation to keep. What would look more beautiful than the girls riding past fields of almond trees and old windmills, with the mountain range in the distance? It was much better than bombing around on a motorboat or a jet ski. Getting from A to B was one thing, but just to drive around aimlessly, using up petrol, stirring up the water, making all that noise? No one ever thought how noise affected marine life. It was like having a night club move into your living room.

Kate had read up on it. Ships used seismic sound pulses fired through compressed air guns to search for natural resources. After surveys for gas off the coast of Spain, researchers found hundreds of octopuses, squid and cuttlefish washed up on the beach. The air sacs around the creatures' heads which helped them balance and orientate themselves in the water had been completely damaged. The article said it was the equivalent of having your inner ear shredded.

"What is it?" Fiona asked. "Not more weird treatments, I hope."

"No, no…this is really fun."

Clare walked out into the garden with an icepack on her neck. Kate grimaced. The girl was currently the colour of a lobster and should definitely not be out and about. And yet…Kate really needed everyone in the shot. She did have Factor 50 in her handbag, and if Clare covered up, surely she'd be fine. In fact, Clare would probably benefit from a little bit of exercise.

"What's happening?" she asked.

"Ouch, are you alright? I've got some great After Sun in my bag," Mel said, going over to examine Clare's burns.

"I'm already covered in aloe."

Kate didn't want to appear cold, but the show really had to go on.

"You'll have to cover up a bit this morning, Clare, but you'll be fine."

"Fine for what?"

"Fine for a wonderful adventure."

Ricardo was looking at her warily. He had known there was going to be a bike ride so there was no need for that face. Yes, she was late, and yes, she should have been here earlier to discuss details, but she also knew he'd done much more complicated jobs in the past. She was sure she'd seen a clip of hens on go-carts before.

"We've got someone waiting for us outside," Kate said.

Fiona's face lit up. "Like a celebrity?"

"Uh...no."

Her face fell. "Then who?"

Kate shouldn't have started off like that. She didn't think poor Pep was going to evoke anything but disappointment now. Fiona had clearly expected a more glamorous experience than she was currently having.

"It's our lovely guide, Pep. He's going to take us cycling through the beautiful Mallorcan countryside."

She waited for them to protest.

"What...now?" asked Clare, looking fearful.

Jem was smiling. "That sounds brilliant."

Judging by the look on Chi's face, she didn't agree. "I don't think I can...I'm still hungover."

"Oh come on, Chi, you'll be fine. Look at you, you've got the perfect cyclist physique," Kate said. She needed to coax rather than order. "It'll be so worth it, you'll see. You'll sweat that hangover out in no time."

"Tomorrow," Chi said. "I'll do anything you want tomorrow."

Kate checked Fiona's face. She didn't look excited, nor did she look displeased. She just looked like she hadn't made her mind up how she was going to react.

"I'm afraid it's now or never."

"Never," said Chi and Clare in unison.

Kate grimaced as they cemented their solidarity with a smile.

"When I said now or never...I meant now or now."

She had to accept she wasn't here to be popular.

TWENTY-FOUR

Day 3
JEM

Jem was relieved to be out of the villa and exploring the island. The atmosphere hadn't been quite the same since her outburst at the restaurant. She should have controlled herself, but all the acting had got under her skin. What was true and what was false? She was Andrew's sister and she should have known. She had felt upset that he hadn't confided in her and guilty because she knew she was partly to blame. Over the years, whenever he had mentioned Fiona, she had always reacted so negatively, shutting down each potential conversation. As far as she'd been concerned she had heard enough about that woman to last a lifetime. Now she realised that all those tentative mentions had been significant. That he had never stopped being obsessed with her. That he had just been waiting for the moment Fiona reappeared in his life and asked him to "Jump".

She'd called her mother from the restaurant.

"What you call obsession, other people call love, darling," her mother had chided her.

"Love makes you happy, not stressed!"

"We saw him two weeks ago and he seemed happy."

Jem had burst into tears. It had been the wine. With so many takes, dinner had taken for ever, and all her little sips had probably amounted to a whole bottle.

"Darling, you need to let Andrew walk his own path," her mother had said, ending the conversation. "This is his journey, not yours. I suggest you go back to that dinner table and apologise to your future sister-in-law."

Jem had said sorry, but although Fiona had told her not to worry about it, her smile had been cool and measured. All Jem could do now was try to be nicer and friendlier with everyone so the next four days wouldn't be so awkward.

It was easier to relax outside the villa. She hadn't relished the idea of spending another day lounging by the pool getting drunk. On a bike, she could get some space from the others and clear her head. She was someone who liked to see and experience new things on her holidays. Mallorca was so beautiful, she had been secretly wondering how she might escape and see it for herself. Luckily, Kate was a bit more interesting than she'd anticipated.

Their guide had driven them to the north of the island, a place called Selva, assuring them it was the flattest area they'd find. He had sorted them out with a bike each and there had been a lot of giggling and exaggeration about the last time they'd ridden. Clare had been particularly repetitive, betraying her nerves. Unsurprisingly she was firmly at the rear of the group now. Jem was leading the hens, keeping up with their guide, who was telling her in broken English about the cycling experiences to be had on the island. He was an affable guy, but she wished he was Ricardo. It would have been really romantic if it had just been the two of them.

The scenery was gorgeous. Flowers seemed to flourish despite the arid ground. Bright pink and red oleanders lined the vineyards and impregnated the air with their fragrance, while vibrant fuchsia bougainvillea sprang over the gates and archways of every self-respecting villa. Beyond rock walls, almond trees were dotted unevenly across fields of dry grasses which shone bright yellow as if the sunshine had leaked into their stems. Jem had thought the trees were olives at first, but though they were short and picturesque, their trunks weren't half as gnarled. The occasional sheep took cover in the shade of their branches. There was little shade to be had on the road, though.

Jem reached for her bottle of water and squirted some of it down her neck just as the jeep pulled past.

"You're going to win the yellow jersey!" Ricardo called out of the car window.

She turned and grinned at him. He drove at her pace.

"Everyone else is dying," he added. "It's thirty-three degrees."

She glanced behind her. Chi and Sam were pedalling side by side, well out of earshot. Their heads were lowered as they took on the incline. With her big white sunglasses, it was difficult to read Chi's expression. Sam was going red in the face, but still managing to keep up a steady stream of conversation. The two seemed to have become close, and now it felt like Jem was the random relative in a group of friends. Further behind them, she noticed Fiona stand up on her pedals and attempt to close the gap.

Jem looked back at Ricardo, the only person who had seemed genuinely happy to see her that morning.

"I bet you're enjoying the air conditioning."

"Not really. I'd rather be outside on a bike."

She smiled. It was good to hear this was his idea of fun too. It made her little daydream of them cycling together seem like an actual possibility. She hadn't been expecting to have a crush on anyone at this hen party, but she was enjoying it, even though the chances of anything happening between them were slim. He was too much of a professional and she too shy to ask for his number. She kept planning to, then chickening out. Perhaps in the airport, before they went their separate ways, it would feel more natural to suggest it. It wasn't like she needed his number now.

"I'm going up ahead to get some scenery shots," he said. "It's so beautiful with the mountains in the distance."

But he continued at her side. In the passenger seat, Mel was checking her phone, either genuinely uninterested in their little chat or pretending to be.

Jem found Ricardo becoming more gorgeous each day. They had had so many good chats about music and travel and bucket lists. He didn't talk about what he would like to do *if* he had the means, but when. He had made her think outside the box about her job. Through their conversation they had arrived at the conclusion that she didn't want to be the person organising courses and talks. The truth was she wanted to be the person on centre stage, running the courses, giving the talks, sharing something of value. She'd just been limiting herself, feeding herself a story about not being good enough.

"*You create your own reality,*" Ricardo had said. "*Start believing you've got what it takes and your life will change,*" which had made her realise how thirsty she had been for someone to step into her life with something worth saying.

It excited her that he seemed more interested in talking to her than the others. It wasn't her imagination. They did seem to gravitate towards each other, finding conversation easy. Their silences weren't awkward. If he wasn't interested, why was he driving at a slug's speed beside her? Mel was still pretending not to be aware they were flirting, which Jem found a little embarrassing.

"I should drive ahead and set up…"

"Off you go then. Chop-chop!"

He looked a little hurt. "Hey, I thought you'd appreciate my support!"

"What support? You haven't even given me a high energy snack."

Mel laughed. Ricardo turned to her. "Have we got anything?"

Mel rummaged around in the glove compartment. "Nope, sorry."

"Worst support crew ever. How am I supposed to win my yellow jersey now?"

"Probably for the best. I don't think yellow would suit you."

"Excuse me!" Her jaw dropped in mock surprise. In real surprise, too. Why wouldn't it suit her?

He laughed at her for taking offence.

"I'm joking. I'm sure you'd look good in any colour."

She blushed. "Thank you."

It was good to see he'd cheered up. For a moment back at the villa, he looked like he'd been about to strangle Kate. It would appear she hadn't given him much notice about the trip.

"I'll see you in a bit," he said.

It meant nothing. And yet it felt sweet. He would see *her*. Never mind anybody else.

"Make me look good!" she called as he accelerated past her and headed off around the bend.

She smiled to herself. Behind her, grumbles floated on the air. She didn't want to hear them. It was a beautiful day and cycling was a wonderful thing to do. She just wanted to enjoy it and forget the reason why she was here.

She stood up on her bike and pedalled her hardest until she'd caught up with Pep.

TWENTY-FIVE

Day 3
CLARE

How could the road be flat and still cause this much pain? Clare wanted a spirit level to check she wasn't being tricked. People said you should trust your body. Well, her body was telling her she was riding up fucking Everest.

She stopped, the bike resting against one clammy thigh, and reached for her water bottle again. The water was evaporating before she had time to drink it. Cycling in this heat was dangerous. It should be illegal. Anyone who did this for fun had psychological problems and should get help.

Clare was aware of Fiona turning around to check on her and then stopping. They were way at the back now. Jem had set off at a speed to rival Chris Froome. It looked like she had her own support car, too. Ricardo's jeep was crawling along the dusty road beside her, ruining the view.

"Are you alright?" Fiona called.

Clare laughed drily. "Oh don't worry about me. I've had a good life."

"Maybe we should cut through the field and see if we can find a proper road to flag down some help."

"Or just throw ourselves in front of a car. I don't think it'd be much more painful." Every time she pushed the pedal, her thighs felt like they were on fire.

Fiona look ahead at the others, who were getting smaller by the minute. Clare wondered if she was wishing she was up ahead and not stuck with the slow coach.

"Go on ahead if you like," she said, not really meaning it.

Fiona's voice adopted some forced enthusiasm. "Come on, you can do it!"

"I don't think I can, but thanks."

"Think of how good you'll feel after this."

Clare felt a brief wave of optimism. "I suppose it's a good pre-wedding workout, isn't it? I'll be able to fit into my bridesmaid dress…"

She got back on her seat and started pedalling. The pain shot through her thighs again, but she gritted her teeth and carried on.

"When are we getting them?"

Talking and exercising really didn't go hand in hand, but she needed something to spur her on. After Clare had nagged her for ideas, Fiona had sent her a link to a gorgeous aquamarine Coast dress and Clare had optimistically asked her to order a size 16. Several times that same evening, she'd told herself to call Fiona back and tell her to make it an 18, at the very least. But in the end, fantasy had won. If she didn't make fantasy a reality then she was going to be in trouble. She stood up in her seat and pushed harder. *Serves you right*, she thought, as her muscles groaned.

"When we get back I'll look into it," Fiona called back, flicking her plait behind her and standing up on her pedals.

"So you haven't ordered yet?"

"No, not yet."

Clare slowed down. Maybe she didn't need to punish herself. Fiona seemed to be speeding up. She concentrated on her friend's size 12 hips and imagined getting to that size.

"How about your dress?" she called, needing a distraction.

Fiona would look fabulous in a fishtail dress, whereas Clare would look like a snake after it had swallowed a bison whole.

"It's much easier if you don't talk, you know," Fiona called back, laughing.

That was true, but Clare wondered if that was the real reason Fiona didn't want to talk. She had a theory that Fiona was feeling nervous about the wedding, and it wasn't her imagination. Yesterday she'd expected Fiona to leap at the idea of looking at wedding blogs beside the pool, but instead she'd reminded Clare about the 'no phone rule' – as if Fiona had ever been a stickler for following rules.

"Whatever you do, don't go looking for one without me. I've always imagined being there with you and knowing it was the one."

"Life isn't like the films, you know, Clare Williams!"

"I think it is. Your proposal was pretty special, wasn't it? Not many people get collected by a driver and then taken to one of the most expensive restaurants in London."

"Jem didn't approve, though, did she."

Clare stopped, out of breath, her energy spent. "Fuck her."

Fiona stopped too. "Yeah, she should be grateful I invited her."

"Exactly."

"All this time I thought she liked me."

Clare frowned. She didn't get why Fiona would have thought that. Jem had never hung out with them when they were younger. If anything, Clare had sensed her disapproval of them for being so girly.

"So is she still going to be your bridesmaid?"

That would be dramatic if Fiona ditched her. Clare relished the thought. She liked the idea of a tighter unit of her, Sam and Chi. Chi was more manageable than Jem.

"I don't think so," Fiona said.

"Really? What do you think Andrew will say? Won't he be pissed off?"

"Maybe..."

"Perhaps you should keep her..."

Perhaps it wasn't worth the confrontation. Jem was going to be part of Fiona's family, after all. She should probably be encouraging her friend to keep the peace. In private they could bitch.

"I'm going to tell her now!" Fiona called back. "Get it over and done with."

"No! Don't be crazy!"

Fiona didn't like thinking about the consequences of her actions. But if she stopped for a moment, she would realise what a terrible idea it was. Clare couldn't see how they would restore good vibes in the villa if Fiona kicked Jem off the bridesmaid list.

"It's not worth it."

The distance between them was growing fast. Clare tried to catch Fiona up but her body wouldn't obey.

"Fiona!"

The week would be ruined. What would Jem do? Would she immediately call her brother? What if Andrew got so annoyed he called off the wedding?

"Fiona! Think about Andrew! She's his sister."

"I was just joking," Fiona called back.

Thank God for that, Clare thought, immediately slowing down.

"I'm going ahead, Clare. See you up there."

Up there? Clare thought angrily. She knew it hadn't been flat. She felt a jolt of panic as Fiona disappeared around the corner. How long before everyone noticed Clare wasn't with them?

Tears of frustration welled up. She wiped at the corners of her eyes, determined not to cry. It reminded her of growing up with her big brothers. They'd never waited for her, never slowed down for her, and she'd often found herself alone and panicking.

The distance between her and the other hens was growing, but Clare couldn't go any further. As she was standing there, feeling sorry for herself, two cyclists in bright red Lycra veered up the road. She wiped her face, hoping she looked like she was just having a relaxed moment rather than a nervous breakdown. The first cyclist, a bearded man in his fifties with the body of a whippet, nodded his head at her as he passed. The second, a woman equally thin and with skin showing years of overexposure to the sun, slowed down and looked at her with concern.

"Are you alright?" she said in an accent straight out of the home counties.

Clare tried to sound breezy. "Yeah, fine. Just taking a little break."

"Are you on your own?"

"No, I'm with a group. A hen party."

The woman looked intrigued. "Cycling's an unusual choice for a hen party in Mallorca. Usually everyone's off to Magaluf."

"We're kind of like an eco-hen party," Clare said, thinking of the director.

The woman looked delighted to hear it. "That's wonderful. Sounds like something we could put in the paper, doesn't it, Greg?"

Greg clearly hadn't wanted to stick around for a chat and was well out of earshot.

"Oh, he's a Speedy Gonzales. We run a news bulletin for the expats. It would be nice to get you in the paper, wouldn't it?"

Red-faced and in unflattering clothing? It felt wrong to say no. The woman was so enthusiastic.

"We're actually on a show," Clare said. "A hen party reality show, believe it or not."

The woman didn't only believe it, she'd already heard all about it.

"Come on, let's walk and talk," she laughed. "I'm Debs, by the way."

Debs started pedalling and Clare felt her heart sink. She had to dig deep to keep up with her new companion. Debs explained how she'd seen the story in the paper about the director who had fallen from a balcony.

"Joanna Kane, she was called," the woman babbled happily. "Does the name ring a bell?"

Yes. It did. Joanna had been the original director who had interviewed the hens all those months ago. She'd been very interested in their stories. Clare had liked her a lot. She had laughed easily and had been curious to hear Clare's predictions for her best friend's wedding. One minute she had been the director, and the next the channel had sent them letters apologising for last minute changes to the team. The new director, Kate Miller, was equally excited to be part of *The Hen Party*. Well, that bit was wrong. Kate couldn't compare to the exuberant, laughing, fun-loving Joanna. Clare was certain that Joanna would not have approved of them training for the Tour de France. If it had been down to Joanna, Clare felt sure they'd be at a beach club being waited on hand and foot.

She and Debs cycled around another bend and the rest of the cyclists came into view. Greg was now on Jem's tail and picking up speed. Far up ahead, Clare could make out Ricardo standing up at the back of the jeep with his camera in the middle of the road. It was as if he was reporting on an actual sporting event and not a motley bunch of hens being far too active for her liking. Clare's legs were giving in. Her breakfast had just repeated on her, and for a moment, she'd thought the sheep shading itself under the almond tree had been a cow. If that wasn't a sign of sunstroke then she didn't know what was. The gap between herself and Debs was growing, so too was her sense of failure.

"I think I need to get off and push," she called after Debs.

"Nonsense!" Debs called back. She sounded like a schoolteacher. "You can do it. Keep breathing. Push! Push! Push!"

Clare didn't have enough breath to argue. She kept her eyes on the road just ahead of her front wheel so she couldn't see it steepening. It helped psychologically. All she needed to do was get up that hill and then she could stop.

With every pedal, she felt her loathing of Kate increase. This was *not* fun. They should have been given options to choose from. All Kate cared about was her stupid show and not the feelings of the group. Cycling in this heat wasn't just stupid, it was unsafe. Clare was seeing cows again. Oh, it was a cow. But that wasn't the point.

Fiona was standing up on her pedals and sprinting.

"I'm not coming last," Clare heard her shout. "It's my hen party!"

Ahead she watched as Sam slowed down, then stopped altogether, the back of her red T-shirt stained burgundy. Fiona overtook her with an excited cheer. Next was Chi, who was losing pace. Fiona got past her too. Clare didn't know where she was getting the energy from. Quite possibly it was generated by the anger she felt on seeing her future sister-in-law riding so smugly up at the front. The guide was a small spec in the distance. He was probably used to riding with people who actually liked cycling and weren't being forced to do it because their director wanted to reduce their carbon footprint. Debs was bored of Clare now and had sped up to see if she could get more interesting material from the others.

The camera was about a couple of hundred metres away. Kate had got out of its way and was standing by the jeep with her bike. If Clare could just get past it with a smile on her face then she would consider it a victory. After that, she was getting a lift in the car.

Fiona waved at the camera, screaming, "Cheer me on, guys!"

Ricardo turned his camera to follow Fiona up the hill. Clare felt herself relax. Perhaps they wouldn't capture her after all. No one wanted to see her big, sweaty self riding a bike.

The others passed by the jeep without a fuss. Debs deviated from the route to go and talk to Kate. The camera was still focused away from Clare, which was a relief. She really wasn't feeling very good at all. The heat was unbearable and her sunburn was sore. She needed to focus on a reward. She conjured up a cocktail full of crushed ice – she would quite happily bathe in a cocktail right now. A big tub of mojito. She closed her eyes and summoned the strength to continue. Instead, she felt the approach of tears. Perhaps she was on her period. People said that women's periods aligned when they were together, and Chi had said hers was due.

Clare slowed down, then stopped again. She considered getting off and pushing.

"Come on, girl!" shouted Debs. "Do it for England!"

Great. Now she was not just embarrassing herself but her country too.

Debs was coming back for Clare on her bike. Her shouting had got Ricardo's attention and he had his lens on her. Clare swore under her breath over and over. Short and rhythmic: *"Fuck, fuck, fuck."*

"Just a little bit more," Debs shouted. "Come on!"

Clare's legs didn't want to do any more. They wanted a massage. In fact, her whole body wanted the luxurious comfort that had been promised. It wasn't fair! She hadn't signed up for this.

The jeep was reversing. Ricardo was coming towards her. Her heart started pounding. *Go away, you stupid man!*

"I'm just taking in the scenery," she yelled. "Mallorca is such a beautiful place, I think I might get married here." And under her breath, "I might die here too..."

She didn't want the nation seeing her giving up. She pushed against the pedals, which felt like rusty levers that hadn't been pressed in a hundred years. Her legs were throbbing. Even worse, her head was starting to swim. There was her breakfast again, trying to escape. She swallowed hard. Just a little bit more. Ricardo was recording her every moment. Her every facial expression.

Was it her head or her hammering heart? She took deep breaths, but they only made her feel more sick.

"That's it!" Debs cried. "Push, push, push!"

Was Debs even real or was Clare hallucinating? Perhaps Debs was the cow she had thought she'd seen but which was actually a sheep.

The sunlight danced across the Jeep. The sunlight danced across everything. Clare's vision was a riot of yellows and oranges. She tried to smile as she came face to face with the camera, but as she did, her stomach lurched. With a horrible gulping sound, she threw up over her handlebars.

There was a moment of stunned silence, and then: "CUT!"

Clare would have liked to have punched Kate in the face. Instead, she threw up again.

TWENTY-SIX

Day 5
KATE

"Cycling," Sharon echoed.

"Beautiful shots," Kate said. "Stunning."

Kate could see Sharon was thinking about it. Her lips were pursed, her eyes narrowed. Then as her face began to relax, another thought struck her and she frowned.

"But weren't they hungover after the night before?"

The laugh escaped Kate. Had there been a morning they hadn't woken up hungover? They'd been lucky that she'd arrived so late and they'd had a bit of a lie in. The pool was a miracle cure, too. It washed off a late night in one swoop. But poor Clare hadn't faired so well.

"They were all great...except one...who puked up in front of the camera."

Sharon grimaced. "Gross."

"Good television, though."

"You bitch," Sharon cackled. "No wonder the girls wanted a break. I didn't know a cycling trip was even planned."

"I didn't want it looking all *Big Brother* with everyone stuck in a house."

Sharon frowned and cast her eyes towards the notes resting on the table.

"They shouldn't have been stuck in the house..."

Kate could see her brain ticking. She was thinking about the yacht. Kate wasn't ready to talk about the yacht.

"Of course we had loads of sea views, as you can imagine," she gushed.

Sharon leant back, the notes untouched.

"But I thought the show would benefit from other scenery too, and the Mallorcan countryside is so gorgeous...plus it led to a piece in a local paper. They loved the healthy hens angle."

Sharon seemed to be weighing this news up, deciding whether she was pleased or not.

"I suppose that's more positive than the last piece about us," she conceded, "although 'healthy hens' sounds terribly dull. What about after the cycling? You haven't told me about any games. You were supposed to have hen party themed activities. It's not a documentary on what to do in Mallorca, after all."

"Yeah, we did a bunch of games that evening."

Sharon nodded. "Good. Go on."

Kate had vetoed the classic game of *Waste Loads of Toilet Paper Designing a Wedding Dress*. Instead they'd done *How Well Do You Know the Bride?*, *Pin on the Penis*, and a *Mr and Mrs* quiz with a video from Andrew answering questions about his future bride. He'd done really well, and Fiona had seemed surprised and visibly moved. It had been a perfect piece of *Hen Party* footage. Hopefully, anyway. Ricardo hadn't been on his game that night. He'd been distracted and had kept nipping out for cigarettes with Jem...except Jem didn't smoke, did she?

Kate's phone vibrated against the table, making her jump. Gabriel.

"Is that the fiancé again?" Sharon asked. "Pass him to me."

Kate felt the butterflies. He'd called her three times in one morning. How sweet that he should be unabashed about chasing her. Or had she left something important at his place?

"Excuse me, I have to take this," she said, getting up suddenly.

Sharon looked exasperated. "Where are you going?"

Kate felt her heart hammering against her chest as she stepped back into the hotel foyer. There was no need to feel nervous, and yet she had a sense of dread. She'd come to feel it often since Matt had broken off their wedding, like she shouldn't risk feeling happy because everything could go wrong at any moment.

"Hello?"

"Kate! Thank God!"

She had an image of him from last night leaning over his balcony, watching the sun set over the sea. It had been another magnificent display of oranges and reds. He had taken off his shirt earlier, and she had admired his trim body, thinking how lucky she was to have bagged such a gorgeous guy. Even if it was just a fling. He'd been so complimentary of her, telling her how beautiful she was, how sexy, what incredible breasts she had. He couldn't believe she was four years older than him.

"What's up?" she said, pushing last night from her mind. She'd definitely left something at his flat.

"What's up?" he echoed dumbly. The cheer in his voice died. "Oh, shit."

"What is it?"

"You just meant to leave quietly, didn't you? You didn't want me to call."

"No, it wasn't like that."

"Why did you leave without saying goodbye?"

"I had to go to the villa. I had to check on the girls. I felt guilty."

"You could have woken me."

"We went to sleep at four in the morning…and you looked so peaceful."

"The look of a man who thinks he's going to wake up with the beautiful girl he fell asleep with."

Kate snorted. How could he be so unafraid to show his feelings?

"It's not funny," he said, grumpily. "And then you ignore my phone calls. What am I supposed to think?"

"No, it's not funny. You're right about that," she replied. "It's a complete disaster."

"Why?"

"This morning when I got to the villa, there was no one there."

"Okay," Gabriel replied. "So, they're still out partying?"

"I don't know, but right now I'm at the Hotel Nixe Palace with the series producer and I have no idea what to tell her."

"I'll get my car," he said. "We'll go find them."

Go find them. He made it sound easy. But it wasn't like she'd misplaced them in a shopping centre. Mallorca might look like a tiny dot on a world map, but 3,640km² was a sizeable chunk of land to cover.

"And who shall I tell her you are?"

"Your Mallorcan boyfriend."

Kate let out a breathless laugh. "Oh my God, don't."

"I might be one day."

"You're mad."

"About you."

She bit her lip. "I suppose you could be the runner..."

"I'm very good at running."

"That's not the kind of runner I meant."

"I know. I'll be there in twenty minutes."

She got off the phone and stood for a moment, aware of her body buzzing. Was he adorable or insane?

Sharon was taking photos of the seaside. She lowered her phone when she saw Kate return and resumed her prior look of exasperation.

"Who was that?"

"The...uh...runner. He's bringing the car around in a bit and I'm going to go with him to get the girls."

"So you didn't lose track of the runner. Well, that's something I suppose."

TWENTY-SEVEN

Day 3
JEM

Jem knew she was drunk as she slipped out into the garden. Not bad-tempered drunk, but the kind of drunk that makes you feel fuzzy and tell people you love them. She didn't plan to tell Ricardo she had feelings for him, but she had specifically slipped out to be alone with him. The glow of his cigarette caught her eye. He was sitting on the back of the bench under the jasmine bush around the side of the villa. She felt a rush of excitement.

"Hey," she whispered. "Am I disturbing you?"

He looked amused to see her. "No. I'm just having a break."

"It got pretty animated in there."

"It generally does with *Pin on the Penis*."

"A classy game."

He laughed. "You enjoyed it."

"Oh yeah, nothing I love more than sticking a penis on to my brother's cardboard cut-out."

"At least it was a black penis. You must have been able to detach yourself a bit from it."

She grinned. It had been pretty hilarious. With each hen blindfolded and spun around five times, the game had been a tough challenge which had temporarily united them all in tears of laughter. Clare had obviously been out of the game too long because she'd stuck it on Andrew's forehead. Fiona had got his nipple, Chi the vintage poster two metres away from his groin. Sam had

202

come the closest, sticking it with gusto into his thigh. When Jem's go had arrived, she had started up a mantra of *"This is not my brother's penis! This is not my brother's penis!"* which had sent Sam running for the bathroom in a bid not to pee her pants.

Jem stepped up to the bench and sat beside Ricardo. His masculine aftershave carried in the air, mingling with the jasmine, and it was a heady mix. She felt like turning her head and kissing him. It would be so easy. But what if he pulled back? She smiled at him. He raised his eyebrow.

"You always look like you're laughing at something," she said. "What are you laughing at now?"

He reached for her hand. She wasn't expecting that. His skin was so warm. The air felt electric.

"Sometimes I laugh because I'm nervous."

Her heart was thumping. She smiled uncertainly. Perhaps it was just the buzz of the cicadas. She swallowed.

"What have you got to be nervous about?"

"This."

Then he leant towards her and kissed her. Just one chaste kiss, but as he began to move away, she pulled him closer, hungry for more. He didn't need any encouragement and soon they were kissing like they'd been resisting the urge since the moment they'd met. She didn't know where the passion had burst from. His hot lips had ignited her whole body. She'd never had much of a libido, yet now she wanted to rip his clothes off. Maybe she hadn't had much sex drive because she'd never met someone sexy enough. His tongue knew exactly what it was doing, and his hands were running up her back and giving her goose bumps.

They heard voices and parted brusquely. She glanced behind them, but no one had come out. Ricardo let out a little laugh.

"We really shouldn't be doing this." He hadn't let go of her hand. "You're so beautiful."

She felt her whole body singing and she kissed him again on the lips to hide the big smile.

"Really," he said, emphatically. "You're the most beautiful girl I've ever kissed."

"Shut up."

"When I saw you, I thought, *that girl is going to have a shit personality.*"

She burst out laughing.

"But nope," he said. "Beautiful personality too."

"You know, I wasn't going to come on this trip," she said.

After Fiona had emailed Jem the hen party invitation, peppered with exclamation marks and happy faces, she'd confronted her brother. She'd told him that she didn't want to get emotionally invested if he wasn't going to go through with it. They'd argued. He'd said that it was serious and that he loved Fiona.

"Do you want to talk about it?"

"I've probably talked about it enough."

Ricardo shrugged. "Do you feel any better about it? About Fiona and your brother?"

Jem wrinkled her nose. "Now I mostly feel guilty. I should have been more enthusiastic. I didn't go to their engagement party. What sort of sister doesn't go to her brother's engagement party?"

"What happened?"

"I was at a work do. I could have got out of it but I didn't want to."

She'd made up some lame excuse then had felt terrible. The next day she'd asked Andrew about it and he hadn't been very forthcoming, which meant it hadn't gone well.

"Was Fiona moody?" she'd asked. He'd blown up in her face. Apparently he'd been the idiot that night, getting angry with Fiona because she'd got so drunk. Now she wasn't talking to him and he said he totally deserved it because he'd been an arsehole. Without knowing the details, Jem had felt furious at Fiona.

"That's what psychopaths do," she'd shouted at him, *"they make you feel like you deserve to be badly treated."*

It had taken her breath away how angrily he had yelled back. *"You only see what you want to see!"* he'd bellowed, before storming out.

She pushed the argument from her mind and shot Ricardo a sad smile.

"Everyone romanticises their relationship because they knew each other as teenagers. But they didn't see how she toyed with him."

"Maybe you're biased because you're his sister?"

"Being his sister I got to see behind the scenes."

"What did she do?"

"She broke him down."

He frowned. Ricardo thought she was being dramatic. Well, it had been. Jem remembered finding Andrew with his fist bleeding from punching his bedroom wall.

"What does she want from me?" he'd cried.

"When they'd been going out for a few years off and on, she told my brother she'd met an older guy…that they were emailing each other."

"About what?"

"Stuff he wasn't mature enough to understand, apparently. Obviously he assumed it was sexual and he asked her to stop."

"Teenage girls are cruel. I'm guessing she didn't stop…"

"She said he didn't have any right to ask her that. She said she wasn't cheating."

"Did he see the emails?"

"No, she wouldn't let him. But she would write them there and then while he was with her."

Ricardo scratched his stubble. "Your brother sounds like he was a bit…"

"…a bit of a walk over?"

Jem could tell by his expression that's exactly what he thought.

"I can't imagine putting up with that shit, that's all."

"She would cry if he got angry. He couldn't bear to see her cry."

Andrew had always been a sensitive boy. He had held all Fiona's troubles in his heart and made them his own. He had endless patience because he blamed all her shortcomings on other people. On her parents. On her friends. Anyone but her.

"What about you? I bet you tortured all the boys," he said, pulling her in and kissing her again. "I bet you were frigid."

Jem rolled her eyes, her cheeks reddening. She hadn't been frigid at all, but she could see Ricardo had warmed to the idea. She should stop talking about her brother. It was probably putting him off. But she wanted to get it off her chest.

"My mum says I have to let go. I have to let him lead his life."

"Sounds about right."

"But it's so hard. I want him to be happy."

"How do you know he isn't?"

Jem tipped back her head, and as she took a deep breath, her nose flooded with the delicious scent of jasmine.

"Oh, I don't know..."

Enough, she thought, *enough*. Andrew was a grown man. She had to trust he knew what he was doing. And if it was a mistake, then she must let him make it. She had to close that book of bad memories; she couldn't carry around all the pain and drama any more. She needed to leave it behind for her brother's sake, and for Fiona's sake. It wasn't fair on either of them. She must let them shed their teenage skin and be the people they were today.

"Isn't family important to you?"

Jem looked at him in surprise. "Of course. So, so important. That's what worries me, that she won't..."

"Won't what?"

Fit in?

She fiddled with a tendril of hair, feeling embarrassed. "I don't know. That she won't make an effort."

Ricardo frowned at her. "Why would you think that?"

It was a good question. Jem only had the past to go on, and she couldn't give one example of Fiona being in any way rude to her family. As a teen, Fiona had definitely been a bit brazen for Jem's family's standards. She'd kissed Andrew in front of his parents and talked openly about which celebrities she thought were shagging each other in front of his grandparents. But she had never been rude. On the contrary, she had always been quite affectionate with them. She had gone to the funeral of Granddad Dougie and people had remarked on how good it was that she was there for Andrew.

Jem shook her head. "Shit. I don't know."

"What's her family like?"

"A bit more complicated. Divorced parents who don't like each other."

"How unusual. Divorcees usually love each other."

She made a face. "Alright, smarty pants."

He grinned back. "Just keeping it real."

Her brother had always painted a terrible picture. He'd said Fiona's mum was an alcoholic and her dad a workaholic. But since then, Jem had worked out they were the throwaway comments of a moody teenager. Fiona's mum was a social butterfly and her dad had been unhappy. They'd realised they weren't suited and gone their separate ways. Jem didn't believe there was anything more sinister to it.

"The crazy thing is, sometimes I feel sorry for her," she said.

"Why? For being engaged to your brother?"

She nibbled softly on her lip. Was that it? Was there a part of her that could understand why Fiona had toyed with Andrew? Because his lack of backbone and his ability to forgive her transgressions over and over again had been so infuriating to anyone with a modicum of pride and self-respect? Hadn't Jem once been furious with him too for letting Fiona get away with such awful behaviour? If he had been a friend instead of her brother, would she really have sat through so many exhausting offloads? No, she would have backed off, cutting the friend out of her life so she wouldn't waste any more of her time feeding his addiction to emotional turmoil.

"I suppose, deep down I know nothing's ever black or white."

"That's true."

They sat in silence, Jem feeling the absence of Ricardo's hand on hers. She wondered what this was. Just a drunken kiss in the dark? It felt like it had got so deep, so quickly. The last time she'd been with a guy had been eight months ago. A brief fling with an engineer before he headed off to Qatar for six months. She'd known it was going to end before it began so she hadn't leapt in with her heart and soul. She feared Ricardo was another nomadic sort. She would have to be careful with her heart, which was still beating faster than it should have been.

"There's so much to see on the island," Ricardo said. "I wish we could go off somewhere."

She lit up at the thought. "Can't we?"

"We have a strict schedule."

"It doesn't feel like it."

Ricardo laughed. "True. Kate is doing her own thing."

"Can't we do ours then?"

"I'm kind of essential to this project."

Jem leant over and kissed him. "Just one afternoon?" she suggested, batting her eyelids.

He ran a hand over her cheek. Her stomach fizzed.

They pulled apart when they heard footsteps. It was Chi, tottering on her heels.

"What are you guys doing out here being all secretive?" she called.

Jem felt her heart sink as Chi wandered over to them, her arms folded. Wasn't it obvious?

"We're playing *How Well Do You Know the Bride?* next," Chi said, hiccupping. "Are you coming?"

"Yeah…in a second…"

Chi swayed gently on the spot. "I think it should be *How Well Do You Know the Groom?*"

"I'd win at that one," Jem said.

"I bet he doesn't tell you everything."

"Pretty much everything."

"Right," Chi said. "See you in there."

She turned and walked away. Next Kate appeared, clapping her hands.

"Ricardo? Come on, guys, you're missing important conversations here."

"I was just having a smoke."

"You've got to give up! Did you know one cigarette butt can contaminate one litre of water so badly fish die in it?"

Jem dug him in the ribs. "Fish murderer."

Ricardo groaned. "I'm not planning to throw it in the sea."

"It all ends up there eventually!" Kate called. "One rubbish bag is being emptied into the ocean every single minute. There's 150 million tons of rubbish in there right now, and by the time you get into the house there will be 151, so hurry up, before we're all intoxicated."

She turned and marched back to the house.

"I think I'm already intoxicated," Jem chuckled.

"Why did I take this job again?"

"To meet me," Jem said, grinning.

"Ah yes."

It was a risky thing to say, she thought later, but his reaction was lovely. He kissed her again.

"It's going to be rubbish not being able to kiss you openly," he said.

She returned to the house in high spirits. Her brother was getting married and the guy she had a crush on had told her she was the most beautiful woman he had ever kissed. It was time to be happy for Andrew. Happy for Fiona. Happy for all of their futures. And perhaps, just perhaps, she'd be pleasantly surprised by what a good couple they made after so many years apart.

TWENTY-EIGHT

Day 3
CHIOMA

"Quick!" Fiona shrieked, grabbing Chi's arm and pulling her through the patio doors. "We're starting!"

Unused to her new heels, Chi reached out to steady herself against the wall. Everyone had told her she looked fabulous in them and she had smiled and pretended to be thrilled by the compliments. But if the group hadn't been so small, she would have slipped out and hidden in her room. She didn't feel fabulous. She felt like a traitor. A two-faced bitch. She had never felt such self-loathing as she did now.

Fiona's cheeks were pink and her eyes glassy with drink. She was wearing a vest top covered in gold sequins. Chi thought how the shimmering plastic discs matched the artificial twinkle of her engagement ring. She breathed in sharply, wanting to suffocate the thought before it spilled out of her. She tried to untangle herself from Fiona's grasp but her friend pulled her in closer and deposited a sloppy kiss on her cheek.

"Love you, Chichi."

She swallowed back the sick feeling in her throat. "Love you too, Fifi."

It was awful. She wished she would stop thinking about it but she couldn't help it. Her online search revealed the worst news. Far from being diamond, the ring wasn't even crystal. It was a cheap piece of costume jewellery from a high street shop, and as far as Chi could see, it would only be a matter of time before Fiona bumped into someone else wearing the exact same one.

"Alright, get your pens!" Kate called, clapping her hands.

"No! Not those!" Clare cried as Kate started giving out normal biros. "I brought these."

She ripped open a packet of glittery pens with wobbly rubber willies on top. Chi felt her heart sink further. She tried to laugh but it caught in her throat.

"I love them!" Fiona cried, grabbing one.

"Great, lots of extra pointless plastic. I'm so glad the message is getting across," Kate said, putting her hands on her hips and breathing out heavily.

"They're reusable!" Clare said. "You can transfer the willy on to any other pencil."

"Oh, that's alright then," Kate muttered.

Jem stepped into the living room with a smile on her face and a noticeable sparkle in her eyes. Ricardo followed her inside. Chi watched him as he went straight for the camera, his face giving away nothing and everything at the same time. They fancied each other. It was so blindingly obvious.

"Can I have one?" Jem called to Clare.

A pen went flying through the air and Jem caught it by the plastic willy.

"Ouch, sorry pen," she giggled.

Jem was in a great mood today, but Chi wondered what she would feel if she knew the truth about her brother.

"Are you ready?" Kate said, glancing over at Ricardo.

Chi tried to clear her mind. She felt so mixed up. Her moments of fury at Andrew were interspersed with confusion. He'd seemed like a good guy. Happy and warm. She hadn't known many people at the engagement party and he'd come to her rescue. She'd felt relaxed in his company, like they'd known each other for ever.

"Question one of *How Well Do You Know the Bride?* Are you ready?"

Never mind the bride, who was the real groom? Was he a good guy who had broken under pressure? Or was he a bad guy pretending to be good?

"You all think you know me?" Fiona cackled. "If you answer any of these questions wrong you will no longer be my friends."

Chi forced herself to join the conversation. "What's your surname again?"

"Ooh, are you changing your name?" Sam called.

"No," Fiona replied without hesitation.

"Aren't you?" Clare gasped.

Her astonishment was so comic and Chi found herself taking pleasure from it. Clare thought of herself as the guardian of everything there was to know about Fiona.

"I think Clare has just lost a point!" Chi laughed. "Who knew that Fiona didn't want to change her name?"

She raised her arm, remembering the conversation they'd had at Pret a Manger. It was the same day Fiona had told her she was getting engaged. It was out of the blue and had turned a dull sandwich into a hilarious lunch break. Fiona was a great story teller, and it had been fun hearing about this man, her childhood sweetheart, who had reappeared and swept her off her feet. Chi had been so positive, so encouraging.

"*People will tell you you're mad,*" she'd told Fiona, "*but ignore them. I think everyone waits too long these days to get married. When you know, you know!*"

"Does Andrew know you don't want to take his name?" Jem asked.

Chi thought her smile looked strained, like she was trying to hide her real feelings.

Fiona shrugged. "I suppose so."

"You suppose so?"

"What Jem wants is that you take *her* name!" Sam called.

"Exactly," Jem said, with a laugh.

Fiona didn't seem to want to go along with the joke. "Sorry, Jem, I'm keeping mine."

"Andrew will be disappointed," Jem said.

"Fuck Andrew," Chi said, the words tumbling out before she could stop them.

Everyone turned and stared at her, the smiles all falling from their lips. Fiona let out a high pitched giggle and put her arm around Chi.

"See, Chi's got my back!"

Chi felt her stomach muscles clench. The nicer Fiona was to her, the worse she felt.

"I'm just saying, it's old fashioned and Fiona should do whatever she wants," she said, trying to justify the outburst.

"Yeah, alright, no need for the potty mouth," Sam said. "Think of Ricardo."

"Oh just cut!" Kate called, groaning. "We've talked about this, for God's sake. Ricardo doesn't exist. None of the viewers have seen him, do you understand?"

215

Sam let out a low whistle. "Shall I go to the naughty step?"

Kate ignored her. "You do realise over a million people will be watching you, don't you?"

The room fell silent and Chi felt a tension bubbling under the surface. They had all been trying to forget that fact so why was Kate always bringing it up?

"I've been trying to let you do your own thing..."

"No, you haven't," said Clare.

"Excuse me?"

"I didn't want to go cycling."

Kate looked exasperated. "Look, I'm sorry if not every activity suits every person."

"It's alright," Fiona called. "All will be forgiven if we go on a yacht."

"A yacht," Kate said. "That's what you want, is it? That's what would make you happy?"

Fiona grinned. "Yes."

Sam and Clare whooped in agreement. Chi smiled, but inwardly she felt miserable. How could she enjoy it?

"Okay, very well," Kate said. She walked over to her handbag and pulled out a folded piece of paper. "But first I want to read out some facts about the environmental impacts of recreational boating."

There was an immediate uproar. No one wanted to hear it. Chi's eyes widened as, unperturbed, Kate stood on a chair and started reeling off the facts. She turned around and saw that Ricardo was looking over at Mel, who was in turn holding up her hands as if to say she hadn't got a clue either.

"She said 'environmental'," Fiona screeched, grabbing Chi's arm. "Come on, we have to have a shot!"

"She said 'pollution'," Clare called, laughing. "Shot!"

Chi followed Fiona into the kitchen where she accepted a shot of tequila, wincing as it hit the back of her throat. Fiona poured out another and Chi hesitated.

"Go on!" Fiona said, chinking her glass against hers. "I just heard her say marine life."

"Marine life?" Chi giggled, uncertainly. "I don't think that was on the list."

"It's on the list now."

Clare flew into the kitchen, screaming, "She said 'environmental' again. Shot! Shot!"

"Quick!" Fiona cried, grabbing the bottle and serving. Tequila flowed over the edges of the glasses and dripped on to the floor. The smell of it stung Chi's nostrils as she drank.

Clare breathed out as she slammed her glass on the table. "Oh my God, that's disgusting. It tastes like nail varnish."

The sound of Kate's voice made them all start laughing. Even Chi found herself relaxing a bit. *Fuck it*, she thought. She wasn't a bad person. She just wanted Fiona to be happy, and the only way Fiona was going to remain happy was if she didn't know the whole truth.

"Have your boobs got bigger?"

Clare's question caught Chi off guard. Everyone turned to look at her chest and she let out an embarrassed laugh.

"No!" she said, pressing her hand down on them. Did they feel plumper? She was wearing her black halter neck with a bikini underneath. Neither was padded.

"They look bigger," Clare said.

"How can they be bigger? I'm like an A cup!"

She felt self-conscious. Her mouth suddenly tasted of metal as if it had just filled with blood. She had read about this symptom on a forum she had stumbled across.

"I don't think they're bigger," Sam said.

Chi felt slightly reassured. "Can everyone stop looking at my boobs, please?" she said, forcing a laugh.

"I swear Kate just said 'turtle'," Fiona said, cocking her head to one side. "Wasn't 'turtle' on the list?"

Chi laughed. "I'm going to the loo."

"One for the road then."

"The road? I'm only going next door."

"Well, Kate's bound to say five more words on the list before you get there!"

Chi carried the shot into the toilet and poured it down the sink. Had she been needing to pee more often recently? That was another early symptom of pregnancy. When she thought about babies, it made her clench down there. Perhaps the tension was making her want to pee.

Perhaps it had come. Perhaps when she pulled down her knickers, she would find a pink stain and it would all be alright. But a moment later she felt overcome with disappointment. Her period hadn't come. There wasn't even the musty odour of possibility of it coming. Her shoulders slumped. Her life was over. She leant down and held her face in her hands, a wave of tequila induced nausea washing over her.

"Chi? Are you still in there?"

The knock on the door made her jump. It was Sam.

"Coming!" she called, getting to her feet.

Chi confronted herself in the mirror as she reapplied her lip gloss. She wasn't going to be beaten. She wasn't a wimp. Whatever happened, she would take it in her stride as plenty of women had done before. She gave Sam a smile when she remerged and decided to wait for her. She wasn't in a hurry to get back to downing liquid poison.

When Sam emerged, adjusting her waistband, she looked surprised to find Chi still there.

"Are you alright?"

The concern in Sam's voice caught Chi off guard. The emotions she had been keeping at bay came crashing over her. She blinked back the tears.

"Oh, Sam…"

"What's wrong?"

How had she got so drunk? When she got back home she would give it up for good. She couldn't start now. That would be like giving up booze on New Year's Eve. She'd said that line to *him*. The memory caught her off balance.

"I can't take much more of this…"

Sam looked sympathetic. "I'm knackered too. If I'm honest, I could really do with a cup of tea and a film."

"No, it's not that…"

"What's wrong? You can tell me."

Maybe she should keep quiet and wait a little longer. If she was going to tell anyone in the house, though, it would be Sam. The fact no one else had mentioned the fake ring since dinner was proof Sam could keep her mouth shut. Plus, she was the only one out of them who had actually been pregnant, so perhaps she would know by looking at Chi's tongue or something.

"It's just my period hasn't come."

Sam looked taken aback. "Oh, right. Are you usually regular?"

"Pretty much."

"Have you been stressed?"

Chi knew Sam was going to ask that before she did. That was the standard question. That's what Chi would have asked too had it been the other way around.

"I don't think it's that."

She held Sam's gaze until the penny dropped. When it did, Sam looked sufficiently shocked.

"Oh my God!" And then, as her mind tried to sort out the facts, "But who?"

"A bloody one-night stand."

Sam's eyes widened. She had probably thought Chi wasn't the type. Truth was, she wasn't. She couldn't believe she had let it happen.

"And the condom broke?" Before Chi could reply, Sam was shaking her head in sympathy. "That happened to me once. It was horrible."

Chi felt too embarrassed to admit they hadn't even used a condom. It seemed absolutely insane now, but at the time they had both been so hammered. It was a miracle he'd been able to perform at all.

"But you got the morning after pill, right?" Sam said, looking hopeful. Chi winced and looked at the floor. Why on earth hadn't she? Because she hadn't had the guts to ask for it? Because she thought the chemist would judge her?

"How late are you?"

"About two weeks."

Thirteen days and counting.

Sam nodded, her brain ticking into action. "Was it on a fertile day?"

A fertile day? Chi had no idea.

"I don't know."

"Don't you have a period tracker app?"

The door of the living room swung open and Fiona appeared, looking the worse for wear.

"COME ON GUYS! The bride doesn't like waiting. But you should know that about me, shouldn't you."

They both struggled to get the smiles back on their faces in time and Fiona clocked that something was up.

"What's going on, guys?"

"Nothing," Chi said.

"Yes there is!"

"No, we're just avoiding Kate a bit longer," Sam said.

"Oh, don't worry, she's shut up now. We're going back to the game."

Chi felt Sam's hand gently squeeze her arm as they headed back into the living room. There weren't enough people in the room for them to have a private conversation, but Sam chose to sit beside her anyway.

"Test," Sam whispered.

"First question!" Kate called.

Chi accepted another shot from Fiona and cradled it in her hand. Even without looking, she knew Sam's eyes were on her and she felt apprehensive that Sam wouldn't be able to contain herself. She regretted opening her mouth. No one could keep a secret like she could.

Sam leant forward. "I don't think you should be drinking," she whispered.

Chi felt her cheeks colour. "Even if I was, it would be too early to make a difference."

"Haven't you heard of..."

Kate shot them a warning look and Sam shut her mouth.

"READY EVERYONE? If you don't settle, I might enlighten you about the horrors of cruise ships."

"YES! WE'RE READY!" Clare cried and Chi winced at the volume of her voice. *Of course Clare's excited*, Chi thought irritably. She was desperate to prove how much better she knew Fiona than the rest of them.

"Number one. Is Fiona more likely to..." Kate began, and then looked around the room to increase the suspense. Chi only felt suspense about wanting to know what Sam had been going to say.

"Recycle or dump?"

There was a baffled pause.

"What sort of question is that?" Fiona asked.

Kate ignored her. "No conferring! Write the answers on the page."

Sam tossed her pen on the floor in front of Chi and then leant forward and whispered, "FASD!" in her ear.

Chi frowned at her. "What's that?"

"Next question!" Kate shouted

"Google it," Sam hissed. "Believe me, you'll want to stop drinking."

TWENTY-NINE

Day 3
SAM

"My worst wedding nightmare would be walking down the aisle and falling flat on my face," announced Fiona.

"Which is what I wrote," cried a triumphant Clare. "Look! You can see for yourself! Word for word."

"And breaking my nose," Fiona added. "Have you got the part about breaking my nose?"

"No, but that's obviously implied."

Sam realised Fiona was waiting for her to give her answer and she smiled automatically and looked down at her page. When Kate had asked the question, her first thought had been about the ring. *Your worst nightmare would be finding out your engagement ring is fake.* She'd felt a shiver run down her spine as she'd imagined saying that out loud.

"I just said spilling red wine down the front of your dress."

"Not bad, but as I would only drink champagne at my wedding, that wouldn't happen," Fiona said, winking.

"Clever woman."

Fiona looked behind her. "Chi?"

Sam glanced worriedly at Chi and wondered whether she had pulled herself together in time to put an answer to paper. She had been observing Chi and she'd noticed her eyes glazing over. Perhaps she should have reassured her and told her it was nothing. All sorts of things could delay a period. Stress about spending a week with people you didn't know. Being too skinny. Flying.

Sam would never forget the time her period had been late and she'd gradually become convinced she was pregnant. She'd kept prodding her boobs to see if they were tender, until in the end they were tender from so much prodding. *Aha*, she'd thought, *tender breasts, I must be pregnant!* She'd tried to analyse how tired she was. It was difficult to know if she was uncharacteristically knackered because she was pregnant, or because she'd been celebrating non-stop since Chris had proposed two weeks earlier.

Another week had passed without a sign of her period and she'd begun to get really paranoid about all the celebratory drinking. A search on Google led to articles that suggested even drinking a tiny bit during the first weeks of pregnancy could lead to FASD syndrome, resulting in physical abnormalities and behavioural problems. Before her baby had even been born she'd already condemned him to a life of being slower and stupider than everyone else. What an awful price to pay for a party.

Sick with worry, she'd finally taken a pregnancy test. For three long minutes she'd waited with baited breath, imagining her first trip to the clinic, where she'd confess her stupidity to a grey-haired doctor with a stethoscope around his neck and a disappointed look in his eyes. He'd shake his head: *"What were you thinking?"*

In the jargon of the pregnancy forums it had been a BFN. A Big Fat Negative. The relief had been tinged with sadness, which had proved to her that she was ready to become a mum.

At the time Chris had told her she would have been fine anyway. *"Think about our grandparents' generation,"* he'd said. No one knew back then that there were things you shouldn't eat or drink when you were pregnant, and the human population had thrived anyway. Still, once you knew, it was hard to un-know, and Sam had been careful after that.

"Uh..." Chi scanned her page. "I wrote...food poisoning."

Fiona frowned. "What?"

"At one of my cousins' wedding everyone got food poisoning from the chicken. Everyone started throwing up half way through the karaoke."

"Are you sure it was food poisoning?" Clare snorted. "Sounds like Jäger to me."

Sam laughed and tried to push Chi's problem out of her mind. If she wasn't thinking about her late period, she'd only be thinking about that bloody ring, and Sam really didn't want *that* coming out. She had regretted telling Chi. But perhaps Chi had forgotten about it now or had assumed she'd been drunk and talking rubbish.

"That wouldn't happen at my wedding because there'd be so much alcohol everyone would be inoculated from salmonella," Fiona said, laughing.

"So I win!" Clare shrieked.

Fiona shrugged. "Yup, unless Jem has an answer?"

Sam looked over at Jem who had been sitting quietly on the armchair with her feet curled up beneath her. She smiled coyly.

"Surely Andrew not turning up to the wedding would be your worst nightmare?" she said.

Fiona did a pantomime act of thinking about it and then shook her head. "Nope. Breaking my nose walking down the aisle tops that."

Obviously she was being silly, but Sam was surprised to see that Jem seemed genuinely irritated.

"You wouldn't be walking down the aisle if he didn't show up," she said. "Or actually, maybe you would!"

"Yeah, maybe I would," Fiona said. "I mean, if I'd already paid for it, why not?"

"Oh yeah, because you're paying for the whole wedding, right?"

Fiona let out a hollow laugh. "Well, I don't think Andrew's monthly salary is quite going to cover it, do you?"

"And yours will?"

"CUT!" shouted Kate. "We're jumping straight to the last question."

"The Bahamas!" Clare cried.

"CUT! I need to *ask* the last question first," Kate said.

Sam looked down at her own answer to *Where would Fiona most want to go on her honeymoon?*

"Caribbean cruise," she said, her voice being drowned out by Clare who felt the need to repeat her answer several times.

Sam noted that Jem's face had gone very pink. She was looking down at her page and her hands were trembling.

"What did you say?" Fiona said, looking straight at Sam. She smiled brightly.

"A cruise around the Caribbean?"

Fiona grinned. "Correct."

"But the Bahamas is in the Caribbean. Doesn't that count?" Clare asked.

"Half," Fiona said.

Clare scribbled half a point on her page, then started very vocally totting up her score. Sam glanced at Chi just as she swallowed back the shot she had been dithering over drinking. Without meaning to come across as utterly judgmental, Sam felt her eyebrows fly up into her forehead. Chi looked back at her defiantly and Sam looked hurriedly away.

Chi probably wasn't worried because if she was pregnant, she didn't plan to have it. Sam thought of baby George and felt a longing in her gut to hold him close to her. She wished she was at home now, on the sofa, with her little family. Suddenly three more days in Mallorca seemed like an eternity. She felt an urge to book herself a flight home.

"Really? A cruise?" Kate said.

The sharpness of their director's tone brought Sam back to the present. The cosy image disintegrated, and in its place was Kate's disgusted expression.

Fiona scowled at her. "What's wrong with a cruise?"

"Didn't you hear anything I said before?"

"Nope. I wasn't listening because I don't care."

"Well you should care! This is your planet."

"SHE SAID PLANET!" Clare shrieked. "Shot! Shot! Shot!"

"They're like floating shopping centres," Kate snapped. "Just think of all the waste produced. Where exactly do you think it goes?"

"WASTE!" shouted Fiona, reaching her shot glass out to Clare who had picked up the half empty tequila bottle.

Ricardo coughed loudly and pointedly. "Permission to cut?"

"Yes please," Sam murmured, rubbing a hand over her face. Even she could see this was terrible television. It had been a rocky night from start to finish and she reckoned they should scrap the whole thing and start again tomorrow.

Kate looked shocked. "No. Not really, Ricardo. Because that's my job, or did you forget?"

The room fell silent as the director and cameraman eyeballed each other. Sam was sure Ricardo was about to storm off, but in the end Kate looked away first and suggested they all take a ten-minute break.

THIRTY

Fiona was fuming. Jem needed to back the hell down before she made a laughing stock of all of them on national television. Why did she think Fiona wasn't good enough for her brother anyway? Andrew and Jem weren't exactly royalty. And even if they were, the monarchy was totally fine about accepting commoners into the fold these days. But they were from a normal family, and once upon a time Fiona had found the sense of normality in the Stephensons' house very soothing. She remembered their mother, Lyn, pouring them glasses of cloudy apple juice and telling Andrew off for not taking his shoes off without undoing the laces. She'd even apologised to Fiona for her son's scruffy hair and the dragging bottoms of his trousers, which she said she'd hemmed herself only last week. Jem had wandered in with her headphones on and given Fiona a friendly enough smile before asking her mum's permission to go to a gig, even though she was at least seventeen.

Life had been more conservative in the Stephensons' house, that much was true. Fiona remembered how she and Andrew had sat out in the garden because he was too embarrassed to hang out in his room. His mum wouldn't like it, he'd told her at the time. She'd tried to kiss him but he'd looked alarmed. What was the big deal? It was just a kiss. But he was worried his mum was watching from the kitchen window. They'd kissed in her bedroom instead. Got to base three in the same week. If her mum had suspected, she never mentioned it.

"*I trust you*," she would say, washing her hands of the responsibility.

Andrew appeared on screen now. Fiona sank down into the sofa, her heart beating fast. He was looking all scrubbed up and smart in a slim fitting grey V-neck T-shirt. He'd had a fresh haircut, too. It was shaved at the side, long on top and parted to the right. His eyes looked bluer than ever as if the film crew had added a filter to enhance them. She remembered noticing that they always seemed lighter in the morning.

She wondered how nervous he was. Andrew hadn't been jealous of her hen trip at all, had immediately said he'd hate to be on television. He wasn't that bothered about having a stag do, full stop. He hadn't been able to shake off friends like Joe, whose humour still depended on taking the piss out of him.

He waved at the camera.

"Hi, future wife! I hope you've been having a good time."

Fiona bit her lip. *Future wife*? It sounded so crazy.

"Aw," Clare said, misty eyed.

Fiona checked the expressions of the others. Chi was staring intently at the screen, Sam was smiling faintly and Jem looked like she was going to cry.

"So I was asked a few questions and I really hope I've got at least one of them right." He bared his teeth in a comical wince. "But if I haven't, just know that doesn't mean anything, really."

"I guess that depends," Fiona said, forcing a laugh. The truth was she didn't want to do this now. The atmosphere was tense; she didn't think it could be repaired.

"So we asked him," Kate said, scrolling on her tablet, "what do you love most about Fiona?"

She paused the video and looked at the bride-to-be. "What do you think he said?"

Fiona tried to ignore the nerves in the pit of her stomach. The camera was rolling and she knew Ricardo's focus would be on her reaction. *Take your time and breathe,* she told herself, remembering Joanna's words. *And for God's sake, have fun!*

What did Andrew love most about her? She smiled as the answer popped up in her head. Her boobs. It was obviously going to be that. He hadn't been able to look her in the eyes when they'd been teenagers. She'd caught him out a million times taking a quick peek, and each time, his cheeks would flush bright red. It was like all his Christmases in one when finally he got to see them. She'd undressed slowly, drawing out the moment he'd been dreaming about since he'd first seen her. He'd touched them so gently, like you might touch a pair of Fabergé eggs.

"Easy," Fiona said, grinning. "My…" and she did a shimmy, so the sequins across her breasts shook a little.

"Breasts?" Kate said, with a laugh. "O-kay."

Andrew looked pensively at the camera. "The best thing about Fiona?" he said. "I think it's how active she is."

How *active*? What was he talking about? She was hardly a gym bunny. She occasionally had a go at a yoga video on YouTube and had owned dumbbells for forty-eight hours after making and breaking a New Year's Resolution within the same timeframe.

"She loves doing new things and taking risks. She loves adventures," he said, flashing a grin. "I'm excited about being part of those adventures."

Fiona could feel herself going red. "I thought you meant a body part!"

"I'm sure he loves your boobs too," Sam said, laughing.

"Of course he loves your boobs," Clare said.

Fiona felt exposed all the same. She didn't want the world thinking her shallow. How could she have known Andrew would answer so seriously?

"Next we asked him: what did Fiona wear on their first date?"

First date? They hadn't exactly had a formal courtship. They'd got to know each other intimately before they'd even set foot outside the close, their relationship proceeding like a traffic light, one minute all go, the next a complete stop.

"Fiona?" Kate pushed.

He'd insisted on having their first ever proper date. They'd gone to Greenwich, away from prying eyes. It had been nice. They'd eaten pancakes in the market with cinnamon and chocolate. He'd got chocolate on her sleeve and she'd been annoyed about that. She wished she hadn't. He'd been trying so hard and it wasn't his fault.

Sleeve of what?

"Fiona? Don't you remember?"

Everyone was looking at her expectantly. She made a fuss of what she was wearing for every occasion and so she was bound to know this. White, it had to be white if she was so annoyed about the chocolate.

"Of course I do!" she said. "I was wearing a white top...and jeans..."

She would have accessorised with bronze hoops, Indian bangles and borrowed her Mum's best leather belt, brown with little gold studs.

Kate played the video.

"She was wearing a white shirt," he said, smiling. "She got annoyed with me because I got chocolate on it."

Fiona smiled back weakly. She felt terrible. "Sorry about that, Andrew. All true."

She reminded herself it was a long time ago and didn't matter now. She couldn't help it, though. She felt a wave of sadness wash over her. It seemed such a shame that it was an imperfect memory when it could have been a perfect one. Life was too short to care so much about food stains on your clothes.

Kate looked pleased. "Very good!"

Fiona cheered herself and took a sip of champagne. Despite the tequila shots, she felt like she was sobering up. These games felt more like a test than anything else and she was looking forward to them being over.

"Wait, but when was that date?" Sam asked.

"When we were teenagers..."

"Shouldn't you be talking about your more recent first date?"

"Yeah," Clare agreed. "We want to hear about when you got back together."

"Pause it!" Sam called. "We want to hear the latest first date."

Fiona swallowed and rubbed her sweaty palms on her shorts. Kate was holding her thumbs up at Ricardo.

Fiona mustered a big smile. "Okay, well…basically, it was the same date."

In her mind, Andrew had never grown up. She had kept the image of him, standing outside Greenwich station. A slim boy with floppy blond curtains, hands deep in his pockets making him slouch, looking the wrong way up the road. She was surprised when he walked out of the station as a man. His eyes were the same, though. Clear blue and happy to see her. She recalled what he had told her when they were teenagers. They were at a house party and cheap cider had loosened his tongue.

"When I saw you, I told Joe, 'I'm going to marry that girl'…"

At the time she had laughed and told him to stop drinking. But she had held on to those words like a precious gift. The fact he had come to meet her after so many years proved he had held on to that teenage prophecy too.

"We had fish and chips," Fiona said. "And reminisced."

She'd told him she had never stopped thinking about him. He'd breathed out, long and hard, and sworn over and over. *Fuck. Fuck. Fuck.* She asked him why it was so bad, and he'd shaken his head in disbelief.

"I dreamt about this," he'd said. *"I just didn't think it would actually happen."*

Fiona didn't go into the detail of that conversation. Instead, she satisfied the hens by telling them how easy it was to be together again and how they were holding hands by the end of their first date.

"Did you get that, Ricardo?" Kate asked.

"Perfect."

After their little tiff, they were being extra polite. It was obvious they wouldn't be working together again in a hurry.

"Back to Andrew, then. Next we asked him: what's Fiona's guilty pleasure?"

Kate paused the video as Andrew broke into a laugh. The frame froze, capturing the moment of his face opening up. Happy eyes. He looked handsome. He *was* handsome. It struck Fiona, not for the first time, how much he'd changed from when he was a timid teenager with fluff on his lips and the odd volcanic spot on his chin.

"Fiona?" Sam called. "What are you guilty of?"

Her cheeks were getting hot. She was guilty of a lot of things that the nation didn't need to know.

"I know!" Clare said.

Fiona felt her chest tighten uncomfortably. What did she know?

"Reality TV?"

Fiona smiled. "That's a good one, Clare."

If only it was just that.

"You can't say Reality TV is your guilty pleasure if you're on Reality TV," Jem said.

The truth wasn't what mattered. What was important here was getting the answer Andrew had guessed.

"I'm a hoarder of all things sparkly?" Fiona said.

"Hardly a secret, Fi," Clare said. "Look at what you're wearing."

That was true. She'd even had the drycleaners sew extra sequins across the pockets of her hot pants.

She racked her brain for a better answer. "I...um..."

I told everyone my mum was an alcoholic and it's not true...she just got drunk at a party once and cried about Dad not loving her any more...

Those emails I said I used to write to an older guy. There was no older guy. I just wrote stuff down and emailed it to myself. I enjoyed seeing Andrew jealous.

My dad is a good guy but he's too weak. Weak like Andrew.

She realised she was holding her breath and let go. This was about secrets that caused her pleasure, not pain.

Kate played the tape.

"Fiona is a competition addict," Andrew said, winking. "Aren't you, love?"

"That's what I was going to say next!" Clare cried.

"She enters everything, fills in every raffle, buys a lottery ticket every week," he continued, laughing at a memory. "She's lucky, too. Well, obviously. That's why she's in Mallorca now and I'm stuck here in rainy England."

"I'm not an *addict*," Fiona protested. "But yeah...I guess he's right."

Kate smiled. "Is he doing better than you thought?"

Fiona nodded. "Yeah...a lot better."

Her heart was racing. She drained her glass and welcomed the alcohol rush.

"He's been in love with her since he was a teenager," Jem said to no one in particular. "Of course he knows her."

Fiona felt butterflies in her stomach. Was it unconditional? Would he love her no matter what?

"To lovely Andrew," Clare said, lifting her glass. "I think he deserves a round of applause."

Or did he have a breaking point? What would it be like to have Andrew hate her? Could she really live with it?

She swallowed back her fears and toasted her childhood sweetheart.

THIRTY-ONE

Day 5
KATE

"Is that the runner?"

Sharon nodded at somewhere behind Kate's head.

"He's a bit older than our usuals, isn't he?"

Kate felt nervous as she turned around, hoping very much that it wasn't Gabriel. What if he didn't act like the runner he was supposed to be?

But it *was* him and she felt a jolt of alarm, which morphed into a much more pleasant emotion. Her crush was getting worse. He looked so sexy, standing there in the doorway to the terrace, scanning the tables with all the calm in the world. He was dressed casually in a navy V-neck T-shirt and crumpled jeans, unshaven and with his dark hair a tangled, gorgeous mess. He definitely looked the part.

He saw her and gave her a measured smiled. It was a good pretence. He knew what his role was in this situation.

"Hi, good morning...I have the car parked outside," he said.

"Great. Good. This is, uh..." Kate faltered.

"Gabriel," he said. He held out his hand to Sharon, who was eating him up with her sharp green eyes.

"Nice to meet you. Are you from Mallorca?"

"No, I'm from Malaga but I've lived here ten years."

"Oh, I love Malaga."

"Yeah, I love it too," he said, smiling warmly.

"I went to the Picasso museum when I was there and this gipsy woman tried to press rosemary into my hand...good luck, apparently, but I'd read they try and get money after that so I declined. I had some delicious fish there. Not at the Picasso museum, obviously. At a restaurant...*El*...*El*...oh, I can't remember."

Kate tried to conceal her surprise at hearing Sharon make time for small talk. Clearly there was an exception for handsome men with good tans and twinkly brown eyes.

"There are some great seafood restaurants here. You'll have to go to La Parada del Mar," he said, plucking the air by his lips to emphasise just how great it was. "You pick what you want as if you were at a fishmonger and then they cook it for you. It's so fresh."

"If only I was here on holiday," Sharon said, straightening up, remembering why she *was* here. "So you know where to find our cast, do you?"

"Your what? Sorry?"

"The girls," Kate said.

He nodded. "Of course. They are in one of three places."

He said it so convincingly Kate found herself believing him.

"Good. I'm glad we have someone on top of the situation," Sharon said. She removed another cigarette from her pack. "Alright, well, off you go." She looked out towards the sea and let out a sigh of resignation. Kate felt like telling her to go for a swim but held her tongue. It would give the impression they were going to be a while.

"Okay, let's go," Kate said.

They didn't say a word until they were outside the hotel, then Gabriel took her hand and squeezed it.

"I want to take you back to bed," he groaned.

She freed her hand as quickly as she could. "Don't even think about it! Sharon sees and hears everything."

"She was nice."

"Yeah, she really liked you. She'll like you less when she realises you're not on top of the situation after all."

He laughed. "She has no idea, does she."

Kate breathed out and shook her head. "Nope."

"And you?"

"Well…I think I know one part of the puzzle. If we find Ricardo, then we'll find Jem."

They got in the car and both lowered their windows at once. A few minutes in the sun and it was already an oven.

"So where are we going?" he said.

Kate thought about the last time they were all together on the beach. She'd been in the sea with her snorkel and her sieve. She'd volunteered to clean up in the water so she could get away from the bickering hens. It had been the wrong thing to do. She knew that now. At the time she'd told herself they'd sort things out by themselves. She'd also done it because she didn't know if she would be able to contain herself.

"Don't you get it? Polluted oceans means polluted food chains which means polluted blood streams. We're going to wipe ourselves out if we don't wake up."

Gabriel had been in the water too, which had made things quite a lot more distracting. One minute she'd been reeling in horror at the plastic soup they were filtering through their nets, the next minute she'd been observing

240

his bronzed body and cheeky smile and entertaining thoughts about how great a team they'd make together.

The hens hadn't settled down. You'd have to have been an inanimate object not to have sensed the tension between them. Sunburn, hangovers, tiredness...or had there been something more? If she had been Joanna Kane she would have been more tuned in. Well, if she had been Joanna Kane, they'd all have been on a yacht sipping champagne instead of at a beach clean-up.

Gabriel was looking at her, waiting for an answer. "North? East? South? West?"

"Honestly?" Kate said, running a hand through her hair, which had become frizzy in the heat. "I've no idea."

THIRTY-TWO

Day 4
KATE

If they'd known their day was supposed to include the morning on a yacht and cocktails at a luxury beach club, they would have been furious. Luckily they hadn't seen the original schedule. Kate had made sure of that. Inspired by Gabriel, she was taking them on an alternative experience which she hoped would open their eyes, in the same way her eyes had once been opened in Greece.

The hens didn't see why they had to arrive at the beach at a certain time, and hadn't taken her instructions to be ready for 9am at all seriously. It was already a quarter to ten and they were only just emerging, bleary-eyed and thirsty. Clare was first, heading straight for the kettle. Sam appeared from the garden in her pyjamas, red-eyed as if she'd been crying. Judging from the phone in her hand, it was because she'd had a conversation with her little one and was missing him.

Kate fought the urge to yell up the stairs. "I'll go wake the others up," she said instead.

Clare eyed her warily. "No, let me. If you go it'll be like waking up to death metal."

"What have I done this time?"

"Um...the quiz questions weren't great."

"The quiz questions?"

"Is Fiona more likely to recycle or dump? That's not a classic *How Well Do You Know the Bride?* question."

242

Kate stared at her. "Why are you still thinking about that?"

Clare looked irritated. "*Still*? It was only last night."

"I thought everyone had fun."

"Seriously?"

A lot of other things had happened after that. Andrew had done well with his answers, Fiona had cried a bit, dancing had happened, only one more glass had been broken...

"Ricardo said you all ended up dancing Gangnam style on the kitchen table."

"That was only for about two minutes..."

"Well, still. Sounds like you had fun to me."

"Well, you weren't there."

"I thought you'd relax if I left early, and from what I hear, you did!"

Kate had left at a quarter to one in the morning, which was as soon as she could. Gabriel had still been wide awake, had answered her text message with an eager phone call. It wasn't all that late for Spain. They'd gone to a bar near the beach and shared a jug of fruity Cava Sangria and chatted until three in the morning. The owner had looked apologetic when he'd told them he needed to stack up their chairs. Kate had wanted the night to continue. It could have. They'd stood there on the pavement, the tug of desire stopping her from leaving after she'd said goodbye. His eyes had searched hers.

"*See you tomorrow?*" he'd asked.

They'd confided in each other. He knew about Matt. She knew he'd had his heart broken by a foreigner who had only been passing through. Perhaps that's why he didn't kiss her. It was stupid, she'd thought as she walked

243

back to her hotel. It was a summer fling without even a kiss.

"What's the problem?" Kate asked, blinking away the image and finding Clare still looking grumpily back at her. "Come on, the sun is shining and I promise we're going to have a really meaningful day today."

"Oh my God...I just..." Clare shook her head. "I just really want to make my tea and go back to bed."

"Why? What's wrong?"

"You didn't feel the tension?"

Kate grimaced. "Look, Ricardo and I are passionate people..."

Clare shook her head. "Not you two. Fiona and Jem."

"Oh." Now that Clare had mentioned it, she did recall a small confrontation between them. But it hadn't lasted very long and it was nothing that couldn't be blamed on too much tequila and not enough sleep. "Are they alright now?"

Clare sighed. "You need to pull something special out of the bag today."

Kate beamed at her. "Believe me, I will. It's going to be life-changing."

"Oh God, you've got that look in your eye..." Clare ran a hand over her face and started to walk away.

"Wait! Where are you going?"

"TO GET DRESSED!"

"Alright, calm down. You only need a bikini and a T-shirt...no need to dress up..."

Clare shot her a withering look. "You're filming this, right?"

"Well, obviously."

"Then everyone is going to dress up, aren't they?"

Oh for God's sake, Kate thought, pressing her fingers over the bridge of her nose. A little voice in her head was trying to tempt her to give up and take the easy route. But it sounded like a meek, defeatist voice to Kate and she found it easy to ignore. It was Day 4 and she was set on finishing what she'd started. It wouldn't be right to start off with a heartbreaking video of a turtle being impaled by a plastic straw, and continue to a shot of the girls all drinking cocktails through half a dozen of the things on a yacht which cost enough to fund a turtle charity for twenty years. No, her first episode, and quite likely her last, would have some integrity.

Admittedly there was another reason why she was particularly determined to get them to the beach clean-up that morning. She had been playing the scene in her head: how they would make their surprise entrance and Gabriel would stop what he was doing, his eyes lighting up, a smile spreading across his face, so evidently impressed...

"How did you manage to persuade them?"

Persuasion would have been preferable to force, but unfortunately there wasn't enough time for eloquent speeches. She reasoned that what would really change their minds was seeing the state of the sea for themselves.

By the time the hens had got into the minivan, no one was talking to each other. Their Spanish driver handed Kate the GPS. She entered the address and handed it back, checked his expression to see what he thought of their destination. He raised his eyebrows but didn't utter a word.

Kate cranked up the radio to lighten the mood and Chi made a point of putting both her earphones in instead of just the one. They were all wearing oversized sunglasses so Kate couldn't tell whether they were giving her the evil eye or not. Ten minutes into the journey, gentle snores told her more than a couple had fallen asleep.

Mel and Ricardo were trailing the minivan in the jeep. They didn't have the address and were relying on following it not to get lost. Their moods were frayed, too. Ricardo wanted to know what Kate was up to this time. Mel was subdued, possibly hungover.

Kate checked the time on her phone. Her stomach muscles tightened with worry. What if they arrived too late? They had distanced themselves from the busy, sandy beaches of Palma and Arenal and were heading further south along the coast which promised a long stretch of rocky coves. It wasn't going to be packed with tourists, that was for sure.

They turned into a quiet coastal town, soon leaving behind a few shops and bars for purely residential streets. There were rows of small Mediterranean villas with gated gardens, palm trees visible behind sun baked walls and terracotta pots of fleshy cacti cemented in place. Except for an old man waiting for his little white terrier to relieve himself beside the tree, there was no one about.

The driver slowed down, looking unsure.

"We are near...I hope," he said.

His expression didn't inspire much confidence. Kate prayed for some sign of life. They took a left and then a right.

"This is the road," he said. "Unless..."

"There!" she cried.

The driver jerked to a stop.

"Sorry," she said, touching his arm. She hadn't meant to shout. It was just an enormous relief to see some sign of life. It had to be them. The motley group had spilled out on to the road, colourful rucksacks lying on the tarmac at their feet. Kate spotted an athletic looking man with a professional camera smoking a roll-up nearby. Local news, perhaps?

The group watched them curiously, no doubt wondering if they had come to help. Gabriel was nowhere to be seen.

Kate turned around in her seat. "Right, we're here."

"Where are we?" Fiona asked.

Clare stifled a yawn. "Who are those people?"

"I told you, we're making a trip down to a special beach," Kate said, getting out of the van.

"With a bunch of randoms?" Fiona asked, her voice turning to a whine. "They all look older than my gran!"

It was true. They did resemble a retirement club, but then it was Thursday morning and most young people were either working or in bed. She wouldn't ring Gabriel just yet. She got out of the car and headed over to the group, feeling a bit stupid. There were seven of them in total – fewer volunteers than she'd expected. It made her feel relieved that she had stuck to her guns and brought reinforcements.

A short grey-haired man with kind eyes smiled at her. There was something about his stance that told her he was the leader of the group. He greeted her in Spanish and she managed a few words. A few words in a language he didn't recognise, by the look of his blank expression. She grimaced and waved to the black jeep which Ricardo was having difficulties parking in a tight space.

"Hang on...my camera guy speaks Spanish!"

The man smiled. "Okay."

"He was born in England but both his parents are Spanish."

"Ah...okay..."

"I'm Kate."

"Josep," he said, holding out his hand.

There was an awkward wait, during which Kate tried to ignore the fact the girls were not getting out of the van. Ricardo finally parked the jeep and went around to the boot to get his equipment.

"Quick! Come over!" she called. "Tell him we're here to help."

Ricardo left the boot open and came over. He greeted Josep with a tense smile and spoke in Spanish that seemed a little hesitant. Kate was about to tell Ricardo to explain that the hens didn't actually know why they were here, but stopped when she saw them emerge from the back of the van.

"This beach had better be special," Fiona called.

"And really close by," Clare added. "My legs are still killing me from that bloody cycle ride. I don't think I'm ever getting on a bike again."

Their bad mood lifted slightly when they became aware of the other cameraman whom Ricardo had engaged in conversation. Kate was vaguely aware of the hens muttering how many points they'd give him out of ten.

"Local news." Ricardo confirmed her suspicions. "We're hoping it's not a long way down."

He shifted his camera from one hand to the other to make a point. His assistant had called in sick with food poisoning and it was Mel who was carrying his camera tripod at the moment.

Josep looked at his watch then spoke to the rest of the group. Ricardo paraphrased the introduction.

"Basically, it's time to go."

The residential road had a gap between two villas with stairs leading down to the coast. The volunteers and hens posed on the paved steps while Ricardo and the other cameraman filmed their guide talking in Mallorquin about what they were doing here. The girls flashed big smiles behind him, miscalculating it for a chance of international fame. Kate almost felt sorry for them.

The low steps took them under an outcrop of pine trees, from where they got a first breathtaking glimpse of turquoise sea. Kate felt her heart soar. It was so stunningly beautiful. She wanted to breathe it in, store it in her brain for all those rainy days to come when she was back home. *Imagine seeing this every day*, she thought, *like Gabriel*. She liked that he appreciated his home.

"That feeling doesn't change either," he'd said to her when she'd raved about the views last night. *"Ten years here and I still feel like I'm seeing it for the first time."*

She turned to look at the hens. But they weren't smiling. They seemed more interested in the amount of rugged rock separating them from the water.

"How are we going to get down there?" Fiona said. "These are not hiking shoes." She held up her foot to show off her sparkly flip-flop.

"At least they're flat," Clare said, miserably.

249

Kate cast her eye over Clare's pretty espadrille wedges and her swollen looking feet which were the same colour as the bright pink flower on the heel.

"Has everyone got sunscreen on?" she asked. She should have got them all to put some on before leaving the house. Then again, she was a director, not a school teacher.

Chi was also in wedges. Stripy red ones which looked too big for her. If Kate had known there would be a little excursion to get to the beach, of course she would have told them to wear suitable footwear. Hopefully it would be a short walk. There was a sandy path ahead of them. She could see someone in the distance coming up it.

"I'm going to film this part," Ricardo said.

She liked to think that he was impressed with the views, even if he was reluctant to show his enthusiasm just yet.

Josep led the way and Kate followed after him, eager to get away from the sarcastic banter between the hens. It was a concern that they weren't raving about the place. The plan had been for them to fall in love, and as a result feel absolutely devastated and moved to help once they saw what was at the end of the trail. Kate didn't quite know what to expect herself. From where she was, the area looked completely unspoilt. But then it was often the case. Sometimes it was only once you were under the water, with your snorkel on, that you saw the conflict between man and nature.

She was concentrating on her footing so she didn't see him until he was close. In a faded green vest that left his nut brown shoulders exposed, legs covered in sand, and sea water stiffening his dark hair, Gabriel looked like he'd been let loose in nature. He waved at Josep, his face breaking into a warm smile, and then he saw Kate and his pleasure seemed to double. So did the pace of her heart. She hoped the girls wouldn't recognise him. She hadn't really thought about what she would say if they did.

"Hello again."

She blushed. "Hi."

He glanced behind her, and his eyebrows shot up when he saw the vision of five girls sparkling and gleaming in the sunshine.

"Wow. The whole party."

He looked impressed.

"I told you I would."

Josep waved his hand between them. "You know each other?"

"We met on a plane."

The rest of the party had slowed down behind them and seemed restless to get on. Josep started to walk ahead. Gabriel hung back and walked beside Kate, even though that meant walking on the rocky part beyond the path. When he took her hand to help her cross a big boulder, she felt her heart drumming in her chest. She wondered if he felt the spark between them.

"So, tell me what else I need to know about Kate Miller," he said, grinning. "We have time."

In that moment, she thought it was a really romantic thing to say. She didn't think that the fact they had time meant the path was a lot longer than it looked.

THIRTY-THREE

Day 4
FIONA

Fiona yelped in pain as another stone slipped under her toes and dug into the sole of her foot. The old woman in the strapless pink swimming costume and beige shorts ahead of her turned and raised an eyebrow before heading on, a satisfied smile fixed to her leathery face. Clearly she was feeling smug because she was having less difficulty than someone so young.

The problem was the soles of Fiona's flip-flops were so thin that they were letting absolutely everything in. She was making an effort to contain herself, though, because Clare was in a worse position having chosen to wear super high wedges.

She stopped to let Clare catch up.

"Did you see who that was?" Clare said, her sunburnt face shiny with sweat. "That man who Kate's with."

Fiona strained to see, but it was all just a blur. She had been prescribed glasses but hated wearing them. She got by without them, although for moments like this she would have been grateful for a bit of detail.

"I'm almost positive it's that man from the plane. The one who got angry."

Fiona frowned. "How random is that?"

"Or is it?"

"What do you mean?"

"I don't know…maybe it's nothing, but…"

She paused for effect. Fiona pushed away the niggle of irritation and followed her thread.

"Go on. What are you thinking?"

"That we came here just so they could meet up."

"What do you mean? Like a date?"

Clare shot her a pointed look. Fiona wasn't buying it.

"That doesn't make any sense. When would they have arranged it? They were only together five minutes on the plane."

"Not much of this week has made sense if you think about it," Clare grumbled. "To be totally honest, it feels like our director has been making it up as she goes along."

Fiona had had the same thought. But she didn't feel like dwelling on it now. She had a massive hangover and was full of regrets.

"Maybe this is what making TV shows is really like."

"What do you mean?" Clare asked. "I'm not just talking about Kate calling 'Cut' every five minutes, I'm talking about the general direction...do you know what I mean?"

"I don't know. I've got a headache."

"You mean a hangover."

Fiona gritted her teeth. Headaches elicited sympathy, hangovers did not.

Clare stopped in her tracks. "Okay, Fi. Do you want to talk about it?"

The question made Fiona feel nervous. She could feel her pulse throbbing in her head. Clare had her hands on her hips and was giving her a look.

"Talk about what?" Fiona asked innocently. She didn't want to talk about anything.

"What you said last night. It sounded like you had some insecurity issues."

Fiona felt her cheeks redden. That was rich coming from Clare. The problem with her best friend was she loved to analyse every drunken phrase like an English teacher deconstructing a poem.

"I was just drunk, Clare."

"You said Andrew was better than you. He isn't better. I mean, he's a great person, but so are you."

Fiona knew she wasn't a great person, but she could live with that.

"He *is* better," she said. "But that doesn't mean I'm insecure."

"Doesn't it?"

"Can we not talk about this now?"

"The thing is...you don't want to talk about anything now."

Clare was right about that. The sun was blazing, and talking and walking were starting to feel like a real effort.

"I don't mean you don't want to talk now," Clare said. "*Now* now. I mean recently it feels like you don't want to talk about *anything*."

"That's not true."

"That's what it feels like. You don't want to talk about Andrew, you don't want to talk about the wedding...sometimes it feels like you don't want to talk to *me*."

Fiona could see there were two ways to go. Either she could deny it all or she could apologise. The latter would probably wrap up the conversation quicker and make Clare feel good.

"I'm sorry," she said. "I just didn't want to think about it for a while."

"But why not?"

Oh, for God's sake.

"I mean, why wouldn't you want to talk about your own wedding? Aren't you excited?"

"Yeah...I just...I don't know..."

Clare's face softened. "Look, I want to make sure you're happy. That's all. I worry about you."

Fiona didn't reply and they walked for a while in silence. She could sense Clare's thoughts buzzing around her head like a bee trying to break through a patio door. *Bam, bam, bam.* She looked out at the horizon. A white speedboat was marking its trajectory across the deep blue sea with a trail of white foam. She wished she was on it. She didn't care where it was going. As long as it wasn't home. Or back to the villa. Mainland Spain didn't sound too bad. Barcelona did have a certain ring to it.

She breathed out. Her mother had had melancholy moments and Fiona had sworn to herself she'd never be so miserable, or so passive. If you wanted magic in your life, then you had to make it happen. She thought about the email she'd received last night. Its timing had been pretty magic. The question was whether she was going to take advantage of what it offered now or save it for when she really needed to escape.

"We'll have to have another hen party when we get back," Clare said. "You deserve one."

Fiona couldn't think of anything she wanted less right now.

"Why do I deserve one?" she asked.

"For putting up with this one, of course."

Fiona smiled. She needed to put Clare at ease. What a waste of a holiday to spend it worrying. Another stone slid up her flip-flop and she yelped. She retrieved it and flung it over the side of the path, where it pinged off a few rocks before settling in a patch of sand somewhere below.

"This better be an amazing beach. I'm talking like one of the top beaches in the world! If it's not, I'm…"

What was she going to do? Have a cry? Call Andrew to complain? She'd promised herself she wasn't going to give him any headaches while she was in Mallorca. It wasn't like he'd rung up to complain about the weather in England. He'd sent a few sweet messages in the evenings, and she'd done her best to limit her texts to words and not envy-inducing photos of palm trees and juicy cocktails. There was no need to rub it in.

"What?" Clare grinned. "What are you going to do if it's not the best beach in the whole wide world?"

"I'm going to ask the channel to pay for a cruise to the Bahamas, that's what!"

"Can I come?"

The thought of being stuck on a cruise with Clare interrogating her made Fiona feel trapped.

"No, I'm going on my own. You hens are all a headache."

"Thanks a lot!" Clare said, clearly offended. "You're not that easy yourself."

Why couldn't Fiona just have said yes? It wasn't as if it was going to happen.

"I'm joking, it's my hangover talking."

Clare didn't reply.

"Of course you can come, Clare. I was joking."

It was no use. She'd hurt Clare's feelings. Clare moved ahead of her, quietly seething. Fiona inhaled deeply and thought how wonderful it would be to get away from the hens and head off on a new voyage where she could pretend to be someone else. A young divorcée, perhaps, hoping to start over. She envisioned herself lying on deck beside a glittering pool, blue ocean as far as the eye could see. Free drinks being delivered by a Federico look-alike.

The image cleared as the path wound up over a boulder and she had to pay extra special attention to her footing. Would a top ten beach be so difficult to access? She very much doubted it.

THIRTY-FOUR

Day 4
SAM

Sam climbed up the rocky boulder and paused to survey the spectacular panorama. In the distance, Palma Bay was swathed in streaky cotton wool clouds, the heat haze blurring the edges of buildings so that it looked like an old postcard which had faded in the sun. It was a different story where they were. Above her the sky was a glorious blue, the sun a flame of gold dancing across the sea.

A warm breeze tickled the hairs on her arms. She breathed in the fresh air, with its hints of pine and rosemary. The thought tugged at her heart that she wished she was here with Chris. The last time they'd been together she'd shouted at him so unfairly.

"If I miss that plane, you're driving me to Mallorca!"

Every inch of her rigid posture had blamed him for the delay. He'd misplaced the car keys. Big deal. It was something she could easily have done, and had done plenty of times only the previous week. They'd argued more in the last six months than they had in six years together, but only now did she feel the repercussions of all those little arguments. They rattled through her and made her feel hollow.

When had she stopped being so laid-back? They'd always been the easy-going couple, taking each other's less appealing idiosyncrasies in their stride. Life was too short to care what end of the toothpaste was squeezed or

258

how the washing was pegged out on the line. It was just great that teeth had been brushed and there were clean clothes. They had always told themselves that they would be chilled parents, they wouldn't try to be perfect. Parenting seemed such a competition, fought out each day with passive aggressive posts on social media. But they wouldn't get involved in any of that, they'd said. Bottle or breastfeed? They'd see how it went. They weren't going to follow a rule book. They would go with the flow. Whatever suited their lives. They wouldn't forget themselves and make every waking moment about the baby.

Sam had forgotten about all those conversations when they were cuddled up in bed, imagining what it would be like to be responsible for another human being. In her desperation to be the best mum, she had become the mum she had wanted to avoid being. She would store this thought to share with Chris. It was a chance to grow.

Fiona and Clare were following the path around and would disappear shortly. Sam hung back, welcoming a moment of quiet. She loved her old friends, but being with them had reminded her why they didn't meet up as often as they used to. When she was with them, she found herself regressing to her old teenage self, being louder, more obnoxious, chasing the banter, drinking more, trying to prove herself. It was fine at first, but after a few days, she was feeling tired of herself. With other friends, she didn't feel like she had to prove how much fun she was. With Chris, she could just be herself, which was a lot quieter and more thoughtful than Fiona and Clare could imagine.

Chris knew Sam's face when she was pretending. It was one of her earliest memories of being with him. They'd been at a party and someone had been talking about Ewan McGregor. She knew it was terrible, but she didn't know who he was. He was as famous as Brad Pitt and George Clooney, she was sure of it. But for half an hour she had nodded and laughed and pretended she knew, and inside her head a faceless man had jumped up and down and gone, "Come on, it's me!"

The circle had broken up, the girls at her side turning to discuss another topic. Chris had stepped forward with an enigmatic smile on his face. He'd held up his phone, and a familiar handsome face had smiled charmingly back at her. Of course, Ewan McGregor, how could she have forgotten?

She'd given him a quizzical look. "Um, yes? I know who Ewan McGregor is."

"Oh." He'd put his phone away. "I just thought you'd…"

She'd grabbed his wrist, leant in close. "No. You're right. I went completely blank."

Honesty from the very beginning. They could read each other. They shared the same sense of humour. Sam didn't want them to become another tired and stressed couple forgetting why they had fallen in love in the first place. Yes, George was full on, especially as he was a terrible sleeper. But some people had five kids and still managed to find time for each other. Not that she knew anyone with five children. She was in the minority with one. Perhaps Fiona and Andrew were going to change that.

She had deliberated long and hard whether to tell Fiona her suspicions about the ring and had decided to keep silent. It was possible that Andrew was really hard up and planned to replace it later. Perhaps Fiona knew but hadn't wanted to lose face. She wasn't someone who liked to admit to shortcomings, and donning a fake ring wouldn't be something she'd want to broadcast. If that was the case, Sam had no intention of embarrassing her. On the other hand, if Fiona didn't know then Sam wasn't going to ruin things for the couple by pulling her to one side and telling her. Ostentatious jewellery wasn't what made a successful marriage, after all.

Sam breathed out and pushed away the jabbering thoughts. She would call Chris later. It would be good to hear his voice. She would tell him how she was feeling, how she thought it was time they stopped arguing over silly little things. She wouldn't let the distance between them grow until it was too late to fix it.

THIRTY-FIVE

Day 4
KATE

"Oh, it's beautiful!"

From the path, Kate could see miles of rugged coastline, one rocky bay after another. The rough surface hadn't put off the sunbathers. She could see them far below, stretched out on brightly coloured towels on flatter areas of stone and pockets of sand, roasting in the sunshine, completely naked. She and the others had been walking for a good ten minutes but they were still high above the water. She hadn't dared look back to see how the hens were getting on. Sensing their anger, she preferred to focus on the positive faces of the volunteers who were chatting cheerfully in Spanish.

Perhaps she was being paranoid. The last time she had glanced back, Sam had been admiring the view from on top of a rock, and Fiona and Clare had seemed to be conversing happily enough. Mel and Jem had been gazing out at the dazzling white yachts sailing across the two tone water. Of the hens, only Chi had looked a bit defeated, taking a break under the shade of a lone pine tree. She had wiped at her face, and for a moment Kate had worried she was crying, but no, she was sure it was just sweat glistening on Chi's cheeks.

Ricardo hadn't looked very perky either. Instead of paying attention to the scenery, he'd had his eyes on the floor and was closing the gap between them.

"I've been coming here since I was a kid," Gabriel told her.

"You poor thing."

He smiled. "I hate seeing it ruined."

"Is it that bad? It looks completely unspoilt from up here."

"You'll see. Josep said the southern wind has brought in lots of rubbish from the coasts of North Africa...rubbish that was probably dumped in rivers close to the sea. They're calling it a *sopa de plásticos*..."

"Plastic soup?"

"Yeah, the currents grind the plastic down into tiny little pieces. I went to a beach recently in the south and the sand had so many bright colours in it because it was full of plastic. We need some kind of filter..." He trailed off with a sigh of resignation. "Anyway, we're going to pick up a lot of the bigger stuff now."

"All together I'm sure we can shift it."

He raised his eyebrows and gave her an admiring look. "You know, I didn't think you'd come. I didn't think this was the kind of thing a British hen party would do."

"I like to surprise."

"Surprise? You mean they don't know?"

Her guilty grimace made him laugh.

"Are they going to be really angry?"

"It's a television show, viewers like a bit of drama."

"Not this kind of drama, Kate," shouted a voice from behind her. It was Ricardo. He'd caught up with her and Gabriel, leaving Mel and Jem trailing behind. His neckline was dark with sweat, his face red and his thick hair was plastered to his forehead. His eyes glinted angrily. She had felt his disapproval over the last few days, but despite the particularly tense moment last night, they had managed to avoid any serious confrontation.

"You worry too much, Ricardo."

It was a flippant thing to say and she wasn't sure why she said it. Probably because she was trying to impress Gabriel with her relaxed and rebellious approach to her job.

"Do you know how much this camera weighs?"

It was his job, wasn't it? If he didn't want to carry heavy things he should have chosen a different career.

"See it as a good workout, a chance to sweat out the beers," she said, pointedly.

She might not be following the schedule but at least she was maintaining a professional attitude. She'd caught him a few times having a cheeky beer in their breaks.

"Do you want to carry it half way?" he said. "I don't want you to miss out on the chance of a good workout too."

Was he implying she was fat?

"Look, I didn't realise it was so far," Kate conceded. "It can't be much further."

"It's about ten more minutes," Gabriel said, sounding sympathetic.

The other cameraman met them as the path weaved around the corner, his face also set in a grim expression. He and Ricardo spoke in Spanish after that. Kate didn't need to understand the words to know they were bitching about the job.

"I'm sorry, I should have told you about the walk," Gabriel said.

She shrugged. "I would have come anyway."

"Your camera guy looks furious."

"It's his default face. He'll be okay."

But a moment later Ricardo put his hand on her back and steered her off the path. Gabriel went to follow, but Ricardo said something to make him change his mind.

"I need to talk about what's happening," he said, gruffly.

"What's the problem?"

He rested his camera on the dusty ground and wiped his forehead with the collar of his T-shirt.

"What are you doing, Kate?"

"I'm taking them to a beach."

"A beach *clean-up*," Ricardo said. "That's why the local news is here. We are here to pick up a load of rubbish from the beach, isn't that right?"

"So what if we are? Is it so bad? They'll still get a suntan, they'll still be able to swim in the sea. The only difference from a normal day out is they'll feel good about themselves at the end of it."

"No, they won't. You can't speak for them. The only person who'll feel good is you. Everyone else will feel like they've been robbed of their prize holiday."

"But this is so much better for them. This experience could not only change their way of thinking but a whole audience of people, too. Isn't that more important? Doesn't it make the job feel more meaningful? Aren't you sick of filming the same old vacuous nonsense?"

Kate didn't think it was possible for Ricardo's face to get any redder.

"It doesn't matter what I think about it, this is not the show!" he cried, shaking his free hand at her.

"Maybe the show needs changing."

"Who do you think you are? The replacement director of another replacement director, that's who. They've trusted you to do a job here and you've gone crazy! Do you understand what you're doing?"

The fire in his eyes was intimidating. She looked away, her heart pounding. Ricardo lowered his voice when he spoke next.

"Look, if you want to lose your job and get blacklisted, that's fine with me, but don't bring me down with you. This is not the brief and you know it. Who do you think you are? Michael Moore? You're a nobody! This isn't going to end well for you."

They were no longer alone. Jem was hovering nearby. Gabriel too had stopped a little way ahead and was standing by the stony faced local cameraman, looking apprehensive.

"We'll do it my way today," Kate said, "then tomorrow we can get back to doing pretty shots with pretty cocktails."

Ricardo shook his head. "It's too late. This isn't going to work. They're going to be furious. We've got to make the most of today while we still can, while the sun is still shining."

"Are you coming?" Gabriel called.

Ricardo snapped.

"No, I'm not fucking coming!"

Despite the argument, Kate hadn't considered he might not come. Now the fear rose up her throat.

"Please, Ricardo!"

"It's really not much further," Gabriel said.

Ricardo glared at him. "I don't know your part in this but can you stay out of it, okay?"

Gabriel lifted his hand in peace. "I'm going on ahead. I need to catch up with Josep."

Kate looked back at Ricardo. "You have to come with us. It's your job."

"No, it's not. I don't know what this is."

"What's going on, guys?" Mel asked. "If we stop, I'm going to lose momentum."

"We're going back," Ricardo said.

Mel's face fell. "Seriously?"

"No, you can't go!" Kate cried.

She was not going to lose control of the team. They had to come. Up until now she had failed to make an impact. This was going to be the game changer. The viewers would see a stunning landscape, and then the awful contrast with the rubbish. Secretly she was hoping it would be dramatic. A pile up of refuse so high it would render them all speechless. It was a hypocritical thought, she realised that, but if that was what it took to give a really strong message, then so be it. She had been kicking herself that she hadn't asked the hens to dress down, but actually them being all dressed up was strengthening the other message: that this problem belonged to everyone and not just a bunch of dreadlocked environmentalists posting scary statistics online.

"We can't be that far," Jem said.

Ricardo shook his head, a look of disgust on his face.

"I'm going back. That's my final decision."

"Ricardo, please…we can make this work!" Kate begged, feeling suddenly desperate. Without him, they had nothing. He ignored her. Mel tipped her head back and silently screamed.

"Shall I come with you?" Jem called after him. It was a telling question. It dawned on Kate that she wasn't the only one on duty who was getting distracted by a dose of romance. She'd had an inkling when she'd found Jem and Ricardo sitting on the bench last night, close enough to have been kissing.

"Jem, tell him to come back," Kate pleaded.

But it didn't look like Jem had all that much influence over the cameraman either. Ricardo hadn't even acknowledged her question. He just kept walking.

"Now what are we supposed to do?" Mel muttered to no one in particular. The other cameraman had gone on ahead, annoyed that he didn't have any choice in the matter.

"I can't believe this," Kate said, shaking her head. "I'm going to ring someone about this."

Ring whom? To tell them what? That her cameraman had bailed out on her because she wasn't following the schedule? Why was she not following it? Oh, because she didn't actually want to be directing *The Hen Party*. She wanted to be directing her own personal project called *Plastic People*, but since she couldn't get any support for it, she was hijacking this show instead.

Fiona and Clare turned up, breathing heavily.

"Where's Ricardo going in such a huff?" Fiona asked. "Is he alright?"

Like she cared what was wrong with him. The only thing concerning her right now was that the camera she wanted filming her was going off in the wrong direction.

Kate forced a smile. "He's fine. We've got..." She didn't know the name of the other cameraman. She waved in his direction, "...our replacement."

268

There. She would ask him to film for them. This experience wouldn't go undocumented.

Fiona had her hands on her hips and was looking past Kate.

"Why is *he* here?"

Kate felt her pulse racing again. "Who?"

She knew exactly whom Fiona was talking about.

"The guy who was throwing beer on the plane."

"He was not throwing beer on the plane! They were throwing beer at him," Kate snapped before she could stop herself.

Everyone gawped at her. She should have controlled herself, but Ricardo's abandonment of the project had left her on edge. She still had time to make things work. Gabriel could be the location manager. Was that feasible? Wouldn't they ask her why she hadn't introduced him earlier?

"He's the location manager."

"Then why didn't you introduce him before?"

"He was afraid you'd throw beer at him if he got too close."

Fiona looked unconvinced. "Seriously? I wish someone would throw beer at me. There'd better be a bloody good beach bar down there."

Clare's face lit up. "Is it like a cave bar? I think I read about a cave bar once, but I can't remember where it was."

Kate's tongue felt heavy in her mouth. Beads of sweat trickled down her back. She had a flask of water in her rucksack. If she dug deep enough she might even find a biscuit, the type that comes free with a cup of coffee. It hardly amounted to a picnic. She hadn't exactly come thinking of having a fun day out. That was a big mistake. Perhaps she should abort the plan now. Admit her mistake. Take the hens to a beach club and drown them in margaritas.

"Come on," she said, turning abruptly. "We're nearly there."

No. It was her duty to show them the consequences of society's greed and thoughtlessness so they could be the change the world needed so badly. It didn't matter if they liked her or not. It mattered that they gave a damn about their planet.

THIRTY-SIX

"So Jem and the cameraman have run away together," Gabriel said, rubbing his chin. "Any other clues, Detective?"

Kate frowned. "Well, I think it's also safe to say wherever Jem is, Fiona isn't."

"Why?"

"According to Clare..."

"Which one's Clare? I was distracted when you were telling me about them...you were naked, remember?"

Kate blushed and rolled her eyes. "The one who threw up cycling."

He laughed.

"It's not funny. She really hates me. They all do."

Gabriel shot her a sympathetic smile. "So who would Fiona be with then?"

"I'm not sure...there was so much tension on that beach. That's why I went into the sea."

Kate recalled the last time she'd seen the hens at the beach clean-up. None of them had leapt into action, although there had been mounds of rubbish everywhere. Not just bottle caps and straws, but also huge lumps of broken toys and sun beds half buried in the sand. The other volunteers had responded enthusiastically, whipping on gardening gloves and distributing black bags. The hens had gathered in the middle of the action, the only people standing tall while everyone else bent over the sand and rocks, fishing out the packages and Styrofoam, comparing their findings in a jolly stream of Spanish.

"I should've got out of the water," Kate said, thinking back to her complete lack of interest in what had been going on. It had been so unprofessional. She'd been in her own little bubble. "I just didn't want to know. If anything has happened to them, I'm going to be in so much trouble."

Gabriel put his hand on her shoulder. "They'll be okay, trust me."

"How do you know? They were so angry with me."

"Not just you. I told you what the witnesses said."

"True...but I put them in that situation. They were exhausted and hungover and hungry."

At some point, Kate had looked up and seen Fiona marching off on her own. She'd thought: *Let her go, see how far she gets before she realises I don't care about her little tantrums.*

According to witnesses, Clare and Chi had argued after that. Clare had then abandoned the beach too, no doubt in pursuit of Fiona. It had been pretty clear from the beginning that Clare was the loyal best friend. Then there was Sam, the other childhood friend. Sam was more cool-headed than Clare. She was a mother, too, and possibly had more of sense of responsibility than the others.

"Sam," she said. "Surely she would know something."

"I can't remember who is who. Have you got photos of them?"

Kate nodded. "Yeah, tons."

"We're going to find them."

"We don't have a choice. The show requires a happy ending."

Gabriel's expression brightened. "Hey, don't any of them have Instagram accounts?"

"I don't know...I'm a shit director who didn't pay enough attention to them."

But she got out her phone anyway and started googling each of their names. There were a few people with the same names, but no clear matches.

"What about the cameraman? I'm guessing he's a visual guy."

"He wouldn't post something if he didn't want to be found."

"Some people can't resist."

"I'm following him as well," she said. "But I don't think..."

She stopped talking as Ricardo's latest pictures came up. She recognised the villa, absent of girls, the focus concentrating on a detail. A flower with a droplet of water on its petal. The texture of the wall. A gecko. But the last one he'd posted was a villa she didn't recognise. It showed a huge rectangular pool with beautiful grey flagstones around it. Two empty sun loungers positioned in one corner invited the viewer in. The Serra de Tramuntana mountain range was misty but visible in the distance. A vision of a luxury holiday. Was it a villa or a hotel?

"It's a photo of a pool," Kate said.

"Let's see." Gabriel took the phone and looked at the picture, recognition dawning. "It's a boutique hotel called Son Ametler."

She stared at him. "You know that from a photo of a pool?"

He gave her back the phone and reached for the GPS.

"No. He's hashtagged it."

Kate looked down at the picture. Of course he had. It was there, plain to see. She was a bad director, but clearly an even worse detective.

"It's thirty minutes from here," Gabriel said. "Shall we?"

He drew her hand away from her mouth as she was about to bite on a nail. She rolled her eyes, but secretly wondered at how familiar it felt to be with him.

"I suppose it's better than driving around at random...not that he's going to want to help me."

"I think he will, especially when he knows your boss is here."

"True."

Kate thought of Sharon Wingman back at the bar. She was probably checking her watch, calculating times as if finding the hens was a sure thing. Mallorca might be a small island, but if someone didn't want to be found, it was big enough to disappear.

THIRTY-SEVEN

Day 4
CLARE

As the hens made it down the last stretch of rocky path, which was less a path and more a test to see whether they shared the agility of a mountain goat, the reason Kate had brought them here became apparent. Clare's focus, which had been firmly on the ground just in front of her feet, landed on a bright pink plastic tampon applicator. With a gasp she stepped aside, her toe pinging against a bottle top which in turn hit a lone yellow flip-flop jammed into the sand. Clare looked up to take in the whole picture. The small bay they had been walking towards for nearly half an hour in thirty-six degree heat was littered with rubbish.

Her jaw dropped. "What the hell are we doing here? This beach looks like a landfill site!"

"Oh my fucking God," Fiona shouted from behind. "You must be joking if you think I'm staying here."

"Was it all washed up or left behind?" Clare called out. Could people really be this disgusting?

"Really? Is that your question?" Fiona asked. "My question is: how quickly can we get out of here?"

Clare gritted her teeth. Yes, that was her question. Why did Fiona have to decide which questions were valid and which weren't? Clare was still reeling from Fiona's mean comment about not inviting her on her Bahamas cruise. Never mind the cruise was only hypothetical. That wasn't the point. Hadn't Fiona seen how hard Clare had been trying to make things better? She was the one who'd bought novelty hen party pens. It might be a little detail, but the best parties were made up of lots of small but thoughtful touches.

Clare pushed on for a few more angry moments before turning around to check the others weren't going to suddenly leave her behind. Chi had slumped against a large rock where the volunteers were handing out black bags and gloves. She had barely said a word all morning; she hadn't been too forthcoming last night, either. Between Jem's bad attitude and Chi's half-hearted one, the evening had been an uphill climb. Still, that wasn't Clare's fault. She understood that Fiona would want to throw *them* overboard, but she couldn't put her in the same category.

Clare looked around for Kate. Why was she a director if she was always trying to get out of directing? She spotted Sam picking her way around the edge of the cove, her eyes scanning the floor, occasionally bending over to pick something up. Was she actually going to clean up?

"Sam, what are you doing?"

Sam looked over at her, frowning. "What did you say?"

"Are you actually picking stuff up?"

She held up something in her hand which Clare couldn't see clearly.

"I've just found a doll's head," she called. "It's like something out of a horror film!"

Clare rolled her eyes. Didn't it bother Sam she'd been brought here? She had always been one of those roll-up-your-sleeves-and-get-on-with-it types, but surely she wasn't just going to accept they'd been tricked into community service?

Clare's gaze moved towards the water's edge and landed on Kate. She was in the process of shimmying out of her dress while talking with Mr Plane Guy. The location manager, apparently, although Clare wasn't buying it. He'd acted like a total stranger in the airport. Why hadn't Kate introduced him before? And why had Kate forgotten all about the hens the moment she'd bumped into him this morning? Clare's eyes narrowed as she watched Kate posing in her red bikini. She *was* posing; definitely holding her stomach in. All the signs were there that Kate was into him. The way she was giving him her undivided attention, hanging on every word.

Kate suddenly glanced back, her eyes searching the hens out. When she saw them, she held up her thumb.

"We're cleaning up this beautiful beach so we can enjoy it," she called with that big smile of hers, which always seemed to come on at the most inappropriate times, as if she enjoyed annoying them all. "Isn't it dreadful what they've done to it? But it's going to feel so good cleaning it up. Thanks so much, girls, I knew you'd understand when you saw it."

Kate was mad, Clare decided. No one in their right mind would interpret any of their expressions as comprehension. Clare was currently trying very hard to murder the infuriating woman with a fierce glare in her direction. Sam's curiosity was the only positive face among them. Fiona was fuming. Chi looked like she was going to lie down on the floor and die.

It wasn't that Clare was completely insensitive to the evident environmental calamity. The place had real potential to be beautiful. It was a secluded rocky bay with a small area of golden sand. To one side, jutting out of the water was a natural stone arch, like something you'd buy in miniature to decorate a fish bowl. It was a romantic escape for couples who liked hiking. The water looked deliciously inviting. Then there was all the rubbish. Human rubbish. Obviously it was terrible and the lazy bastards who had disposed of all this stuff so irresponsibly deserved a massive fine.

"It's terrible, isn't it," Sam called over to her.

Plastic bottles and sweet packets and bottle tops were strewn like confetti. There was a fold up chair, battered and broken, and a black flipper lodged in the sand. Clare spotted a faded green lilo and an orange hula hoop, a child's tricycle and half a dozen aerosol cans. All of it was just sitting discarded across the intimate little beach. The bushes were peppered with packets and broken bits of yellowed Styrofoam.

"Terrible!" she called back, and thought about picking a few bits up herself, but her high wedges had made her back ache and she felt she needed to sit down first.

Were they really needed? The volunteers were equipped with gloves and bags, and right now they weren't exactly begging the hens to join in. Then again, it wouldn't hurt to pick up a few bits and bobs. It wasn't what she'd envisioned doing on a hen party, and certainly not what Fiona wanted to do. Right now, though, Clare didn't particularly feel like getting excited about what her best friend wanted. In fact, she would pick up a few bits just to annoy her.

"I'm not picking it up," Fiona snapped. "We didn't leave it here. The government needs to sort it out."

Clare ignored her and scanned a small area beyond her feet to see if there was anything clean that she wouldn't mind picking up with her bare hands.

"Have you seen my engagement ring? It's not an engagement ring for picking up rubbish!"

"You could take it off," Clare suggested to irritate her. "My pocket has a zip, I can keep it safe for you."

"I'm not taking it off to clean up some beach!"

"You don't have to shout at me. It's not my fault."

"I'm not shouting at you. I'm shouting at the situation."

"It feels like you're shouting at me."

"I'm tired and hungover."

"And that's my fault?"

"Clare, I said I was sorry!"

"Alright..."

She would forgive Fiona in a minute. She bent down to undo her buckles, thinking what a relief it would be to get out of her wedges.

"I'm sure it'll be alright if you keep the ring on," Chi said.

Clare turned to frown at her. Chi had lowered down to a squat and was resting her head in her hands now.

"Of course she's got to take it off," Clare said. It was annoying that even when she was angry with Fiona, she was thinking of her best interests. Wearing diamonds to pick up rubbish was completely stupid, and if Chi was a real friend and not just a workmate whom Fiona hung out with at lunch breaks, then she wouldn't have been so blasé about it.

"I can make my own decisions," Fiona cried, sounding, Clare thought, like a real diva. "Obviously I wouldn't wear this ring to pick up rubbish."

"I think it would be alright if you did," Chi said quietly.

"Chi? Are you feeling okay?" Clare thought she looked pale, which was quite something considering Chi was half Nigerian. She caught Fiona's eye and they frowned at each other, momentarily united. Clare forgave her for the Bahamas comment.

"Chi, shss, love," Sam called. "Best not to give out advice when you're still drunk, okay?"

"I know diamonds are tough, but I don't want to scratch the band," Fiona said.

"Exactly," Clare said.

Chi cleared her throat. "I hate to say this, but I think you could get another one quite easily from a shop we all know pretty well."

"Seriously, Chi, shut the fuck up!" Sam shouted.

Clare might have thought Chi was just acting weirdly if Sam hadn't shouted like that. It was totally out of character. Sam didn't shout at people. She teased them, laughed at them, argued with them. But Sam was staring at Chi with a fierce look in her eye like she was trying to tell her something. It definitely didn't feel right. Clare looked at her best friend. Fiona's face was bright red, but Clare wasn't sure if it was red with anger or embarrassment.

"Right, very funny, because my ring's from Accessorize," Fiona said with a fake laugh. "Ha-ha. Good one."

Clare felt a flicker of relief. There was no substance to Chi's words. Of course there wasn't.

"It's not a joke," Chi said.

"Chi," Sam warned. "That's enough."

"For God's sake, you're still drunk, aren't you? I forgot you turn into a psycho when you drink tequila," Fiona said, trying to smooth things over.

But Clare didn't think Chi invented stories when she was drunk. She suspected it was the other way around and Chi was more likely to tell the truth.

The confession came a moment later.

"It's £12.99 and yes, it is from Accessorize. I looked it up online. I'm so sorry."

A price and a shop name. It was so specific. They all turned to Fiona. Her mouth was frozen open. It was awful to watch her try to get the words out. She sounded like she was choking.

"What do you mean you looked it up?"

"I couldn't stop thinking about it."

"You're not making any sense and you know it," Fiona snapped. She looked like a cornered animal – there was anger in her eyes, but also fear.

Chi's head slumped and her shoulders shook. "I had to tell you, didn't I? How could I not tell you?"

Beyond them, Kate waved a butterfly net and called out above the sound of the waves, "Who else wants to dive for rubbish?"

As if they weren't dealing with enough of the stuff on shore.

THIRTY-EIGHT

Day 4
CHIOMA

Why couldn't she have kept her mouth shut? Why couldn't she have buried this secret alongside the other?

"Ignore her, Fiona," Sam said. "She's delirious."

Perhaps she was. Her head was swimming in the heat. She didn't feel good at all. She had felt awful last night, too. In the early hours of the morning she had leant over the toilet bowl, feeling her insides churn. It was the feeling of being sick but not being able to be sick. A voice told her she was pregnant. She'd felt too awful to care. A numbness had washed over her. She'd finally made herself throw up, her face crumpling at the pain of stinging acid reflux.

"You know what's wrong!" another voice had snapped at her. She'd been here before, standing over the toilet bowl with a twisted stomach. It wasn't a hangover. It wasn't *just* a hangover. Fully clothed, she'd collapsed on to her messy bed, oblivious to the bottle of sun cream and makeup bag jabbing into her back. She'd fallen into an uneasy sleep and had woken up feeling afraid.

"What if she's right?" Fiona said, her lip quivering. She held her ring hand against her stomach, her other hand covering it. "What if he doesn't love me?"

"Of course he loves you," Clare said.

It didn't look like Sam could bear to tell Fiona the truth. It was up to Chi.

"She's just winding you up," Sam said. "Aren't you, Chi?"

This was it. Her chance to laugh the accusation off.

"It's not very funny," Clare said.

Not it wasn't. It wasn't funny at all.

A middle-aged volunteer approached the rock Chi was leaning on and bent down to retrieve a broken bucket wedged down the side. She cast an eye over them, her forehead twitching with questions she didn't have the ability to formulate in English. Why were they standing around and not helping? Chi didn't think she was physically able to pick up rubbish. She felt nauseous. Any amount of bending over and she'd be throwing up again. She wanted to get far away from this beach full of tension and collapse somewhere cool and quiet.

"I can't pretend any more," she said, not daring to look at Fiona. How much longer would this be dragged out? Was the truth worth this much discomfort?

"Just stop it!"

Clare again. She was losing her mind with this turn of events – Clare who craved the perfect hen party more than Fiona did. She was looking at Chi as if she wanted to extinguish her like a mosquito. Then there was Sam, Fiona's other childhood friend, who was happy to deny the truth for an easy life. They thought they were such wonderful friends.

"That's it! You're not staying in the villa," Clare snapped. "You can go find a hotel because you're no friend of Fiona's, I'll tell you that for free."

The confession was hopeless without Sam. Chi looked at her, imploring her to come clean.

"You know I'm telling the truth. *You* told me."

Sam gasped, horrified to be put on the spot. "I just said I thought it felt light."

She was backtracking now, but she'd been certain the other night.

"Which is why I looked into it…I had to be sure…Why would I joke about this stuff?"

Fiona was standing there, trembling. It dawned on Chi that their friendship wouldn't survive this day, and that she had known this for some time now.

Clare suddenly picked up a small stone and lobbed it at Chi. It missed and bounced off the rock and hit a volunteer who turned and shouted something at them. Chi straightened up in surprise.

"You're going to stone me now for telling the truth?"

Clare would refuse to believe the ring were fake even if a jeweller told her, so eager was she for the week to go smoothly.

"I don't need this shit!" Fiona exploded. She turned away from them, her fishtail plait swishing around her neck. As quickly as her slippery flip-flops could take her, she made her way back up the rocky path.

"Fiona, wait!" Clare called after her.

Sam threw Chi a dirty look. Chi looked down at the floor, her heart drumming against her chest.

"How could you land that on her like that?"

Soon it would all be over and Chi wouldn't have to see any of these girls again. For now, the guilt clawed at her.

"Fiona!" Clare called. "I'm going after her. She's going to be so upset."

She staggered back up the beach, her footing clumsy in her high wedges.

"Chi, why?" Sam snarled. "What did it matter if it was real or not? It's just a piece of fucking jewellery!"

"Because it's the truth. The truth matters."

"But...but...maybe you should have spoken to Andrew and listened to his side of the story."

They both turned to look up when they heard the sound of Clare losing her footing and a few loose stones falling. She had stopped where the path had begun to steepen.

"Fiona!" She was out of breath, sunburnt and, from the tone of her voice, close to tears. "Wait for me!"

If Fiona was hurting badly, maybe she needed to be alone. Clare would only make it worse.

"Let her go, Clare," Chi called. "She probably needs some time alone."

That was the wrong thing to say. Whatever energy Clare had used on the walk down to the beach returned with force. She spun around and charged at Chi. Chi just managed to stand up properly as Clare threw herself at her, thumping her fists clumsily against her, hitting her shoulder, her hip, her stomach.

"You bitch!" she shouted, over and over.

Chi lifted her arms in self-defence, blocking the poorly placed punches. There was a part of her which felt pleased to be hit. Perhaps if she really got hurt, she'd be forgiven.

"Stop it, Clare!" Sam cried. "Get off her! Stop it!"

Chi wasn't going to hit Clare back. She'd be her punch bag if that's what she wanted. She winced as Clare's knuckle collided with her breast and tried to dodge the next blow which struck her in her stomach.

"Clare! Leave her!"

It was Mel's voice. Between them, Sam and the sound recordist pulled Clare off Chi. Clare stood there panting, her face and neck blotchy and red. Chi straightened her T-shirt and resisted rubbing the tender spots where she knew bruises were going to appear.

"I'm not sorry!" Clare shouted at her, then burst into tears.

"Look, it might be true, Clare," Sam conceded, reluctantly.

"So what?" Clare sobbed. "Does it matter?"

"Hey, whatever it is, it's going to be alright," Mel said, her voice soft and sympathetic. She rubbed Clare's arm, but Clare shrugged her hand away and stalked back up the path. They let her go. This time she didn't stop.

"I'm going after her," Mel said after a few moments. "She seems really upset."

Sam kicked a stone, shaking her head like she couldn't believe what had just happened.

"This is the worst possible outcome," she muttered to Chi. "I should never have said anything to you."

The volunteers murmured around them, the waves washed back and forth. Chi held the words in until the silence grew too heavy between them.

"She needs to know who she's marrying."

"It's just a ring!" Sam said.

"It's not just the ring…"

She looked at Sam meaningfully. Sam looked back at her and understood nothing. Chi took a deep breath, wishing wholeheartedly that she had never opened her mouth in the first place.

"The one night stand I told you about…"

But she couldn't bring herself to say his name. Sam's eyes narrowed as she began to comprehend the full extent of Chi's revelation. The disgust on her face was worse than any of Clare's punches.

"How could you?" she hissed. "It was Andrew, wasn't it? You slept with Andrew."

THIRTY-NINE

Day 4
JEM

Jem almost didn't go after Ricardo. He'd given her no clear signal that he wanted her to follow and she had wondered if he would think her a fool for chasing him. Torn, she'd watched him striding up the path, the muscles in his back straining under the weight of the camera, his T-shirt patchy with sweat. Mel had turned back too and was trailing with the tripod, her head lowered.

A niggling voice reminded Jem that she was on a hen party, not a holiday, and she couldn't just abandon everyone. She twisted on the spot, not committing to turning back or moving forward. The thought of joining the hens and missing out on seeing Ricardo made her feel weak with disappointment. There didn't seem much point going to the beach without him. He was the only one who ever seemed pleased to see her. Everyone else tolerated her. They had just this moment walked past her and not one of them had uttered a word.

She couldn't blame them. She shouldn't have taken it all so seriously last night. They were only games, but she'd acted as if they were battles to be won and had made things awkward for Fiona. She would have apologised this morning but her future sister-in-law had not moved away from Clare for a moment. Jem didn't know if she was making it up, but she was sure Fiona was refusing to look at her. Even if she did get Fiona alone, would a verbal apology really cut it? At the very least, she needed to buy Fiona some flowers…

Jem looked back down the path towards the sea. The last volunteer had disappeared around the rocky corner. The pull to do her duty and follow the hens eased a little. Now to ascertain how annoyed Ricardo might be. Was he annoyed with everyone or just Kate?

He had been in a bad mood by the end of last night. It had been a messy evening full of bickering and suspiciously long toilet breaks, where endless running taps had tried to drown out muffled sobs. Kate had interrupted the hens constantly, requesting them to start again as if they had started somewhere in the first place. Then Chi had got a headache and had insisted on going to bed, but not before the hens had dedicated ages persuading her to change her mind. At a quarter to one in the morning Kate had declared it a wrap for the day, and Ricardo had given up, slipping out into the garden to smoke a cigarette.

Jem had come out to find him and he'd eyed her warily as she approached.

"You didn't make that easy, did you," he'd said.

She'd felt so stupid.

"I know, I'm sorry."

She hadn't been able to read his face.

"I shouldn't have come."

"I think Fiona would agree with that."

He'd exhaled, cigarette smoke spiralling into the night sky. The moon had glowed through the jasmine branches, and beyond, the pool shimmered. It had been another warm, balmy evening; the only cool draught had been between them.

"I'll say sorry," she'd said. "I'll try harder."

"If you genuinely forgive her for whatever she was like to your brother all those years ago, you won't have to *try*."

She'd raised her eyebrows. "That sounds very wise."

His face had softened and he'd reached out and put an arm around her. She'd moved along the bench, snuggling up against him, her heart swelling with relief. How could an arm around your shoulders feel more intimate than a kiss?

Jem pushed her sunglasses up on to her head and blinked in the sunshine. Mel had stopped in her tracks and was leaning over the tripod, taking a breather. Ricardo had disappeared around a sandy boulder. Soon she would lose track of him. If she left it any later he would reach the car first and drive away, and that would be the end of that.

Jem subscribed to the belief you shouldn't abandon your girlfriends for a guy. But these girls were hardly her friends. She had only got to know them these past few days. Except for Fiona. But hadn't Ricardo said himself that he was sure Fiona wished Jem hadn't come? On the other hand, the chemistry she had with Ricardo was the most exciting thing to have happened to her in years. It had kept her awake last night, feeding her daydreams. She'd tried to persuade him to stay but he'd insisted on heading back to the apartment he shared with Mel, joking that he'd already put his reputation as a professional in grave danger by kissing her in the first place.

Mel looked up when she heard the sound of feet crunching against the gritty sand. She didn't look surprised to see Jem and shot her a tired smile.

"He's a speedy bastard," she said.

Jem smiled, feeling self-conscious. She didn't know what the quiet sound recordist thought about what was going on between her and the cameraman. Right now, Mel didn't look like she was in the greatest of moods.

"So is everyone coming back?"

"I don't think so," Jem said.

"It's worth the walk then?"

"I didn't get that far." Jem nodded at the tripod. "Do you want me to help?"

Mel looked like she was thinking about it and then she passed the tripod over. "If you think you can manage."

It was heavier than Jem had expected but she tried not to let on.

"I don't really need to go," Mel said. "And to be honest, I don't feel like hearing him rant. He's pretty pissed off."

"Yeah, I know."

"With good reason."

"Yeah...it's quite a walk."

Mel breathed out. "Oh, it's not just the walk."

"Kate?" Jem offered.

Mel didn't need to answer that one – the expression on her face gave her away. Jem shot her a grim smile.

"I'm guessing you won't be working together again."

"No, because Kate won't be getting another job after this one."

"That bad?"

"Not on this show, anyway. Although don't say I said anything."

"Of course I won't."

Mel nodded. She pushed her escaped fringe around her ear. "Hey, I think I might join the girls. I take it you don't mind going after Ricardo alone?"

Jem blushed. "No."

"Good luck...he's got a terrible temper."

"Thanks..." Jem was feeling more confident that she could soothe him. "You heard the beach is supposed to be full of rubbish, right?"

Mel rolled her eyes. "You didn't think Kate was going to do something normal, did you?"

"Poor Fiona...not that I've been very nice."

She expected Mel to agree with her.

"Personally I feel sorry for Clare," she said.

"Clare? Why?"

Jem didn't have much time for Fiona's biggest fan, but between Clare's sunburn and the cycle ride, she could understand why someone would pity her.

"She tries to be so enthusiastic and I don't think Fiona really appreciates her."

"Maybe she tries too hard."

Jem was growing concerned about Ricardo's absence. He was no longer in sight and she felt a pressing need to catch up with him. She was sure there had been only one path, but it hadn't been a very obvious one.

Mel sensed she was distracted. "You'd better go."

"Sorry...I don't want to get lost..."

"I don't know what we're going to do about this show."

Jem mustered a sympathetic smile. She couldn't say she had ever been looking forward to seeing herself on television. If someone told her it was to be cancelled, she would have felt nothing but relief.

"We've got three more days, right?"

"Things are falling apart."

"It'll be alright. Everything will get back on track, you'll see," Jem said, not believing it for a second. Her rush of optimism was down to the thought of soon being with Ricardo.

"If you don't kidnap the cameraman," Mel said, her nostrils flaring.

Jem laughed, her cheeks reddening. "I don't know what you mean."

She could feel Mel's eyes on her as she raced up the path. It didn't stop her breaking into a run, the tripod banging against her legs. She didn't care if Mel thought her desperate. It would be terrible if she missed Ricardo. But would he drive off knowing Mel had been following him? Had he known Mel had been following?

She felt a burst of pleasure when she caught sight of him. He was taking on the hundred odd steps up to the residential road.

"Hey you!" she called.

He didn't look up at first, so lost was he in his thoughts. When he heard her, his face cleared of the clouds. He turned and the smile he gave made her heart leap for joy. He lowered his camera, sat down on the step and waited for her to catch up. It took her another few minutes to get to him. She stuck her tongue out as she climbed the last couple of stairs.

"I left my hat in the car!"

His face fell. "Seriously?"

She laughed. "No, of course not."

"What are you doing here then?"

"Take me with you."

"But I don't know where I'm going yet."

She shrugged, her smile coquettish. "I don't mind where. It's the company I'm interested in."

He grinned. "Come on then, let's get out of here."

FORTY

Kate had told Gabriel everything she knew, which amounted to a rather chaotic description of a bunch of women who had been at odds with her grand masterplan of upping the tone of the show.

The conclusion she'd initially drawn when she'd emerged from the sea to discover they'd all abandoned the mission had been simplistic. Since they hadn't thought the beach clean was fun, they had made a unilateral decision to bail out. If there had been alcohol they might have stayed a few extra minutes, but since all the beer bottles and cans were either empty, corroded or both, they had seen absolutely no sense in picking them up.

Kate had lost her temper big time. The memory of what she'd done made her blush. She'd acted like a petulant child.

"What is it?" Gabriel said.

"I did something I'm not proud of…"

"You were just trying to make a show with more significance."

"I'm not talking about that," she said, feeling embarrassed.

"What is it?"

"I dumped a pile of rubbish in their pool."

He looked confused. "When?"

"After the clean-up I went to the villa to see if they were there."

"Just before you met me?"

"Yeah, I took a detour there before I went to my apartment to change."

"But they weren't there?"

"No…and I felt so angry that they couldn't have spared five minutes to help that I got a bin and tipped it into the pool."

He gasped. "Kate, that's terrible!"

"I know. I just assumed they were partying. I didn't believe it was more critical than that."

She hadn't taken the volunteers' report very seriously. The middle-aged woman in the strapless pink swimming costume had looked like a gossip. All that talk about the fighting between the fat one and the black one had seemed like an exaggeration. Kate might have been in the sea, but she felt pretty sure a punch up would have caught her eye. Her interpretation of their disappearance was clear: they were selfish and insensitive. In retrospect, she had been a little short sighted in more ways than one. An eye test would be on the cards once she sorted this mess out.

"I regretted it as soon as I'd done it," Kate said, running an anxious hand through her dishevelled bob. "I acted insane…no wonder…well…"

No wonder Matt had backed away all those years ago. He'd obviously seen this impulsiveness in her. It was her way or no way. Gabriel didn't ask her what was of no wonder. Maybe he didn't recognise the expression.

"I understand why you did it," he said.

"Yeah, to teach them a lesson. It was stupid...all it would have achieved would have been them hating me more..."

"Right. Because they never saw it," he said, nodding.

"Exactly. All I've done is make work for some poor cleaner."

Kate turned to look out at the fields of almond trees whizzing by beside farmhouses with sunken roofs and broken windmills. It was so beautiful and yet she couldn't enjoy it. The seriousness of the situation kept coming at her in waves.

"We're going to find them," Gabriel said.

She was biting her fingernails again.

"Finding them is worrying me as much as not finding them."

"Don't say that. You definitely want to find them."

True. But what would they tell Sharon? Was there any way Kate could convince her to get back on a plane without talking to the hens? Could she pay them to smile and wave and feed the channel a story in which she didn't come across as completely inept?

They turned off up a narrow country road. The wheels crunched over the gravel. Up ahead she saw another wooden sign for the boutique hotel with a bunch of grapes carved into the wood.

"This is it," Gabriel said.

They slowed down as they turned into an unpaved car park. The hotel was a converted farmhouse with a gorgeous stone facade partly concealed by creepers. The uneven paved entrance was decorated with terracotta pots full of pink and purple petunias in full bloom. A young, fresh-faced couple were putting helmets on ready for a day out on their bikes.

Kate recognised Ricardo's rental at once, and her heart leapt into her throat.

"Oh God. That's his jeep."

She felt a stirring blend of nerves, anger and relief. She wanted to have a go at him and simultaneously felt fearful that he was going to be the one having a go at her. He had every right, too. They might have made a good team if she'd let him in. She'd scrolled through his Instagram account on the way over. He was quite the environmentalist himself, judging by his #naturelover posts.

Kate didn't wait for Gabriel to park before jumping out and heading for the red double doors. The cyclists greeted her with curious smiles and she caught a few words in German. She stepped inside the cool reception area of red flagstones. A fan hummed as it spun from the thick oak beams above. There didn't seem to be anyone about. There was a bell on the counter, but she didn't ring it. Instead she crossed the room towards the glass double doors opposite, which were ajar.

She stepped outside into a beautiful manicured garden protected by tall, dark cypress trees. There was a stylish lounge area, tastefully furnished with white wicker chairs and distressed wooden tables. Candles sat in clear glass vases filled with sand and shells. Further on grey stone slabs provided a path down the gently sloping hill. She followed it past the pines and fragrant orange trees, and was rewarded with a view of the misty mountain peaks in the distance. She sensed the proximity of a pool and kept going.

At the end of the path, the photo she'd seen on

Instagram became a reality. The only difference was there were people in this version. There they both were: Jem sitting on the edge of the pool, Ricardo in the water playing with her feet. Like a couple on their honeymoon and not the deserters that they were.

Kate took a deep breath. She would not get angry. She needed to get everyone back on her side. If she didn't, she would be going home with her career in tatters.

Jem spotted her before Kate could think of anything clever to say. Her jaw dropped.

"Oh," she said, her hand covering her mouth. "We've been found."

Ricardo turned. The fight was in his eyes.

"How did you know we were here?"

Kate held up her phone. "Instagram."

His cheeks reddened. Jem let out a snort of laughter. "Really, Ricardo? Instagram?"

"Good detective work," he said with a shrug.

"Thanks."

There was no need to mention Gabriel right now.

"So?" she said. "Having a break, are we?"

"Yeah, pretty much," Ricardo said. He was no longer touching Jem's dainty feet. Instead, he slopped the water between the palms of his hands. Kate had expected a bit more of a reaction than this. He was supposed to leap out of the pool and say he'd had his fun and was ready to finish the job.

"Right," she said, "and how long are you going to be?"

He was under contract! He had to finish the job.

"I'm sorry, but it was ridiculous."

"What was? Walking ten minutes down to a beach?"

299

She heard the sarcastic edge in her voice and swallowed. She needed to be empathetic. It had been a long walk and his equipment had been heavy.

"You think that's all it was?"

"Okay, so it was more like twenty minutes."

"I'm not talking about the walk."

She knew that, but she still asked, "What then?"

"It's not a hen party. They're going to want a hen party, Kate. I don't know what the hell you're doing."

"It might not be an ordinary hen party," Kate countered. "But we've had lots of great drama, haven't we?"

Jem shook her head and muttered, "Wow" under her breath.

"Great drama?" Ricardo echoed incredulously. "Have you ever seen an episode of *The Hen Party*? Great drama in this show does not mean one injured stripper, some homemade games, clay fights and a day at a rubbish dump!"

"Sharon Wingman is here," Kate blurted out.

Ricardo's eyes widened and he glanced up towards the hotel. "Where?"

"Back in Palma. Well, Cala Major. I avoided meeting her at the villa."

Ricardo frowned. "She called me earlier but I couldn't hear her properly. I didn't realise she was here. What does she want? What have you told her?"

"Who's Sharon Wingman?" asked Jem.

"The boss," Kate said.

The revelation didn't elicit much reaction from the hen. Kate took a deep breath. What did Jem have to worry about anyway? She wasn't the one who had to face up to Sharon.

"So what did you say?" Ricardo asked.

"I said we were taking a much-needed break."

Ricardo pulled himself out of the pool, water streaming off his broad back, and stood up, squeezing at the side of his shorts.

"And what did she say?"

"She said we'd better get filming soon."

"I bet she did."

Was he going to make her beg?

"We need to get going."

Ricardo looked annoyed. "Fine."

"Do we have to?" Jem murmured, looking pained. They both ignored her. Ricardo was looking at Kate with a warning in his eye.

"I'm going to need more communication from you and we need to start making this look like a hen party."

She let out a weak laugh. "Yeah, well that's going to be a bit tricky."

"Only tricky if you keep trying to push your agenda."

"No. It's going to be tricky because we've only got one hen."

Jem's eyes darted up from the surface of the pool. She looked surprised.

"Yes, you," Kate said.

"What happened to everyone else?"

"I don't know," Kate replied. "I was hoping you'd help me find out."

Jem gawped at her. It was a look that made Kate's heart sink. Clearly while she'd been gallivanting with the cameraman, Jem had given little thought to the whereabouts of her fellow hens.

FORTY-ONE

Day 5
SAM

The woman from the airline finished tapping in the information on to her computer and looked up with a practised smile.

"Any suitcases to check in, madam?"

"No. I've only got this, actually," Sam said, holding up her small handbag. "This is a bit of an impulsive flight home."

The woman gave the bag a cursory nod. Sam felt a little put out by her lack of emotion. Clearly she'd been in her job too long. If Sam had been the air stewardess she would have wanted to hear the full story. She would have been intrigued to hear why this passenger in front of her had arrived in Mallorca with a suitcase and was now leaving with nothing more than her passport, wallet and phone.

"You can check in online next time," the woman said, handing her the boarding pass. "That way you don't have to queue."

Feeling less sure of herself with every passing minute, Sam headed towards the security check. She was trying hard not to think about the others, veering between feeling high on rebellion and fear that she was being selfish. She'd never done anything like this before. Quite possibly she would have worked off some steam if she had stayed at the beach yesterday and focused on picking up rubbish.

Who was she kidding? How could she have carried on as if everything was normal? She had needed to get away from Chi; she'd felt physically sick just looking at her. Even now, the thought of her made Sam's blood boil. How could she have agreed to come on Fiona's hen party after what she'd done? It was unthinkable to Sam. The hypocrisy of celebrating the love of a couple knowing you had tarnished it beyond repair.

Sam didn't know where things could possibly go from here. All she wanted to do was get home and cuddle up to Chris. He would know what to do, because right now she couldn't think straight. If *she* couldn't, what sort of turmoil was poor Fiona in?

First off, the revelation about the ring. Sam hadn't been brave enough to mention it. In fact, she'd wanted to tie duct tape around Chi's mouth when she'd brought it up. Sam had spent the best part of forty-eight hours convincing herself there was some acceptable reason why Fiona was donning costume jewellery rather than the 2.5 carat diamonds she'd been claiming the ring to be. So Chi thought Sam was a coward. Well better a coward than a two-faced cheating bitch. Chi's was a secret so awful Sam had decided to leave instead of be the one to relay it. Telling someone that one of their best friends had slept with their fiancé was possibly the most unenviable task she could imagine.

Although Chi hadn't actually confessed. She hadn't said, "*Yes, I had sex with Andrew.*" Sam felt a spark of hope. It didn't last long before a voice of dark reality extinguished it. Chi hadn't needed to spell it out. It had been obvious in that look and the admission that she'd been really drunk and emotional.

Sam had watched Chi, her shoulders shaking with sobs, the bruises from Clare's angry punches starting to show up on her arms. She had looked so pathetic and broken. But Sam had fought against feeling any pity for her. Chi had known who he was. She had put herself in that situation and she had only herself to blame.

Clare had stormed off without knowing the awful truth and Mel had followed her with unfathomable concern, as if Clare was the wronged party and not Fiona. Sam and Chi had been the only hens left on the beach. Two women in bright summer clothes having an emotional meltdown in the middle of a beach clean-up. A few volunteers had looked their way, but most had already come to the conclusion that the strange British girls were in a drama of their own. Since the tears weren't related to the girls getting injured collecting refuse, they didn't need to engage.

Sam had turned to look at the sea where their stupid director had been frolicking with her fishing net, trying to save the world from one plastic bottle cap at a time. Oblivious. Completely oblivious. She wondered what would become of this episode. Could *The Hen Party* really create something watchable from this wreckage? Could the channel show it if the couple weren't even together by the end of it?

A hand touched her arm lightly and made her jump. "Are you going?" A woman in an expensive looking beige jacket pointed towards the security scanner where an officer was waving for Sam to come through.

"Oh, sorry. I was miles away."

She hurried on, forgetting to take the coins out of her pocket and causing the machine to beep. She didn't even have a cardigan – she was going to freeze when she arrived in London. Kate had better not complain about packing her stuff up and getting it back to her. A big part of this was Kate's fault. If she hadn't put everyone under such strain...

Then again, what did Chi sleeping with Andrew have to do with Kate's baffling style of directing? Sam hadn't asked Chi any details.

"I can explain," Chi had said.

Why? Why had Chi wanted to confide in her? Why did she think Sam was somehow less a friend to Fiona than the others? They might not see each other often, but they'd grown up together and that meant a lot in her book. Sam had felt revulsion at the thought of hearing a detailed confession, like she'd be a part of it if she knew too much. She'd shaken her head.

"Please, don't."

Chi had looked hurt. Sam had got a kick out of it. Chi couldn't just go through life doing terrible things and expect sympathy.

"I'm getting out of here," she'd said.

She hadn't had a plan. It had formed as she'd walked back up the path. It had taken half an hour for her to find a cab, but at least she'd had her wallet on her and could pay for it. Otherwise she would have had a serious problem.

The villa, when she'd got to it, was locked. She had thought the housekeeper might be there or a cleaner. The house certainly needed a clean after last night's party. She'd waited around for some time, pacing up and down the street, hoping to see Ricardo's jeep. As the heat had taken its toll, she'd grown unbearably thirsty. She had decided that she'd had enough of Mallorca and couldn't wait any longer to get off the island. And because she had never emptied her handbag, and still had her passport in her inside pocket, it seemed that she would be able to do just that.

The only available flight was the following morning, so she'd booked a hostel, turned her phone off to save some juice, and had been in bed at nine o'clock, an insanely early hour according to the rest of the island.

FORTY-TWO

Day 4
CHIOMA

Now that Sam had left her, Chi felt like she could breathe again. She steadied herself against the rock and coaxed herself to take some deep breaths. The shock of telling the truth still had her heart pounding in her chest. The heat and thirst weren't helping and she felt giddy on her feet. A part of her welcomed the thought of passing out – the same part that yearned to be pitied, to be rescued from the guilt.

She wished it was the end, but in reality it was only the beginning. Once Fiona heard what Chi had done, she'd declare war on her. Going to work would be hell. Thank God they weren't on the same floor and would be able to avoid each other.

Would Fiona tell their colleagues? The thought made Chi catch her breath. Andrew's part in it wouldn't matter. They didn't know him, had never met him. But they knew her. They'd trusted her to be a decent person. Her reputation would be in tatters. She would become the woman who shagged her friend's fiancé. A stereotype from one of those daytime TV shows.

Chi squeezed her eyes shut against her growing panic. She would apply for a new job. It would be alright. Perhaps it was for the best. There wasn't much room to grow in her current one and a new challenge might be good for her. For a fleeting moment, she felt optimistic. Then a voice reminded her that looking for a new job was a full time job in itself and it could take the best part of a year to find one.

Perhaps it wouldn't be in Fiona's interest to broadcast Chi's reprehensible behaviour. It wouldn't exactly reflect well on her that her fiancé had been so easily tempted at a time when he was supposed to be most in love. She wouldn't want to be the poor victim whom people felt sorry for.

Chi hadn't meant for it to happen. There. Did that help? But she *had* been flirting. That didn't help. The thing was she'd assumed Andrew to be incapable of cheating so she'd let her guard down. She'd thought as a newly engaged person, he would realise that she was hammered and was only being touchy feely because that's what she did when she was drunk. Except that she'd had none of these thoughts consciously at the time. It had all been a blur of drunken elation and hormones.

The engagement party had taken place in a cocktail bar in Kensington, a venue kitted out in chrome and cool blue lighting. Friends only, no family. Fiona had said they'd do something later with their parents. Andrew had told Chi he would have even invited second cousins once removed if it had been up to him.

Chi had arrived an hour late, her bright red dress and gold heels attracting a number of looks. It was either her outfit or her skin colour. As usual with this part of town, everyone was white and she was in the minority. She headed straight for the bar for something to take the edge off her nerves. She'd already had a few drinks at home, but she felt naked without a glass in her hand.

A young man in a crisp white shirt had appeared in front of her with a bottle of pink fizz and a couple of flutes.

"Hi, I don't think we've met," he said. "Glass of champagne?"

She gave him a big, appreciative smile. "Has anyone ever said no to that question?"

He laughed. "You are here for the engagement party, right?"

"I am, I am..."

He was blond with sparkly blues eyes, like someone out of a boy band. His hair was shaved at the sides, long on top, gelled to one side so stiffly it looked like a gale force wouldn't spoil it. He beamed at her. He had great teeth.

"What's your name?"

"Chioma, but everyone calls me Chi. I'm a friend of Fiona's. We work together."

He poured her a glass and she felt a thrill. She hadn't had much luck on the dating front. She definitely had to work harder than this usually to get a guy to buy her a drink. On her last date, the monosyllabic sod had said he'd forgotten his wallet, only to rediscover it when he'd reached the train station to go home. She had begun to wonder if there was something wrong with her. But this man was giving her a good feeling. His smile seemed so guileless and she was attracted to his unaffected confidence.

"Who are you then?" she asked.

"Someone you should know," he said, giving her a wink.

She bit her lip as the smile spread across her cheeks. *Someone you should know.* What did he mean? That he thought they should get to know each other? She was up for that.

"I should, should I?" she laughed.

He frowned. "Um, yes. You really should."

Wait…did he genuinely mean she should know who he was? She felt a jolt of alarm. Shit. Had they met before at a party? But when? How? What was he doing here? She hadn't come into contact with many of Fiona's friends. Perhaps he had arrived very late at some party where Jägerbombs had already sent her brain cells off on holiday.

And then Fiona appeared at his side.

"Chi, you made it!" she said. "Oh my God, you look so glamorous! You're not supposed to upstage the bride-to-be."

He'd put his arm around Fiona. "Hey, I can't believe you've never shown Chi a picture of me. Shouldn't I be in your profile picture on Facebook?"

Then she'd understood. Her uneasiness vanished, replaced by disappointment which she hurriedly pushed away. So that was why he had been so confident. Because this was his party and he'd already secured his girl.

"I've changed mine," Andrew added.

"Yeah, well, I'm not as soppy as you!" Fiona retorted, nudging his arm off her.

Engaged. The moment you're supposed to be most in love? The only time Chi saw Fiona 'head over heels' was later that evening because she'd drunk too much.

310

The volunteers were talking nearby. The youngest of the group was pulling at a tangle of mesh caught under a rock behind her. Chi watched for a while, her brain disconnected from what she was seeing until another woman bent down beside him and helped him get the rest out. Their eyes met and she knew his question. What was she doing there if she wasn't going to help?

She couldn't stay. Volunteering might make this lot feel better about themselves, but Chi doubted it was going to help her. She needed to get away from it all. She needed to lie down somewhere and be alone. Kate was in the sea with her mask on, bobbing in and out of the waves. There was no point calling out to her.

Chi headed back up the path, humming a tune she could only remember a tiny part of. Her mouth was dry and she longed for a cold drink. Money? Did she have any money? She rifled through her bag in alarm, exhaled when her fingers made contact with her bus pass sleeve where she kept her emergency American Express card. She wasn't completely hopeless after all.

She took a while to get back up to the road. Several times she had to stop and lean over, because she was pretty sure she was going to be sick. The nausea passed each time and she cheered herself on with the promise of an ice cold drink.

When she got to the residential road it was completely empty. Tears pricked her eyes and she swallowed back a desire to break down and sob her heart out. She didn't know where she was or how she was going to get out of here. A tougher voice in her head told her to pull herself together. It was Mallorca, not the Sahara Desert.

She walked up the road in the direction she felt sure they had come from. At some point they had passed through an area with shops and a bus stop. There was bound to be a cashpoint there too.

A while later, Chi was seriously considering ringing on a doorbell when she saw a woman's head appear above a wall and then the rest of her pass through a garden gate, a set of keys jangling in her hand. Chi quickened her step.

"Excuse me!"

The woman whipped her head around, her feathery black hair bouncing over her jowly face. She didn't answer, but stopped where she was, eyeballing Chi with an air of suspicion.

"Do you speak English?" Chi asked.

The woman visibly relaxed. "Yes. I'm very good at it, in fact, because I'm from Yorkshire."

Relief flooded through her. "Oh, thank God."

"Are you alright?"

"No," Chi said, and felt the approach of tears again. "I'm a bit lost."

"Oh dear. Well I'm heading to Palma Nova," the woman said. "It's the town beside Magaluf...does that help? I can give you a lift if it does."

Magaluf? It sounded like the perfect place to get lost. No one would go looking for her there. Kate had vetoed the place.

"That would be amazing. Thank you so much."

The woman aimed her car keys at a blue Honda and its headlights flashed.

"No need to thank me. Go on, jump in then."

Once inside, the woman turned the radio on and Chi was grateful she didn't ask a million questions. She leant her head back against the headrest and let the memory wash over her again. She wasn't the only one to blame. Andrew had to share the burden of this guilt.

If only Fiona had paid him some attention that night, maybe things would have played out differently. But she hadn't. She'd barely spoken to him. Chi had found herself stuck to his side instead, enjoying the banter. She should have gone off and spoken to other people, but there was no one there she had felt particularly drawn to. She had met Clare, who was in the group of girls following Fiona around the bar, a couple of times, but neither of those times had she felt much warmth from her.

"So had you been planning to propose for a long time?" Chi had asked Andrew.

He'd blushed. "I've been imagining it for years, but in the end it didn't happen quite like I thought."

"No?"

"It surprised me how it happened."

She could have pushed him for details, but she found she didn't really want to hear them. She felt deflated at the thought of such romance. It seemed cruel that falling in love wasn't something that could be guaranteed for everyone, that it was completely and utterly down to chance. Would she ever be the centre of someone's world? Would anyone love her as much as Andrew loved Fiona?

"Do you smoke?" he'd asked.

She did when the mood took her, and it did in that moment, so they squeezed through everyone and headed outside on to the pavement where already a number of smokers were huddled together.

"I'm going to quit," Andrew said. "On my wedding day."

Chi raised an eyebrow. "Isn't that like giving up alcohol on New Year's Eve?"

He'd laughed. He laughed easily. She liked the way it made her feel. She'd wondered if he was enjoying her company as much as she was enjoying his. He hadn't made much effort to go off and talk to other people, either.

"I want a baby," he said, his cheeks reddening again.

"Wow," Chi said, taken aback. "Already?"

"Yeah. Why not? It would be fun."

She laughed. "Really? No one ever describes having babies as fun."

All Chi heard was that they tied you down and tired you out.

"I know it'd be knackering and stuff, I'm not a complete idiot, but I think I'm old enough."

He was swaying slightly. A happy drunk. A mellow drunk. She wished she was one of those. But she could feel the impatience in her toes, wanting to dance. The doors opened and she caught the beat of a song she loved. It was torture to have to stay still. She sipped her drink. One more and perhaps she'd go home. Before she did something she regretted.

She thought about asking him whether Fiona wanted a baby so soon. There were plenty of questions she could have asked. The words were ready in her mouth, but she didn't say anything. That's where the disloyalty began. The fact was she didn't want to drop Fiona's name into the conversation because she didn't want him thinking about her.

Andrew nodded at her empty glass.

"Another bottle of the pink stuff?"

No. She shouldn't. She should go home, but she was already feeling reckless. She wanted to lean forward and kiss his lips, moist with champagne. The thought made her shiver. She had to talk to other people and leave Andrew alone.

"You cold?" he said, misinterpreting her shiver. "Come on, let's go inside."

"Alright...one more and I think I'd better be off."

Famous last words. When had one more ever been one more?

A few hours later, she had been dancing in the bar. Not alone, so that was fine. There was a little group of them. Smiley girls whose names she couldn't remember. Handbags and coats were piled up in the middle of their circle. She was having a good time. She wasn't going to go now, not when she was having fun. When was the last time she'd danced?

Half an hour must have passed when Andrew appeared by her side. She momentarily forgot herself, clutching his arm and beaming with pleasure as if she hadn't seen him for ages. A second later, she registered his expression. He looked a mixture of worried and annoyed.

Why had he gone to her? Because Clare had gone home on the last train and he thought Chi was a great friend of Fiona's.

"She's being sick in the toilets," he said. "Can you help her?"

Chi had felt a rush of superiority because she wasn't drunk. Because she thought that, unlike Fiona, she could control herself.

Fiona had collapsed in the corner of the girls' toilets, her dress bunched up to her waist, a ladder in her tights creeping up her thigh. Chi splashed her face with water and Fiona groaned and said she just wanted to sleep now. Fewer than twenty minutes ago she'd been fine. *It must have been the shots*, Chi thought. It had happened to her before several times which was why she tried to avoid shots as much as possible. One minute you were drunk but aware of everything, the next minute you were unable to function and your memory had been erased.

Andrew came in, too impatient to wait outside the door. He was furious when he saw Fiona, shouted at her as she lay there dribbling.

"Come on, you've got to try to stand up, for fuck's sake!"

Chi remembered her cheating ex-boyfriend yelling at her once too, his voice sounding like it was coming through a funnel from a long way off. She'd been so drunk that her tongue had been dead in her mouth, making talking impossible. She felt pity for Fiona and urged her to drink water, but it spilled down her chin, a string of spit spinning like a spider's web from her prominent front teeth.

"We've got to get her home," Andrew said.

We. Not I.

It took an hour to get a taxi. One look at Fiona and taxi drivers sped up. It was a cold night and Chi only had a light coat. Andrew offered her his jacket as she stood there shivering. Perhaps he thought Fiona was oblivious to the cold.

Finally a cabbie stopped for them. Andrew gave the driver Fiona's address.

"I live in the other direction," Chi said.

"Shit."

She should have got out. Instead, she said she'd sleep on the sofa. It was Saturday tomorrow and she wouldn't have to work. It wasn't that she didn't want to leave Fiona. She didn't want to leave Andrew. From the way he looked at her, she didn't think he wanted her to leave either.

Another moment passed where she could have set things straight.

"She's impossible," he said. "I must be mad."

They had put Fiona to bed and were in her kitchen. Instead of going to sleep, Andrew was opening a bottle of white wine. It was only midnight so it wasn't too crazy, but Chi felt like she had walked through a door marked *Danger*. Accepting the glass, she was sure she heard the door click shut behind her.

"She was just excited," she said.

"Was she?" Andrew said. "Because didn't you notice she blanked me all night?"

Reassure him. That's what a friend would do.

"She wanted to talk to everyone," Chi said. "You two are going to have plenty of time to talk to each other."

He frowned. "Yeah...I just wish we could talk now..."

They took their wine into the small living room. Chi thought about sitting in the recliner to mark some distance, but the sofa looked so much more inviting. She sat down, drawing her legs beneath her. He sat down beside her, resting the bottle on the floor. They were going to drink it all. It was inevitable. Her head was swimming. He connected his phone to the speakers and selected a playlist. Coldplay's *Viva La Vida* started playing, stirring up the mood. She swayed a little bit, her body instinctively wanting to move with the beat. She forced herself to stop.

"I just wish she was more excited," Andrew said. "I feel like I've been waiting for this for my whole life."

Chi laughed. "Oh my God, you're so dramatic!"

He blushed. "Okay, not my whole life. But I always fancied her."

"So what's the problem then?"

"I don't know," he said. "I thought it was never going to happen and I'd got used to the idea, you know…"

"What changed?"

"Well she showed interest again suddenly. It felt like a miracle. I was so happy."

"And now?"

"I'm happy, but…I don't know how to explain it…"

She waited for him to try. He didn't. She nudged his thigh with her foot.

"You got cold feet?"

He held her foot still and didn't let go. She felt a shiver of anticipation rush up her leg. She willed his hand to slide up her ankle, up to her calf, to find her thigh and keep going. Then a new song came on, a new voice that was deep and yearning. *Take Me to Church* by Hozier. It was slow but her body still wanted to dance.

"I like this one."

She got up. Unsteady on her feet. She was drunker than she'd thought. He was watching her as she swayed dreamily to the music. She felt sexy. She closed her eyes.

"You dance really well," he said.

She should have stopped. She should have gone to bed. But it was too late. She'd missed the window a while back. She still thought he was incorruptible.

"I can't dance on my own," she said, grinning.

She reached out a hand and pulled him off the sofa. He stumbled into the middle of the room, letting out a breathless laugh.

"I can't dance," he said, but he didn't resist her.

If Fiona had woken up and come into the living room, what would she have seen? His hands resting on Chi's hips, her arms draped loosely around his neck as they moved. She could smell the wine on his breath; his eyes were misty with drink. They were so close. The music was soulful and longing. The drink swilled around her head. She felt herself melting, turning to liquid. He was so beautiful, so interested.

Their lips knew what to do. That first touch, it was like lighting a spark. The passion was ferocious. They fell on to the sofa, hands battling with zips and buttons. No words were spoken. Chi's hands ran over the soft shaved back of his head. He cupped her face, drawing her close. They broke off, breathless. So serious. No laughing now. No banter. No flirting. It was intense, like the music that wrapped around them as if they were in the climax of their own film. His lips worked their way down her neck, her shoulders. He helped her out of her dress, unclipped her strapless bra.

She rode him. With her hands cupping his knees behind her, her head turned up to the ceiling and her eyes closed, she chased that promise of ecstasy. She thought of all the past hurts, all the guys who had let her down, and then there was this one who was kind and wanted her, and she wanted him, and she was driven by so much lust and desire that she overlooked the fact that he was forbidden.

He could have been anyone. He should have been anyone. Anyone else but him.

Afterwards they stayed a moment, breathless and spent. Their eyes met, but she couldn't read his expression. She disengaged herself and hurried to the bathroom to clean herself up. The guilt didn't set in then. The drink was still coursing through her veins and she couldn't think.

When she got back to the living room, she found he had put his trousers back on and had fallen asleep. There was no way she wanted to be around when Fiona woke up. She got dressed quickly, ordered a taxi, and soon she was being driven away from the crime scene. By the time morning came, she had already begun the burial process. It was the only way to deal with something so awful. She buried it deep down and promised herself she would never tell a soul.

She hadn't spoken to Andrew since.

FORTY-THREE

Day 4
CLARE

"Fiona! Wait!"

Chi should be the one walking away with her head hanging in shame. Not Fiona. Not the bride-to-be. Clare hadn't been able to stop herself lunging at Chi. It had been like hitting a rake. Hard and unyielding. Clare had probably done more damage to herself. Her hands felt a little tender. Chi, on the other hand, hadn't even winced. Probably because she was like the Tin Man: no heart at all. What a bitch!

Thank God the camera hadn't been rolling for her outburst. Vomiting and now fighting…Clare was hardly setting a very good example for her primary school children. If her colleagues…no, if the *parents* of the kids at her school ever got an eyeful of her behaviour on the television, she'd be out of a job.

"Fiona! Wait!"

Was the ring fake? Had Fiona thought they'd all be fooled by a cheapo from Accessorize? Now Clare thought about it, she was sure she'd had her own doubts when she'd seen it the second time. She was fully aware her old friend was capable of pulling off a stunt like that. Fiona had always been the type to lust over things she couldn't afford, drooling over the adverts in glossy magazines to the point she'd become boring to be around. Clare could remember her cutting off the tags of a black and gold dress she'd bought for a fiver in Brixton market, and then later at a party telling everyone it was Giorgio Armani.

Fiona was a show off. She hated to lose face. If the ring was fake, then she would be feeling very embarrassed right now. If she had known the truth then she should have confided in her best friend. Clare would have helped her with the charade. Clare would have understood. It wasn't like Andrew was a big earner. It would have made sense to buy a placeholder ring and save the money.

Clare had been about to give up the chase when she saw that Fiona had come to a halt. Her shoulders were shaking. Was she crying? Clare felt a rush of affection for her oldest friend. Fiona could be very sweet when she was upset. She was easy to love during those moments. She softened and seemed genuinely grateful to have Clare at her side. Perhaps, with the tears, the lovely Fiona would come out. Not the nasty one who had told Clare she wouldn't be invited on a cruise to the Bahamas.

Fiona's face was crimson. Wisps of frizzy golden hair stuck out like a halo around her head. She was looking out at the sea, her eyes wild and unseeing.

"It's alright," Clare said, opening her arms to hug her. "Come here, it's alright."

Fiona's lips curled. "No, it's not, is it. No it's fucking not. This whole thing is fucking ridiculous. It's been the worst week of my life."

"I promise we can have another hen party when we get home and it will be amazing."

They would do it properly. Clare would organise it. She'd book something fancy like afternoon tea at Claridge's. There would be champagne and cupcakes and fun hen party games. It would be just how Fiona wanted it. Neither Chi nor Jem would be invited, obviously.

"No way," Fiona said, shuddering. "I can't think of anything worse."

Of course she would say that now. Clare would change her mind, though. She just needed to get back home and have a good night's sleep.

"Don't worry, we wouldn't invite Chi or Jem. I'd organise it for you."

"I don't want one! I don't want any of this!" Fiona barked, and she abruptly twisted the ring off and lobbed it out across the rocks.

Clare let out a horrified gasp. It dawned on her in that split second, as the ring sailed through the air, that Fiona might be capable of tricking them with a cheap ring, but Andrew would rather sell an organ than admit he couldn't afford what she wanted.

"What have you done?" Clare cried. "Chi has to be wrong. Andrew would never do that to you."

"Go get it if you want it so badly!" Fiona shouted at her. "You're so fucking clingy, it's probably the nearest you'll ever get to an engagement ring."

The words were like poisonous darts. They sank into Clare's chest and paralysed her to the spot. Fiona was already walking away, her arms swinging as if she hadn't just crushed her friend like a beetle.

While Clare stood there, reeling in shock, someone took her arm. She turned as Mel went to hug her.

"Fuck her," the sound recordist whispered in her ear. "Seriously. She couldn't tell a diamond if it hit her in the face."

323

"Oh my God." Clare breathed out the pain in her chest and sank into Mel's embrace. "Did you hear what she said to me?"

"Yeah, I got the tail end."

"How could she say that?" Fat tears rolled down her hot cheeks and soaked into Mel's T-shirt. "I'm her best friend. How could she say that to me?"

"She doesn't deserve you," Mel said, holding her close. "Breathe, babe. Deep breaths."

A moment passed and Clare became aware of Mel's slim body against her own big, sweaty one. Mel's slender hands were stroking her back. Clare pulled away, feeling self-conscious, and wiped her face. She'd expected Sam to come and comfort her, not Mel, who had been a complete stranger a few days ago.

"I should find the ring," she said, taking a tentative step off the path. "She's going to regret that so much. It will be like the time she threw away a gold bracelet from her dad. Oh God, you should have seen her."

"Clare, leave it."

"I have to find it."

"No, you damn well don't. Didn't you hear her? You think she's your friend? I'm sorry, but she's not, and you can't go on letting her treat you like this."

"But what if it's a diamond?"

"Then Fiona will be back in five minutes on her hands and knees. Meanwhile, you and me will be chilling out, enjoying this island how you were supposed to."

Clare laughed in surprise. She wasn't sure why Mel had singled her out of the girls, but it felt good to have someone giving a damn about her for a change.

"And how are we supposed to be enjoying the island?"

"For starters, we need to get away from here."

Did she really mean leave the other hens behind? Could they actually escape?

"Don't you have to work?"

Mel snorted. "I don't think there's any filming going on today, do you? Kate's lost her mind."

"Should we go back to the villa?"

"Is that what you want to do?" Mel asked, levelling her eyes at Clare.

Clare thought about the state they'd left it in. She wouldn't mind jumping into the pool, but it would be nice to get away from everything for a while.

"Where else could we go?"

She didn't fancy roaming around town. It was too hot for that.

"You can come back to mine if you like?"

Clare didn't know why the suggestion made her feel awkward. It made sense. Mel shrugged as if to say it was no big deal either way.

"The apartment has a pool...and a shower..."

"A shower sounds good."

Clare didn't want to be in the villa when Fiona and the others got back. She wanted her best friend to feel awful about what she had said. Her ex-best friend. She would turn her phone off for a while and show Fiona how it felt to be on the wrong end of the silent treatment.

Ricardo had taken the jeep but Mel was unfazed. She called a taxi which arrived ten minutes later. Clare relaxed in the back of the car. It felt good to have someone taking charge. As she stared out the window, Mel reached over and squeezed her hand.

"This might be a blessing in disguise. You've seen her true colours."

"I don't know...love is blind," Clare said, turning to look at her. Mel raised her eyebrows, an uncertain smile on her face.

Had it been friendship or something more? Clare had never dared answer that question. As they sailed down the motorway, she felt the pressure in her chest lighten, the burden of caring about Fiona start to lift. It was over. She was free. Free to care for someone else.

They got out near Mel's apartment block to buy wine and something to eat from the supermarket. Then they climbed the hill and weaved through the car park to the entrance. Mel commented on the absence of Ricardo's jeep. They had been sharing the flat. Clare was relieved he wouldn't be there. More relieved still that Jem wouldn't. She didn't have the energy to deal with that woman.

"Here we are," Mel said, pushing open the front door which led straight into a sunny living room. "Check out the view."

Clare stepped out on to the balcony. She could smell the smoky aroma of barbequed meat wafting over from somewhere, and the sound of laughter. People on holiday, without a care in the world. The sea was just visible in the distance, separated from them by bushy Aleppo pines and terracotta roof terraces.

"You hungry?"

"Starving."

"Yeah, Kate isn't very good at...well..."

"At her job," Clare finished.

They had a lot to say about that. Mel brought out the wine and bowls of crisps and olives. She told Clare how excited she'd been about the job and how it was now her duty to warn other sound recordists about Kate. Clare's stomach grumbled loudly and she blushed.

"I'll shove the pizza in the oven," Mel said, heading back inside.

"Can I stay here for the rest of the week?" Clare joked.

"Fine by me…but you'd have to stay in my room."

Mel winked. Clare laughed, although her stomach was flipping. She settled down in the recliner on the balcony and tried to feel normal. They were just chilling out together. Two girls. It was totally relaxed. Normal. So why was she feeling nervous all of a sudden?

"Feel free to offload," Mel said, coming back outside.

Clare took a cooling sip of wine. "How long have you got? Fiona and I…we've been friends since we were little."

"I'm not going anywhere," Mel said with a reassuring smile. "And there's a lot of rubbish in the Mediterranean so Kate's going to be quite a while, too."

"Where do I begin?"

By the time she'd finished the first glass, Clare was crying her eyes out. It seemed ridiculous how much crying she could do. It wasn't as though she had consciously held it in over the years, but the reservoir gates must have been holding more back than she'd thought.

"Sorry…oh God…I don't even know why I'm crying…"

Mel leant down at Clare's side, her silky hair coming loose from behind her ear and falling across her cheek. She put an arm around Clare, squeezing her shoulder.

"Don't apologise, honey," she whispered in her lovely Australian accent.

Clare realised that this girl was gorgeous, and this girl wanted something more from her than she was saying. Clare had sensed it earlier. She had sensed it in the comforting stroke of Mel's hand on her back at the beach, and she had read it in her eyes when she'd asked her if going back to the villa was what she *really* wanted…

It was Clare who instigated it; Clare who leant in quickly, before she could stop herself, to kiss those pretty pink lips. Clare had dreamed about kissing Fiona before, but didn't everyone imagine kissing their friends? Mel kissed her back, and Clare felt weak with relief. Her lips were so soft and gentle. This wasn't a battle of tongues like the last snog Clare remembered, in a night club with a random with writhing hands. Mel's tongue knew where to go, how to dance with her own. Her lips weren't pressing forcefully against hers, but moving with hers in perfect harmony. Clare felt she could do this for hours.

Mel broke off, breathless, her grin big and beautiful.

"Wow…you're the best kisser."

Clare blushed with pleasure as her ego received a much needed boost.

"It takes two…"

"Seriously…wow." Mel raised her glass. "A toast to Fiona's hissy fit?"

"Oh don't…"

"Sorry. Too soon?"

"Too soon."

Mel kissed her on the cheek. "Well I'm glad I followed you."

"Yeah…I might have thrown myself off the mountain otherwise."

"You wouldn't have got very far. That sea was bloody miles away."

Clare laughed. "True."

They finished the bottle of wine with their pizzas. Conversation flowed easily and they had a laugh speculating over what everyone might be doing. They both agreed that Kate needed a reality check and they would keep their phones off for the evening. It would be good for her to worry about them, to realise she needed them all. Fiona would be alright. She was as tough as nails. She always had been.

At sunset they headed to the sea for a night swim. It was magical. The black water swallowed them up, warm and delicious against their skin. They kissed with their arms around each other, their lips salty and wet.

When they got back, Ricardo still hadn't appeared.

"He must have wanted some privacy," Clare said, pointedly.

"I don't blame him. Jem's hot."

"Hey," Clare said, prodding her. "She's also a stuck up cow."

"Aw, I don't think she's that bad," Mel said, thoughtfully. "I think she's just a protective sister."

It was funny to feel jealous like this. Clare didn't know what was going to happen tomorrow between them, but she didn't want to think about it. She was tired of being the sensible one.

"Are we terrible?" Clare said as they snuggled in bed later. "Shouldn't we have rung Kate?"

"I did."

"When?"

"Just before when you were in the shower. I tried five times. Phone's off…"

"Wow. She really did lose the plot."

"We'll ring tomorrow," Mel said. "I don't want to think about it now."

Clare felt the kiss on the back of her neck. It made her skin tingle.

FORTY-FOUR

Day 5
KATE

"They obviously all went out together on a massive binge," Jem said. "What time did you go to the villa last night? Maybe they've only just got back."

"They're not there. And from what the volunteers on the beach said, they went off separately."

"You haven't seen them since the beach?" Ricardo asked, incredulous. "You didn't think to check on them last night?"

Kate felt the heat pour into her cheeks as a vivid image of her chucking rubbish into the pool flashed into her head. "Yes, I did think to check on them. I went to the villa in the afternoon and they weren't there. I didn't go back in the evening because I thought we all needed some space."

Ricardo and Jem had become distracted by something behind her. Kate turned around. Gabriel was coming down the stone steps.

"I take it he's your 'space'?" Ricardo said, with a flicker of amusement in his eyes.

Kate was about to say, "*You* can't talk," but stopped herself.

"This is Gabriel," she said instead, keeping her voice measured. "He's been a great help."

"Any news?" Gabriel asked.

Kate shook her head. "No, they haven't been in touch with any of the hens either."

"I hope they're alright," Jem said, looking concerned. She was out of the pool and rubbing herself down with a towel. "If anything happens to Fiona, my brother will kill me."

Kate was going to point out that Jem hadn't cared much about Fiona when she'd walked out during her proposal story. Or when she'd ruined Fiona's hen party games by being so argumentative. But her attention was distracted by her ringing phone. She braced herself for the worst.

"Kate Miller speaking…"

There was an intake of breath on the other end of the receiver. "Oh Kate, you're there…it's Mel."

"Mel! Thank God! Where are you? Are you with the others?"

Kate took a few paces towards the shade of a palm plant. The cool spot barely ensconced her feet. She could feel everyone's eyes boring into her back.

"Just with Clare. Why? Where are you?"

"I'm…it doesn't matter where I am. Where are you?"

"We're at my apartment."

Why were Mel and Clare together? Why was Clare not with Fiona? Kate thought the two of them were inseparable.

"Wait…so Clare hasn't been back to the villa since the beach?"

"No…" Mel said, hesitantly. "There was an argument."

"Between who?"

"Between Clare and Fiona for starters."

For starters? Kate pushed a hand through her tangled hair. She thought the person most likely to argue with everyone was standing at the edge of the pool in front of her.

"Chi said Fiona's engagement ring was fake."

Kate blinked in the sun. "What?"

"Yep, you heard me. She said she'd found the same one on Accessorize's website."

"You can't be serious. How did Fiona respond to that?"

"She got pretty mad. Clare tried to console her but Fiona was a complete bitch to her and then threw the ring away and stormed off."

Kate's hand flew to her mouth as she thought about that sparkly rock that had set off a less sparkly twinge of envy in the pit of her stomach. How could Fiona have thrown it away? This was a disaster. No wonder Andrew was getting on a plane. She must have broken off their engagement.

"Why would Chi say that?" Kate asked. "Why would Fiona believe her?"

"I don't know...maybe it's true..."

"Is Chi a jeweller?"

Mel didn't reply. She obviously thought it was a rhetorical question. Kate racked her brain and vaguely remembered Chi's job being something in marketing. She took a deep breath. She had to control herself and not take her frustration out on the others.

"Alright. Well if you can think of anywhere they might be, call me."

"I know where one of them might be."

"Oh yeah?" Kate said, looking over at Jem. "Where?"

"With Ricardo."

Kate smiled grimly. "Correct."

"You're with her?"

"I am. Two down, three to go."

She got off the phone and stared out at the mountains without seeing them. She thought back to the conversation with Andrew. He had been crying. But what had he said exactly? That he'd made a mistake but he loved her. Could he have been referring to buying Fiona a fake diamond ring?

"Who was it?" Ricardo asked.

Kate paced back to the pool and took a good look at Jem.

"Tell me. Do you think your brother would buy Fiona a fake ring?"

Jem's eyes widened in surprise. "No, of course not!" And then uncertainty crept into her voice. "I mean, I don't think so...but then again, Fiona always was pretty demanding." She narrowed her eyes. "Why? Who's saying that?"

"Apparently Chi saw the exact same one in Accessorize. Fiona has since lobbed it across the beach and gone AWOL."

Jem reeled back in horror. "She just chucked it?"

"Apparently."

"That's awful! How could she do that?"

"Can you call Andrew?" Ricardo suggested.

"She can try, but he might be on a plane," Kate said, passing Jem the phone. "He called this morning and said he was on his way over."

Jem's jaw dropped. "Please tell me you're joking! She chucks away his ring and now she's summoned him? Nothing has changed. Nothing. Has. Changed."

"I'm not joking," Kate said. "I also have to tell you that when I talked to your brother, he said he'd made a mistake and he was sorry."

Jem paled at the news. "You didn't ask him what he'd done?"

"Yes but he hung up."

Jem covered her mouth with one hand, Kate's phone forgotten in the other. Ricardo shot Kate a look that suggested he didn't think Andrew was innocent either.

"He was under pressure," he said, softly. "Men do crazy things under pressure."

"Oh God. What if it's true? And all this time I've been such a bitch to her," Jem murmured. "We need to find her."

"We need to get Fiona and Andrew back together," Kate said. "They need to be kissing as the sun sets on Mallorca."

Ricardo laughed. Kate frowned at him. She couldn't see how he could find anything funny at this point.

"Finally you're thinking like Joanna," he said. "Finally you get the show."

Kate kneaded her temples. It wasn't just the show she had to save, it was her future in the industry. Word got around fast. She needed a miracle or some very good acting to sort this mess out. Who would be willing to stand up for her, though? Ricardo? Mel? The hens? She couldn't think of one sure ally among them.

Jem had the phone to her ear. It seemed to take for ever for him to pick up.

"Andrew?" she cried. "Where are you?"

Kate fought the urge to grab the phone from her. Gabriel's hand gently touched her back and she stopped jiggling up and down.

"It's going to be okay," he reassured her.

"Not it's not."

"It's not life or death."

"It kind of is...for my career."

"Maybe it's the beginning of something else."

He might be right, but now really wasn't the time for contemplating a career change.

"What's happening?" she mouthed.

"Slow down," urged Jem. "She's broken up with you? So you have talked to her?" She covered the receiver. "She broke up with him by text, apparently."

"Ask about the ring," Kate hissed.

Jem glowered at her. "Yes, we'll come over and collect you right now. We're on our way."

FORTY-FIVE

Day 5
SAM

"I can't wait to see you," Sam said.

"What time are you boarding?"

"Any minute now. We're waiting for the last lot to get off the plane...they're coming off now."

Chris had sounded half asleep when he'd answered, but he'd perked up at the sound of her voice. She'd felt a relief to hear the enthusiasm. He'd reassured her that she was doing the right thing by coming home early. He'd also admitted that he'd stopped himself sending her messages telling her how much he'd missed her because he hadn't wanted her to feel guilty for taking a holiday.

She'd filled him in on everything that had happened. He'd never been much good at extracting gossip, but he loved to hear it. Sam already felt guilty for sharing it all so eagerly. It was like a tabloid paper getting excited about someone else's tragedy – horrible but quite a scoop. It was terrible, yet it made her appreciate her own life.

"I guess there won't be a wedding then," Chris said. "Or if there is, Chi definitely won't be invited."

"Oh God, can you imagine?" Sam groaned at the thought. "I wouldn't marry you if you'd slept with one of my best friends."

"Good job I didn't tell you then."

"Ha. Shut up."

"Love you."

"You too."

"Are you boarding yet?"

Pale-faced passengers were coming off the plane from Gatwick in dribs and drabs with bags and prams and noisy kids. She watched, relieved that she wasn't part of the stag party inexplicably dressed as *frauleins*. Wasn't it a bit early for Oktoberfest? They were red-faced, and Sam suspected they were sedated by a previous hangover.

"No. People are still coming off our plane..."

Two couples weighed down by hand luggage struggled to manage their party of under-fives. A crying kid slid across the floor in protest, his baby sister choosing that moment to vomit over her mum's shoulder. Sam looked on in sympathy, and felt a pang of need to cuddle her own child, who had always puked up at inopportune moments.

She was still thinking about baby vomit when she caught a glimpse of him. Sam froze, only her eyes widening. Andrew looked anxious as he walked through the gate, a black sports bag slung over his shoulder. Impeccably dressed as he always was in a crisp pale blue polo shirt and chino shorts, he glanced around him for the way out.

"I'll ring you back, love. I have to go. I've just seen Andrew."

"Don't make a scene. It might be a load of bollocks, remember. You hardly know Chi."

She might not know Chi, but she knew a guilty face when she saw one. She got up off her seat and headed after him. He was dithering in front of the baggage reclaim sign.

"Andrew!"

He frowned at her like he didn't know who she was.

"It's Sam."

Recognition dawned, and with it, little pleasure.

"Where is she? What are you doing here?"

"I was on the hen party, but it collapsed."

"I didn't buy her a fake ring. The shop must have conned her. I don't know why she's so upset with me."

"Don't you?" she cried. Then remembering her husband's sane advice about not making a scene, she lowered her voice. "You don't think you've done *anything* wrong?"

He looked scared then. "What did she say?"

"Nothing *she* said. Chi, on the other hand..."

Bingo! If she'd had any doubts, they left her as she watched the colour drain from his face.

"It was an accident," Andrew stammered. "We were wasted. It was a one off. It should never have happened."

"But it did."

He rubbed his hand nervously over his mouth, looking like he was about to speak then changing his mind. Then he changed it back.

"Why would Chi tell her?"

"She didn't," Sam said. "Fiona walked off once she found out the ring was fake. Only I know your dirty little secret because Chi clearly has more of a conscience than you and couldn't keep it a secret any more."

He frowned. "So Fiona doesn't know?"

"I don't know if she does now."

Andrew ran a hand over his face and swore so loudly heads turned.

"Where is Chi?" he asked.

Sam felt her opinion of him drop even lower.

"Chi? No idea. You shouldn't be worrying about her, though. It's your fiancée you need to be worrying about."

"I know. She must have found out because she broke up with me."

"You've spoken to Fiona?"

"She broke up in a text message," he said, his voice cracking. "I've got to find them."

He didn't say goodbye. Sam watched him go, feeling unsettled by the encounter. She didn't know what to think.

She dialled Chris's number again, wanting to hear his comforting voice. She couldn't wait to get home.

FORTY-SIX

Day 4
CHIOMA

The Yorkshire woman pulled up her car beside a souvenir shop with rails of brightly coloured towels and inflatable sharks and crocodiles bobbing up and down in the light breeze. She studied Chi's face with a look of maternal concern and asked her if she was positive she knew where her apartment block was. Chi reassured her and got out, making sure to look like she knew where she was going.

Once her saviour had gone, Chi relaxed her shoulders and wandered towards the beach front. All around her she heard English being spoken. She heard accents from Liverpool, London and Glasgow. It was like a part of Britain had been scooped up, dusted with yellow sand and left to enjoy some sunshine. So much white flesh on show, so much of it turning pink.

She stopped at an ice cream truck and bought a bottle of water, drained nearly all of it in one go, pulling it away from her lips with a gasp. A wave of tiredness washed over her, tugging at her eyelids. She just needed to sleep for a while and then she'd sort herself out.

She kicked off her wedges and picked her way through the sunbathers, across the hot sand until she found a spot that looked safe from crying kids and ball players. Without taking off her clothes, she sank into the sand, shoved her bag under her head and closed her eyes.

How long she slept, she didn't know. She was startled into consciousness by a plastic ball bouncing off her head. It drew a cry from her and she sat up, feeling disorientated. For a moment she was back at the rocky cove and Clare was hitting her. She rubbed the tender spots on her arm, a part of her almost enjoying the focus of the pain.

A male voice swore loudly nearby and her thoughts cleared. She was in Magaluf. A lovely lady had driven her here.

"Are you alright?"

He was built like a rugby player: broad shoulders and a thick neck, which made his head seem too small and square. He had a Space Invaders tattoo on his right pec. It might have been cool if the edges had been a little sharper.

"How many fingers?" he asked, holding his hand up. He had a stubby nose and thin lips. His eyes were kind, though. Behind him a bunch of guys were laughing less sympathetically.

"Three," she said, her brain kicking into gear. "Like the number of beers I'm going to need to accept your apology."

He looked surprised and then delighted. When he grinned, his stubby nose creased. He was a five out of ten.

"You're on," he said. "I'm Phil."

Chi pushed away the worry that she was being reckless. She suspected Phil hadn't managed to convert Magaluf into Shagaluf yet and thought this might be his opportunity. Really she should get a taxi back to the villa. Sooner or later, she would have to face Fiona, but the thought made her stomach clench in fear. She couldn't go back. Despite the heat, she felt a cold shiver run down her spine. She felt far too sober for a confrontation.

She forced a bright smile and got a flashback of Andrew telling her what he thought of her smile. A *great* smile; a *mischievous* smile; a *smile that made you laugh even though you didn't know what you were laughing at.* Why would he say that to her at his own engagement party? You couldn't go around saying that to people!

Chi battled to bury the memory as Phil introduced her to his three mates. It was the last day of their holiday and they were going to end it with a bang.

"What about you?" they wanted to know.

"Why are you all billy no mates?" the one called Diesel scoffed. He was the hottest of the lot with tanned olive skin and shiny black hair that fell in a perfect wave over his face. Half Cypriot, half Italian, he had been born and raised in Essex without a trace of a foreign land in his accent, which was a shame. His twenty-one-year-old body had been sculpted in the gym. He knew he looked good and oozed a confidence that swung between being attractive and appallingly arrogant.

"I'm taking a break from my mates," she said, trying not to let his comment bother her. "I'm here working on a TV show."

That piqued his interest. "What's it about?"

"Girls having fun on the island."

Their eyes widened, their dirty minds immediately imagining a kind of fun that involved pouting lips and PVC corsets.

"Wow," said Phil, gazing at her. She could tell he fancied her. His eyes kept dropping to her arse. "That sounds amazing."

Shame it wasn't.

"So you're like famous?" Diesel wanted to know.

He wasn't impressed yet, but it wouldn't be hard. She just needed to keep on pretending as she had been pretending all week. She could be a famous actress if that's what would make her forget for a while. She shot him a coy grin and shrugged.

"Well obviously not famous enough, because you guys don't recognise me…"

"No, I think I do…"

The one called Steve sat down beside her. "And are your other friends as hot as you? Because maybe you should call them up and tell them to come down."

She laughed, and Phil looked like his prize was being taken away from him. She felt sorry for him. He might have the body, but she wondered if he ever got lucky when he had such predators for friends.

"So," she said, giving Phil her full attention. "We have a date with three beers, don't we?"

He looked thrilled. A voice told her she could bring herself to snog him if it came to that. She'd kissed worse. He *did* have the body. She wouldn't let it get any further, though. If he insisted, she'd tell him she was on her period. *If only she was.* Another awful thought she had to beat off. Among strangers was no place to have a breakdown. She had to keep it together.

They had a few cans of beer on the beach, and then, dizzy with alcohol and too much sun, they headed slowly back to the lads' apartment, stopping off to bulk buy bottles of Smirnoff and WKD. Chi could hear the music pumping from the bottom of the street. The air was sizzling with the anticipation of the party ahead. It felt raw. Dangerous. Again the voice inside her head urged her to get a taxi back to the villa. And again, fear stopped her.

The lads' apartment was a mess of open suitcases and wet towels and clothes strewn all over the place. There were phone chargers trailing from every socket and empty bottles near the bin, waiting for someone with initiative to chuck them inside. Diesel lined up shot glasses along the bar in the kitchen. Glassware was a notch above what Chi had expected from them.

"What are we having?"

She noticed the bottle of tequila by the sink. He ignored her question and poured it instead. There were five glasses, so he was counting her in even though he wasn't showing any interest.

"Come on, then!" he bellowed when he was done.

The others were getting ready. Phil was in the shower. She could hear the boiler working hard. Steve had suggested she go in with him and save on water. Phil had looked worried, like she might actually do it. But no. She'd laughed him off. Steve was like a hyena on the prowl, all crooked teeth and hungry eyes.

"I'm not fucking waiting!" Diesel yelled again.

"Come on, then!" Chi said, perching on the bar stool. She picked up a glass and chinked it against his. "Cheers."

Diesel eyed her, making up his mind about her.

"Cheers," he said.

They knocked it back. He let out a cry, like he'd achieved something important, and slammed his glass down on the counter. She placed hers down without the fuss. No one else had reappeared yet.

"Come on, you bunch of pussies!" Diesel yelled.

Their eyes met. At exactly the same moment they picked up a second glass. His face lost some of its hard edge when he laughed and his eyes crinkled. Chi suddenly thought of Andrew again and felt as if a huge weight was pressing down on her shoulders. *But I liked him!* She wished she could shout it out at the top of her voice. *I really liked him!*

"Wait up, you greedy bastards!" Steve yelled.

The rest of them piled in around the counter, spruced up and stinking of too much aftershave. After the shots, they headed out on to the balcony. They drank ready mixed bottles of Smirnoff and listened to dance music from a phone plugged into mini speakers. Chi leant over the balcony and stared at the glimmering pool. Phil stood so close their arms were touching. She was aware of the little hairs on his arms.

"I don't want to go back," he groaned.

No doubt he was expecting her to commiserate. But she didn't say anything. She didn't fancy him. She decided she wouldn't be snogging him. His teeth were small and he showed too much gum when he smiled.

"Do you?" he said. He was clutching at a conversation.

"I don't want to think about it."

"Yeah…me neither," he said, trying to deduce from her neutral smile whether that meant he was going to get lucky tonight or not.

On a balcony below, a bunch of girls were having their own little get ready party. The guys watched on as they walked in and out of their apartment in their tiny shimmering bikinis, nursing tall glasses of something mixed with orange. Chi felt unthreatened by them. They were normal looking girls with muffin tops and unremarkable faces disguised with lashings of makeup. One of them brought out a bottle of Jack Daniel's and Steve whistled. The girls looked up.

"Party at your place then?" he called down.

"Yeah, alright then," one of the them shouted up. "Jump over."

Steve lifted his leg, got his foot up on the balcony rail. The girls shrieked.

"Don't be an idiot," Phil shouted, reaching out for him.

"Obviously I wasn't gonna," Steve said, pushing him away.

"We're going out in a minute," one of the girls said. "Pub crawl. You can come with."

"Yeah, maybe," Diesel said, acting nonchalantly.

Of course the guys wanted to go. Within seconds they were talking about which one they were going to bang. Chi wondered if any of them had had sex on this holiday or if it was all bravado. Phil kept telling them to shut up as if Chi was going to be deeply offended by their lewd comments. She couldn't care less. It was better for her if they were concentrating on getting these girls. It took the attention off her.

They met up outside the apartment block with noisy introductions that showed the alcohol had already hit their bloodstreams. Chi and the girls passed compliments back and forward. *Nice dress. Nice shoes. Nice boobs.* Phil told the girls Chi was famous. They wanted to know more.

"Not allowed to say," she said, giving them an apologetic smile. "I signed a non-disclosure form."

In the back of her mind, a harsh voice reminded her they wouldn't be so friendly if they knew she had slept with her friend's fiancé. She had broken the laws of sisterhood. The thought made her heart feel so heavy that she sought to bury it in booze.

First stop was an Irish bar. Another line of shots was demolished in seconds. Chi went with the flow, losing herself in the music. She felt Phil's arm on her waist. Diesel was dancing with a girl in a scrap of fluorescent orange polyester. Chi wanted both and she wanted neither.

"Another drink?" she said to Phil.

"What you having?"

"Do you like rum?"

This would be her last night on the booze. After this, she was done with it for ever.

"Double?" he asked.

The voice which had been urging her to get a taxi back had gone quiet.

She grinned. "Oh, go on then."

She'd be able to take it. She'd been practising all week.

FORTY-SEVEN

Day 5
JEM

Ricardo drove the three of them to the airport. The location manager or whoever he was got into car and went his own separate way. Not before giving Kate a kiss on the cheek, though. Not two kisses, either, which would have been standard, but one sweet peck. Jem was convinced there was something going on between them. But now was not the time for speculation. There was a more important relationship up for inspection. That of her brother and Fiona.

Outside the airport, Ricardo pulled up at the disabled parking bay.

"I'll do a few circles and meet you back here," he said.

Jem leapt out of the jeep and hurried towards the automatic walkways, Kate following close behind. Their progress was slow, hindered by stationary tourists who had no intention of speeding up their journey home. Jem weaved in and out of them, stepping over their bags and ignoring their disapproving mutters. The airport entrance was packed with crowds of recently disembarked passengers getting to grips with where they were. A line of brightly coloured coaches awaited them, their drivers hovering on the pavement, sucking the last bit of life out of their cigarettes.

She spotted Andrew straight away, standing to one side of the sliding doors, casting furtive glances around him. He looked so young. It was his clean shaven jaw and overly groomed hair, and the way he held his shoulders like he wasn't quite sure what he was supposed to be doing and was ready to shrug off a mistake. He glanced up, sensing the storm coming his way. When he saw Jem, his face crumpled and his lips started to tremble.

"Andrew!" she cried.

He flew into her arms. "This is the worst day of my life," he murmured into her shoulder. How many times had she heard him say that? Too many to count and yet it still affected her. He was her little brother. She hated seeing him suffering, whether he was to blame or not.

Kate was standing too close. Jem could sense her agitated presence and wanted to tell her to leave them alone.

"We really should get going, there's nowhere for Ricardo to park."

At the sound of Kate's voice, Andrew stepped back, shaking off the lost boy look.

"Are you the director, then?"

"I'm afraid so," Kate said. She held out her hand and he gave it a weak shake. "Kate Miller."

Jem took her brother's arm. "Come on."

He looked fearful. "Is she in the car?"

"No."

He nodded. Relieved? Jem couldn't tell.

"So you haven't found her yet?"

"No," Kate said. "I don't think she wants you to find her, either. Something about a ring?"

"I'm sure he can explain," Jem said. She tried to ignore the doubts sloshing around in her stomach. Her brother had never been a saint. And yet when it had come to Fiona, he had always tried so hard.

350

"I didn't buy her a fake diamond ring," he said as they hurried back towards the car. "I would never do that."

Jem heard the earnestness in his voice and believed him.

"So they conned you?"

"No," he said. "I didn't buy her any ring."

Jem faltered. She leant on the moving banister of the walkway and frowned at him. "What do you mean? No ring at all?"

"Come on!" Kate called as the jeep came into view. Jem got into the backseat with her brother, Kate taking the front seat.

"Hi, I'm Ricardo," Ricardo called, highlighting the fact they'd all ignored him.

"The cameraman," Jem added. She almost winked at her brother to signal that the cameraman was a little more significant to her than they were making out, but caught herself in time. It was totally inappropriate to reveal her fling while her poor brother's romantic dreams were collapsing around him.

"He didn't buy a ring," Kate filled Ricardo in.

"Who did then?"

"She told us you did, Andrew," Jem said. She squeezed his arm. She hated this. "She said that you presented her with it after you took her to Gordon Ramsay's restaurant. Did you really book that table a year ago? I couldn't believe it when she told us!"

He pressed his fingers against his eyelids. He was too choked to speak.

"What is it?" Jem pressed.

"I said I wouldn't tell anyone."

"Tell anyone what?"

He turned to look at her, tried to tell her telepathically for a moment before finally opening his mouth. "I didn't propose to Fiona. *She* proposed to *me*."

Jem heard the words but it took her a moment to get their meaning, like when you pick a bunch of scrabble letters and for a second can't even find a three letter word.

"What?" she said. "When?"

"After the Born and Bred festival we went to."

Where? In fact, forget where! Jem was still trying to get her head around Fiona proposing. If it was at a music festival then there was a strong chance they'd both been drunk. But still, a proposal was a proposal and it came from somewhere. All their relationship had been about him chasing her. Now Jem was supposed to believe that Fiona had put herself in a position of vulnerability. Then again, perhaps she hadn't considered rejection a possibility. It was Jem's brother they were talking about, after all.

"Wait, that festival was in June," Kate said.

Jem looked at her. "So?"

"Yeah, it was the first weekend," Andrew said, his eyes darting everywhere but refusing to make contact. "I wasn't really enjoying it so we walked off…went and sat somewhere with some beers. We shared a packet of crisps. She just blurted it out. It doesn't sound very romantic, does it."

It certainly was a long way off from what Fiona had told them.

"But it was kind of amazing. To have her ask me to marry her. I just couldn't talk, you know. I think I started crying."

Jem had no doubt he'd started crying. All that pent up emotion. She thought the therapist had helped him get it all out of his system.

"No, it can't be," Kate said.

"You think I was hallucinating?" Andrew replied, annoyed.

"No. It's not that."

"Then what's the problem?"

"The channel informed Fiona she was the winner back in April."

There was silence in the car. Ricardo started coughing. Jem could tell he was trying to mask a laugh and liked him a bit less for it.

"What are you talking about?" Andrew said.

Jem turned to look at him. He had gone very pale. She couldn't bring herself to say it.

"It means," Kate said, "that Fiona won a hen party before she'd found herself a fiancé."

FORTY-EIGHT

Day 4
FIONA

Fiona climbed the last of the stone steps and arrived back on the residential street where the hens had begun their walk. The minivan had gone. So too had Ricardo's jeep. The spark of adrenalin had gone out too, well and truly. She leant heavily against a garden wall, the rocks digging into her back, and breathed in deeply. Her legs were aching and her mouth was dry. She would have done anything for a can of ice cold coke.

It had come as a shock that Chi had noticed her ring wasn't the luxurious piece of bling she had sworn it to be. She'd been worried about Jem guessing they were just cheap diamantes, but not Chi. Chi didn't have expensive tastes. Chi didn't have an eye for what looked classy and what didn't. She bought earrings that would have given anybody else ear rot. She thought no one noticed that her gold bangles were peeling.

Fiona wondered what the hens were saying to each other now, whether they were bitching about Andrew or whether they thought she had been the naïve fool. It was total humiliation. Definitely grounds for breaking up with your fiancé.

At least, it would have been if he'd bought it. It wouldn't be long before Andrew started telling everybody that he hadn't. Next he would reveal that he hadn't even proposed. There was no way Fiona was sticking around for that. She was fetching her stuff and

354

getting out of here. It looked like she'd be using her next win after all. Next stop: Barcelona. The email had arrived just in time. There were ferries leaving from the port every evening. She'd have to pay for her own transport, but at least the accommodation would be free, plus it came with a welcome bottle of cava and a complimentary spa treatment. A real treatment this time, not an excuse for embalming someone with dead grass.

Fiona tried to turn on her phone but it was dead. She swallowed back the nerves. Without a phone, she had no Google maps. Luckily she had something more important. She dug her hand in her pocket and her fingers wrapped around the key to the villa. She'd leave it under the mat for the others before she left. She just hoped they weren't planning on going back early.

It was a long day waiting for the ferry to leave. Worried the hens would return at any moment, Fiona had wasted no time packing. At the last minute she'd grabbed the wrought iron candelabra from her bedside table and some of the crystals off her chandelier and had stuffed them in between her clothes. She figured she'd get a little something off eBay for them and the channel wouldn't even notice the extra charge. It was the least they could do. She'd put so much on the line for this holiday and it had been one huge disappointment.

She regretted the extra weight later. Walking down the seaside promenade hadn't been much fun with the heat beating down. One of the wheels of her suitcase had buckled under the weight and she'd had to drag it noisily behind her while battling with her bulging handbag.

She'd felt like an idiot arriving at the beach with so much stuff, but what else could she do?

She'd lain between her bags, barricaded in from the rest of the sunbathers, and topped up her tan. It hadn't been all that enjoyable. She'd been on edge every time she'd gone for a dip in the sea to cool off and had kept looking back to check on her things. If anyone nicked her passport, it was game over.

At a restaurant near the port she'd made a magazine and a can of coke last two hours. The waiter had given her the evil eye when she'd plugged her phone charger into the restaurant's socket but hadn't told her she couldn't. Once the phone was charged, she couldn't bring herself to turn it on.

By the time she boarded the ferry she felt like she'd pulled an all-nighter. A cabin had been too expensive so she'd hauled her suitcase across the lounge and sunk into one of the cushioned seats. The boat had been busy and the bar had been buzzing with people wanting to stretch out their holiday with one last evening of merry-making. She'd felt self-conscious, sitting there alone with nothing to do. But tiredness won out in the end and she'd fallen into a broken sleep.

The trouble was, she couldn't blank it out of her mind. What she'd done was going to have consequences, but she reasoned that the consequences were manageable. She wasn't going to lose her job or her flat, so on some level nothing really significant had changed. Yet when she thought of Clare, she felt anxious. Something told her she had gone too far this time.

Fiona didn't switch her phone on until she was settled in her hotel room in Barcelona. Even then she hesitated.

It was easy to make up a story in your head when you didn't have to listen to other people's versions of it.

A barrage of messages and missed calls and voicemails came in all at once. She felt tempted to switch it off again. Instead, she scrolled through the notifications. There were ten missed calls from Chi alone.

It had been cruel of Chi to point out the ring was fake so publicly, and yet Fiona couldn't help feeling a wave of guilt at knowing how terrible she must be feeling now. Fiona's intention had never been for anyone to get hurt. Even Andrew. Yes, she'd proposed, but she hadn't tricked him into thinking she had changed. She'd been distant and cool. It wasn't her fault that he was such a martyr.

She dialled her voicemail and braced herself.

Andrew first, wanting an explanation for her text message.

"You can't just send that. We need to talk about this. Ring me."

Delete.

"Fiona, it's me again…whatever I've done…"

Why did he think he'd done something? Why did he always think it was about him? Had he learnt nothing over all these years? His actions didn't dictate her life.

"Please ring me…"

She knew she should feel terrible but the neediness in his voice was such a turnoff.

Delete.

"Fiona, it's me. Chi. Sam probably told you already…look, nothing I'm going to say is going to make this better…I'm so sorry…I don't know what's wrong with me…"

Fiona covered a hand over her ear to hear better. Chi sounded drunk.

"We'd had loads to drink…I know that's no excuse…"

Who was she talking about? Had someone else put her up to telling her the ring was fake? Was it Sam?

"…he was confused because you blanked him and I…look, I can't excuse it…"

Fiona's heart thumped in her chest as she began to understand what Chi was trying to say so inarticulately. This was not the apology she had been anticipating. This was a confession.

"…we didn't mean for it to happen…"

They had slept together. Andrew, who Fiona thought was so besotted with her, incapable of hurting her in any way, had slept with Chi on the night of their engagement party. She was in shock. She leant forward in her seat, covered her face, and wondered whether she would cry.

"I hate myself, Fiona, probably more than you hate me…"

Inside, Fiona's brain was going berserk. This was good, wasn't it? This meant he was the bad one, not her. This meant she wouldn't have to lie to any of her friends and family about why they were no longer getting married. His infidelity was a gift.

Despite the reasoning, she wasn't feeling any better. In fact she felt sick.

"I'm outside on this balcony thinking why don't I jump?"

Do it, Fiona thought, feeling a burst of anger. *Just fucking jump, you bitch!*

How could Chi have been so two-faced? How dare she come to Fiona's hen party having cheated with her fiancé? Because as far as Chi was concerned, Andrew had been Fiona's fiancé…

But his infidelity was a gift. Fiona had to keep saying this to herself like a mantra.

"They're doing it on the other balcony...massive party...I don't know who they are...it doesn't look all that far, you know..."

Fiona lifted her head, connecting with what Chi was rambling on about so drunkenly. Surely she was just trying to scrape together some sympathy. There was no way she was actually going to jump, was there?

"I don't know how I could have done it...I keep asking myself...I'm not that kind of person...It just...it just happened..."

The noise in the background had been gradually getting louder. Men's deep voices had joined together in a forceful chant: *"Jump! Jump! Jump!"* Girls shrieked and laughed in the background.

Chi's voice dropped to a whisper. Fiona could hardly hear her.

"I'm so sorry, Fiona...I fucked up...but I'll get out of your life now and maybe you'll be able to make it better..."

Fiona pressed the phone to her ear, panic rising in her throat. The line cut out and she gazed at the screen, her mouth open in shock. She didn't hesitate. She rang the last person she thought she'd be reaching out to.

She rang Kate.

FORTY-NINE

Day 5
KATE

Kate scratched the back of her neck, the rough edges of her bitten nails drawing red lines across her skin. Sharon's eyes looked like they were going to pop out of her head. Any minute now she would burst a vessel and squirt blood across the room like a horned lizard. Except the horned lizard did that in self-defence and Sharon was rearing up for attack.

"I have never in all my life dealt with such incompetence," Sharon hissed. She kept sitting down, then standing up again.

They had reconvened at the villa. The housekeeper had let a band of cleaners in and they were working quietly in the background, picking their way through the building with black bags, brooms and mops. Behind Sharon, Ricardo coughed uncertainly.

"I think we can still make it work," he said.

Sharon's maddened gaze landed on him. "You do, do you? With no bride-to-be, one hen in the UK, one run off with the sound recordist..."

"I'm still here!" Mel piped up. "And Clare didn't run off. She's upstairs."

Sharon ignored her.

"...and one hen in hospital, and one sister-in-law hen who is no longer going to be the sister-in-law?"

Ricardo licked his dry lips. "The audience doesn't need to know all that."

Sharon looked incensed.

"What are you suggesting?" she said. "Shall we get some animators in? Maybe we could do a Roger Rabbit episode...yes, we can draw in the characters that have gone missing! Perhaps Fiona can marry a cartoon character at the end. Bravo, all sorted!"

Kate noted that she was on the periphery of this conversation, that Sharon couldn't bear to look at her.

"It's not all bad. We do have some decent stuff. Plus, there's loads that can be done in post-production," Ricardo said, his voice calm, his nails pulling at his shredded cuticles. "I've got a few ideas, actually."

Sharon stopped pacing up and down and folded her arms. "Go on, genius, I'm listening."

Ricardo inhaled sharply and leant back in his chair so far the front legs rose up. "Well, for starters I'd suggest new audio...a shot of a plane landing...silhouettes of the couple meeting at sunset on the most beautiful cliffs in Mallorca...a voiceover of the groom saying he couldn't wait to see her so he came over..."

"Wouldn't that make him sound really possessive?" Kate said.

Sharon narrowed her eyes at her. "Don't say anything. I'm not ready to hear your voice."

"It's not Kate's fault they broke up," Ricardo said. "I mean, as far as Fiona was concerned, they were never together."

Kate was surprised to hear him come to her defence and hoped her expression looked sufficiently grateful.

"It *was* her fault," Sharon snapped. "Everything is her fault! Fiona was prepared to act all the way through it quite happily."

Kate couldn't argue with that. Fiona had definitely been up for playing a role, and no doubt would have seen it through until Sunday if Kate had stuck to the schedule and pampered them properly.

Sharon's phone, which had been vibrating at five minute intervals, started ringing loudly. She checked the screen before answering it.

"Yes, it's me...Ricardo thinks we can save it..." She charged towards the patio doors and out into the garden. "Ricardo, the DOP," they heard her bark. "*Ricardo.*"

"Bunch of clowns," muttered Ricardo. "I've been working with them for three years."

Kate let out a deep breath. "Do you really think this can be sorted out?"

Ricardo was gnawing his lip. The feet of his chair had banged back down on to the tiles and he was leaning forward, tapping a nervous beat with his hands. Now that Sharon was out of the room he didn't look so confident.

"Maybe," he said. "They have the money for a fantasy."

Mel poured herself a glass of tap water and stood there sipping it. The atmosphere was tense. Kate knew she was seething. This was supposed to have been a great job. Mel had been so excited when they'd first talked on the phone, telling Kate how relieved she was to be getting out of the studio of a badly paid television show. Now she saw herself being associated with the worst episode of *The Hen Party* ever made. She thought Kate was a selfish cow but she was too polite to say it.

"I'm going to see how they're getting on," she said.

Kate nodded. "Right."

Mel headed upstairs where Clare and Jem had begun packing up Sam's belongings. The two remaining hens had greeted each other civilly, but Kate doubted they were going to be meeting up in England any time soon.

"Have you spoken to your agent?" Ricardo asked.

"No. I daren't."

Kate didn't add that her agent had only rung her once in the last three months and the call had been about this job. She didn't add that she thought the next phone call would be to suggest they parted ways.

"Everyone's allowed one bad experience, right?"

Kate didn't want to think about what awaited her back home. Instead she thought of Gabriel. She thought of the incredible coincidence of their encounter under water. It was a story she could imagine them both telling all their friends, in a dimension where all their friends knew each other. She let herself imagine him looking gorgeous in a pale grey suit and fitted waistcoat. He was holding a microphone and standing at the centre of a long table decorated with white roses and lavender, a full silver service and little name cards. Well if you were lucky enough to have it as your story, you would tell it on your wedding day, and even though everyone had already heard it, they would want to hear it again because it was so incredibly perfect.

A wedding daydream. A good one for a change. The first one in a long while that didn't end with the groom not turning up. It might be just a daydream, but last night hadn't been. The memory of it made the hairs on her arms stand on end. He'd met her at the entrance of his well-kept apartment block. She'd just come back from the villa where she'd tipped the rubbish into the pool and had been feeling on edge.

"Before we do anything else..." he'd said, and he'd put his warm carpenter hands on her cheeks and kissed her. *"Now I can breathe."* She'd made a decision then and there to leave her fury outside the door.

They'd cooked together, talking easily about what they were good at, their specialities and their guilty pleasures. They'd eaten with the balcony doors wide open, the warm breeze bringing in the earthy smell of pine. Afterwards they'd lain in his double hammock, drinking bottled beer, watching the twinkling light of the city across the bay. It had been perfect. At one point she'd half-heartedly mentioned she should be getting back, and he'd laughed, because it was so obvious she had no intention of leaving.

"Oh, God," she murmured. The thought of returning to London was making Kate's stomach ache.

Ricardo assumed she was talking about Sharon. "I know. At this rate we won't get anything done today either."

Another ten minutes passed. A cleaning lady washed glasses at the sink nearby, one earphone dangling down her chest. Ricardo picked at the peeling logo on his T-shirt. Kate thought about asking after Jem, but decided she'd missed the window to be his friend. They weren't even going to be colleagues after this. Ricardo wouldn't be recommending her for a job, and she wouldn't want to work with him and be reminded of the mess she'd made.

At last Sharon pushed through the patio doors. Her cheeks were flushed, but she looked a little less furious.

"Alright," she said. "They want a magical ending. What time's sunset?"

FIFTY

Day 5
CHIOMA

Chi was awake but she didn't want to open her eyes. She knew it was bad. Her body ached. Her head throbbed. Her arm was encased in something hard. She guessed it was a cast but she wasn't ready to see it. She could hear the hum of fluorescent lights, could feel their white glare penetrating her fluttering eyelids. There was a squeak of soles. The rustle of clothes. Someone was sitting nearby. She prayed it wasn't her mum.

She waited for whoever it was to go and leave her alone with her shame. In the silence she became aware of her laboured breathing. She tried to slow it down but it made her want to cough.

Couldn't they see she was asleep?

She knew she was in a hospital. The smell of disinfectant was masking another of boiled chicken and human sweat. It reminded Chi of weekends spent visiting her grandma when she was slowly dying of cancer. Chi would sit in a corner of the hospital room with her colouring book while her mum sat by her mother's side, reading passages from the bible. She remembered feeling relieved when they'd stopped going.

Chi couldn't remember getting here. Had an ambulance come for her? Had the paramedics delayed heading to a more serious emergency because of her stupidity? Did she have blood on her hands?

Broken memories flashed into her head. She saw herself on the beach flirting with the boys. She remembered Phil touching her arm a lot when he spoke, but not knowing how to make a pass. Back at the apartment, Diesel hadn't shown any interest in her so she'd tried to get his attention by drinking shots. So stupid. Why had she cared what he thought? He was an arrogant twenty-one-year-old who could hardly string a sentence together and probably had an STD.

After the drinks on the balcony they'd headed out into town. She had already been drunk, but somehow she had managed to keep going. There'd been an Irish bar, a cocktail bar, a sports bar...there had been tequila shots and sickly-sweet rum. Phil had tried to kiss her and she might have kissed him back, but she couldn't be sure. She vaguely remembered warm lips on her skin but not wanting to lose herself in them. The music had saved her. She'd wanted to dance, not kiss. The girls from the other apartment had adopted her as their new friend. She remembered screaming with laughter. She remembered falling over. She remembered someone helping her up on to a bar top to dance to Justin Bieber.

Chi wanted to curl into a ball. Instead she lay still and listened. Whoever it was beside her, they were still there. If it was a hen, they were only there out of a sense of duty. She couldn't think of one person in the group who would be there out of sympathy. All of them would think that she'd brought this on herself. She hoped no one had filmed her climbing over that balcony and...

Chi opened her eyes to stop the memory taking shape. The person in the chair sprang out of it with a gasp.

"Thank God for that!"

Andrew was standing at the side of her bed looking like he'd stepped out of a Marks and Spencer's summer catalogue. White shorts and a pale blue polo shirt that matched the colour of his eyes – eyes that were now looking at her with something between surprise and relief.

"You almost gave me a heart attack," he said.

If he was here, then he was not with Fiona and that meant she had ruined everything.

"What are you doing here?" Her voice came out hoarse. Her throat was burning as if someone had forced a cactus down it. She was right about the cast. Her arm was a block of white up to the elbow. It was of some small comfort it was her left arm.

"I'm checking on you...you could have died. The others came earlier, but you were still out."

She wished they hadn't come. Chi could imagine them talking about her in the corridor in hushed voices. *Slut. How could she have done it?* She closed her eyes. The tears bubbled up and rolled down her cheeks, leaving a cold trail.

"Don't cry," he said. "You didn't die, so that's good."

He laughed nervously. When she didn't try to wipe away her tears, he leant forward and wiped them away for her so gently it made her heart ache.

"What's Fiona going to think of you being here?" she said. "Shouldn't you be running after her apologising for that ring?"

She watched his face. She couldn't read him. He looked tired, but resigned. He didn't look like someone who was falling to pieces.

"I didn't buy her that ring. She bought it herself."

Chi frowned. "So she knew all along it was...what it was."

"Yep, she knew what she was buying. She lied to us all."

"But..." It didn't matter, did it? If she'd wanted to use a ring out of a cracker it wouldn't have mattered. Their lie was infinitely worse. "What about what we did? Will she forgive you?"

Andrew pursed his lips and smiled grimly. "It doesn't matter now."

Chi couldn't understand how he could be so calm. The future he had been imagining had just gone up in smoke.

"She's probably breathing a sigh of relief we stopped her looking like a lunatic," he said.

It hurt to frown. Chi lifted her hand and touched her face. Cuts stung beneath her fingertips.

"She never meant to marry me."

Chi dropped her hand to her side and gave him her full attention. What he was saying didn't make any sense.

"She just needed a fiancé for a competition." He pressed his lips together and smiled weakly. "I've been a complete fool."

"I don't understand."

"She proposed to me after she was selected for *The Hen Party*."

Chi stared at him, open mouthed. "No...Are you serious?"

"She was going to dump me straight afterwards."

"Oh my God."

"She rang Kate and confessed the lot. She's in Barcelona now...won something there too, apparently."

The news was shocking. The thoughts rumbled around Chi's head. In all the pain, she felt relief that she would be able to let go of her guilt, that what she had done wouldn't define her for the rest of her life. She could start again.

"I'm sorry," she said. "I'm sorry about everything."

He squeezed her hand. "Me too."

"I should never have come but I thought it was the only way to get over it, to pretend it hadn't happened."

"It doesn't matter now."

"I feel so ashamed."

She looked down at her cast and felt a strong wave of self-loathing.

"You're going to be alright, you know."

His concern made her feel tearful.

"I'm such a car crash..."

He didn't reply. He seemed pensive. She was sure he was agreeing with her in his head. When he looked up again, his eyes were brighter.

"You know what I think?" he said. "I think some of us have to fuck up badly before we get on the right track. I don't regret what we did now. I mean, I know it was wrong, but I think I was trying to sabotage our relationship so I could escape."

Chi thought back to that night and how easily they had fallen into each other's arms. How passionately they'd kissed as if desperate to forget everything beyond that room.

"Fiona had me on a chain all these years. I'm finally free."

He looked at her in a way that seemed to promise so much. She felt a ripple of hope race through her. If this was rock bottom then the only way was up.

"What's going to happen to the show?" she asked.

He rolled his eyes. "If it was up to me, it would all be cancelled and there would be no memory of this horrible week."

"Won't it be?"

"No. The show will go on."

A nurse came in to announce visiting time was over and Chi didn't get a chance to ask how the show could possibility go on. Andrew kissed her on the cheek and said he'd be back in the afternoon.

"You'll be let out tomorrow morning," the nurse said to her. Before she left the room, she placed a pack of sanitary towels by Chi's bed. "It never comes at the right time, does it."

FIFTY-ONE

The view at Cap de Formentor was one of the most breathtaking Jem had ever seen. The majestic grey cliffs jutting into the sea gave the impression they had been there since the beginning of time. At the lighthouse, tourists leant over the stone balustrade of the terrace in anticipation of the sunset. If she'd been alone with Ricardo, she would have walked back down the winding road and chosen a quieter spot as they watched. That wasn't to be. Ricardo had been working since the crack of dawn without so much as a lunch break. She had tried to make him eat a sandwich and he'd taken a few distracted bites before turning away, absorbed in the project. He was currently explaining to the actors what he wanted from them.

The girl was the same size as Fiona. She had the fleshy hips and the round shoulders. A hair and makeup lady had given her a fishtail plait. Her face wasn't going to be in focus so it didn't matter that she didn't have Fiona's small upturned nose or puckered lips. The actor playing Jem's brother was the same build, had the same slick haircut. Other people might believe it was him from behind, but she knew Andrew's shoulders had never been so relaxed.

The tourists grumbled when they were asked to move along for filming. A few selfie sticks kept creeping into the shot until Sharon paid the tourists to go elsewhere.

The fake Andrew and Fiona climbed on to the balustrade and sat side by side. The audio was going to be added on later. Sharon hadn't decided what it would be yet. *"I want to spend the rest of my life with you…"* or *"You complete me…"* Something desperately romantic. Something that Andrew and Fiona would definitely not be saying to each other any time soon.

Jem felt she could breathe properly again knowing that her brother had avoided being trapped in an unhappy relationship. He was free. For now. But she wasn't putting money on him enjoying his bachelor status very long. Andrew's concern at hearing Chi was in hospital had seemed quite extreme for someone he'd only ever met once. Jem hoped he wasn't going to fall in love again before he even made it back to England.

She broached the subject with Ricardo later that evening. Once the fictional happy ending had been filmed, they were sitting side by side on the bench under the jasmine bush where they had first kissed. She felt the tension between them and the butterflies multiplied in the pit of her stomach.

"So was this a *what happens in Mallorca stays in Mallorca* thing?"

She was trying to play it cool. She didn't feel it, though. Her hands were clammy and she felt out of breath. Ricardo probably had flings wherever he travelled and she couldn't attach much meaning to it. It had been wonderful, though, sneaking secret kisses on this very bench; running off to that beautiful hotel; trying to make love in a secluded bay where the fishes had nipped at their legs, forcing them to break apart, laughing. It was the most intense and romantic experience she had ever had.

"No," Ricardo said, meeting her eye and looking so serious she felt fearful of his reply. "I was thinking what happened in Mallorca could also happen in England if we wanted it to."

Jem stared back at him, her heartbeat racing.

He raised an eyebrow. "What do you say?"

Her smile gave her away. He knew what she was going to say but she said it anyway.

"I guess that could work, too," she said, only just managing to stop herself breaking into a happy dance.

FIFTY-TWO

Day 7
KATE

Kate stuffed her toothbrush into her wash bag, did one last check under the bed and in the cupboards, then zipped her suitcase shut. The time had come. Any minute now a taxi would be arriving to pick her up. She had thought telling Gabriel not to take her to the airport had been a clever move, but now it just seemed stupid. It would have been so good to spend one last hour with him. Yesterday's goodbye hadn't felt right. She had been miles away, worrying about her future instead of enjoying the present with him. Her resolve not to cry melted and a big, fat tear slid down her cheek. She washed her face in the bathroom, gritted her teeth at her reflection and headed outside.

At the airport she waited in the queue to check in her bag. She recognised Clare shuffling forward ahead of her, wearing a white T-shirt with tiny flowers on it. It had a wide neck and Kate winced at the raw sunburn which had already begun to peel. Mel appeared with bottles of water and handed Clare one. They were travelling together, then. Jem had probably extended her flight to tag along with Ricardo while he took extra shots of beach clubs and nightlife. Sharon had ordered it, and there had been more phone calls and more exasperated mentions of Kate's name.

The queue moved along slowly. It was one of the few times she would have been happy to be told the plane

374

was cancelled. Kate would have welcomed another day to sort out her thoughts. What was she going to do now? Would she ever work again? Mel would no doubt feel it her duty to warn other sound recordists and would post it on one of those online forums set up by crew to look out for each other. *Hey, guys, you don't want to work with Kate Miller…*

She looked away as Mel and Clare passed by so they didn't have to go through the palaver of small talk. If they saw her, they didn't stop. A few moments later she was at the check-in desk, handing over her passport

"Where are you flying?"

Kate hesitated too long.

"London Gatwick?" the woman suggested.

Kate could see the journey in her head. Arriving to rain lashing against the plane window. Walking through the doors to find the pickup point packed with people holding cards with names on them, not one of them her own, because no one in London was waiting for her or knew when she was due back. She would roll her suitcase across the airport, thinking it may as well be her heart she was dragging behind her. She would arrive home in a blur of regret, look in the mirror and her face would smirk back at her. *What happened to that great opportunity?* She had blown it. She wasn't one of those fearless Greenpeace activists; she was just a wannabe.

But then she thought of picking up rubbish on that secluded beach and the sense of wellbeing it had given her to be actually doing something practical. Just because she hadn't converted a hen party into a party of environmentalists didn't make her a failure. The only thing that would mean failure was giving up on herself.

Failure would be believing she was powerless to do anything at all.

"No," she replied.

"Well that's the only flight we're open for. Madrid isn't until this evening."

"I've changed my mind." She took her passport back. "Thank you. I've decided to stay."

The woman raised an eyebrow and chuckled. "Okay…not ready to face reality, are we?"

"I'm thinking of redefining my reality."

The woman's smile dipped uncertainly. She probably thought Kate was drunk. Kate did feel a bit altered as she left the queue. There was a voice of panic telling her to go back, not to be so stupid. But what was the point of going back to a path that wasn't leading her where she wanted to go? Was she just going to follow it because it was there?

Last night Gabriel had told her about the oceans' initiative programme at the sailing club which taught kids about the effects of plastic on marine life. The organisers were looking for volunteers to train and help at their summer boot camp.

"Who has money to volunteer?" she'd asked, dismissing the idea straight away. But now she realised she wouldn't have to give up everything she'd learnt as a director. She could take a few days to visit production companies and get a sense of how much work there was. And if there wasn't any work, then she could always get a job in a bar in the meantime. The rent would be half the price it was back home. She could live a simpler life.

Kate stepped outside and the warm caress of another beautiful morning in Mallorca made her feel a little better. She thought of Gabriel, the first man she'd fallen in love with since Matt had broken her heart. There was no guarantee of a happy ending, but then there never was. It didn't mean you shouldn't try. It didn't mean you should stop putting your heart on the line.

She dialled his number. He picked up after a few rings.

"I was hoping you would call," he said. "Are you checked in?"

"No. I've been thinking about what you told me...about that volunteering programme..."

She heard his intake of breath.

"Hold that thought," he said. "I'm coming to collect you!"

She laughed. If she'd needed any more encouragement, that was it. All her doubts drifted away as she waited in the sunshine for her new man and the rest of her life to begin.

EuroWeekly News

Reports have confirmed that the woman in the balconing incident last weekend was another member of The Hen Party reality show. This comes two months after the previous director, Joanna Kane, was concussed in a similar accident.

Hen, Chioma 'Chi' Ademola, had abandoned filming to party in Magaluf and had attempted an ambitious jump into a neighbouring balcony whilst heavily under the influence of alcohol. The show, which was being filmed on the island, has been reported to have had several complications.

Ademola was said to have deserted the other hens after a dispute. Rumours that she slept with the bride-to-be's fiancé are yet to be confirmed. The bride-to-be was unavailable for questioning and is mending her broken heart in Barcelona. There are also reports that two other hens were having sexual relations with the crew. One hen also accused the director of trying to hijack the filming to make an environmental statement.

Sharon Wingman, the series producer, denies all reports and says that the new episode will be a celebration of love and romance.

Acknowledgements

Continued thanks to all the people in my life who support me on this writing journey. To my parents, my brother, my family and friends, and all the kind strangers on social media - I'm so grateful for your encouragement.

I started this book several times and there's a chance I may have been grumpy at some point during the deletion of many thousands of words. Therefore, I feel special thanks are due to my nearest and dearest, my wonderful husband.

I also want to thank Joanna Penn, a writer and entrepreneur I have yet to meet. Her publishing podcast really inspired me to take an important new step in my career and make this book happen.

Thank you, reader, for choosing this book. It wouldn't be the same without you.

If you are setting off on a hen party any time soon, I hope it goes smoother than this one!

More Books by Emily Benet:

Shop Girl Diaries
Short Stories for Busy Adults
The Temp
#PleaseRetweet

Find out more about Emily Benet:

www.emilybenet.com
www.facebook.com/EmilyBenetAuthor
www.twitter.com/@EmilyBenet